The Sarah Puzzle

Annie-Laurie Hunter

The Sarah Puzzle

ISBN:148393571X

ISBN-13:978-1483935713

DEDICATION

<u>The Sarah's Puzzle</u> is dedicated to all the real people in my life who have made this work of fiction possible.

March 27th   7:45 am

"Tony, we've got a kid up here."

Tony replied on the walkie-talkie, "What do you mean you've got a kid? Tell it to get out of there!!"

"No, Tony, she's little. Call the cops. We need the cops. You've got to see this. Just call the cops."

"What am I supposed to tell them?"

"Tell them we have a kid living here and she is little."

"What is she, on drugs?"

"I don't think so, Tony. But this isn't right. Something's going on here and you gotta see it."

With that, Bartolo stopped talking on the walkie-talkie and looked at the attic and the child within it. She was sitting in a small pile of blankets, just waking from a deep sleep. Clearly, she had made this attic her space. It was clean around her blanket in contrast to the years of dust coating the rest of the attic floor. The window had been cleaned. And there was a clean pathway to the window from her little nest. Besides her nest and a single backpack, the attic was empty. There was none of the usual detritus of a vacant building. No bottles, no drug paraphernalia, no remains of illicit encounters. There was just the child and her little nest.

But now she was fully awake and beginning to panic. "Hey there, no one is supposed to be up here. We're supposed to start taking this building down today. What's your name?"

There was no response from the girl. "Hey, my name is Bartolo. My friends call me Bart. I'm glad I found you. We're taking this building down. You can't be here anymore. My friend Tony is calling for people to come and help you to move out. Can you tell me your name?"

But as the sun rose and lit the room, Bart saw her eyes and knew she wouldn't answer. There was terror on that face. He backed away.

He was standing at the top of the stairs watching her and speaking quietly when two NYPD beat cops and Tony came up behind him.

"What'cha got, Bart?"

Bart half turned to them without taking his eyes off the girl. "She hasn't said anything. I backed up to here 'cuz she looks really scared." The two cops looked in and one started to enter.

"Hey, what're you doing up here? What's your name?"

And with that she took flight. One second she was in a ball on the floor; the next she had grabbed her bag and flown towards the window.

"No!" they all screamed at once. But before they could react, the window was open and she was gone.

"There's a roof! There's a lower roof under that window," exclaimed Bart. The four men ran to the window and sure enough, the girl was on a flat roof a few feet below the window.

"That must be how she's been getting in. The door was locked down below. I broke the lock to get in for the final walk through."

"Okay, kid. Just stay there." The officer keyed his radio. "We need backup. We have a ten year old female runaway on a roof."

The second officer called to the little girl, "Hey, look at me. What is your name?" Bart attempted to hold the girl's focus. "Hold on kid. Just stay there. Just stay where you are. Alright? It's going to be okay."

The second officer called, "We're going to get you to a safe place. What's your name? Look at me."

But she was off again. She went over the side of the parapet wall and was gone. They rushed forward to watch her descent.

"She's coming down the outside, south side of the building," the officer reported into the radio. One of the officers went through the window in pursuit.

Using the brick spacing as toe holds and finger holds, she scrambled down with obvious practice and in moments was running through the alley. Officer Joe Hogan, a young beat cop, caught her as she rounded the corner. As his arms encircled her, she lashed out furiously, moving in all directions at once. He held her arms tight, braced her head in his shoulder and swiped his foot around her legs to take her feet out from under her so that he could take her to the ground and restrain her. She didn't stop fighting until her hands were cuffed, her feet shackled, and she was free from his arms. Her quaking body was carried to the back of a squad car. She had not made a sound.

Hogan reported to dispatch, "We need a female officer for transport."

"You okay?" his partner Pete Sheehan asked.

"Yeah, never had a kid fight like that. She on something?"

Pete looked at the child. "I don't think so. I think she's scared of something or someone. Where are we going with her?"

Sergeant Macintyre arrived on the scene and fielded the question. "Let's take her down to the precinct and we'll figure out who she is. Do we have a female officer in route to transport her? Who found her?"

"I did." Bart and Tony were walking to the crowd of officers who had responded to the call for back up. "We're taking down the building today and I was doing the final walk through. I checked the attic. She was sleeping up there. I packed her blankets. These and her bag are all she had. What's going to happen to her? Is she a runaway?"

Sidestepping the questions, the Sergeant asked, "Did she say anything?"

"No, she hasn't made a sound."

The Sergeant looked at the small girl in the back of the squad car. "Hey, what are you doing? Hogan, wasn't she cuffed in the back?"

"Of course she was cuffed in the back. Why?" He looked in and found her hands still cuffed but in her lap.

"Oh, come *on*, kid. What are you, Houdini?"

March 27th   8:30 am

"Sarge, we gotta take her out to re-cuff her."

The Sergeant looked at the child squirming in the car. "Let's wait until we get the female officer here. She needs to be restrained and I don't want to hurt her. God, she's skinny. She's too small for the cuffs. That's how she got out."

Hogan looked in on her and spoke quietly. "Look at those wrists; I'm surprised she hasn't gotten her hands out."

"Oh, shit! You spoke too soon. She *is* out!"

The Sergeant nodded at Joe Hogan. "Call for a bus. We can't transport her. She's out of control. We need restraints."

Pete Sheehan called, "Let's see if we can calm her down."

"Damn, she looks like a caged animal. This isn't right. She isn't just some little street kid and she's not acting like she's on drugs."

The Sergeant spoke to the child through the front seat of the car. "Hey, kid, let's settle down. We want to take you out of the car so you don't hurt yourself, but we can't do that with you jumping around like that. Nobody's going to hurt you. You need to just calm down. Don't take your shoes off. Leave the shackles on. Hey, look at me. Stop taking your shoes off."

Hogan sighed, "Sarge, we're going to lose the shackles."

"We need to get her out of there and do a physical restraint. Hogan, are you up for holding her?"

"Yeah, let's do it against the side of the building."

"You ready? We're gonna pull her out. Sal, grab those cuffs. We don't want her throwing them. Mark, Kevin, you take her out and Hogan is going to restrain her. Get ready for her to bolt. She's a runner."

"Tom, you need to document this: everyone who touches her, the times, everything. By the book folks; let's see if we can do this without anyone getting hurt. Hogan, secure your weapon first." He handed his gun to Pete, who secured it in the car trunk. "Are we ready?"

"Ready!" the officers replied in unison.

They opened both doors to the squad car. Sal reached in from one side and grabbed cuffs that were lying on the seat. Mark and Kevin reached in and each grabbed an arm to pull her out. They expected resistance but instead she rushed them. The shackle was around one ankle and it clanked against the frame of the car as she lurched forward. She ran head on into the wall of officers, dropping low so as to go through their knees. But they were well trained and caught her and picked her up.

"Hold on, kid. You're not going anywhere. Settle down."

But she didn't stop struggling, even as she was placed against Hogan's body to be restrained. He sat on the cold but dry sidewalk and wrapped her arms with his own, trapped her head against his shoulder and wrapped his legs over hers in an attempt to safely secure her. Sal took the shackle off the second leg.

Sergeant knelt down to try to talk to the still quaking child.

"Settle down! We're not here to hurt you. But you're not running away, so settle down. Let's try to make this easy on everyone. We're going to take you to the hospital to make sure you're okay. Officer Hogan is going to sit here with you until the ambulance gets here. Just relax. Just sit right there and relax."

Officer Hogan could feel her quaking even under her winter coat. Every muscle was rigid with fear. Her stomach was heaving, and her breaths were short and ragged. She hadn't made a single aggressive move. She hadn't bit or spat or kicked. She was not like any child he had ever come across before. And as he restrained her, he started speaking to her gently, trying to sooth her.

"Shhhh. It's okay. I have you. You're safe. You've had a tough time but you're safe now. Shhh, relax. Take a deep breath. Let's do it together."

He took a deep breath and let it out slowly. "Shhh. Let's do that again, nice and deep." He took another deep breath, modeling for her and trying to connect. Her breathing didn't change and she made no signs of relaxing. She wasn't fighting him, but she was watching everything, waiting for the right moment to make her move. Hogan continued talking softly. "Shhh. Relax. We're going to take good care of you. Once we get you checked out and make sure everything is okay, we can get you some breakfast. Bart says he woke you up. You must be getting hungry. What do you like for breakfast? How about some pancakes? Do you like pancakes? You strike me as a pancake kid. Melted butter and syrup. How does that sound?"

The quaking hadn't changed, but he was able to hold both of her arms with one of his and brush her long blonde hair back away from her face and lean the back of her head against his shoulder. He noted with some surprise that her hair was clean and he could smell shampoo. He looked down at her, "Shhh, that's better; you can see better now."

"How about another deep breath? Nice and deep."

But despite his modeling a deep breath yet again, she did not follow his lead.

While Hogan was restraining the girl, the Sergeant was looking in her backpack. "Let's see if there is anything in here that will help us get a handle on this kid. Toothbrush and toothpaste in a zip lock bag. She's not the typical street kid. Washcloth and soap in a zip lock. She's definitely not typical. Hair brush. We have a change of clothes and a water bottle. There is water in the water bottle. Did he say this bag was all packed up when he first saw her? This kid is on the run. But there's no I.D, no pictures. No money? Did you check her pockets?"

"Yeah, they're empty."

"She has no money. Check her shoes. Was she sleeping in her shoes?"

"Yeah, she was just like this."

"Okay, kid, we're just going to take your shoes off of you. Grab her other foot. Hey. It's okay." She tried to pull her foot away from him. "Nothing."

"Kid, do you have money stashed someplace?" But she didn't respond.

"How long do you think it's been since she has eaten?"

"I don't know. She's really skinny."

"Leave her shoes off," Sarge commanded.

6

March 27th   8:45 am

"Here's the bus. Hogan, you're going with her." The Sergeant nodded at the paramedics, "Let me talk to the paramedics about what we have."

"Shhh, we're going to go to the hospital now so we can make sure you are okay," Hogan did his best to reassure the child. The first paramedic approached briskly but calmly. Hogan felt her fear level increase and responded by tightening his hold on her just before she again tried to bolt.

"Whoa, Nelly. Hold on kid," the paramedic said as the tiny blue eyed waif glared at him and fought for her freedom.

"Shhhh. Calm down."

The paramedic spoke cheerfully, "We're the good guys. I just need to listen to your heart and make sure you aren't hurt anywhere." He reached forward with the stethoscope and she began to flail again. He backed off. "Okay. Are you hurt anywhere?"

She made no discernible response but the flailing quieted. "Shhhh. It's okay. It's okay… We're all going to be fine. That's better," cooed Officer Hogan.

The first paramedic conferred with his partner. "How are we going to get her on a gurney?" Then, turning to the gaggle of cops, "She's wild. Is she on something?"

"We don't think so. I think she's feral," Pete chimed in.

"Come on, this isn't the 1800's. We don't have feral children in the 21st century. And this is a city, not some forest with wolves."

"Look, she isn't speaking, and she isn't stupid. She's terrified of every one of us. She doesn't have any drugs or money on her and she's clean. She's…what? Eight or ten maybe? Look at how skinny she is. But her clothes aren't too big, so she didn't just lose weight. She's living in the attic of an abandoned building but she gets to the attic from an outside window. I don't know who she's hiding from or why but whoever it is has scared her good." Turning to the paramedic, Pete continued, "Now, how are we going to get her from where she is to the gurney?"

"Let's get a person on each leg, one on each arm and Hogan you take her head."

Hogan addressed the child, "Alright, little one, we are going to put you on that stretcher. You just relax and let us move you. You can't get away and this will be a lot easier if you just let us do it. Okay?"

"Alright, everyone ready? On three: one, two-" and she exploded. In that moment when everyone was preparing to lift her, she contracted in and exploded out. It was a futile attempt, but the paramedics now understood why this tiny eight-to-ten year old was being restrained. "Get her on the gurney. Let's strap her down."

"Shhh hold on kid. It's going to be okay. Can you give her anything to calm her down?

"I don't dare. Not without a tox screen."

"Let's just get her secure and get her in. Let's go both arms and both legs. Here, let's get her knees and waist and chest. Alright, now let's get her hands and feet. Settle down kid. Settle down."

"Shhh, I'm right here. I'm staying right here, kid. Settle down." Joe Hogan stroked her head.

During transport, the paramedic radioed in to prepare the emergency room staff for an upcoming challenge. On arriving the triage nurse asked, "Is this the stray child?"

"Yeah, where do you want her?"

"Take her to nine. We have it ready."

Officer Hogan kept his hand on her forehead as she was wheeled to a small psychiatric intake room with an observation window.

The triage nurse asked, "Do we have a name?"

"No."

"Age?"

"Eight to ten."

"Female?"

"Yeah. Well, we think so, we haven't really looked."

"Has she said anything?"

"Not a sound," answered Officer Hogan. "Can you give her something to calm her down? She's been quaking with fear since we caught her. I'm surprised she hasn't passed out by now."

The nurse responded, "We'll see what the doctor says."

The doctor arrived. "Let's try taking the chest strap off. Okay, I am going to listen to your chest." As the stethoscope was brought towards her, her panic rose again, and she contorted herself to move away. "We're going to have to strap her down again. Let's get a bed in here and full restraints. We need a full tox screen and call Pediatric Psych."

She was transferred to the hospital bed. Blood was taken and people filed out. Officer Joe Hogan and his partner were left with the scared waif.

In a quiet, easy manner, Joe spoke. "You're having a tough morning, aren't you? How about a drink of water? You must be thirsty. I know I'm thirsty. Pete, why don't you grab us a couple of waters and a straw for my friend here?"

"I don't know what you're so worked up about but as soon as we get you settled in, Pete and I are going to work on finding out who you are and where you came from. You can help us out. How about you tell us your name?"

"If you're hiding from someone, we can protect you. Are you hiding from someone? Where are your parents?" He looked at her and then shook his head and smiled warmly. "Oh, heck, you're not going to tell me. You win. They're your secrets. How about we just sit here together for a few minutes?"

Pete returned. "I have three waters and a straw for the little lady." Hogan adjusted the bed. "Let's sit this bed up a bit. That's better. How about some water?"

Hogan held the straw to her mouth. She flinched and drew back but then took a small sip. Hogan took a deep swallow of his. "You've worn me out, kid." He turned to his partner. "Thanks, Pete. I needed that." Then, addressing her again, "You want a little more?" He brought the straw to her lips again but this time she did not sip. "Okay. No more water. I'm just going to set it here and you can look at it if you want some more."

"How about we play a game? I am going to say something about Pete or myself and you need to look at the right person. Alright, let's try an easy one. Which of us has blond hair?"
But her gaze went to the door as the psychiatrist and nurse entered.

"Anything?" the psychiatrist asked.

"She took a sip of water."

"Okay, let me talk to her." Pete and Hogan stepped out.

"So, I understand you were living alone in a building."

She made no response.

"How long have you been living there?"

No response.

"How old are you?"

Still there was no response.

"Let's test her ears." The doctor moved behind her and she started to quake. Then he clapped his hands and her flinch assured them that she could hear.

"Okay," he said, once again moving into her sight line. "We took some blood from your arm. Do you know what it told us?" He paused as if she would respond but then continued, "It said that you have not been eating very well. You need to stay here so we can get you some good food." She did not acknowledge him in any way. "Are you hungry? No, I don't imagine that you are. I think that right now you're too scared to be hungry. We are going to give you some medication so that you don't feel so scared. Then you can take a little nap and when you wake up, you can have a nice meal. Is there anything you want to tell me?"

There was no response.

"No? Okay, I will check on you later, after you've had a nap. Nurse." Before she had a chance to pull away, she was given a shot and almost immediately went into a restless sleep.

Once she was sleeping, the nurse started an IV and a pediatrician performed a full physical exam before moving her to the pediatric medical unit. The Administration for Children's Services was notified that a child had been brought in.

March 27th   10:30 am

Hogan and Pete began the search for answers.

Before leaving the hospital they took her picture and her fingerprints. "Let's start back at the attic. We need to look at that before they knock it down. God, that kid was strong." Joe continued talking as they approached the squad car. "Someone has got to know who this kid is. Have you contacted social services? Missing persons? She must be in the system."

"I just sent the picture to both missing persons and social services," Pete said as he opened the door.

Back at the building, Bartolo met them at the front door. "How is she? Did you find out who she is?"

"She's sleeping and no. We need to take a look in the attic and see if she left anything up there."

"I checked the whole place up there after you left. There is nothing up there. You guys were outside when you were here before so I'll show you the way."

From the top of the stairs, it was clear that there would be nothing. The only footprints in the dust were Bartolo's and the other officer's. There were no small footprints, just a clean pathway from the clean window to the clean rectangle on the floor where she had been seen sleeping. "She's not a stupid kid. Look at this. In all this dirt, she didn't leave a single foot print."

"Bart, how many times have you been up here?"

"Just today. The door was padlocked and no one had the key. We were told there was nothing up here and the only reason I came up today was to do the final walk through. You know, you have to walk the entire building before you take it down. I guess now we know why."

"How long since there's been electricity?" Pete asked as he looked around the attic.

"At least a couple of years. It's been condemned for five years. The roof is collapsing over there and the water running down has taken out all the floors and ceilings in the front of the building. That kid picked the one building that even the crack heads don't go in anymore."

11

"And I bet she was the one who put the padlock on the door. Just in case."

"Had you ever seen her before?"

"No."

"Okay."

"Hey, can we go ahead with the demolition? I mean, I care about the kid, but we have a deadline."

Pete looked at Bart, "Hold on a second, let me check for you."

He called in and got permission to proceed with the demolition.

March 27th   11:45 am

"Let's ask around." Hogan and Sheehan spent an hour asking the shop owners and the few neighbors if they recognized the runaway. Most of the shop owners recognized her as a child of the neighborhood, but they had never seen her with an adult and she had not spoken to them. No one knew her name or where she had come from or even had a clear idea as to how long she had been around. She had never stolen anything, caused alarm, or even inspired much curiosity. She was a ghost child.

Three blocks from the building was a public library.

"You think?"

"She has to go somewhere. It's public and they have running water." They approached the counter and showed the checkout librarian the picture. "Have you seen this child?"

"Yes, is something wrong?"

"Do you know who she is?"

"No, I don't know her name, but she comes in here and reads over in the corner. She is a strange child."

"Strange how?"

"Let's go into the office. She acts like a war veteran or a released prisoner. She always sits with her back against the wall. She is hyper-vigilant and she doesn't seem to go to school. She's here instead. But she didn't show up today. Is she okay?"

"She's safe. How long has she been coming here?"

"Well, it was maybe September the first time I noticed her. She may have been coming in before then but it was summer vacation so I might not have noticed her."

"So, seven months?"

"Yes, I guess so. It's hard to believe it's been that long; she hasn't grown or changed much." She looked out the office window at the empty corner table before explaining. "She still hasn't spoken to anyone or let anyone get near her."

"So, she was always fearful?"

"She is well beyond fearful. She only stays if her table is available, so at first she wasn't here very often. But we did some rearranging and reserved the table for her. Now, when we see her at the door one of us removes the reserved sign and places anything we want to give her at the edge of the table. Then we stand back."

"How close can you get to her?"

"She gets more agitated if anyone is within 10 feet and bolts if anyone gets within 5 feet of her. We just don't try anymore. We do what we can for her but don't press her limits. We have come to an understanding. We leave her be and she will stay here."

"She reads?"

"Yes. That is how we can communicate with her. We set out books on her table and she reads most of them."

"So, she isn't slow?"

"No. Of course, we can't test her in a formal way, but we can tell how well she can read by how fast she goes through the books and how many times she reaches for the dictionary. She seems to be reading at about a 9th or 10th grade level."

Pete looked shocked. "She uses the dictionary?"

The librarian smiled, "Yes and she reads both novels and non-fiction. Other than being terrified of people, she seems quite bright. Although I have never seen her read about fantasy or about animals she won't encounter here. In that way, she *is* limited."

She looked again at the table where the mysterious child often sat. "She is reading for information. She even reads fiction to figure out the world."

"Let me guess; she's read Anne Frank."

"Oh, yes. Based on her choice of books, she seems to identify with the Jews in the Holocaust and the slaves on the Underground Railroad. But she has also read about the Japanese internment camps and the civil rights movement. The turning point for us was when she read "*My Side of the Mountain.*" We all felt like the librarian who was watching over her. Actually, that was the book that started her accepting our gifts."

"What kinds of gifts?"

"She is so thin that we have worried about her nutrition. We gave her whole food—fruit, vegetables that don't need to be cooked, granola bars, and canned foods. She won't take anything that isn't whole or isn't sealed. She is very paranoid."

"You are the Ziploc bag person?"

"I suppose. Is she okay? What happened?"

"And you never called anyone?"

"Oh, we thought about it. We talked about it many times. But a kid that scared? She is running from something and we decided that the best we could do was to provide sanctuary for her. When she is here, she is safe and warm and no one is hurting her. And she has never shown signs of physical abuse. We don't know if she is already under treatment somewhere and we were afraid that if we called someone, she wouldn't consider this place safe anymore."

"So, you *didn't* call because you care?"

"Well, yes, not calling you or child services has been agony for all of us. In the beginning, we figured we would befriend her and find out what the story was before calling the right authority. But that never happened. She never spoke".

"So, she has no library card?"

"No. She never takes anything out. She reads here and re-shelves her own books. When she leaves, it's as if she was never here. Where is she? Please tell me what happened."

"She is at the hospital. She was living in the building over on 9th that they are taking down. They found her in the final walk through."

"Is she hurt?"

"No, just terrified."

"She was living alone? We always assumed she was living with an adult. She was always clean. Can I see her?"

"We'll let you know. Is there anything else you can tell us that might help us find out who she is? Did you notice which way she came from or which way she went when she left? Do you have any idea where she went when the library isn't open?"

"No, but you should know she reads how-to books and magazines on hunting and urban wildlife."

"Okay, thank you. We'll be in touch."

They left the library thinking about what the librarian had said. "Let's go back to the hospital and check on her and check in with missing persons and child services."

March 27th   3:00 pm

She was still sleeping in the pediatric unit when Hogan and Sheehan arrived back at the hospital.

"Doc, how is she doing?"

"Well, we did a full exam while she was under. I don't think we could do it otherwise. She is clean and she doesn't have any bugs. She's a bit malnourished. She only has a few typical bruises from before today. She is going to be covered with bruises from today. They are just starting to show." Seeing the officers bristle, he continued, "Relax; they're exactly what we would expect from how she was fighting."

He took a breath. "She has had multiple broken bones that have healed on their own. Judging from the types of breaks and the way they healed, we are looking at child abuse. But since they were not set, she may not be in the system. The last break was at least 3 years ago."

"Can you tell how old she is?"

"Based on her teeth, she is at least twelve. We did a hand x-ray and it suggests we are looking at closer to fourteen. There is almost no pubescent development yet, but she is severely underweight so that may be skewed. My best guess is between twelve and fourteen."

"Wow, we thought like eight or ten." Pete looked amazed.

Joe reported, "We just came from the public library. The librarians have been giving her food for the past seven months. She reads but doesn't speak and she is paranoid there too. It sounds like her behavior today is normal for her."

"Well, we'll see what happens when she wakes up. We're going to keep her sedated overnight so we can keep the IV in her. We'll try letting her wake up tomorrow and see how she does. Maybe by then we will know who she is."

As they were leaving the hospital, Joe's phone rang. "Hogan"

"Your kid's prints are in the system."

"You're kidding, you've got a name?"

"No, they're unknown prints tied to a four-year-old unsolved murder of a John Doe in Westchester. We're sending the file down to you."

March 28th   9:00 am

Joe Hogan returned to the hospital in the morning and met with Dr. Reuben Feingold, a pediatric psychiatrist assigned to the Jane Doe. "I got a file from Westchester. Her fingerprints were found on a knife that was used to kill a John Doe up there. They don't know what the circumstance of the homicide was. He wasn't found for about week after it happened and they have never identified him. The animals had pretty much cleaned up the mess."

"How did they find fingerprints?"

"It hadn't rained so her fingerprints in the blood on the knife were still there. We've checked missing persons and there is no one reported missing that matches her description. The national missing child data bank doesn't have her. No child or social service agencies have a record of her anywhere in the tri-state area. So, we don't know who she is. We don't know who he is. We don't know if or why she killed him. And we don't know if she could ever speak. Can't you test to see if she can speak?"

"We have. There is no physical reason for her silence. But if she witnessed a murder or committed a murder, she could well be scared silent. You said this was four years ago? Where has she been for four years? How can a child be lost for that long?"

"I guess it's our job to try to find that out. Thanks Doc."

The IV was removed from her arm and Jane Doe was allowed to wake up. She immediately dressed herself in clothes that were laid out for her, and then she made her bed and climbed under it. She was furtive but followed the directive to get into the wheelchair and offered no resistance as she was moved from the pediatric medical unit to the pediatric psychiatric unit and directly into a therapy room. She climbed out of the wheelchair when the seatbelt was released and moved away from the attendant.

A tall, medium-built man in his early forties, with dark hair and dark suit, entered the room. "Hi. I am Dr. Feingold. I would like to talk to you."

She sidestepped away from the doctor without actually looking at him.

"First, I have a message for you. Officer Hogan, the policeman that brought you here yesterday, met the librarian at the library you go to. He wanted you to know that they are concerned about you. They said that you have been going there for a long time and that they care about you. But they don't know your name. We would like to know your name too. We don't know what to call you."

She sat down and curled up on the floor, half sitting, and half kneeling. She made no response and did not acknowledge knowing the librarian.

Gently he continued. "Yesterday while you were sleeping we did some tests. You can talk. But I guess talking seems a bit scary right now. Sometimes, it is easier for people to draw about what they want to say, or write about it."

She did not acknowledge him or his words and he continued pleasantly. "I am going to leave some things here for you. Here are paper, crayons, a notebook, and a pencil and a pen. I am going to leave them here. I will stop by later and we can talk again."
He stepped out of the room and saw a friendly middle-aged woman coming down the hall.

"Theresa Myers, how are you?"

"It's good to see you, Doc. Are you working with my Jane Doe?"

"I just started. Let's go in the observation room and see what we have."

Dr. Feingold and the Children's Services worker watched as the small long haired child looked at the paper and started rocking.

Theresa asked, "Is she autistic? Why is she rocking like that?"

"No, she's not autistic; she almost looks like she is davening." Brightening, he said, "I think I know who she is. I need to make a phone call."

"How do you know who she is?"

"My rabbi talked to me a few years ago about a little girl who started coming around the temple. She never spoke. He asked me about how to handle her muteness. They tried including her as much as they could without parental consent but then the executive director pushed parental consent and medical paperwork and she stopped going there."

"You think this is her?"

"We'll know soon. Theresa, I want to keep her here. She is in no condition to go to a regular facility and I don't think you have a facility that is equipped to handle her."

"If you're willing to have her, I'll talk to my supervisors and try to make it happen. No one has come forward to claim her."

"I don't think anyone will. Did the cops tell you she was involved in a murder four years ago? She would have been somewhere between eight and ten years old then. She has a story. I would like to help her tell it."

"She's yours. You have my contact information. I am going to need weekly visits and reports on her progress. I am supposed to meet with her but I don't think that's going to do her any good right now."

Theresa left to pave the way for her Jane Doe to receive the care she clearly needed.

Rabbi Cohen was out of town for a meeting. He assured Dr. Feingold that he would stop by the hospital as soon as he returned.

March 28th   2:30 pm

After meeting with his other patients, Dr. Feingold returned to the therapy room. Jane Doe had been given lunch but had only eaten the items that were pre-packaged. She had not left the room to explore the unit. Instead, she was sitting in the same ball, half sitting, half kneeling, ready to spring into action.

"How are you doing?" He paused to observe her. "I see you're a little scared by me being in the room with you. How about I sit over here?" He sat in a chair away from the door and a distance from the girl. "Do you see any toys in here that you would like to play with?"

No response.

"You are allowed to play with any of them. Did you know that?"

She just sat, kneeling on one leg but with the other foot on the ground.

"It's been a while since you've played with toys, hasn't it?"

He waited a moment, but there was no reaction.

"Sometimes toys help us to help children feel better. Let me show you how this works." He took a 50 piece puzzle off the shelf and showed her the box.

"You are like a puzzle. It is a very pretty picture but right now it is in all these pieces." He dumped the pieces onto the table and started moving the pieces around, sorting as he spoke. "My job is to help you put all of your pieces together so that you can be whole. Right now we are sorting out the pieces. We need all the edge pieces so we can build the framework. We know some of your pieces. Maybe you can help us understand them better." He spoke and moved puzzle pieces. "The librarian told us that you read very well. One of those pieces is where did you learn to read?"

She did not move or look at him.

"Did you go to school?"

She began to look around the room.

"The librarians also said you are very careful about cleaning up after yourself. I wonder who taught you to be tidy and what happened to that person?"

Still, she quietly surveyed her environment without acknowledging the doctor or his words.

"You have been hiding for a long time, haven't you?" He paused, "You have been very careful about not being found." He moved the puzzle pieces around some more and connected two pieces. "For us to work together, we need to be honest with each other. So, I'm going to be upfront with you. We know you had something happen to you four years ago. We took your fingerprints when you came here and they match fingerprints that the police found four years ago."

She did not show any reaction.

"So that is another piece of the puzzle that we need to put in place." He attached another piece to the puzzle. "And if you were in Westchester four years ago, where you have been for the past four years?" He paused. He looked at the puzzle pieces on the table and then at her.

"There are lots of pieces that we need to put together. So we are going to be spending time together so we can do it. But for now, I am going to leave you alone to just relax and play."

Dr. Feingold left the therapy room and joined the other staff members who were watching from the observation room. From the observation room the multidisciplinary team could see that she was sitting and gently rocking. Dr. Feingold addressed Mike, the senior attendant, "How has she been when she is alone?"

"Just like she is now; she relaxes when people leave and tenses slightly when they enter. You have to watch for it though, it's subtle. Watch her feet, she draws her toes up as she tenses; other than that, she's not showing anything. I wouldn't want to play poker with her. What are we going to do with her?"

"For now we are going to watch her. We know she has been physically abused. But for her to be this non-reactive and paranoid, she has probably suffered severe long-term abuse. I am guessing that she is in survival mode. Once she starts to feel at all safe, we may be dealing with post-traumatic stress disorder."

Nancy, the head nurse, looked at the little girl gently rocking. "What staffing do you want for her? I imagine that she needs one-on-one but isn't that going to stress her more?"

"I want one-on-one but I want the staff to keep their distance. I don't want to stress her but I want her watched. I want your best staff with her. I have a feeling that she's going to be a handful once we start working with her."

"Should she be on suicide watch?"

"Not yet. She is still in survival mode. We may need to change that along the way, but for now, I don't think so. I think we need to work on getting her comfortable here."

Over the next two days she was guided through the daily routine of the unit. She ate in the dayroom and attended group therapies. She outwardly complied but did not participate, gave nothing of herself, and was always vigilant of her surroundings.

Nancy commented to Dr. Feingold, "I feel like we are all under surveillance. She doesn't miss anything."

For meals she ate only prepackaged food and the staff worried about her nutrition. They called the nutritionist who provided sealed cans of supplement shakes. She drank them only if she saw someone else drinking one and she was allowed to choose hers from a group.

Her natural schedule was not compatible with the unit schedule. She slept for several hours from about 6 pm until 10 pm and then was up until nearly 4 am. Then she slept until 9 am. This broken sleep pattern was difficult for the staff and played havoc with the meal schedule. On the third night, she was kept awake in the evening and sent to bed at 9 pm in hopes she would sleep through the night. She did fall asleep for a while.

April 2nd   3:40 am

"This is security. We have a girl in the north stairway: blonde, jeans, blue shirt and a backpack."

"Check Jane Doe."

"She's not in her room."

The security officer entered the stairway on the second floor in time to intercept the escaping child.

"I've got her," he reported into his radio. Addressing the child calmly, "It's is a little late to be going out, isn't it?" She started to bolt but with deft hands he captured her shoulder. "Hold on. You belong upstairs."

He turned her gently and guided her back up the four flights of stairs. "Come on. Let's get you back up there. It's okay. How did you get out? Did someone leave a door open?" He paused as they climbed a flight of stairs, "They know they aren't supposed to leave the doors open." They reached the sixth floor and he led her through the fire door. Looking up, he saw one ceiling tile out of place.

"Oh, I see. That's very clever. We've never had a kid try to escape through the drop ceiling."

"How did you get up there?"

She just stood still, looking down.

"You're not going to tell me, are you?"

Bending down and looking in her face, he said kindly but sternly, "Look, kid. Don't do it again. We have the stairs on surveillance. We are pretty particular about making sure our patients stay where they are supposed to be. That's our job. We're here to make sure you're safe. It's your job to stay here and deal with whatever it is you need to deal with. Everyone needs to do their job. Okay? Okay."

And with that, he unlocked the unit door and sent her back inside.

"Here you go folks; one stray kid. See if you can keep her inside from now on." He nodded at the staff and with a smile he resumed his rounds.

The child was returned to her room and assisted back into pajamas. Her backpack and clothes were removed from her room, as were her sneakers. She lay down in the bed as directed but sleep was not on her agenda. She looked around the room and her eyes darted back and forth. Finally, she climbed out of her bed and scurried furtively out of her room.

She went into the therapy room, ignoring the night staff person who was chastising her for escaping and telling her to go back to bed. She found the pad of paper and a pen, sat on the floor in the far corner of the room and started writing.

I don't want to die. I know you need to kill me and that I deserve it. I have been hiding for four years because I don't want to die. But I know that is what has to happen and I am going to try to be brave enough to do it. You wanted to know where I have been for four years. I started out in the woods but then I took a train into the city. I came into Grand Central Station. There were so many people and no one noticed me. I started to think that I was invisible. The first place I slept in the city was in a closed train platform. I went to sleep under the platform overhang. But the rats woke me up when they ran across my legs. I haven't ever tried to sleep in a tunnel again. I hate rats. There are so many rats in the city. I don't think most people notice them. But at night, they just walk around like the people do during the day. Sometimes I still kill them with my slingshot. I practiced on the rats so that I could kill the squirrels and the pigeons. A gun would be faster but people would notice a gun.

I have been in the woods on the north end of the island and in abandoned buildings, and on playgrounds, and in public places. Sometimes I ate at soup kitchens but other times I got food from trash cans, hunting, eating berries, and vegetables from people's gardens. I tried collecting acorns, but it is hard because the squirrels get them first. I have eaten the squirrels and the pigeons but not the rats. I don't like rats. I don't like rats at all.

I moved around the city the first summer. Part of the time I was on the northern end of the island. It is wilder there and I could practice with my slingshot during the day and go swimming and people left a lot of food in the trash at the park. I liked the little red lighthouse. But then it started getting cold and I moved south. Some of the buildings have steam heat and the pipes are warm. It took some time to find the warm places and sometimes people would find me and chase me out. I stayed in churches. Old churches have lots of hiding places. But they don't have food. Temples are warm too. I like the temples because they are open all day. There is a Rabbi that I like. At first he used to see me but pretend that I wasn't there. When no one was around he would talk out loud and sometimes he would sing to me. And he would leave me food. I was his secret. He talked to me and didn't ask me anything. I liked that he pretended that I wasn't there. People would come to see him and he never told anyone that they were being watched. He told me that I could go to Hebrew school and that if I didn't want to talk that I could just watch. So, I learned Hebrew. I went to Hebrew school for a long time. In the mornings and on Friday nights I went to services. But then a man told me that I had to have papers filled out by my parent to come back. I didn't go there anymore. I liked being there.

But Rabbi Cohen taught me to read in Hebrew and he talked about God and Talmud. He said that the questions to many answers are in the Talmud. Sometimes what he said was all backwards. He was funny that way.

The answer for me is very clear. I have to be killed. I am not like Daniel or Job. They were innocent. I am not innocent. I'm not even like Sarah in the bible but Rabbi called me Sarah. I miss him. I think that if the Rabbi helped me anymore he would be in trouble. I don't want him to be killed, too.

She stopped writing as Dr. Feingold entered the therapy room.

"I hear you had a bit of an adventure last night. I see you have the notebook. They said you have been writing since you got back. Is there something you want to share?"

And with that she stood up. Biting her lip and closing her eyes, she handed Dr. Feingold the notebook. He read what she had written while she stood in front of him, braced for certain death.

"Sarah? Is your name Sarah?"

She nodded and then shook her head.

"So the rabbi called you Sarah but that isn't your real name. "

She nodded tentatively.

"And do you want to tell me your real name?"

She shook her head slightly and winced as if expecting to be hit for her defiance.

"Do you want to be called Sarah?"

She nodded.

"Then Sarah it is. Do you want to see the rabbi again?"

Shrug.

"Is that a yes, but you do not want him to be in trouble?"

She nodded.

"Sarah, you have had quite an adventure over the past four years."

She stood quietly with her head bowed.

"Have you spoken at all during that time?"

She shook her head and looked at him.

"And before then, did you speak?"

She shrugged her shoulders non-committally.

"You are a very brave person. Not many people would face death the way you are. Are you sure that you will be killed?"

She stood still and with a very scared but trying-to-be-brave face, she nodded.

"Do you think that you deserve to die?"

She nodded slowly.

"Sarah, you wrote that the answer was clear for you. You wrote that you have to die. The only time the Torah calls for death is murder. Do you think that you deserve to die because you have killed someone?"

She nodded again, somewhat relieved by his understanding.

"And you have not spoken since you killed the person?

She nodded again.

"Sarah, no one is going to kill you. We have a lot of work to do together." He paused and then added, "I will tell you that Rabbi Cohen has been very worried about you. He isn't going to be in trouble for helping you. Would you like him to visit you?"

Sarah nodded.

"I will let him know you're here. It may be a few days before he comes to visit because he is out of town in a meeting." She looked at him quizzically.

"You weren't a secret. Rabbi Cohen saw you, like all children, as a treasure. He never wanted to lose you and has been very worried about you since you stopped going to the temple."

For the first time he saw a spark in her eye.

"I am proud of you, Sarah. You have done something that very few kids could ever do. You have done so much by yourself. I hope that you will let us help you now. I know you will tell me the truth. Will you stay here willingly?"

She nodded slowly.

"Okay. Here is your notebook. How about you get some breakfast and I will see you tomorrow?"

She took her notebook and left the room, not believing that he was not going to kill her and knowing that her time was limited for getting her story on paper before the execution.

Sarah, as she was now to be called, ate breakfast and spent the rest of the day writing. She stopped long enough to eat meals, but then returned to her task until bedtime.

April 2nd   1:00 pm

The first summer I was sleeping on playgrounds and in little holes and I was finding food from the trash cans. I learned how to shoot a slingshot. I practiced on rats until I could shoot them really good, then I started to kill pigeons. I can hit them in the head and knock them out and then wring their necks. The first time I did it I threw up and I cried. But a few days later I tried again and I did it okay. Cleaning the bird was really gross. But I was hungry. So I did it anyway. I kept telling myself that they are just little chickens and people eat chicken all the time. I still hate the feeling of the bones crunching in my hands but now I can do it fast and I don't even have to think about it. Rich people used to eat pigeon and they called it squab. So, I think about them being flying squab and I pretend that I am a rich kid like Eloise.

I like squirrel better than pigeon. But I couldn't kill them with just pebbles. I needed shot for that. I got BBs at an army navy store. And then I could shoot squirrels. Squirrels don't run around at night and you can't kill squirrels in public so I don't get to eat squirrels very often. But sometimes I can be in parks without people and the squirrels will be out and I can get them.

But after the first summer, it started getting cold and I knew that I couldn't just sleep on a playground when there was snow.

I started walking south and checking out empty buildings along the way. I would go into any building that I could get into. Some of them had people in them and I left right away. Other buildings were really scary and I didn't go in them at all. I stayed in some of them for a few days but they didn't feel right and I moved on. I didn't have a real plan. I just wandered. But then one day I found my building. I went in the basement and I found the little room. I think it was an access hole or something, but I am not really sure. It was just the right size for me and there was a steam pipe running along one wall. It was dry and warm. The whole building was empty and a lot of the floors weren't safe so people weren't going to be coming in there. The roof was collapsing so it would rain in the building but there was a drain in the floor so the basement stayed dry. I used the floor drain for my potty. The rain helped keep everything clean, sort of. So, I moved in.

I found plastic at a construction site and I put it down on the floor. I got a metallic sheet at the army navy store in the camping section and I put that down. That helped the floor be warmer but it was still really hard. I was checking dumpsters one night and I found packing peanuts. That is when I had the idea of a packing peanut bed. I took them home but they just spread everywhere and made a mess. So, I found a board that was a floor plank and I cut it so I could fit it tight in the room. Then I started finding more peanuts and filling up my bed. I put a tarp over the peanuts so I didn't track them all over the place. And I found a strawberry shortcake sleeping bag on sale at the thrift store. So that was my bed. I still collect packing peanuts because they squish down.

The first night I went into the laundry there was only one person there and she was a lady who was busy washing clothes. I went to the little washing machine and emptied all my clothes into the washer. Then I put in the money and started it up. I didn't have any soap but I figured that just putting them through the machine would be better than washing them on me in the fountains like I had been doing. That method doesn't really work very well and they were pretty stinky when I put them in the washing machine. Well, the lady came over. I was getting scared but she smiled and she said, "You need soap to make clean. You have soap?" I looked around for the soap machine. She said, "I have. One scoop you need. Tonight, I help."

"Taina Ortiz help little girl. Little Girl have name?"
She was the first person that had helped me directly all summer. I am trying to write this the way that she talks even though it isn't right writing. I could understand what she meant and I didn't want to be rude, but I couldn't   talk.

"You no speak?"
I shook my head.

"*Taina Ortiz calls you Blanca. Blanca hair, Blanca girl. You be Blanca, 'kay?"*

And that is how it started. The first night I just washed my clothes and dried them. Taina helped me fold them. My whites weren't white anymore and most of my clothes were really worn. But she didn't make fun of them. Instead she said, "You get all dark clothes. You wash together, not turn grey."

When she helped me fold my short sleeve shirts she said, "Time for long sleeves too. Getting cold for short sleeves and short pants."
"Your mama have warm clothes for you?" I shrugged. She just talked about the nice warm clothes she saw at The Second Hand Store. She said I look like I will need size 8 now. "Size 8 when you get new clothes."

I didn't tell her that I didn't have a mama. But I did go to The Second Hand Store and they did have warm clothes. I got 3 pairs of jeans and 3 long sleeve shirts and a jacket. I went to Jack's and got underwear and socks. I got them in dark blue so I didn't have to try to match them and I could wash them all together. I was glad she told me what size to buy because I really didn't know and I couldn't have asked to try them on.

I also got laundry soap at Jack's. I had forgotten how nice it is to have clean clothes and I didn't want to be without them again.

I went back the next week with some of my new clothes all dirty. When I came in the door Taina saw it was me and she started smiling, "Blanca, you come back! Good we wash clothes. And look you dress warm. Good girl. We wash clothes. I loaded my clothes into the washer and she touched my new blue socks. "Good Girl, no grey clothes for Blanca." I put my soap in and she told me I did a good job. Then she pulled shampoo of her bag and said, "While clothes wash, we wash hair. Come lay down, Taina wash Blanca hair, she feel so clean with clean hair."

What else could I do? I lay down on the folding counter. Taina washed my hair. It was starting to get long by then and the only thing I had done all summer was to get it wet when I went swimming in the Hudson River and in the playground sprinklers. I didn't realize how bad it must have smelled, but she never made a face about it. She just got it wet and washed it twice. I never had anyone wash my head like that before. She scrubbed so hard then she put conditioner on it. The conditioner smelled like coconut. I felt so clean and wonderful. Then she combed my hair out. I had been trying to comb it but it had sort of gotten away from me a bit and I had some pretty big snarls. But Taina didn't yell at me and she didn't hit me. She just talked to me about her kids and how she used to brush their hair every day. And that she missed getting to do it because they were all grown up. She said I was a gift; "A little Chiquita to help." I thought she was calling me a banana for a long time. But she was so nice about it and she wasn't scary. So, the next week when I went I was okay when she took my shirt off of me in front of the washer and gave me a bathrobe to put on. She said it was her little girl's a long time ago. Now I could wash all my clothes and we would wash my hair and then she had me sit with my feet in the laundry sink and I had my first bath in about five months. She scrubbed me down that first time. I needed the help. I didn't realize how dirty I was, but my dirt had dirt on it. She even had me sit in the laundry sink so she could wash my back. She let me wash my own privates. Then she dried me with some amazing, fluffy, soft towels. And she combed out my hair. It went much faster this time because I had been combing it every day. I could keep up with it since it was clean and tied in tails most of the time. She said she was proud of me for the job I was doing, "Not many kids wash their own clothes." After my clothes were clean and dry, I got to put on hot clean clothes for the first time in months and Taina put the robe and towels in the washing machine and said, "Now no one know. Taina help Blanca and no one knows."

I came back every week and washed and dried my clothes, washed my hair and took a bath. She always helped me with my hair and washed my back but other than that I took care of myself. It didn't take as long as the first time, so we had time to just spend together. She showed me how to fold clothes and we would fold all the other people's clothes together. That was really her job, washing people's clothes that were left at the laundry. She did it in the middle of the night so that the machines were there for people who wanted to wash their own clothes during the day.

Sometimes she would trim my hair and sometimes she would cut my nails. But mostly we just did the usual routine. She talked about her kids and grandkids. We washed lots of clothes and folded lots of clothes. Sometimes she spoke in English and sometimes she spoke in Puerto-Rican. She started explain the words when she used them but it got so I didn't need the explanation. I don't know if I could speak it, but I can understand it. Anyway, I started helping her more and she started giving me money for working for her. She said that I made up for the time it took to wash my hair because the rest of the work went faster. And we would stop and eat. She said it was her lunch time and she was hungry. She brought the best food. So, one night a week I had a bath, washed my clothes, washed my hair and had a really good meal. But I missed this week and Taina doesn't know where I am. I wish I could let her know that I am okay.

April 3rd   9:30 am

Dr. Feingold sat down with Sarah in the therapy room.
"Sarah, I am told that you are doing a lot of writing."
She nodded.
"Is it helping you feel a little more relaxed?"
 She looked into his eyes, nodding.
"I am glad that writing is helping. But I am a talking doctor and I would like you to tell me about you and your life. We can start wherever you want but I want us to be honest with each other. Can you try?"
She once again looked into his eyes but did not answer.
"Is that a maybe?"
She looked at him and tilted her head to the side. Then she picked up a puzzle piece and placed it in the corner of the puzzle.
"Hey that's great. You have the corner piece."
She placed another piece. She took a deep breath. Her entire body shook as she placed a third piece and whispered, "When?"
"When what?"
Sarah shut her eyes, took a deep breath, and whispered, "When kill me?"
"No one is going to kill you. But I'd like to talk with you about why you think I am going to kill you."
"Someone has to do it." She was panting with the effort of speaking.
"Why does someone need to do it?"
"It's the rules."
"I think we have a puzzle to put together before anyone can plan your execution."
"Sarah puzzle or picture puzzle?" She asked in broken speech.
"The Sarah puzzle. I think you could put this puzzle together in about 5 minutes, yes?"
"Yes." And she put it together quickly as he watched. Her hands moved as if she already knew where each piece went.
Dr. Feingold smiled as he watched. "Sarah, that was great. Putting the Sarah puzzle together may take a little more time. Do you

think we can work together on it?" Stepping back Sarah looked directly at Dr. Feingold, bit her lip, and nodded.

April 5th   10:30 am

Rabbi Cohen returned to New York and called Dr. Feingold. "So, when should I see if you have my Sarah?"

"I already know that I have your Sarah. And she wants to see you. When can you come by?"

"How is this afternoon?"

"That would be great. She has missed you and would like to see you again."

When he arrived on the unit, he was greeted by Dr. Feingold and led to the therapy room where Sarah was sitting on the floor, writing.

"Sarah, someone is here to see you."

Sarah looked up and smiled before her face clouded over with fear.

"Sarah, look at you. Have you been hiding here all this time? I was worried when you stopped coming to temple. You are well?"

"Sarah, you look surprised and worried," Dr. Feingold observed. Sarah looked at Dr. Feingold and nodded.

Rabbi jovially exclaimed, "Look, she nods. For me you didn't nod, for him you nod."

Sarah smiled.

Rabbi returned the smile and, bumping Dr. Feingold's arm teased, "For me she smiles. A smile is better than a nod. I get the smiles."

"Sarah, do you want me to explain to Rabbi Cohen why you stopped going to temple or would like to save that for another time?"

Sarah looked quizzically at Dr. Feingold, *How do I answer that question with a nod?*

"Sarah, watch me." He put one palm down on his upturned flattened palm and said "now." Then he slid the top palm across the bottom palm and pushed it away. "Later."
Sarah understood immediately. She thought for a minute. Looking at both men, she closed her eyes and signed "Now."

"Okay. I think we all need to have a seat."

Dr. Feingold explained that Sarah had been living alone for the past four years and that she had not spoken because she had killed someone and she didn't want to die. And that she stopped attending temple so that Rabbi Cohen would not get in trouble too.

"That is very kind of you, Sarah, to care so much about your old rabbi. You are such a good girl. Did Dr. Feingold tell you that I will not get in trouble for being your friend, even if you did kill someone?"

She nodded.

"And you would like this old rabbi to visit you?"

She looked at him and nodded.

"Then it shall be. Shall we work on your studies? You haven't practiced your aleph bets, have you?"

She shook her head ashamedly.

"Have you said your morning prayers like I taught you?"

"You taught her to daven?" Dr. Feingold asked.

"She learned that part on her own. But prayers? Prayers, I teach."

"How is your schedule on Thursday afternoon, Sarah?"

She looked at Dr. Feingold quizzically.

"I think Thursday afternoons would be a fine time for Hebrew School. I will put it on her calendar."

"Ah, you are her social secretary, too?" Turning to Sarah he said, "You are in good hands Sarah. But I must leave now. Thursday, two o'clock, sharp."

Sarah walked down the hall with Rabbi Cohen. She was stopped about 10 feet from the locked door by the staff, who knew she would run if given the chance. He turned to her and held her hands against his chest and then hugged her. As he did it he sang out "Rab-bi Hug." Then he placed a hand on her head and offered a blessing. Sarah allowed herself to be hugged and blessed.

April 6th   10:00 am

Sarah had been in the hospital for 10 days. She was speaking regularly with Dr. Feingold but only sporadically with the staff. It was Friday morning; there was more noise and staff on the unit than usual. The parent of another patient called to report that, for the second time, she had seen that a staff person had not allowed Sarah to eat dinner. After several short meetings, a group of hospital administrators and Theresa, the ACS worker, went into the observation room. Dr. Feingold brought Sarah into the therapy room.

"Sarah, have a seat. We need to talk about something important."

Sarah sat in a chair at the table and shrunk down as if expecting to be yelled at. "Sarah, have you been eating dinner?"

She shook her head "No."

"Did you want to eat dinner?"

She looked at the doctor and nodded.

"Why didn't you eat dinner?"

Haltingly she explained, "I wouldn't talk to Stephen. I can't eat dinner until I speak up and ask for my tray."

"Did Stephen tell you that you can't eat until you talk to him?"

She haltingly repeated his words. "Mute my ass. You'll talk when you get hungry. You can have your dinner when you say, 'May I have my dinner, please?'"

"Why won't you talk to Stephen?"

"Scary."

"Are you saying Stephen is scary?"

She nodded and said, "Mean."

"Stephen is mean?"

She nodded again.

"So you won't talk to him because he is scary and mean?"

She looked down and nodded.

"Have you eaten dinner here at all?"

She looked at him and nodded.

"When?"

"Days off."

"So, you have only eaten dinner if Stephen is having a day off?"

She nodded again.

"Sarah, if anyone tells you that you can't eat, I want you tell me or the nurse in charge. Can you do that?"

She nodded her head and relaxed.

"Thank you, Sarah. You can rest assured that you will be eating dinner from now on. Okay?"

She nodded.

"I need to talk to some people and, speaking of food and eating, I believe you have cooking group."

April 6th   3:00 pm

Cooking group is funny. We make funny food and we never cook. We put peanut butter on crackers and we put peanut butter on celery. And we put frosting on cupcakes, but we don't bake the cupcakes. We just put frosting on them. We don't cut anything up because we can't have a sharp knife and we don't have a fire and the electric stove is shut off at a box that is locked. I would like to cook on the stove. It would be nice just to boil water to make some bouillon like I used to make when I lived alone. That isn't really cooking either, but it's better than peanut butter on celery.

Yesterday, she put raisins on the peanut butter on the celery and called it ants on a log. Clearly, she has never actually tasted an ant because she would never call it ants on a log and expect us to eat it if she ever did. I tried eating ants because I read that people in other countries eat ants. Other countries must have better tasting ants than New York ants.

April 6th   3:00 pm

The call came on Joe Hogan's cell.

"Hey, Officer Hogan, it's Bartolo. We were doing the asbestos removal and we found where your kid had been living."

"Really? I thought she was living in the attic?"

"No, there is a false wall in the foundation. She has a heated apartment down here. There's food, clothing, sewers, and a little stove—the whole works. She even has a teddy bear. The kid set the whole place up nice. You want to look at it before we wreck it?"

"Yeah, I'll be right down."

Hogan arrived at the building a short time later. Seeing the small bunker he sighed, "We need to take pictures of all of this and then pack it up. This is amazing. Do you think she did this all herself?"

"I think she did. Look—she has a saw and a hammer; everything here is either found or recycled. She could put this all together. It's simple but makes do. I think a lot of kids could do this if they thought about it. But they never need to think about it. Here, look at this bed. She has a frame that she nailed together and she filled it with packing peanuts. What softer, better insulated mattress could she have? Look at the shelf with the clothes. They are all clean and folded. The bed is made and her bear is sitting guard. All her food is in metal containers. Oh, and look what we have here; she has weapons."

"What?"

"She has a slingshot and a can of mace. I bet one is for one type of rat and one is for the other. And look at the white line all around the room. That's why there are no bugs; Boric acid. This kid is really something else."

"You said she has sewers?"

"Yeah, check this out. See that bucket? We noticed it when we did the walkthrough but didn't think about it. That bucket was right under the hole in the roof. So, she has rainwater. And over here there is a floor drain attached to the city sewer system. See that old enamel bowl? It's a chamber pot. She could use that, drain it down the pipe and rinse with clean rain water. The cover comes right off that pipe. She has sewers and clean water."

Bart surveyed the basement with vicarious pride in the child and asked, "Is she doing okay at the hospital?"

"Yeah, the doctor says she is starting to respond a little. She has a long way to go. Let me take her clothes and her bear to her."

"My guys can pack this room up. We need to make sure it's asbestos-free before she gets any of it. Can you come back on Monday and pick up her bear and clothes? We'll store everything else. We'll keep it safe for her. I feel like we are tearing down the poor kid's house. You tell her that me and my crew feel bad about tearing down her house and we will make her a special room wherever she goes. You tell her."

"I will."

April 9th   8:00 am

The investigation of Sarah's actual identity had gone nowhere. Despite a street canvas and news exposure, no one could give any substantive information as to who Sarah was or where she had once lived. Officer Hogan was back on his beat and the hope of finding out more about Sarah's past was no longer on his mind when a call came into Missing Persons.

"Missing Persons"

"Hello? Little girl, she no come two weeks now."

"What little girl?"

"Little girl come every week to wash clothes. I help her wash hair. Do laundry. She no come two weeks. I worry."

The officer took the caller's information and relayed it to Officer Hogan. "I think I found someone who knows your Jane Doe."

It was early in the morning when Officer Hogan contacted Taina Ortiz at the 24 hour laundry six blocks from where they had found Sarah.

"Who is the little girl?"

"I call Blanca. Blanca hair, Blanca girl. She no speak. She come every week in the night and wash her clothes. I help her wash her hair. But she no come two weeks."

Officer Hogan showed her a picture of Sarah. "Is this the little girl?"

"Yes, Blanca. She okay?"

"She is okay. She is safe. She's being well cared for. How long has she been coming here?"

"Tres anos." Three years. "She come in the night, always alone. I help her wash her clothes and we wash her long hair. I brush her hair for her; long, blonde hair. I make her food. She sweet girl. She okay?"

"Do you know where she lived?"

"No, she no talk. She no talk. She always alone. But she never hurt. She not look too sad. Maybe her mother sick, not can take care of her good. I help her. You tell her Taina Ortiz ask for her. Miss her. I go see her? You tell Taina where Blanca, Taina go visit."

"She is in good care now but I will get a message to her that you called about her. Can I give her a way to contact you?"

She gave him her number and assured her that she would do anything she could for her Blanca.

"Thank you for helping her. I will tell her that you asked about her."

"Wait! Her name, I call Blanca but what her real name?"

"I wish we knew. But for now anyway she is being called Sarah."

"Sarah. I call Sarah too."

April 12th   Two O'Clock, Sharp

Rabbi Cohen arrived on the unit to find Sarah reading a book from the unit library. "Sarah, are you ready for Hebrew School?"

Sarah looked up and smiled, "Two o'clock sharp?" Rabbi Cohen, who had never heard her voice before, laughed. "It's two o'clock sharp. Come, I have books for you."

They sat in the day room reviewing the letters which Sarah said aloud for the first time. After working with letter and words, Rabbi asked, "It's been a long time since you were at temple. Do you still remember your prayers?"

Sarah nodded. "But, I never said them out loud. I don't know if I can."

"How about if we say them together?"

Sarah nodded and the Rabbi started slowly. "Baruch Ata, Adonai...." And together they completed several prayers Sarah learned during her time at temple and Hebrew school.

When they finished, Rabbi Cohen stood. "I need to go now but I am going to leave these books with you. Rabbi Hug?" Sarah nodded, and he held her hands against his chest, embraced her and sang out "Rab-bi Hug." Then he placed his hand upon her forehead and blessed her.

Sarah was smiling when she was stopped 10 feet from the door by the staff.

"You can say good-bye from here."

April 13th   11:15 am

I am in so much trouble. The pet therapy lady came here today. I hate her. She is so way too much sunshine. I think she needs to drink about four fewer cups of coffee before she comes here. Today she brought bunnies and baby chickens. The staff told me that I had to go join in. I didn't want to but they said I had to go so I went and sat in a chair. The therapy lady asked me if I wanted to hold a bunny. I shook my head. She brought it over to me anyway and told me to pet it. I shook my head no. She started rubbing the bunny against my arm and asking me if it felt soft. I pulled away. Then I tried to leave but she stopped me and put a chick in my hands. I wrung its neck and handed it back to her. She screamed and the staff came and she told them that I killed the chick

Nancy looked at the chick and at me and said "To your room". If I remember correctly, that is where I was when this whole thing started. But, why did I kill it? I wasn't going to eat it. I mean, I have killed pigeons lots of times but only to eat them. Today was different. That therapist made me think about before. They would ask if what they did felt good. "That feels good doesn't it?" "You like that don't you?" "Feel how soft that is?"

I keep seeing pictures in my head. Pictures of before. I don't want those pictures.

Tears streamed down Sarah's face as she sat in the corner of her room with her notebook on the floor next to her.

"Okay Sarah, it's okay. Let me get you a washcloth." Nancy wiped Sarah's face and asked if she was okay. Sarah nodded.

"I know you feel bad about killing the chick. I'll let Dr. Feingold know what happened. I'm sure that he's going to want to talk with you."

Sarah just looked at her and wondered how someone who is supposed to be so smart could be so clueless.

"Tough day, I hear. Do you want tell me what happened or do you want me to read first?"

"Read." She handed him the notebook and he read her latest entry.

"So crying wasn't remorse for killing the chick like they told me?"

Sarah shook her head, "No. I don't care about the stupid chick."

"Is seeing pictures of before new for you?"

She nodded.

"Now that you are in a place that is safe you may start remembering what happened to you when you were younger. We need to talk about the pictures."

She nodded.

"Are you ready for that?"

She nodded and looked him in the eye.

"Where would you like to start?"

"At the beginning."

"Okay. What was the beginning?" Dr. Feingold encouraged.

She sat still for a moment, biting her lip and readying herself. Then, slowly, haltingly, she started to speak. "I was asleep but I felt something cold inside me and it woke me up. I think it was his finger. A man was telling Zeke that it's important to start while I was asleep. He was talking about me being asleep and relaxed…and…I don't know what. But he said something about wanting me nice and relaxed. Then when I started to wake up, he was supposed to tell me it feels good. He told Zeke I was good because I clenched. I didn't know what clenching was."

Dr. Feingold remained silent and she continued in halting and broken speech. "Well, that's what you want. He told Zeke to only use one finger and don't let anyone fuck me yet. Then he pushed his finger into me and I squeezed hard against it and he started laughing and took it out and hugged me and told me I was a good girl."

"Do you know who this man was?"

"I don't know who he was but sometimes when I woke up he was there and he was telling Zeke what else to do to train me. Zeke listened to him then he did whatever the man said to do."

"Who was Zeke?"

"He was Zeke."

"Was Zeke the only person who took care of you or did you have other people taking care of you too?"

"Just Zeke. He made my food and got me dressed and tucked me in bed."

"Was he your father?"

"I don't know. I guess so. I didn't have anyone else."

"What else would you like to tell me about the beginning?"

"Sometimes it wasn't just that man or Zeke touching me. Sometimes he had friends over and they would talk about the training. They would be sitting in chairs and on the couch and they just gave me to each other. After a while I would fall asleep."

"Do you know how old you were?"

"No. I think it happened a long time ago."

"Were you wearing a diaper or under pants?"

"I was wearing underpants but before we had company Zeke took them off and Zeke would put special lotion in me."

"He put special lotion inside of you?"

Sarah nodded, "So I wouldn't get sore."

Sarah paused and then said, "I must have been pretty little because I remember bumping my nose on the on the couch arm when one person put me down and I tried to stand up."

"How do you feel talking about this?"

She shrugged, "It's okay."

"You feel okay talking about this?"

"Well, it was all blurry in my head when it happened. And it's kind of blurry and mixed up now."

"Did it make you feel like crying?"

"No. Those were different pictures."

"Do you want to talk about those pictures today?"

She shook her head. "Can we do it tomorrow?"

"Are you going to be okay tonight if we wait?"

"I don't know."

"I am going to write an order for the staff to give you some medicine to help you with the pictures in case you need it tonight." He took out a piece of paper and wrote on it. 'I need medicine, please.'

"If you need the medicine and you are having trouble talking, you can give this to the nurse. You did a great job today. You need to take it easy tonight. Okay?"

She nodded.

"And Sarah?" She stopped and looked at him. "No more chickens, okay?"

"Okay. No chickens."

"I am proud of you."

"We have more talking do, huh?"

"Yes, but not tonight. We will talk tomorrow."

April 14th   10:30 am

Officer Hogan entered the unit and approached Dr. Feingold. He caught the eye of Sarah, who was sitting in the day room. Sarah went white before his eyes.

"Doc, what's wrong with the kid?"

Dr. Feingold looked at Sarah and saw terror in her eyes. "Oh, no. Sarah, it's okay."

"Sarah, stop." But true to form, she didn't stop. She flew into her room, jumped onto the window sill, onto the armoire and into the drop ceiling.

Joe Hogan followed her, "Sarah, what's wrong?"

Right behind Joe was Dr. Feingold. "Sarah, he is not here to arrest you."

Sarah looked down and said, "Chicken."

Officer Hogan responded, "Hey, I'm not a chicken. I just don't have a reason to arrest you."

"No," Dr. Feingold chuckled. "Sarah killed a baby chick yesterday during pet therapy. I would bet she thinks you are here to arrest her."

"Sarah, I'm not here to arrest you." He climbed onto a chair and looked into the ceiling space. "Wow, how did you know this was here?"

"It's not her first trip up there."

"Why does that not surprise me? Look, I brought you some of your stuff. Why don't you come on down so I can give it to you?"

"My stuff?"

"Yeah, I have your stuff. Come on down and see. I have your clothes and your money and your bear. I didn't bring your sling shot or your mace in here but we have all the rest of your stuff packed up for you."

Sarah looked down from the ceiling.

"No arrest?"

Office Hogan looked at Dr. Feingold. "It's your call, Doc. Is she going to skate on the chicken?"

"Well, she is going to have a lot of work to do because of that chicken but you don't need to arrest her for it. Come on back down."

And she did, setting the ceiling tile squarely back in place.

"Can she actually get out?"

"Sarah, what is the answer to that?"

She shook her head. "I can get into the stairway. Security is watching. I can't leave."

"So, you climbed up there knowing you couldn't escape?"

Haltingly she said "Just because I couldn't escape doesn't mean you could catch me."

Officer Hogan let out a laugh. "You are something special."

"They were getting ready to tear down the building and when they were emptying the basement, they found your house. Have you told the doc about your house?"

She shook her head.

"Doc, I have pictures." He handed the pictures to Sarah. "Here you go, these are copies for you. Bartolo, he is the man that found you, packed up all of your stuff, except the bed—nice bed, by the way. They are storing everything for you. When you get to wherever you end up, he and his crew have offered to make your room very special for you. But we wanted you to have your clothes and your money now. And your bear said that if you were here, he wanted to be here too."

"He talked to you?"

"Hey, what can I say? How could he resist? But he's just like you; he wouldn't tell me his name either."

Sarah took the bear, hugged it, and smiled at Officer Hogan. "Cody. He wanted to be a Kodiak bear so I named him Cody."

"Where did you get him?"

"Street fair. I bought him."

She looked at Dr. Feingold, "Can he stay?"

"He can stay."

"It looks like we have a lot to talk about. Did you build this all by yourself?"

She nodded. "I bought the saw and the hammer. Rocks didn't work very well. So I bought the hammer. I found most of my stuff but some things I bought."

"Well, Bartolo said you did a great job. He and his crew were very proud of you." Turning to Dr. Feingold, he pointed to one of the pictures.

"Doc, see how clean this all is? She kept everything this clean in an abandoned building."

"I didn't build the room or the door."

"Yeah, but you found them and you used them. You did a nice job. Now, I need to take off. Are you going to stay out of the ceiling?"

She shrugged and smiled.

"I just have one question. If you had your little house in the basement, why were you in the attic?"

"People had started coming in the building and I didn't want to get trapped in the basement. So I put a lock on the attic door and I slept there when I got home late at night."

"That's one mystery solved."

Officer Hogan shook hands with Dr. Feingold and left.

"That was nice of him to bring you your clothes and Cody. I will send the nurse in to get your clothes inventoried and checked in. We are going to need to put your money in a safe so that it doesn't get stolen. But you will have a signed receipt so you will get it back when you leave the hospital. We will talk in a while; I have some things I need to do now, okay?"

She nodded and looked at Cody.

April 20th   12:30 pm

Cody became Sarah's constant companion. With him by her side she began to engage in the unit activities. Sarah visited the dayroom more frequently, sat in rooms with other people and ate snacks even when they weren't prepackaged. She began to speak more freely with staff and the other patients. This morning, however, she appeared to have woken up the wrong side of the bed. She was generally grumpy and uncooperative in therapy. She was irritable during lunch and accidently dumped her tray on the floor. Mike, her favorite day staff person, started toward her and she ran for her room, quickly crawling into the ceiling. Rather than chasing her, Mike let her be, telling her they would talk about it when she came down.

She was in the ceiling for about 15 minutes when Mike checked on her. "Sarah, you okay up there?"

Sarah crawled out of the ceiling and collapsed onto her armoire. "Help."

"Sarah, what's wrong?"

She touched her head and then her stomach.

"You feel sick?"

She nodded and closed her eyes.

"Can you climb down?"

She shook her head, and then held it in her hands.

"Sarah, I am going to lift you down. Are you okay with that?"

She nodded.

He lowered her from the armoire and set her on her bed. She lay back with her eyes closed and coughed. Mike felt her forehead and called, "Nancy."

Nancy came in. "What's wrong, Sarah?"

"She has a fever."

"That explains this morning."

"Sarah, I need to take your temperature. I am going to put this in your ear. Just lie still."

"102. Sarah, does anything hurt?" She touched her head and her stomach.

"Do you feel like you are going to throw up?"

She nodded weakly then touched her eyes.

"Your eyes hurt."

She nodded and pointed at the window.

"Light hurts your eyes?"

She nodded. She began to shiver.

"Okay, Sarah, you have a fever. Let's get you into your pajamas and get you into bed."

"Mike, can you get a bowl for Sarah while I help her get into her PJ's?"

Nancy helped Sarah change into her pajamas and climb into bed.

She was asleep almost immediately.

Nancy called the pediatrician who examined her half an hour later and, after running a test, pronounced it the flu.

She woke up few hours later and was sick to her stomach. Betsy, the evening nurse, came in and helped her get cleaned up and changed. Before they finished, she was sick again. And so went the evening. At 10:00 p.m. Betsy started an IV to hydrate Sarah and get medication into her.

She slept through the morning. Waking at noon, she was able to eat a piece of toast.

A few hours later, Mike checked on her and brought her a Popsicle.

"Sarah, how is the tummy doing?"

She nodded.

"Are you feeling a little better? Do you want to try sitting up?"

She hesitated, but then nodded and started to sit up. "You still okay?" She nodded slowly.

"Good girl. How about a Popsicle?"

Sarah looked bewildered and betrayed as she pulled away from Mike. "Sarah, what's wrong?"

She looked panicked. "Okay, no popsicles. Let's put this way over here. Do you need the doc?" She continued to pull away.

"Okay, I am going to get him for you. You stay here on your bed. You are in no condition to climb in the ceiling.

Mike went to the door and asked Mary to get the doctor.

Doctor Feingold arrived. "Mike, Sarah, what's going on?"

Mike said, "I was helping Sarah get up and I offered her a Popsicle and she started looking worried. I thought she probably needed to talk to you."

"Sarah, do you want talk here or do you want to go into the therapy room?"

She touched her bed. "Okay, let's stay here."

"I'll get you a chair." Mike left and was back in a moment with a chair for Dr. Feingold. "Let me know if you need anything."

"Sarah, you really don't look very well. Do you want to lie back down?"

She nodded. He helped her back into bed and tucked her in. Then he asked, "What do you think Mike meant when he asked if you wanted a Popsicle?"

"Chicken."

"It's part of our chicken work?" She nodded.

"Is it what someone asked you when Zeke and his friends did things to you?" She nodded again.

"Okay. That is enough for now. We will talk about what happened when you feel better. But for now, we need to work on you getting better. Can you handle Jell-O?" She thought for a moment then nodded. "Is there any other food that you should not be offered?"

"Hot dogs and kielbasa," she croaked.

"Okay."

"Is there anything that you really want to eat?"

"Chicken bouillon."

"Sarah, do you know that Mike did not mean what people used to mean when he offered you a Popsicle?" She nodded.

"Did he scare you?" She nodded again

"Are you still scared of Mike?"

"No, he got you for me."

"Good. Now, Sarah, you know that you are safe here. No one is allowed to touch you or make you do something that is wrong. You know that, don't you?" She nodded.

"If anyone ever makes you feel scared about anything, I need you to promise that you'll tell me. Can you do that?" She nodded.

"Tell Mike I'm sorry?"

"How about you tell him?" She nodded and looked for Mike to come in the door.

"Mike, can you come in here?"

Mike walked towards Sarah's bed. "I'm sorry I got scared of you."

"I'm sorry that I scared you. Are you feeling okay now?"

She nodded and sighed.

"She would like some chicken bouillon if you have some. And Jell-O is a safe food. I am going to put a few foods in her chart that she can't be given. Sarah, work on getting better and I will see you tomorrow."

They left the room and Sarah quickly went to sleep.

In the hallway Mike said, "Doc, I am really sorry. I didn't mean to scare her. I didn't know."

"It's okay, Mike. You handled it well and now we have a better picture of what she is dealing with. We also know that she is able to understand intention."

"What do you mean?"

"You're a safe person for her and your innocently asking her a question from her past shook her up, but she still sees you as a safe person. She can separate her past from now. She has the potential of actually being okay. She can learn to trust and therefore she can develop relationships and be a healthy adult."

"So, this turned out to be okay?"

"Yes. It's just another opportunity for therapy."

"Oh, you said there are other foods she can't have?"

"She said hot dogs and kielbasa."

"What the hell is wrong with some people? How can you do that to a kid? Sometimes I just want to hug these kids until they don't hurt anymore. Wouldn't that freak her out?" They both chuckled and shook their heads. "What kid likes bouillon?"

"I don't know. But it's simple to make and hot and cheap. So, it makes sense that she would like it if she was living alone all that time."

"Well, let me get her some bouillon. She'll probably wake up for it."

April 27th   4:00 pm

Once Sarah recovered from the flu, the treatment team decided that she had stabilized enough to begin schooling. She was given a long series of tests to determine personality, IQ, and scholastic achievement. Nothing could be done with complete accuracy because no one, including Sarah, knew when she was born. For the sake of testing, she was scored as a 13 year old, the age that she was likely to be. She found the testing to be both fun and tedious. In some areas she excelled and in others she performed miserably. She had incredible visual-spatial relations, problem solving abilities, and a very high overall IQ, but she had almost no knowledge of history prior to Colonial America. She could read at a high school level but her knowledge of math was only 5th grade. Not surprisingly, she showed very poor verbal expression.

The most encouraging aspect was Sarah's ability to engage in the testing. She was able to stay on task and talk to the psychologist throughout the process. It was also encouraging to realize that her limitations were due to environment. Sarah had never been exposed to television, so any cultural questions and allusions were simply outside of her experience. Within her sphere of knowledge, her achievement soared.

Putting together an educational plan involved mixing remedial lessons and gifted enrichment. Sarah was assigned a tutor and spent several hours a day in lessons. Between lessons, group therapy and her daily sessions with Dr. Feingold, Sarah did not have much free time. But one afternoon three other girls about her age were in the dayroom talking about cheerleading and practicing routines and dance moves when Sarah entered.

One did a split within 6 inches of the floor. The next tried and got a little closer. The first girl called to Sarah. "Can you do a split?"

Sarah shrugged.

The girl asked, "Did you ever?"

She shrugged again, not really understanding why she was being asked this.

"Do you want to try?"

Sarah spoke quietly, "I used to go all the way down but you can't do a split with pants on and where is the split stand?"

"There is no such thing as a split stand. Cheerleaders do splits with pants on all the time."

The second girl said, "You're weird, Sarah. You probably can't do a split at all."

Julia, Sarah's primary evening attendant, heard the exchange and took Sarah with her into the hall. "Sarah, don't mind the girls, they have had very different experiences from you. But I think you need to talk to the doc about this. Let's go find him."

Julia led Sarah into the therapy room where Doctor Feingold asked, "Sarah, what's happening?"

"The girls were doing splits but they have their pants on and they don't even have a split stand."

He invited Sarah into the therapy room. "I don't think I have ever seen a split stand. What does it look like?"

"It's a piece of wood with like a plastic *thing* sticking up and you have to do a split so it goes inside of you."

"Who taught you to do splits?" Dr. Feingold found himself speaking, even though he could not hear himself over the pounding of his heart.

"Zeke."

"Did Zeke take your clothes off of you?"

"He just took off my pants and shoes. You need socks so that you slide better on the floor. Then he would hold my hands and I would do a split onto the split stand."

"And he held your hands up over your head?"

She nodded.

"Did it hurt?"

"Sometimes, but we had to practice so that it wouldn't hurt. Then, when he had parties I wore a pretty dress and I did it for everyone. They would clap for me. And Zeke would be happy."

"And you liked to make Zeke happy?"

"Everything was better when Zeke was happy. But if he wasn't happy then he hurt me. I didn't like that."

"But you didn't mind doing splits on the split stand?" He asked while breathing to maintain his outward composure.

"It was okay. I only did it when I was little."

"And it made Zeke happy."

"Yes, he was proud of me when I could do something and it was part of training."

"What did you think when you heard the girls talking about doing splits?"

"Confused. I haven't done splits in a long time and why would they want to? Are they in training? Aren't they kind of old for that?"

"How old were you? "

"I don't know but I was as tall as one leg."

"Were you as tall as a counter top?"

She thought and then said, "My nose was at the counter top of the kitchen."

"So you were about 30 inches tall." He held up his hand at about the right height.

She looked at it and nodded. "That's about right. How old is that?"

"About 3 or 4"

"How old am I now?"

"We aren't really sure."

"Do you know when your birthday is?"

"What's a birthday? I have read about them, but what are they?"

"Was there a day with a cake and candles when you became one year older?"

"I don't remember one."

"We looked at how you have grown and we know that you are more than twelve and less than fourteen. Do you know what is in between 12 and 14?"

"Thirteen."

"Does that sound about right for how old you are?"

"I guess so. I never thought about it. But I was little then, wasn't I?"

"Yes, you were."

She thought for a few moments and then, changing the subject, she said, "I have homework tonight. Miss Matthews is a slave driver."

"What's on the agenda for tonight?"

"Dividing and multiplying fractions, and simplifying them. It's pretty simple but I have to do a lot of them. Then I have to read about Egyptians and life on the Nile."

"Well, I guess you'd better get to it. I will see you tomorrow."

April 28th   11:00 am

"Sarah, yesterday you talked about the split stand and you said that you only did that when you were little. Did Zeke have you do something else when you were bigger?"

"When I was older, the guys took turns lying on the floor. Zeke would hold my hands to lower me down but then the men would hold my stomach and move me up and down."

Dr. Feingold felt his stomach churn but maintained a calm demeanor as he asked, "How did you feel when this was happening?"

"Sometimes it hurt but usually Zeke put stuff inside me first so that I would slide. I would still be sore the next day but Zeke would put cream on me so it didn't hurt too much."

"So, Zeke had you do splits onto other men but he made sure that you didn't get physically injured."

She nodded.

"Do you think that Zeke took good care of you?"

"I guess so. He made people be nice to me and he was careful not to hurt me. And he bought me pretty clothes."

"So he made sure people were nice to you and he bought you pretty clothes."

"Yeah, isn't that what most people do if they take care of you?"

"Yes, I suppose it is." He was dismayed by her simple acceptance of her life but continued. "Sarah, you said that Zeke would lower you onto men that were lying on the floor."

"Yeah?"

"Sarah, did they have their pants undone?"

She nodded.

"And you were lowered onto their penis?"

She looked at him quizzically and said "Onto their mansicles. But first I had to make it stand up." She continued calmly. "You know the rule, 'Popsicles melt; mansicles grow.'"

Dr. Feingold took a deep breath and pulled back in surprise but recovered quickly, "You sound like you didn't like this part?"

"Mansicles smell weird and they don't taste good. And sometimes it made me gag. That's why I didn't like mansicle training."

Fighting to keep his feeling in check and remaining externally neutral, he asked, "What did you have to do for training?"

"Well, first I just had to suck on a Popsicle and make it all go without biting it or it dripping on my hands. That part wasn't too bad. But sometimes I had to put a whole hot dog in my mouth without biting it or gagging and choking. Then Zeke would take it out and if it had teeth marks he would yell at me. And when I could do that, I had to do it with a Kielbasa."

She paused and sighed, then continued. "After I could do the Kielbasa, then Zeke had me do practice on him. He had to train me right so that I would do it right and I could earn top dollar. I had to practice on him every morning so that I would stay in practice. The hard part was swallowing when he exploded. But he said that it was really important. He said that the best little girls could swallow and not leave a drop. Sometimes I would cry or gag but then he would put me on the split stand and tell me to sit there and think about whether I wanted to be a good girl. Then he would get me and let me try again."

"He was a patient but demanding teacher. And it sounds like you were a good student."

Suppressing his growing horror, Dr. Feingold tried and failed to understand the life this child lived. But they had both had enough for the day and he changed the subject.

"How are you doing in your school work here?"

"It's okay. Math is harder than I thought. And there were a lot of people who lived a long time ago."

"Why don't we stop for today and let you go do your math homework?"

May 3rd   11:00 am

"Some nights I didn't do splits at all. Sometimes, all I had to do was make the mansicles grow. But then they would hold my head and it would be hard to breathe and then it would like explode and Zeke would tell me I had to swallow it all. And I had to come up smiling. Sometimes I wanted to cry but Zeke said if I ever cried during my work, he would show me something for crying about. He would always say, 'These men were paying good money for you to make their mansicles grow and you should be glad that you are learning a trade.'" She leaned back in her chair. "I didn't like those nights. And I didn't earn as much money."

"Zeke gave you money?"

"No, Zeke had a book and he kept track of all the money that I was earning and was going to give it to me when I had something to buy. I got paid $1.00 for every mansicle and $2.00 for every split. I didn't work every night. But some work nights I earned just $10 and some nights I earned $25 or $30."

"That's a lot of work. Have you done that work since you were on your own?"

"No. Do you want me to do splits for you?"

"No, I don't. I don't want you to work here at all. Not like that."

She read his disgust. "Are you mad at me?"

"No, I am not mad at you. I am very angry, but I am not angry with you at all."

"You're mad at Zeke, aren't you?"

"Yes. I don't like what Zeke did. But I think we have done enough talking for today. Why don't we stop for now and talk some more tomorrow?"

"Okay."

She went into the dayroom and began working on her homework, and preparing for her Hebrew lesson and visit from Rabbi Cohen at two o'clock, sharp.

May 4ᵗʰ   9:30 am

Sarah confided to Dr. Feingold, "I got mad at Zeke too."

"Why were you mad at Zeke?"

"He wouldn't give me my money that I earned. I had been working for a long time but he wouldn't give me any money. He wouldn't even show me the book anymore. And then he started getting mean."

"How was he mean?"

"He just started changing. I had to practice almost every day with him. I had to do mansicles and then lower myself onto him and practice rhythms. I had to do my routines and he would get mad if I didn't do them right. But then sometimes I couldn't get him to explode inside and then he would hit me or hold my arms back so they hurt until he could explode. Sometimes he went in my butt. That hurt a lot but it made him explode."

Dr. Feingold sat listening, dumbfounded.

"Once he exploded he would forget about me for a while."

"He wouldn't do practice sessions?"

"No, we still did the practice sessions twice a day but he stopped making food for me and even buying food. And he didn't buy me clothes except for work clothes." She explained, "I had to have pretty work clothes. And he was getting mad a lot and yelling at me a lot. Like one day I spilled milk all over my blue velvet dress. He twisted my arm really hard and it made a weird sound inside and it didn't work right for a while and it hurt for weeks. But I still had to work that night and I couldn't cry."

She took a deep breath and let it out before continuing. "For a long time if he couldn't explode he would grab my arm. I wasn't allowed to cry. I had to breathe the pain away and tighten and relax my stomach muscles until it stopped hurting. Zeke liked it when I was in pain because he exploded faster."

"So Zeke wasn't taking very good care of you anymore."

"No, he was hurting me and we always moved around before but now we were moving around a lot and Zeke used to be with me when I worked but now I was alone with the men and sometimes it hurt. It was scarier when I was alone with the men but they liked it better. Sometimes they took all my clothes off of me. Zeke had never had me do that. Even when we practiced, I was never all naked."

"And now you had to be naked in front of the men."

"It felt different without any clothes on. And it was a lot scarier without Zeke in the room. Sometimes they would get on top of me and I would get scared that I would get mushed."

She looked at the doctor and continued, "Sometimes it was hard to breathe if they lay on top of me and once I passed out from a guy being on top of me and I couldn't breathe at all. Another man choked me once until I passed out. That was really scary."

She was trembling as she continued. "Sometimes people would give me stuff that made me feel weird and the room would get all different. One time I saw the music on the radio. And when the guy exploded I blew up too and I was all over the room. I was everywhere and I could see myself in the man's lap." She shook her head as if clearing the memory. "That never happened again though, just that one time. It was really weird."

"So, working alone was not feeling safe?"

"No."

"Were you working a lot more?"

"I was working almost every night. Some men just paid for mansicles but most people paid for a half hour. Zeke was supposed to pay me five dollars for a half hour. Sometimes, there would be group of people and they would have a party with me. I don't know what I was supposed to get paid for that because Zeke just said that he had it in the book. But he wasn't showing me the book anymore and I lost track of the money that he owed me."

Sarah sat back for a minute then said, "We didn't have a car anymore and we had to change hotels every few days. Then a guy got mad at Zeke because Zeke didn't pay him enough for something and Zeke said that we needed to hit the road. We went into the woods and I told Zeke that I wanted my money. I told him that if he gave me my money that I could go stay someplace and I could even give him some so he could pay that man. He hit me. He never hit me in the head like that before."

She paused. "I found out what they meant about seeing stars. I couldn't even move or hear. And then I realized that Zeke wasn't ever going to give me my money. I was doing all the work and he was spending all the money and he wasn't even using it to buy food."

"It sounds like things were getting pretty bad."

"That last night we went into a town and I had to work. I did a bunch of half hours and a few mansicles and a couple of splits. When I finished, we started walking out of town. All I had was my back pack. Zeke was really freaking out. He was coming apart and he was really scared of people following us. We had to go through the woods, not on the roads. Zeke had always been really careful about people following him. He taught me about picking up after myself and making sure I left everything so no one would know that I had been there. But now he had a knife out and he was really scary."

"Sarah, are you okay to continue or do you want to stop for today?"

"I think I need to tell you now."

"Are you okay?"

"I'm okay." Stoically, she continued. "After we had walked for a few hours, he told me that we needed a practice session so he could sleep. He was holding the knife when we started but after I got on top of him he let go of the knife to hold my hips and guide the rhythm. We did it for a while but he was having trouble exploding so he made me get off and he went into my butt. He still couldn't explode so he turned me around again. It still took a while but he exploded. When he did, I picked up the knife and I stabbed him in the chest. His eyes opened wide and he looked at me but he didn't say anything. He just took a big breath and then his whole body did this weird jerking shuddery thing and he peed in me and then he was dead." Sarah was visibly shaking. Dr. Feingold was breathing to maintain a calm exterior.

"What did you do?"

"I just sat there. I don't know for how long but at first I couldn't move. Then, I started shaking and I threw up and I pooped and I pooped and I pooped. I thought I would never stop. Then I got scared."

"I think anyone would be scared."

"I took Zeke's wallet and my back pack and I just started walking. I walked all night. When I found a stream I cleaned myself off, but when the sun came up I still didn't look very good. I couldn't get all the blood and poop off of my clothes. I went swimming again and then I laid out on a rock to dry and I fell asleep. I woke up with a sunburn and a headache. My clothes still looked awful. The sun hadn't made them clean. I drank some water and I threw up again but then I drank some more and I started feeling a little better. I wandered around in the woods for a few days before I heard the train. I found the train station and there was a donation box out in front with bags of clothes. I went through the bags and there were clothes that fit me so I put them on and I put the rest in my back pack."

She stopped and looked at the doctor. "That was stealing, wasn't it?"

"All things considered, I think they went to a good cause."

"I threw the messed up clothes out in the trash. And I took all the money and I threw Zeke's wallet away. Then I came to the city."

"How do you feel about killing Zeke?"

"Killing is wrong and that's why I have to be killed."

"Do you still think that you should be killed?"

"Yes. It's the rules. If you kill someone, you have to be killed."

"Are you sorry that you killed Zeke?"

"What do you mean?"

"Do you wish that you didn't kill him?"

She shrugged, "I did kill him."

"But do you ever wish that you didn't do it?"

"There wasn't anybody else to do it for me. I had to do it."

"Why?"

"Because he was getting really crazy and he would have killed me if I didn't kill him first. It doesn't really matter if you think about it because now I have to die for killing him. But at least it won't be a surprise. And I did get to live by myself for a while."

She paused and looked at Dr. Feingold. "God must not be too mad at me because there have been a lot of thunderstorms and He hasn't hit me yet. I'm not sure what He is waiting for. Maybe He wanted me to tell someone what I did before He kills me."

"Sarah, do you think that God is going to kill you or people are going to kill you?"

"Is there really a difference?"

"That is an interesting question. Why don't we tackle that one on another day?"

"No more chicken work today?"

"No more chicken work."

May 7th   11:00 am

Therapy had become focused on understanding Sarah's history. But it was clear to Dr. Feingold that the possible medical ramifications of the abuse she endured had to be addressed. "Sarah, before now, have you ever been in a hospital or been examined by a doctor?"

"No, just here."

"Have you ever had a shot?"

"Just here."

"I want to make an appointment for you to be examined by a doctor."

"But you're a doctor."

"Yes, I am a doctor, but I am a talking doctor and I want a doctor to look inside of you and to make sure that you are okay. Will you let a doctor look in you where the men put their fingers?"

Sarah stopped talking and slowly backed away from Dr. Feingold.

"Sarah, what are you thinking?"

"Are you going to pay me?"

"What?"

"Are you going to pay me? Zeke didn't pay me and I don't want to get cheated again. So if I am going to work for you, I want to get paid up front."

"So you think that I am going to let people do to you what Zeke did, that I am going to rent you out to other doctors?"

"Isn't that what you just said?"

"No, that is not what I want at all. Sarah, you can get very sick inside from people doing what they did to you. I want a doctor to examine you and do some tests to make sure that you are healthy."

"So you can rent me?"

"I am not going to rent you out. And I am not going to let anyone else rent you out. There is to be no renting or selling people here. I just want you to be healthy."

"Do you promise?"

"I promise there will be no renting or selling."

"What do I have to do for the test?"

"There will be a nurse with you—you can take Nancy if you want. You will go into a room with a special exam table and you will take your pants off. Then you are going to lie down on the table and put your feet up in metal foot rests called stirrups."

"Are you sure this isn't the same as with Zeke?"

"I am very sure. The doctor is going to put a plastic speculum inside of you and then he will be able to see inside."

"What's a specu'um?"

"A speculum is a piece of plastic that goes inside of you and opens."

"Okay, that is different from what I did before."

"He is going to put a few long Q tips inside to take swabs. That might feel a little weird but it won't hurt."

"Okay?"

"He is also going to use a wooden tool to scrape the skin on your cervix—that is a place inside. It might feel weird but it won't hurt either."

"Okay?"

"He is also going to need to take swabs from inside your butt and from your throat."

"He isn't going to put a Q-tip in my butt and then put it in my throat, is he?"

"No. Different Q-tip."

"Okay."

"Sarah, there is a part of the exam that may feel sort of like with Zeke but different. I want you to try to trust me on this."

"What?"

"The doctor is going to put his finger inside of you and press on your lower abdomen at the same time."

"Why?"

"He needs to feel what your organs feel like to tell if everything is okay. Your job is to just lie still and relaxed."

"I'm not supposed to tighten?"

"No, this is where it is very different. You are going to just relax and let him do the exam. He is going to talk to you and explain to you what he is doing."

"What do I do when he explodes?"

"He isn't going to explode. He isn't even going to take his clothes off. He really is doing this to make sure you are healthy. He isn't doing it to explode. Sarah, I know you aren't really sure about this, but are you willing to do it?" She nodded.

The exam was set up for the next afternoon.

May 8th   11:00 am

Sarah was quiet and restless the next morning in therapy.

"Are you worried about the seeing the gynecologist?"

"The what?"

"The gynecologist. That is the type of doctor that you are going to see today."

"They have a name?"

"Yes, a doctor that makes sure that girls and women are healthy is called a gynecologist."

"Is there a special doctor for boys and men?"

"Yes, that doctor is called a urologist."

"Are urologists women?"

"Some of them, but most are men."

"What about gynecologists?"

"Some are men and some are women. As it turns out, yours is a woman."

"Really?"

"Really. When I made the appointment for you I asked if there was a woman gynecologist available and there was. I thought that might be more comfortable for you."

"So, you really aren't going to rent me out?"

"No, I'm really not. How do you feel about that?"

"Relieved. But how am I going to pay my room and board here?"

"You don't pay room and board here."

"How are you going to get paid?"

"The state of New York is taking care of that for you. *You* don't have anything to worry about."

Sarah went with Nancy for her first gynecological examination that afternoon. It was as Dr. Feingold described it and Sarah tolerated it well. She was able to let the doctor know when the palpations were painful and remain relaxed during the rest of the exam. She was even able to adjust with the change in the exam when she was also given a sonogram and blood tests.

May 9th   11:00 am

In therapy Dr. Feingold and Sarah discussed the procedure. She seemed to be doing well with it so Dr. Feingold moved on.

"Sarah, we have talked a lot now about what Zeke did with you. But what did Zeke call you?"

"Zeke always called me 'Marcia, Marcia, Marcia.' Most people just called me pretty girl. But Zeke called me 'Marcia, Marcia, Marcia.'"

"What was Zeke's last name?"

"He used a lot of names. But the name on the license that I threw away was Smith."

"Do you remember what state the license had on it?"

"It said New Jersey."

"Was your last name Smith or something else?"

"I think it was just 'Marcia, Marcia, Marcia.'"

Realizing he would get no more information, he said "Okay and I suppose you don't want to be called that anymore?"

She shook her head no.

"Then we will keep calling you Sarah."

May 14th   9:00 am

The tests results came back. Sarah had multiple sexually transmitted diseases, including latent syphilis and pelvic inflammatory disease secondary to gonorrhea and chlamydia. It was unlikely that she would ever be able to bear children. Fortunately, the diseases could all be treated and no further damage would be done. She had also been exposed to HPV and would have to be monitored for cervical cancer. The good news was that Sarah was not HIV positive.

She was given antibiotics for the infections after being told that the doctor had found several infections needing treatment. Her increased risk for cervical cancer and likely infertility were withheld until a time when Sarah was more ready for that information.

"How come I am sick if I don't feel sick?"

"More than half of women who have these infections don't feel any symptoms. You are just one of the people who never show the signs."

"Am I going to be okay?"

"The medications will take care of your infections."

"Did I get the infections from Zeke, or from the other men?"

"I don't know if Zeke was sick but at least some of the men were sick and got you sick."

"How come Zeke didn't take me to a doctor and get me medication?"

"If he had, he would have ended up in jail."

"Where would I be?"

"You would have been taken to some place safe."

"Like here?"

"Like here."

"And you aren't going to rent me out when the infections are gone?"

"I am not going to rent you out ever."

Within a week of finishing the antibiotics, Sarah started climbing under her bed to sleep and hiding in the armoire or in the bathtub. The staff redirected her and noted her behavior change. But when questioned, she would just shrug and turn away.

Sarah's general affect was cautious and flat. The staff often commented that she acted like she was dead inside. She was cooperative and easy to have on the unit because she just complied. She was self-sufficient and responsible. Once given her schedule, she followed it, working on her schoolwork and going to groups as planned. She superficially participated in the activities and did whatever was asked. She was clearly a reader; she read the books in the unit library without discrimination. She was quiet and introverted but did not laugh or cry. There was very little sense of who Sarah really was. But one thing was clear; she was very concrete.

"How much money was there in Zeke's wallet?"

"There was $452.00."

"And that was the money from one night of work?"

"I think so. I think Zeke was cheating me. Men gave him a lot more money then he said I was getting paid. And he never paid me any money. He owed me a lot of money and he never paid up."

"So, when you came to the city you had $452.00?"

"Well, when I started out I did, but I had to buy a train ticket."

"Oh, yes. The train ticket, how could I have forgotten that you needed a train ticket?"

May 18th   11:00 am

"Sarah, you read and write very well. Did you ever go to school?"

"You mean regular school?"

"Yes, regular school."

"No, regular school is for regular kids; I'm not a regular kid."

"So how did you learn to read and write?"

"I don't know. I don't remember not reading and writing."

"Really?"

"Zeke and I would read together and I remember him reading one page and me the next. But I don't remember not reading."

"What is the first book that you remember reading?"

"James and the Giant Peach. The giant peach rolled over the mean aunts and James was free. Zeke said we were free too: just him and me in our very own peach."

"You sound like that is a happy memory."

"I liked doing things with Zeke. We went places and did stuff together. We went to the playground all the time and he helped me go across the monkey bars and he taught me to swing by myself and go really high and he taught me to climb ropes in case I needed to climb down from a peach. We went shopping together and we counted everything. It was just fun."

"So, Zeke made learning just a fun part of life?"

"Yeah, and we played a lot of games."

"Like what?"

"Well, we played what color house."

"How do you play what color house?"

"He would say which house I had to pick and then I had to say what color it was."

"What do mean?"

"Like the fifth house to the right of the green one. And I had to find the green house and count 5 houses to the right and say what color the house was. Sometimes that game got really hard. You had to listen really carefully and then follow it step by step."

"And Zeke was happy if you got it right."

"Yes."

"Sarah, your face just changed. Are you remembering something?"

She nodded slowly.

"Can you tell me what it is?"

With a very quiet tone she replied, "I did something wrong. I don't remember what I did wrong. I remember Zeke was really mad and he called me a little shit. And he picked me up and he tipped me over and he put dish soap in my butt and then he squeezed a bottle of water from the refrigerator in my butt and then he put me down in the middle of the kitchen floor and told me to stand right there and don't move a muscle. I was okay for a minute but then my stomach started to hurt and my legs hurt really bad and I had to go potty but he said not a muscle so I stood as still as I could and I tried to hold it but then I couldn't and it went everywhere and my legs wouldn't work and I fell in it and I got it all over me. I was covered in poop from head to toe. But I didn't cry. And Zeke said. 'See, I told you that you were a little shit. There is nobody who is going to love a little shit like you except your Zeke.' Then he showered me off and gave me a nice warm bubble bath and wrapped me in a towel to show me how much he loved me."

"How does remembering that make you feel?"

"I feel all shaky."

"You're shaking now. What is making you shake?"

"Remembering how hard I tried to stay still. But I couldn't do it."

"Sarah, no one could do it. Zeke knew that you couldn't do it. Why do you think he did that to you?"

"So I would listen to him. I didn't want to ever do that again."

May 20th   10:15 am

Sarah was speaking well in most situations but would stop speaking when she was anxious. The staff learned to use her ability to speak as a barometer of her emotional level. She was required to respond to staff and nodding or signing were accepted without comment. Her speech was often missing in therapies where she was doing activities she had never done before.

"In art therapy today we are going to be working with clay. So take a piece of clay and have a seat at the table."

Sarah took a palm sized piece of clay and sat down.

"Before you can make something with the clay, you have to warm it up and work it. So you can roll it or kneed it. Sarah, have you ever worked with clay before?"

She shook her head.

"That's okay. You are getting a chance to try something new." Sarah was tentative but she too began working the clay, feeling it soften and mold in her hands. After a few minutes of working the clay, the patients were told that they could make something with it. "You can make a bowl, or a sculpture," the teacher offered. Sarah looked at the piece of clay and started forming a little chick. She formed the body, then the head and the beak. She worked on the nose hole and the eyes and was starting to create the downy feathers when she was told that it was time to clean up. She shook her head.

"Yes, Sarah, it is time to clean up."

She shook her head again.

"Sarah, we can save your chick for next time but we need to stop now. Look, we can put a wet paper towel on it and put it in a baggie. I will be here tomorrow and you can work on it some more then. But for now, you need to stop. Let's wrap it together, good. And let's put it in this bag and put your name on it. We will put it in this cabinet and lock it up so it will be safe. Tomorrow, you can hollow the chick out so that it can be fired when it is all dry and then you can glaze it and fire it again and it will stay forever. Is that what you want to do?"

Sarah thought for a few moments and then touched a yellow piece of paper. "You want to know if you can glaze the chick yellow?" She nodded.

"Yes, I can get yellow glaze for you. Now let's wash the table. And then you need to wash your hands for lunch."

Sarah ate in silence and then worked on a puzzle by herself in the therapy room.

Dr. Feingold entered the therapy room. "Hi, Sarah. The staff says that you have been very quiet today. How are you feeling?"

Shrug.

"Does this have something to do with art therapy today?" She nodded.

"So let's talk about it."

"We had clay and we could make anything we want."

"Um hum."

"I am making a chick."

"Like your chick?"

She nodded.

"What made you want to make the chick?"

"They make statues for people who died."

"Yes they do."

"Well, he was a therapy chick and he died doing therapy. He needs a statute, too." And with that, tears began streaming down Sarah's face. Sarah's tears became a torrent as sobs wracked her body. She cried in silence, not understanding her feelings of remorse and gratitude. The doctor sat quietly, letting her cry without interruption until she began to calm.

"You are grateful to that little chick."

She nodded.

"And you want to honor him."

She nodded again.

"Do you think that that chick was a special chick?"

"How many therapy chicks do you think get killed in therapy?"

"Well, you have a point there. I don't suppose there are many. Sarah, are you sad that you killed the chick?"

Sarah put her chin in her hands and thought for a few minutes before replying. "It's complicated."

"Yes it is. How about if we try to sort it out?"

"I don't feel bad about the pigeons and squirrels that I killed because I ate them. And it isn't the same as killing a mockingbird. They were food and I used them for food. And I don't feel bad if I break something that is a tool if I am using it right. I might not like it but I don't feel like I did something wrong."

"I hear a 'but' in there somewhere."

"Well, the chick was a therapy chick and you and I have used him in a lot of my therapy but I don't think that it was quite what he expected."

"You don't think that he intended to have his neck wrung to start your therapy?"

"No. I think it was a little extreme."

"Do you know a word for what you are feeling?"

"No."

"Do you know the word 'remorse'?"

"That is when you feel bad about how something turned out, right?"

"Yes."

"That isn't it. I'm glad about how it turned out; I just wish he didn't have to die to start it." She stopped and brightened as she said, "Hey, he was a catalyst. Like in chemistry, he started the whole thing rolling but got wiped out in the process. What is a word for you're sorry that he was the unlikely little catalyst?"

"How do you know about catalysts and chemistry?"

"Zeke's friend Steve told me about it. He made a lot of money at his laboratory."

"Did you ever go to his laboratory?"

"No. And Zeke told him he was never to bring his product to our house. But Steve told me about how he uses catalysts to make reactions happen and that the catalyst is all used up to get to the next step."

"Well, I am going to have to think about your little chick being a catalyst and I think we have done enough work for today."

May 25th   9:45am

Sarah approached the pet therapist. "Excuse me."

"Yes, Sarah? Are going to be joining us for pet therapy today?"

"No. But I wanted to know if the chick that I killed had a name."

"Well, no, he didn't have a name yet, why?"

"I was just wondering. I'm working on something and if he had a name, then I thought I should include it."

"Do you want to give him a name?"

With obvious condescension, she replied, "No. I don't name tools or food. But, thank you."

It took Sarah weeks to finish the chick, but finally the art therapist brought it back from the kiln for the last time. Sarah cradled it carefully in her hands.

"Are you happy with what you made?"

Sarah nodded. "Thank you, it's just right. I already made the plaque for it."

"Can I see?"

"Yes, but don't tell anyone."

She showed the little plaque and platform to the art therapist.

The next day, the pet therapist came to the unit. Sarah and Dr. Feingold asked her to come into the therapy room. She was rather surprised by the invitation but accepted.

"Sarah has something for you."

"I know that you were very upset when I killed the little chick. And I know that you think that I got away with killing something. But, he was a therapy chick, and that is not the same as a regular chick. I am not going to say that I am sorry because that chick made it possible for me to do way more therapy than I would have done if I just gave him back or just pet him. But he did go above and beyond the call of duty. So, I made a statue of him and I would like you to have it." And with that, she presented the pet therapist with a bright yellow ceramic chick on a little wooden platform with careful lettering: "Therapy Chick- He Gave His Life for the Cause."

The therapist looked dumbfounded. "You made this for me?"

"No, I made it to honor the chick. But since he was your chick, it seems fitting that you should have it."

"Thank you. I don't know what to say. This is such a surprise. Will you be coming to pet therapy now?"

"No. I haven't finished working on the first pet therapy session yet."

"What?"

"I think what Sarah means is that that little chick did not die in vain. It has been an integral part of the therapy that we have done and will be part of our therapy for quite some time to come."

Once again, the therapist was speechless. She sat thinking for a few minutes and said, "Sarah, I am very touched that you have given me this tribute to the chick. But I am not the rightful owner of this statue. It is you who have honored him and you should keep the statue. I had no idea how much work that little chick had done. I am glad that you let me know."

She stood. "Now, I need to go do some more pet therapy with other children."

Sarah watched her move towards the door. "I hope you don't get presented with any more statues."

"Thank you, Sarah."

After she left, Sarah looked at Dr. Feingold and said. "Where should we put him?"

"Where do you want to put him?"

"He should be in here, but other people come in here and I don't want him to get hurt. How about if he lives in my room and comes to visit here sometimes?"

"That sounds like a good plan."

June 7th   10:00 am

Outside of the hospital, the search continued to find Sarah's identity. Even with the name Zeke Smith, there was no confirmation of his identity and there was no record of a Marcia Smith within her age range who was unaccounted for within the tri state area. Theresa Myers had gone to court and had Sarah declared a ward of the state when she was found. But as time progressed, the need to make a proper long term plan for her care became more pressing. Although it was clear that Sarah needed to be in the hospital initially, the unit was meant to be a short term unit and there was mounting pressure to determine the most appropriate long term placement.

Theresa met with Sarah weekly as part of the requirements for a child in foster care. Sarah was cordial but distant. Theresa brought Sarah new sneakers with Velcro closures. She also brought her new pajamas. Sarah was very reluctant to accept the items and in the end, Theresa began placing any new items in her room.

The District Attorney wanted to close the case in Westchester. Sarah had been assigned a lawyer with whom she met with several times. Once she was able to actually speak to the lawyer, she gave her statement regarding Zeke's death. The DA met with Theresa and the lawyer and read Sarah's statement and report from Dr. Feingold. The DA wanted to meet Sarah before he made his final determination of justifiable homicide.

Despite Dr. Feingold's objections, a meeting was set up with all parties. The Westchester DA, the lawyer, Dr. Feingold and Theresa Myers met first. Dr. Feingold stressed that Sarah did not understand the abuse that she had endured and that it was very important that she not know it yet. He reminded them that they would be meeting in the therapy room in order to provide the most comfort to Sarah. The lawyer and the DA agreed and Sarah was brought into the room and introduced to the DA and the stenographer.

"Sarah, do you know why we are having this meeting?"
She nodded.
Her lawyer addressed her, "Sarah, you remember that we discussed that in this meeting you need to use your voice."

"Okay. I know why we are meeting. It's so you can decide when it's time to kill me."

Although the DA had read the reports about Sarah's belief that she would be put to death, he was still taken aback by her earnestness.

He spoke calmly to her. "Well, before we can make any determinations about the future, I need to hear from you what happened. So, can you tell me what happened so that I can make a decision about how to proceed?"

"What do you want to know?"

"I have a report from Dr. Feingold about your life and I have a few questions. You said that the person that you killed was named Zeke. How was Zeke related to you?"

"I don't know; he was just Zeke."

"Did you ever call him dad or was he your father?"

"No, I always called him Zeke."

"Did Zeke say that you were his daughter?"

"He said that I was his little meal ticket; is that the same as daughter?"

The DA grimaced and said, "Not usually."

"And Zeke said your name was Marcia?"

"No, he called me 'Marcia, Marcia, Marcia.' He never called me just 'Marcia.' And he called me his little shit. But that wasn't a nice thing."

"No, that wasn't a nice thing."

"Dr. Feingold said that your, um, Zeke did training sessions with you. What did you do during your training session?"

"Well, there were two kinds of training sessions. I did mansicle training in the morning."

"Every morning?"

She nodded, "I mean yes."

"And what did you do for mansicle training?"

Matter-of-factly she explained, "He would wake me up and I had to make his mansicle grow and then when it exploded I had to swallow the explosion and then lick it clean."

"Could you excuse me?" The DA stood up and quickly left the room. Dr. Feingold looked at Sarah and said, "I'll be right back, you just take a break."

He followed the DA out of the room and showed him to the nearest bathroom. The DA barely made it before he threw up. He emptied his stomach and then had to deal with dry heaves every time the vision of Sarah filled his mind. After some deep breaths and practiced steady breathing, he began to regain his composure.

Dr. Feingold gave him a wet paper towel.

"I have prosecuted scum for 35 years. I have never had a child express that act in those terms. My God, she is so innocent."

"She has no idea what she has done or what she was trained to do and she is not ready to know. For her sake, please don't let her know how depraved what she was forced to do is."

"She really has no idea?"

"None; she has no knowledge of sex. These are just acts that she was trained to do, just like other kids learn ballet or football."

"She really thinks that we are going to kill her? We should be giving her a medal!"

"I don't think that she is ready for that. It will be a stretch, but she might be able handle knowing that it is okay to kill if it is to preserve your own life. Are you going to be able to continue?"

"If that little girl can get through this, then damn it, I will too."

They reentered the room and the DA apologized for leaving. "I must have eaten something that didn't agree with my stomach." Sarah had been working on her homework during their absence. "What are you working on?"

"Just a worksheet for school; math problems. I am behind in math so I have to catch up." She set the workbook aside.

"Sarah, you said that you had two practice sessions during the day. What did you do during the second session?"

"Zeke would tell me that it was time to practice and I would do my pants dance,"

"Pants dance?"

"I had to walk toward him taking my pants off along the way. You have to take one step at a time and for every step you work on taking your clothes off so you have to take little steps and you do this shoulder thing. It would be easier to show you. Do you want me to show you the pants dance?"

"No, I get the idea. What did you do next?"

"Then I had to undo the snap and unzip Zeke's zipper and pull down his pants and then push his chest so that he fell backwards onto the bed. Then I had to grow the mansicle and then I would climb onto Zeke's lap so the mansicle was inside me and he would hold my hips and then we would do rhythm practice until he exploded."

Dr. Feingold asked, "Sarah, what would happen if Zeke had trouble exploding?"

"Sometimes he would bend my fingers back or my arms so that I hurt."

"So, he would hurt you if he didn't explode during your practice?" The DA picked up the line of questioning.

"No, he would hurt me so that I would breathe the pain and make it all go to my muscles so he could explode."

"Sarah, can you share what else Zeke did if he couldn't explode during rhythm practice?"

"I would have to get up and then go back down with the mansicle in my butt."

"Did that hurt?"

She nodded, then, remembering that she was supposed to speak in this meeting. "Um, yes but it made him explode. It's important to make people explode."

"Why is it important?"

"Because the men, that's what they are paying for and you have to give people what they are paying for. Practice sessions are to ensure that you have a quality product." She droned just the way she had heard it many times.

"I see."

"So, let's talk about the day when you killed Zeke."

"Okay."

"What had you been doing in the days before the incident?"

"Zeke had been getting really mean. And it was a lot harder to get him to explode so he was hurting me more and after he did explode he would just ignore me and not feed me or anything. And he let people take me into rooms alone. Before, anytime I was working Zeke would be there and he made sure that when I did splits that I was on the mansicle and I always wore a dress. But now I was alone and I had to take all my clothes off and get under the covers and men would lie on top of me. It wasn't the same anymore. Zeke wasn't taking good care of me. Then a man got really mad at Zeke because Zeke didn't have enough money. So we left town and we were walking in the woods and I told Zeke that if he gave me my money, then I could let him borrow some of it to pay the man."

"Hold on a second; let me understand this, what money was yours?"

"I was supposed to get paid $1.00 for mansicles, $2.00 for splits and $5.00 for a half hour. But Zeke was holding my money for me."

The DA took his hands off the table so Sarah could not see that his knuckles were white with rage.

"When I asked for my money, Zeke hit me so hard I saw stars. And that was when I knew that Zeke wasn't going to give me my money. He was cheating me."

"Then what happened?"

"We got to another town and I had to work that night. I worked until it was really late and then we walked through the woods and out of town. We walked for a long time and then Zeke said that we had to have a rhythm practice session so that he could get some sleep."

"So, I grew the mansicle and we did the rhythms but he didn't explode so I got up and put the mansicle in my butt and it still took a lot of rhythm work and then he turned me around again and put it in my front and finally he exploded. I picked up his knife and I stabbed him in the chest and he opened his eyes and then shuddered and did a jerky thing and then he was dead. That's what happened. Except for the gross stuff."

"The gross stuff?"

"When he died he peed inside of me. And then I pooped a real lot."

The DA sat for a moment trying to compose himself. At last he spoke.

"Sarah, you are correct that you killed Zeke."

She looked him in the eye fully, expecting an execution date.

"What do you think would have happened to you if you had not killed Zeke?"

"He would have killed me."

"What makes you think that?"

"He wasn't like before and he wasn't doing very well. He had the knife with him all the time and sometimes I was afraid of him."

"Could you have run away from Zeke?"

"No, he never left me alone. I was either with him or with a customer."

"What about when you took a shower or went to the bathroom?"

"Zeke gave me my baths and he watched me go potty. He always checked to make sure I was clean."

"So, you had no choice but to kill Zeke in order to live?"

"I don't know how to answer that."

"I am sorry; I did make that complicated, didn't I? Do you believe that you needed to kill Zeke?"

"Yes."

"Why?"

"If I didn't kill him, he would have killed me."

"Sarah, there is a difference between killing and murder. In New York State, we only kill people under very special circumstances. Let me assure you that this was not one of those circumstances. In fact, we have a term for what you did."

"You do? What is it?"

"When someone kills another person in order to stay alive, it is called 'justifiable homicide.'"

"What's going to happen to me if I justifiable homicided?"

"Well, in the State of New York and in Westchester County, which is where this took place, I am given the power to look at a situation like this and to determine if it is justifiable homicide."

He paused. "After listening to your account of the events and reading the police reports of the scene, I have concluded that this is justifiable homicide." He looked at her, "Sarah, justifiable homicide means that what you did was not wrong. Staying alive is very important. What you did, you did so that you could stay alive. Therefore, there is no punishment. Westchester County will not punish you in any way for what you did. What you did was not wrong."

Dr. Feingold asked, "Do you understand?"

She shook her head no. "What about 'thou shall not kill and if you kill someone you will be sentenced to die?'"

"Well, the actual words are 'thou shall not murder.' The Bible and New York State recognize that sometimes a person has no choice but to kill. One of those times is for what is called self –preservation. In other words, it is okay to kill to keep oneself alive."

Dr. Feingold addressed Sarah. "Sarah, how are you feeling now?"

"Confused."

"I'm not surprised. You have thought for a long time that you deserved to die for what you did."

The DA asked, "Are you relieved that you aren't going to die?"

"No, I feel weird." Then she stood up and passed out.

"Get the nurse. Sarah, Sarah?" Dr. Feingold was at her side and checking her pulse and airway.

"Is she okay?"

"I think she's just overwhelmed."

"Should I stay or go?"

"Let's give her a minute."

Sarah started to move and began flailing. Dr. Feingold held her wrists to prevent her from injuring herself or him. "Sarah, open your eyes. Take a deep breath and open your eyes." Sarah started panting but she looked at Dr. Feingold. "Take some deep breaths. You're okay. We have a lot of work ahead of us but you are okay. Can you sit up?"

He released her wrists as she calmed and she sat up and looked around, surprised to find herself on the floor. "Sarah, can you sit back at the table?" Slowly, she returned to the table.

The DA concluded the meeting. "Sarah, I want to thank you for speaking with me today. You are one of the bravest people I have ever met. Today, you have allowed me to close a case that has been open for a long time. For that I thank you. Now, I hope that you are able to feel more relaxed knowing that you are not going to be killed. I want to wish you all the best."

Sarah looked at him, dazed.

"I can see that you are tired so I won't keep you any longer. But if you ever have questions about this matter, your lawyer will know how to get in touch with me. For you, my door is always open."

The lawyer walked out of the therapy room with the DA. The stenographer finished her record and then followed them out the door.

Sarah sat, quaking.

Nancy went to Sarah's side and suggested she get into pajamas to could rest. Sarah allowed herself to be led to her room. She was assisted with changing her clothes and then Mike brought a chair in and sat next to her bed. Sarah lay silent and insensate.

Dr. Feingold went into the nurses' station. "We need to put her back on one on one staffing. They are to make sure she does not get into the ceiling tonight. She may well become suicidal. I don't want her hanging herself on the girders. I am also writing an order for medication in case she becomes violent."

"Doc, what happened?"

"The DA explained that she committed justifiable homicide and that she is not going to be put to death."

"Shouldn't she be relieved?"

"He just broke her strongly held delusional belief. The central tenet of her life was just found to be false. In other words, he just pulled the rug out from under her. Now, the question is, how far is she going to fall and have we done enough groundwork that she can get through this?"

He went into Sarah's room and stood near the foot of her bed. "Sarah?"

She looked in his direction, unable to focus on him.

"I am going to give you some medicine to help you sleep tonight. Tomorrow we are going to do some more talking." Sarah was unable to answer.

He looked Mike and said, "Get her a vest. Sarah, we are going to put this vest on you tonight so you are secure overnight."

Mike put the restraint vest on Sarah and secured her in the bed.

"Don't leave her alone."

In the morning Sarah was still in the land of nowhere. She was catatonic. She was placed on an IV and was catheterized. She was never left alone. And so she continued for four days. Then, as if a switch was flipped in her mind, she became violent and the period that the staff had braced for was upon them. Sarah fought and struggled with herself and anyone that came near her. She clutched Cody one minute and flung him away the next. She was remained restrained for her own safety and medicated to quiet her to the point that she was less likely to hurt herself or the staff.

June 14th   8:30 am

After three days of fighting, she woke quietly. Mike was on watch when she opened her eyes. "Good morning. How do you feel?" Sarah looked at Mike with very sad eyes. "You've had a tough couple of days. Do you want a drink?

She nodded.

"Okay, I have some water here for you." He gave her the straw for the cup of water and she took a sip. "Are you ready to get out of bed?" She looked at Mike and then at the bed. She tried to sit up and realized that she was restrained by the vest. She touched the vest and looked at Mike.

"We wanted to make sure you stayed safe. I am going to have Nancy come in here for few minutes. Okay?"

Sarah just watched him as he went to the doorway and called to Nancy.

Nancy came in. "Good morning, Sunshine. It's nice to see you awake. How do you feel?"

Sarah merely looked at her.

"Yeah, I know that feeling. You're still half asleep and not quite right in the head. Are you feeling sort of cobwebby?"

Sarah nodded.

"You've had some medicine that will be leaving your body pretty soon. You're going to start feeling better before long. Now, you have been sleeping for days. We didn't want you to have a wet bed and we knew that you would not want to wear diapers, so we used a tube so that you wouldn't get wet. Are you ready to be able to get up and go to the bathroom on your own?" Sarah nodded. "Okay. Then I need get a few things and I will be right back to take the tube out."

Mike brushed the hair away from her eyes. "While Nancy is taking care of you, I'll get you some breakfast. Are you hungry?"

She shook her head.

"Do you think you will be able to eat something if I get it for you?"

She nodded slowly.

"Okay, Nancy will get you ready and I will get you some breakfast."

Nancy returned with a procedure tray. "Okay, Sarah. This may feel a little funny, but it isn't going to hurt. I just need you to lie down." She talked as she worked on removing the catheter. "And then we drain this and take it out. All done. Are you okay?"

She nodded.

"Okay, we need to keep you in bed until Dr. Feingold talks to you. But if you need to go to the bathroom, you just let us know and we will take you. And look at that breakfast."

Mike adjusted her bed so that she was sitting up and brought her tray to her.

Sarah looked at the food and took a few bites before lying back on her bed.

Then Dr. Feingold entered the room. "Good morning. I heard that you were awake; how do you feel?"

Sarah stared blankly at him.

"Not into talking yet, are you? That's okay. Is Cody okay?" Sarah looked the bear and patted his head.

"Sarah, if we let you get out of bed, will you stay here with us?"

She nodded.

"Do feel like hurting yourself?"

She shook her head.

"Okay, we're going to try taking the vest off. If you have trouble staying here or you start to hurt yourself or anyone else, we're going to put the vest back on. Do you understand?"
Mike untied one side of the restraint as Dr. Feingold untied the other. Dr. Feingold sat down. Sarah got out of bed and sat on the floor in front of him and reached for his belt. He caught her hands and held her back from her intended destination.

"Sarah, what are you doing?"

She looked pleadingly and whispered hoarsely, "Practice."

"You want to have a practice session with me?"

"Practice, now."

"Sarah, I am not going to practice with you. I will talk to you about how you are feeling but I don't practice with my patients."

Sarah didn't know what to do with herself.

"Do you miss Zeke?"

"Practice."

"Do you think that if you practice you will feel closer to Zeke?"

She nodded and tried to move towards the doctor. He was holding her wrists and was able to guide her back gently. Mike stood by, ready to step in if needed.

"It sounds like you are grieving for Zeke and you want to go back to a familiar routine. Do you feel like if we practice you will feel better?"

She nodded emphatically. "Practice. I want to practice."

She tried again to move toward him, but he held her firmly.

"No, Sarah. I will not practice with you. Zeke is dead and you feel very sad, but practicing is not going to help you feel better."

"Zeke is dead." Tears formed in her eyes as she choked out the words.

"Zeke is dead," he repeated. She put her face in her hands and began crying. He was still holding her wrists. They were very close together when she whispered, "I don't know what to do. I just want to practice. I want to practice so Zeke will come back."

"Zeke can't come back. Zeke is dead. Practicing is not going to bring Zeke back." He nodded to Mike to get Cody. Mike handed the bear to the doctor. "When you feel sad or alone, you can hug Cody." He placed Cody in her arms and wrapped them around the bear. Holding Cody, and resting her head against the front of the doctor's knees, she cried for the loss of the only caregiver she had ever known.

When she calmed down, Mike stepped out and asked Mary to help Sarah back into bed.

Sarah complied willingly and Mary sat with her until she fell asleep.

Mike and Dr. Feingold left the room and went to the nurse's station. Mike said, "This is going to make staffing difficult."

"I know, but we can't have her alone with any male staff while she is awake and she still needs to be on one to one protocols. I want her restrained at night."

"Do you think she has any idea what she is doing?"

"You mean does she know that she wants to engage in sex? No. She is a little girl who misses her father and wants to recreate the activity they shared in order to feel less lonely. If they had collected stamps, she would be looking at stamp books. Unfortunately, if we don't handle this right and get her beyond this, she is going to be a nymphomaniac."

"No pressure, right?"

"Yeah, no pressure. I need to get orders written up."

"This is really going to be tough on the staff."

"It's not going to be easy on her either."

June 14th   2:15 pm

After lunch, Mary and Mike were with Sarah in her room. Sarah went into the bathroom. Mary positioned herself at the door. Sarah finished in the bathroom but started to come out without her pants on.

"Sarah, you need to put your pants on."

"Practice time."

"No, Sarah, it is not practice time."

"Split practice." She looked at Mike. "Be Zeke."

"No Sarah, I am not Zeke and I am not going to pretend to be Zeke. I will stay in here with you and Mary only if you put your pants back on." Sarah looked confused and hurt. She moved toward Mike and tried to push him so that he would lie down on the bed.

He held her wrists and said, "No, I am not Zeke. I will not practice with you. Now put your pants on."

Sarah looked at Mike but could not understand what was wrong. "I know that you miss Zeke. But I will not practice with you."

Mary stepped in, turned Sarah away from Mike and guided her into her clothes and then back onto the bed. "Sarah, when you feel sad you can talk about feeling sad, or you can write about it, or you can cry or you can just lay here on your bed and hold Cody. But you cannot have practice sessions with anyone here. Do you understand?"

Sarah slowly nodded.

"Now, I think you have time for a nap before dinner. Why don't you and Cody lie down here together and see if you can get a nap?"

June 16th   2:15 pm

Over the next few days, Sarah began attending therapies again. She gained some mastery over her desire to recreate her relationship with Zeke. She spoke to Dr. Feingold about Zeke and remembered their time together. Sarah was still monitored one on one, but she was allowed to be with staff of either gender.

Slowly, she started to work on her schooling. She was working in the day room when Mike came in and introduced Greg, a new attendant. "Sarah, this is Greg. Greg, this is Sarah. Sarah is on one on one staffing. Sarah is not much of chatterbox but she should respond to you either by nodding or speaking. She has been her for a while and she is very co-operative so we've decided to keep her."

Sarah smiled. Greg left the room and Mike turned back to Sarah and said, "No practicing with the new guy. You hear me?" And he smiled at her, letting her know that she was okay in his book. She smiled back and then went back to her homework.

June 18th   11:00 am

Sarah was sitting on the floor in the therapy room. This was her most comfortable position. "How come I miss Zeke now? He has been dead for four years. How come now? How come I didn't cry when it happened?"

"Sarah, you have been too busy just staying alive to stop and grieve. I think you can see that grieving is hard work. You couldn't grieve and do all that you needed to do to survive before now. Here, you have people who will take care of you so you can have those feelings."

She sat still, looking at the floor and thinking, so he continued. "How are you doing with those feelings?"

"Well, I haven't tried to have a practice session in a while. So I guess that's good. I still miss Zeke. And I still hurt. It's my own fault."

"What's your own fault?"

"It's my fault that I miss Zeke. I wouldn't miss him if I didn't kill him. I wish I didn't have to kill him. Why did he have to get so scary? Why couldn't he just stay regular?"

"You are angry with Zeke for changing things."

"Yeah, he was supposed to take care of me and he wasn't anymore."

"How wasn't he taking care of you?"

"He wasn't feeding me anymore and he wasn't keeping me safe when I worked. I was a good worker but his job was to manage me and the people. He wasn't doing it very well anymore."

"Sarah, do you think that there are many kids that worked like you did?"

"Sometimes there was another kid. So, I don't know. I never thought about it."

"Sarah, what if I told you that there are very few children who worked like you did?"

"How come? Weren't they good at it?"

"Actually, most people don't train children to do splits or mansicles."

"Is that why I wasn't regular?"

"Yes. How does that feel to know that your lifestyle wasn't regular?"

"It seemed normal to me."

"It did seem normal, didn't it?"

"Yeah."

"Sarah, I am going to tell you something and I want to you to try to stay right here with me. Are you ready for this?"

"I guess so."

"The training that Zeke put you through—the mansicles and the splits and hiring you out to people—is child abuse. Zeke never took good care of you."

Sarah sat in stunned silence. "But he didn't hurt me. He was always careful so that I didn't get hurt. How could he have abused me if it didn't hurt?"

"Sarah, little girls are not supposed to be hired by men to do what you did. I want to teach you some words. What you call mansicles is called fallatio. Can you say fallatio?

"Fallatio? How come Zeke didn't call it fallatio?"

"Probably because Zeke trained you to do fallatio when you were very little. After teaching you with a Popsicle, the term mansicles was something that would have made sense to you."

"Do you have a little girl?"

"No, why?"

"So, the reason that you wouldn't do practice sessions with me wasn't because you had already practiced at home?"

"No. I didn't practice with you because men who care about little girls do not have them do fallatio on them."

"Zeke didn't care about me?"

"What Zeke did to you was wrong. So, even though you didn't know it, Zeke was never taking good care of you."

"But he trained me."

"Yes, he spent a lot of time with you and gave you a lot of attention. But what he was teaching you was wrong and allowing people to pay for you to do fallatio on them was wrong."

"Was I wrong? Am I bad? I did a lot of fallatios."

"You are what we call an innocent. You did what you were told to do. Before now, you didn't know that children aren't supposed to do fallatio. Therefore you are blameless and innocent. If you performed fallatio now that you know it is wrong, you would be doing something wrong."

"What about splits? Are they wrong too?"

"First you need some words. Regular splits are called intercourse. Intercourse with children is against the law. All of the people who had intercourse with you could have been put in jail. When Zeke or other people put their penis in your butt, that was called sodomy. It is also illegal."

"Even if it only hurts a little?"

"Even if it doesn't hurt at all."

Sarah contemplated this new information. "So, if Zeke was never good to me, how come I miss him?"

"Because he was what you knew. Everyone misses what they know." Sarah sat quietly for a few minutes. "Sarah, how do you feel right now?"

"I feel okay. How come I feel okay? You just told me that everything I have ever known was bad and wrong. How come I feel okay?"

"Sarah, Zeke died four years ago."

"Yeah."

"You were earning quite a bit of money working for Zeke, correct?"

"Well, I earned $452 that last night that I worked but he never gave me my money before then."

"Was that night a usual work night?"

"Yeah."

"How come you didn't work again after you killed Zeke?"

"I didn't want to. I didn't like the work. And Zeke wasn't there to manage everything and get my customers."

"Do you think that somewhere inside you knew that it wasn't good for you?"

She thought quietly then looked up. "Maybe. I didn't like how I felt after I worked. I didn't want to do it anymore."

"So maybe, somewhere inside, you already knew I what told you today."

"Is it okay that I feel happy?"

"Yes, it is very okay."

"We aren't finished working, are we?"
"No, but we are finished for today."

July 1ˢᵗ   9:00 am

Sarah seemed to have turned a corner. She was attending and participating in her therapies, progressing with her Hebrew studies, and working well with Dr. Feingold. She had been in the hospital for almost four months and it was well into summer. The rest of the kids on the unit were on summer vacation but Sarah's school year continued. She needed both the continuity of the routine and the opportunity to catch up with peers. Theresa, her Children's Services worker, had met with her weekly to build their relationship and monitor her progress.

During an expanded treatment team meeting Rabbi Cohen expressed his congregation's interest in supporting Sarah in her life beyond the hospital. "Three years ago, the Executive Director told Sarah she needed paperwork completed by her parents to continue in Hebrew School. He could not allow a child to attend without parental consent, an emergency contact, and medical records. No one imagined that Sarah was living alone. When the congregation found out that Sarah was alone all that time and that they had turned her away, they were horrified and remorseful. They had in essence closed the door on Elijah. In Judaism, one does not close the door on someone in need. And when one sins against another, restitution is made. Before, Sarah attended our Hebrew school. Now, the congregation has created a scholarship for her to attend our day school so Sarah can attend our school rather than a public school."

The education staff decided that she would attend the sixth grade because that most accurately reflected her academic level and was most compatible with her physical size. Also, in sixth grade she would have more daily continuity rather than the disruption of changing rooms for each class. Some of the teachers already knew Sarah, as did many of the students from when she attended Hebrew school. The difficulty was in finding appropriate housing. Although she was doing well, she could not be safely placed in a household with children because of the likelihood that she would either abuse or be abused. A two parent household posed the risk of her trying to replicate the relationship with Zeke with the husband. However, handling Sarah alone was too much of a challenge for one person. Sarah needed two foster parents with special training to deal with her extensive special needs. Theresa finally came across foster parents who offered a possible solution: Maria and Amber, a married couple who lived in the Village within blocks of the temple and school. They both had extensive training with sexually abused children and both worked jobs that allowed them to be available for Sarah. They had been intensive short term foster parents, but were willing to make a long term commitment to Sarah. Dr. Feingold offered to continue to work with Sarah on an outpatient basis.

Socially, Sarah didn't fit in anywhere. She did not know how to relate to her peers, having no mutual social experience. She did not know how to play games or sports. She had no idea about the latest bands, current TV shows, or clothes that were in style.

The hospital staff engaged Sarah in games. It was baseball season and she began watching games with other patients and staff. Officer Hogan had been checking in on Sarah whenever he was at the hospital. He enjoyed watching her come out of her shell and really admired her spunk. When he was told that she didn't know sports, he volunteered to watch games with her. On some evenings off he brought a bag of chips and some soda and watched a ball game with her in the day room. She learned the rules of the game, how to root for her team, and how to yell at the ump. Most nights they called it a game after the fifth inning but occasionally she was allowed to stay up until the end of the game. Sarah was able to be comfortable with Joe Hogan and he was comfortable with her. As a visitor, unlike staff, he could hug her and share high fives. Their relationship was avuncular and very happy.

After seeing how well Sarah could handle physical affection, the staff let down their defenses a bit. One morning, when Sarah approached Mike and asked, "Rabbi-hug?" he acquiesced. Thus began a routine of receiving hugs in the morning and evening. Sarah could receive one hug from each staff member if she asked first. It was a non-sexualized, age appropriate physical contact and Sarah handled it well. She was able to be touched and held and feel cared about as a person rather than an object. The staff found this to be a nice way to express their feelings of caring towards Sarah also.

She had come a long way in a very short time.

Sarah's socialization was becoming the main focus of her therapies. Her school lessons included sports development and sports history. Now attending gym, Sarah learned how to skip rope, dribble a basketball, and to throw a baseball and a football. She learned to interact with other children on the unit.

Interestingly, staff noted that Sarah could not speak and play at the same time. While Sarah was a noisy fan, she was a silent player. The physical therapist instructed Sarah to count out loud while dribbling the basketball and playing hopscotch. It wasn't a success.

A few very worldly girls Sarah's age came into the unit. They were constantly dancing. So, with great trepidation of the staff and with close supervision, the girls taught Sarah to dance. Sarah took to it like a duck to water. She knew about routines—she had been doing them her whole life. This was just another routine. Before very long, Sarah mastered all

the dance routines the girls did. The three girls were allowed to watch dance videos on the children's stations and imitate the routines. But as will happen with girls, the discussion turned to boys and celebrities. Sarah covered her ignorance well about the celebrities, but it was clear that she was going to need more information.

Part of Sarah's school work had included watching the national news; now she was also to watch a celebrity news show.

She found it exhausting. After a week of watching celebrity updates, she asked if she had to keep watching about all the people. Other than pet therapy, she had never asked to not do something.

Miss Matthews asked, "Why don't you want to watch that show?"

"It's inane."

"Nice word usage."

"It was on my list last week. That show is really noisy and flashy but they don't say anything important. It's all about people dressing up. They don't really do anything. I like the news better. The news is about things that are happening and about people who are doing things. If I get famous, I want it to be for something that I did instead of how I look."

"Do you want to be famous?"

"Not really. I want to do something good for the world but I don't think I want to be famous. I wouldn't like all those cameras taking my picture all the time."

She was allowed to stop watching the celebrity news as an assignment but encouraged to use it as a resource to know what other kids were talking about.

July 5th   5:12 pm

Sarah was watching the national news in the dayroom while she was eating dinner and saw the Westchester DA. "Hey, I know him. He came to see me."

Jill, a fourteen year old with a history of drug use and delinquent behavior, sneered at Sarah as she retorted, "No he didn't. Why would someone on TV come to talk to you? You're making it up."

"He came here and he talked to me because I justifiable homicided Zeke."

"You what?"

"I justifiable homicided Zeke."

"You killed somebody?!!"

Sarah nodded.

"No way!! Are you here 'cuz you killed someone?"

"I don't know. I thought I was just here because it was where they brought me."

Julia, the evening attendant, entered the day room and asked what was going on.

"Sarah said she killed someone."

"And?"

"She is lying, right? You can't be here if you kill someone."

"We are not going to discuss why any of you are here. But let me assure you that Sarah is not here because she killed someone and you are in no danger. Got it?"

"Sarah's a liar!" Jill sang out.

Julia ignored the outburst and looked at Sarah. "Sarah, why don't you come with me?"

Sarah was very confused but followed Julia to her room. "Okay, now that we are alone, why don't you tell me what happened?"

Sarah took her through it. "She thinks I'm a liar."

"Yes, she does. But we are going to let her think that. And she thinks that you are getting in trouble right now. And we are going to let her think that too."

"But I am *not* a liar."

"No, you're not."

"So, why are we going to let her think that?"

"We're going to let her think that because she understands liars. She knows how to lie and she knows that her friends lie. She's comfortable with lying."

"You're confusing me."

"Sarah, does it really matter to you what she thinks of you? After she leaves, you're probably never going to see her again. Do you really think that she'll remember if you did something that everyone around her did?"

"Probably not. People don't remember the usual. You're going somewhere with this, aren't you?"

"Sarah, not many people have committed justifiable homicide. The kids here don't even understand what justifiable homicide is. You would be very memorable and she would have a lot of feelings and confusion that she doesn't need right now. It would be better for both of you that she think that you are a liar than know that you committed justifiable homicide against Zeke."

Sarah looked at Julia and tried to understand. "We all know what you did and we understand it. But it isn't something that other kids are going to be able to handle very well. So, to make it easier for you and them, we aren't going to tell them."

"So, what I did was a secret?"

"No, it's not a secret. What you did is known by everyone who needs to know. And it is a matter of public record. So, it is not a secret. However, it *is* private. That means that you don't need to tell anyone about it. And telling kids is just going to really confuse them. Do you understand?"

"I think so. You don't want me to mess up their heads because they are already sort of messy or they wouldn't be here."

"Close enough. Are you ready to go back out and play?"

"Yeah. She's going to think I got in a lot of trouble for lying, isn't she?"

"And we're going to let her."

Sarah went back to the dayroom and worked on her homework.

July 9th   8:30 pm

Sarah was in her pajamas and was ready for bed. It was routine for one staff person to tuck her in and say goodnight to her. Julia and Molly took turns so that Sarah had continuity even with staff having days off.

Molly was tucking Sarah in and sat down to talk to her about her day.

"Molly?"

"Yes?"

"You know Mike?"

"Day time Mike?"

"Yeah."

"Of course I know Mike. What about him?"

"Does Mike like me?"

"Of course he does, why?"

"Remember when I used to want to practice?"

"Yes."

"Mike wouldn't practice with me. He said he doesn't practice with little girls. Does he like little girls?"

"Yes, he likes you. No, he won't practice with you, and you, my dear, are heading into chicken work. You know who you need to do chicken work with?"

"Dr. Feingold."

"I will leave him a note for you."

"Okay."

"Good night, Sarah."

"Are you working tomorrow?"

"Yes. I will see you tomorrow afternoon."

"Okay, goodnight."

July 10th   11:00 am

"I got a note that said we have some chicken work to do."

Sarah, who had learned that therapy work was done in therapy and not with the staff, said, "Yeah, but I didn't know that it was chicken work when I asked Molly about it."

"Well, do you want to tell me what you asked?"

Sarah was fidgeting on the floor. "Mike said that he doesn't practice with little girls. He didn't say that he doesn't practice. So, who does he practice with?"

"Do you remember the words that I taught you about practicing?"

"Yeah."

"Okay, do you remember the word 'intercourse?'"

"Yeah."

"Sarah, intercourse is usually done when two adults love each other and want to express that feeling."

"Why?"

"People and all mammals are designed to engage in intercourse in order to make babies."

Sarah was dumbfounded. She sat speechless for a few moments then took a breath, started to ask a question but stopped.

"Sarah, are you still with me?"

She nodded and then, finding her voice, she asked quietly, "Where are we going to put them all?"

"All what?"

In a near whisper she responded, "All the babies. Where are we going to put all the babies?"

"What babies?"

"If you have intercourse you make a baby. I had a lot of intercourses. Doesn't that mean that I am going to have a lot of babies?"

"Fortunately, at least for now, you are not going to have any babies. We need to talk about how bodies work."

He started to explain the female reproductive system and was pleasantly surprised when she knew how girls develop into women. "How did you know that?" he asked.

"Taina explained it to me and she told me that someday my tummy would hurt where my pants are and that I would bleed and that it's okay and not to be scared and how to use pads so it doesn't make a mess. And she said that in a few days it would stop bleeding. And that it would happen every month after it got used to happening. She didn't say anything about intercourse or babies, though. She just said that I would have bleeding times and that I am going to get boobs."

"She did a very nice job explaining your upcoming growth to you. If you have questions about it along the way, I want you to know that you can ask me and we can talk about that, okay?" Sarah nodded. "She didn't talk to you about where babies come from?"

"No."

"Okay, so you learned how your body is going to grow. And you know what intercourse is. After your body has grown, when people engage in intercourse, they can make and have a baby. Not every time, but under the right conditions it is possible."

"So I can't have a baby till I have intercourse after I start bleeding?"

"That is correct."

"And the intercourses that I did don't count."

"Correct."

"So what does this have to do with who Mike intercourses with?"

"Sarah, most people only have intercourse with other people who are adults. It is part of how adults who love each other share their love."

"What does intercourse have to do with love?"

"If you do it right, everything. But one of the rules for doing intercourse the right way is that you have to have mutual consent. Children cannot consent, so people do not have intercourse with children."

"And grown-ups have intercourse just because they want to?"
"Yes."

"And do they have to?"

"No, they do it because they like it."

"Are you sure?"

"Yes, I am sure. I have given you a lot to think about, haven't I?"

"Yeah, you could say that. So, men are supposed to have intercourse with grown up women?"

"Yes. They are supposed to have intercourse with grown-ups."

"And the grown up women have a choice about it?"

"They only do it if they want to."

Sarah sat still and quiet for a moment and then asked, "Which planet did you fall off of?"

"This is pretty weird stuff, isn't it?"

"I never thought about grown up women having intercourse. Do they do fallatio and sodomy too?"

"If they want to. Some people like it and some people don't." Sarah was sitting very still and thinking hard. "Sarah, what are you thinking?"

"I hadn't thought about liking it or not liking it. It was just what I did because I was supposed to." She was silent for a few moments and the doctor let her sit with this new-found information.

"Is intercourse different for grownups than what I had to do?"

"It is very different."

"How come it has the same name if it's different?"

"Well, it does and it doesn't. Each act has the same name but in total, what you did is called child sexual assault or pederasty and what we are talking about now is called having sex or making love."

"They don't sound anything alike."

"They aren't anything alike. And we are going to need to spend some time looking at the differences. Sarah, this is something that we may need to revisit over time. We are going to talk about it some more over the next few sessions, but as you get older, we are going to need to visit it again. I want you to know that it is okay for us to come back to something again that we have already talked about, okay?"

She nodded. "Can I ask you a question?"

"I'm almost afraid, but go ahead."

"Do you make love with a grown up lady?"

"What would you think about it if I did?"

"I don't know. I am still trying to picture grown women making love."

"Why is that so hard to imagine?"

"They are so much bigger than me."

"And…?"

"Well, a lot of times the men would say that I was great because I was so tiny. They said they never had such a tiny little girl that could fuck so well. And sometimes they said I was light as a feather and tight as a drum. They can't say that about grown up women, can they?"

"Perhaps not, but when you are making love with someone it isn't all about their body. It is about who they are as a person and how you feel about them."

"I don't get it."

"Not yet, but you will when you are older."

"Promise?"

"Sarah, I hope with all my heart that you understand it fully. But for now, let's put this chicken away for the day."

"Okay."

July 13th 2:00 pm

Sarah met with her child advocate several times over the month of July to prepare for a visit to family court. Sarah needed to be assigned a birthday and a legal name. She asked that her first name be Sarah but she had no idea about a last name. She had no sense of a birthday. Since Rabbi Cohen had given her the name Sarah, she decided to talk to him about it.

"Rabbi, I need a last name."

"Do you have any idea what you want it to be?"

"I don't know. What would be a good name for me?"

Rabbi Cohen had given this question some thought already.

"How about if you took the last name 'Miller'?' Sarah Elizabeth Miller. What do you think?"

"I like it, but how come Miller?"

"I have been thinking about a name for you and Miller is the third most common Jewish surname in America and it can be either Jewish or Christian. You have been raising yourself Jewish, but I don't think you were born Jewish and I want you to be able to make your own decisions about who you are. Miller is a name that will serve you well and let you be whoever you grow up to be."

"What do you mean I have to choose who I am?"

"You are preparing for your bat mitzvah. That marks your becoming an adult. But when you are 16, you will be given an opportunity to decide if you believe in Judaism or if your beliefs are aligned better with another group. You may find out as you grow up that you are, in your heart, Christian."

"And you want my named to be Miller so that I can be Christian even if you're Jewish."

The rabbi nodded and smiled.

"How come you are spending a lot of time teaching me if I might not be Jewish?"

"Because a rabbi is a teacher and you have asked to learn. Sarah, love is not about owning someone. It is about allowing someone to truly be themselves."

Sarah sat quietly, thinking about what her rabbi said. "Okay, Sarah Elizabeth Miller. I am going to have to get used to having names. What about a birthday? I have to choose one."

"Usually when a person has a birthday assigned they are given January first."

"But that is already a holiday. Can I have a birthday that isn't a holiday?"

"Sure. Do you want a winter birthday, or spring or summer or fall?"

"Can it be in the spring?"

"How about May?"

"May sounds good. Is May fourth a good day?"

"May fourth sound like a very good day, Miss Sarah Elizabeth Miller."

"I have to call my advocate and tell her. I have to go to see a judge next week. I need to have a name and a birthday so I can move out of here."

"Sarah, once you come back to temple, we would like to have a naming ceremony for you. Do remember us having naming ceremonies for babies?"

She nodded.

"A naming ceremony is the way that we welcome children into our congregation. We were never able to do that for you before. Would you like that to happen?"

"But I am not a baby."

"No, but we can have a party for you getting a name and a new start."

"That sounds like fun. Can my foster parents come too?"

"Absolutely."

"Does everyone at temple know what I did?"

"No. They know that you have had a tough time of it and they know that all this time that you were coming to temple you were living alone, but they don't know what you needed to do with Zeke or how that ended."

"Because it's private?"

"Because it is private."

July 19th   2:30 pm

Sarah did not go to family court. It was decided that it would be easier for her to have the judge meet with her at the hospital. It was a quiet meeting and she was able to speak well for herself, after which she was officially Sarah Elizabeth Miller with a birthday of May fourth. The only question the judge had was based upon seeing Sarah for the first time. He asked if Dr. Feingold was sure that this diminutive child was indeed 13. Dr. Feingold explained the medical evidence for her age and the plan for her to be placed in the sixth grade. The judge asked if anyone had an objection to her being assigned the age of 12. Everyone at the meeting looked surprised. The judge explained that lowering her age would give her an extra year of entitlement to foster care and education, and it would lessen the gap between her peers and her. Everyone agreed that it would be in Sarah's best interests and Sarah officially became 12 years old.

Nancy had ordered a cake and the unit celebrated the occasion. The judge and advocate even shared in the festivities for a few minutes before departing.

It was a good day for Sarah.

July 26th   4:30 pm

Sarah and several other patients were in the dayroom waiting for dinner. NY1, the Time Warner news station, was on the television, an odd but not unheard of event on the unit. Sarah murmured, "Wow, this is better than cartoons." She was just about to ask if anyone knew what was for dinner when a breaking news banner flashed across the screen. "This just in: a NYC police officer was shot this afternoon. Officer Joseph Hogan was shot when attempting to apprehend a suspect in a store robbery. He has been taken to Bellevue hospital for treatment. There is no word yet on his condition."

Sarah stared wide-eyed at the television for 30 seconds, then bolted into her room, grabbed Cody and flew into the ceiling. She was so quick that no one realized she had gone. In seconds she catapulted through the ceiling, dropped in front of the stairwell door and began running down the stairs.

Security picked her up on the monitors as soon as she entered the stairway. Officers were dispatched and the unit was notified that they had a runner. She was intercepted when she ran straight into a security guard at the last landing. He caught her and tried to hold her but she pulled away and pointed at the door.

"Hey, you can't go out. You need to be upstairs."

Sarah shook her head, looking frantic and pointing at the door. Dr. Feingold raced down the stairs to find out what had happened.

"Sarah, where are you going?"

Sarah looked at him and then pointed at the door emphatically. The security guard let Dr. Feingold take the lead and positioned himself between Sarah and the door.

"Sarah, did something happen?"

She nodded and pointed at the door again.

"Did someone do something to you?"

She shook her head and pointed at the door.

"Are you feeling safe?"

She nodded.

"Okay, something happened but it didn't happen to you, correct?"

She nodded and pointed at the door.

"Okay, Sarah I want you to take a deep breath." She complied, although it was a bit raggedy. "One more breath and then I want you to find one word that will help me to understand what is wrong and why you need to go out that door."

Sarah took a deep breath, panted a few times and said "Bellevue."

"Bellevue. You're trying to go to Bellevue."

She nodded and grabbed his hand to pull him with her. And he understood.

"Sarah, let's go upstairs and make some phone calls. They're not going to let you into Bellevue right now but let's go see what is happening. Come on."

She shook her head and looked plaintively toward the door. "Yes, Sarah. Let's make some phone calls. We'll find out what is going on."

She acquiesced and they climbed the stairs only a little less quickly than she had descended them.

Mike was getting ready to leave when he saw Sarah come in the door with Dr. Feingold. "What's wrong?"

"She thinks Hogan is at Bellevue." Sarah pointed to the TV. They turned and saw the announcement. Sarah was quaking with anxiety. They went into the nurse's station and Mike held Sarah while Dr. Feingold called the precinct. While he was trying to find someone who would tell him about Hogan's condition, Sarah, who was facing Mike and was being held by him, started reaching for his belt. She was shaking with worry. Mike gently drew her hands away, turned her around and brought her up to sit on his lap.

"Sarah, I know you are scared. I am right here with you. You don't need to practice." She started rocking and he held her against his chest and restrained her. "You are feeling scared and worried. You really care about Officer Hogan and we know that. He is your friend. Dr. Feingold is going to find out how he is."

She struggled against him in frustration but he calmly held her while containing his own worry that this could end very badly. While Dr. Feingold was on one line, the other phone rang and the nurse answered it. She put the person on hold and motioned that it was for

Dr. Feingold. He took the call. "Doc, this is Pete, Joe's partner. He told me to call you. He said don't let Sarah watch the news."

"She has already seen it. How is he?"

"He was shot in the chest and the arm. His vest took the chest shot. He is going to be fine. He will be out of work for a while and I don't know just how bad his arm is, but his life is not in jeopardy. He is really worried about Sarah. I'm sorry it took me so long to call. They have taken him to surgery. It's been total chaos around here and I just got a free minute. He asked me to relay a message to her."

"Okay."

"He said to tell Sarah that he might have to miss this week's ball game but that he'll do his best to be there next week and he's counting on her to root for the right team even if he isn't there to keep an eye on her."

"I'll tell her. Can you call here and keep us updated? You can leave messages with the nurses and they will keep Sarah updated with the progress reports."

"I'll do that. How is she doing?"

"She's very worried. When you see him, you can let him know that we had to stop her from going to Bellevue on her own to see him. Thanks for the call, Pete. Please, let us know when he is out of surgery."

"I'll do that."

Dr. Feingold turned to Sarah. "Sarah, Joe was shot in the arm. He is in surgery now but is going to be okay. He has a message for you." He relayed the message and she smiled through her fear and worry.

Then he asked, "Have you been rooting for the wrong team?"

Mike shook her playfully, "Say it ain't so!"

She relaxed slightly with the humor and jostling but then turned around in Mike's lap, held her head in her hands and wept. Mike held her until she quieted.

Calmed, she climbed off his lap, looked at him then touched her head to his chest, backed up and went into the therapy room. Mike looked at Doc quizzically. "Did she just say thank you and I'm sorry?"

"I think that could be an interpretation. She says a lot when she doesn't speak, doesn't she?"

"She is something else. Is she going to be okay? Do you want me to stay?"

"I think we can handle her tonight. You're on tomorrow, right?"

"Yeah, I'll be here."

"Thanks for getting us this far; you are really good with her. I'm going to stay until Joe is out of surgery."

"I'll see you tomorrow."

Molly took Sarah's dinner into the therapy room. She was sitting on the floor rocking when Molly entered.

"How are you doing?"

Sarah nodded.

"Here is your dinner. Do you think you can eat something?"

Sarah shook her head.

"How about some chicken bouillon? That will be nice and warm and I know you like it."

Sarah nodded and Molly went to make it for her.

Dr. Feingold went into the therapy room and sat at the table. "What are you doing?"

Sarah looked like she was talking silently but she was rocking. "Sarah, are you praying?"

She nodded and then continued with her prayers. After a few minutes she stopped and got up and sat at the table with Dr. Feingold. "I'm proud of you."

She looked at him questioningly. "I'm proud of you because you have done a very good job of caring about Joe. You are a good friend to him." Sarah just sat quietly. "How are you feeling now?"

She whispered, "I'm tired, and worried, and quiet inside. I ran out of prayers."

"What do you mean?"

"I said all of them that I remember. Is Joe going to be okay if I can't remember any more prayers? Rabbi Cohen could make sure he gets better because he knows lots more prayers."

"Sarah, Rabbi Cohen does know lots of prayers, but God can hear the prayer in your heart just as well as Rabbi Cohen's. Prayer isn't about the words; it is about the heart that is saying them."

"Does Rabbi Cohen know that?"

"Does Rabbi Cohen know what?" Sarah looked up to see Rabbi Cohen standing in the doorway.

"It's not Thursday two o'clock sharp."

"No, it is not Thursday but I thought perhaps you would have a use for me."

"We do. I ran out of prayers."

"Well, I have brought some. Have you had any word on how your friend is doing?"

Dr. Feingold explained, "He was shot in the arm and he is in surgery and he is going to live but they don't know how bad the arm is yet. We are waiting for Pete to call."

Molly brought the chicken bouillon in to Sarah. "Hi Rabbi, can I get you anything?"

"No, I'm fine."

"Doc?"

"I'm fine too, Molly. Thanks for asking."

Rabbi Cohen sat at the table. "So, what was it that you were asking about when I came in?"

"Dr. Feingold says that prayers aren't all about the words; it's about what is in your heart."

"What, you're doing my job now?"

"Just pinch hitting in your absence. I'll let you set her straight."

Addressing Sarah, he explained, "The Doc is right. Prayer is about what is in your heart. You can say all the words beautifully, with perfect elocution and pronunciation. But if you don't add your heart, the words are nothing. The words of prayer are like a pretty box into which you place your heart. What God treasures is the gift of your heart, not the box."

"Can we say the prayer of healing together? Your box looks better than mine. Maybe God will pick that present first?"

"It will look even better if we can get the doc to say it with us." They started the Mi Shebeirach and before they finished, three other people who were on the unit had joined the prayer. At the Amen, Sarah looked up and saw the others. They went back to their work but she sat with tears streaming down her face.

Doc gave her a tissue and she wiped her face and asked, "Do you think it worked?"

Rabbi Cohen took her hand. "Sarah, prayers are not like presto magic. Prayers are what we hold in our heart to guide us and comfort us. You are very worried about Joe. You have said prayers for him to heal well. You are showing your love and that is what God is all about."

Dr. Feingold looked at her thoughtfully. "Perhaps you would like to make a present for him for when he wakes up; maybe a picture? Maybe while you draw him a picture you can drink your drink and eat some dinner."

"I don't know what to draw."

"Well, you know Joe. What would he like?"

"He likes baseball and likes to play basketball with his friends. Maybe I will make him a basketball hoop and tell him that I 'hoop' he feels better."

"I think that would be a slam dunk."

She worked on the card and they all talked while they waited. Sarah and Rabbi Cohen filled Dr. Feingold in on what she was learning in Hebrew school.

Then Sarah asked, "Is it my fault that Joe got shot?"

Rabbi Cohen jumped on this one before Dr. Feingold. "You left here today?"

"Only after I heard that he got shot."

"But before he got shot, where were you?"

"Here, doing my school work."

"Did you hire someone to shoot him?"

"No."

"Did you know that there was going to be a robbery?"

"No."

"Then how could it have been your fault?"

"I don't know. I just felt like it must be."

Now it was Dr. Feingold's turn. "So you felt like somehow you were responsible for the shooting even though you know that it isn't possible."

"Am I stupid?"

"No. You are caring and conscientious. People who are caring and conscientious often have the feeling that they should have prevented something that they could not prevent. The problem is if you start to believe it. Let us both be very clear about this. Joe getting shot had nothing to do with you. You will in your life have enough things that will be your fault; you don't need to take on things that aren't your fault."

"You'll let me skate on this one?"

"No, I let you skate on the chicken, this one you are free of. It isn't your fault."

At last, the call came in that the surgery was complete. Surgeons removed the bullet lodged in Joe's humerus and he would be fine once the bone healed.

Doc relayed the information to Rabbi Cohen and Sarah. Sarah was relieved and pleased.

"Now, Sarah. I need to know something and I need you to tell me the truth."

"Okay."

"Are you going to try to leave tonight?"

"No. I'll stay here. I can't see him tonight anyway, can I?"

"No, you can't. They wouldn't let you in. And I think that we have all had enough excitement for one night. You look exhausted. Why don't we have Molly pack you into bed? In the morning we will call and get a progress report together."

"Okay, but I need a Rabbi Hug first." She hugged Rabbi Cohen said good night and went to bed.

She slept through the night knowing that her friend would be okay.

July 30th   10:15 am

Joe was out of the hospital in just a few days. On his way home he stopped in to see Sarah. She ran to him and gave him a warm heartfelt hug. "Wow. If I get hugs like that, I am going to have to get shot more often."

"No!" She stepped back and hit him playfully. Then she looked at his arm in a brace and sling. "Does it hurt?"

"Yeah, it hurts a bit. They have me on some medication that helps. But it makes me tired. I can't stay but I wanted to let you know that I am okay."

"Did you get my picture?"

"Pete brought it to me. Thanks, kid."

"Rabbi Cohen helped me say prayers for you. I started to pray by myself but I ran out and he helped me and so did Doc and a bunch of other people."

"You prayed for me?"

She nodded.

He had tears in his eyes when he bent down and hugged her. "Sarah that is the most wonderful thing you could ever do for me. Thank you." He kissed her forehead as Dr. Feingold came down the hallway.

"Hey, how are you feeling?"

"I'm okay. The arm is going to need some time. I guess I'll be seeing one of your cohorts."

"Yes, I guess you will. It is a good opportunity to heal the inside as well as the outside."

"Well, I have my inspiration right here. If she can do the work she has done with you, I can do my work. Doc, thank you. Sarah said you prayed with her." The Doc looked a little sheepish. "I'm touched, Doc."

He continued, "I wanted Pete to call right away so you could tell Sarah what happened. I was glad that she was with people who would take good care of her."

"She's a keeper."

Sarah looked up at Joe, "Did Pete tell you I almost made it out of the hospital?"

"He did mention that you tried to escape."

"They caught me at the bottom landing. I only had about ten more feet. If we were on the 5th floor I would have made it."

"It was a good try."

"Can you come watch the game on Friday? If you are here they let me stay up late."

"I can only do five innings, kid. I am on the DL."

"Five is better than none."

"I better get going. I have to do some resting."

Dr. Feingold started him toward the door, "Let me walk you out."

Doc and Joe left the unit.

"Is she doing okay? I was so worried about her."

"She was worried about you, but yes, she is okay. Joe, I want to talk to you about your relationship with her. Not now, but maybe next week when you have had some more time to heal. She has special needs and I want to talk to you about them."

"Okay Doc. Look, I am tired now, but I'll tell you right now, I love that kid. I want to be in her life. I want to show her how a real man treats a kid. I know I can't adopt her. But I can be good to her and I can help her as she grows up. She's a hell of a kid."

"Joe, you are on pain killers, aren't you?"

"Yeah."

"So you are saying things you probably wouldn't usually say."

"Yeah, probably."

"Joe, you have good intentions and she needs people like you in her life. Let's spend some time talking about how you can help her and what to do when she gets into difficulties. Okay?"

"Okay, Doc."

"See you next week."

"And I'll see Sarah on Friday night."

August 2nd   9:15 am

Sarah's handling of Joe's shooting was a clear demonstration of just how far she had come. She was able to communicate throughout the incident and she was able to engage in appropriate behavior and find solace in it. Sarah was ready to move to a less restrictive environment. Maria and Amber came to meet Sarah. The plan was for them to meet daily for a week to get to know one another and talk about ground rules before Sarah was discharged. They met with Sarah alone and with Dr. Feingold. They also met Rabbi Cohen and Joe. "We've never had a kid come to us in such a planned way." Amber said when talking to Dr. Feingold. "Usually they show up with an hour's notice and the clothes on their backs."

"Unfortunately, that is usually the case. But if they had done that with Sarah, she would have been gone within an hour of arriving. She has lived on her own for four years."

"Is there a reason why she's so tiny?"

"We've been looking into that. She has barely grown in the five months she has been here and we have been keeping tabs on her food intake. She should be growing. We are following up with an endocrine study. So far we haven't found anything abnormal; she may just be late getting started in puberty but we are going to need to monitor it."

He continued, "We've actually been blessed that she hasn't started puberty yet. Her mind is that of a latency-phase or elementary school child, so everything is concrete and black and white. In a way, it is easier on her. And it is easier for us to lay groundwork. We are going to have our hands full when she actually hits puberty and everything goes haywire."

"So, you aren't going to push her into puberty because it's easier on you?"

Dr. Feingold chuckled, "It's not about me, or you; it's about her. If she can build a solid foundation, she can make it through adolescence. But if she were to hit it now, with her very limited and confused understanding about the world… well, with the hormone storms that she will have, she might either end up dead, on drugs, or a prostitute. I would prefer that she come out of this mess whole and happy."

He continued, "I know that we have a very limited time to lay the foundation before the storm comes. I plan on being with her throughout the storm, but the better the foundation, the better off she will be."

"I get it. Is she promiscuous?"

"Not really. When she gets upset she will want to do what she calls practicing—she will try to undo someone's pants in order to perform fallatio. Here she can be easily redirected. She has done it with me and a few of the staff. For whatever reason, she hasn't tried it with Joe. And he seems to have a handle on her. She needs to be monitored when they are together. I don't want him getting in over his head. That relationship can be very good for her if he can hold his boundaries, but if he doesn't, it will really mess them both up."

Amber asked, "How about the rabbi?"

"I have known Rabbi Cohen for years. He talked to me about Sarah when she first showed up at the temple almost four years ago. He named her Sarah. He adores her and he has a good handle on her. He can be a good resource for you. Her teachers already know her. They were the ones who worked with her tutor to design her schooling this summer so she can enter the sixth grade."

"I thought she was very bright and 12. Why are you putting her in sixth grade?"

"Good question. She is small, even for a sixth grader; she has never been to school except Hebrew school; she is just mastering speaking, and she is has almost no social experience. By putting her in sixth grade, we can allow her to fit in physically with her peers, she will have the security of one classroom of only 15 kids, and she will be on more even footing socially. Also, Rabbi Cohen thought she was a year younger than she is, so she started Hebrew school with the kids who are in sixth grade now. These kids know her and she them."

Maria asked, "What do we need to do special for her? Does she cut or have nightmares or wet the bed?"

"Not yet. I am not saying those thing won't happen. She may be fine or she may become very disruptive at some point. For now, she doesn't have many feelings. You will notice that she is very easy going and complies with almost everything. At some point, that's going to change. What we don't know is how. For now she needs to work on communicating. She isn't required to speak here. However, she has to answer the staff. Usually, she is speaking pretty well, but if she is upset, she loses speech. When that happens, she needs to nod or sign. She has been taught some very basic signs but usually she will gesture or write. You should have the same rules for her. She should be expected to keep her room clean and do whatever household chores you assign. She should be responsible for telling you what she needs. For now, she is actually an easy kid."

Amber and Maria spent time with Sarah. She showed them her hospital bedroom and introduced them to Cody. Then they sat down. "They say that I am going to live with you."

"How do feel about that?"

"Mostly it's okay, but how come?"

"What do you mean?"

"Why do I need to live with you? Why can't I live by myself again?"

Maria fielded this question. "Well, because you're a kid and we want you to be able to go to school and have grown ups to help you out and guide you."

"I was doing a good job of taking care of myself."

"Yes, you were. And we expect you to take good care of yourself at our house."

"What do I have to do for room and board?"

"You need to keep your room cleaned up and keep your stuff picked up and go to school."

"That's all?"

"Well, you'll probably need to help with the kitchen and the laundry and run the vacuum from time to time."

"That stuff is easy. What about renting me?"

Amber spoke up, "You want to know if we are going to rent you out?"

She nodded.

"We aren't renting you out to anyone. We don't rent out kids. And we don't do wrong things to them."

"So, why do you want me to live with you?"

"Amber and I don't have children and we like children so we have decided that having foster children would be a good way to have children and help a child who needs a place to live. We get to help you grow up and you get a place to live. It works for all of us. Are you willing to give it a try?"

"Can I talk to Dr. Feingold before I make up my mind?"

"Of course you can."

"Okay. I'll tell you tomorrow."

August 2nd   11:45 am

They left and Sarah climbed into the ceiling. Mike found the ceiling tile out of place when he looked for her a few minutes later.

"Sarah?"

He got a chair and climbed onto the armoire. He looked into the ceiling and saw Sarah sitting with Cody just a few feet away. "What are you doing up here?"

Sarah was crying. "I want to go home."

"Home where?"

"I don't know. I want to be home with Zeke and I want to go back to my little home but neither one is there. I like here and I have to leave. I don't know if I will like Amber and Maria's house. What if I hate it?"

"How about if you come on down and we can talk about it. Doc is still here, do you want talk to him?"

"He wants me to live with Amber and Maria. How come he doesn't want to keep me here with him?"

Doc walked by the room and saw Mike on the armoire.

"Mike?"

"Sarah is concerned about leaving us."

"Sarah, come on down, let's talk." Sarah came down, wiping her tear stained face with her sleeve.

"Are you trying to leave?"

She shook her head. "I just wanted to be alone."

"Do you go up there that I don't know about?"

"You mean that I don't get caught?"

"Yeah."

"A couple times a week. I just need to be alone. There are too many people here and sometimes I just need to be alone."

"You're having some feelings. Shall we talk about them?"

They walked together to the therapy room and Sarah sat at the table. "How come you don't want me anymore?"

"I do want you. You're going to come see me at my office almost every day. But you don't need to be in the hospital anymore and you are ready to go to school."

"But I know here."

"You didn't when you got here. You learned here. And you learned how to make your little house a home. You can make a home again with Amber and Maria."

"What if I don't like it?"

"Then we will work together so that it works for you."

"What if they're mean?"

"Then you will tell me or Theresa."

"What if school is too hard?"

"Then you, your teachers, Amber and Maria and I will work it out."

"What if I am scared?"

"Then we will talk about what is scaring you."

"What if Zeke comes there?"

"Zeke is dead, he can't go there."

"But what if he finds us and he isn't dead anymore?"

"Zeke will always be dead. He cannot come back, not ever."

"Because I killed him?"

"Because you killed him." Sarah sat at the edge of her chair, closed her eyes and began rocking. She looked like she was thinking hard and expressing anxiety.

"Sarah, what are you feeling?"

"I want to practice and I'm not going to. I am not going to."

"You're containing your anxious feelings?"

The tears started again but she stayed in her seat. "I'm scared and I don't know what to do."

"What are you scared about?"

She began crying in earnest but choked out, "Living with Amber and Maria."

"Why does it scare you?"

"Because I don't know what it'll be like. I never lived with grown up women before."

"But Molly and Julia put you to bed at night and you like that, don't you?"

"Yeah."

"And Nancy has cared for you when you have been sick, and you like Nancy."

"Yeah…"

"What is the 'but' you aren't saying?"

"Am I going to get trained?" Her tears were slowing.

"Are you going to have to go through some training like Zeke made you get trained?"

"Yeah."

"No. Amber and Maria are good people and they will take good appropriate care of you. But Sarah, if they ever did something that made you uncomfortable; you know that you could tell me?"

She nodded. "Will I come back here?"

"If you ever need to come back here, then you will come back. Will you miss here?"

She nodded, "I like here."

"I think you are going to like it at Amber and Maria's even more."

"Are you sure?"

"I'm pretty sure."

"Okay, tomorrow I'll tell them that I'll live with them."

August 10th   11:45 am

Sarah was discharged on Friday morning. She had one last session with Dr. Feingold in the hospital and he assured her that he would see her at his office on Monday morning. She could tell him all about how the weekend went. She was anxious but ready when Amber and Maria came to pick her up. They took a cab to their apartment and Sarah had her first look at her bedroom. The walls were a typical creamy white, but the furniture was a light pine and the rug on the floor a deep blue. Maria led her into the room. "We thought we would let you pick out your own bedspread. And of course you can hang posters to decorate the walls." They helped her put her clothes away and Cody took up his position on the bed. Sarah carefully placed her chicken on the dresser.

Amber, who was helping her unpack asked, "Did you make that?" Sarah nodded. "It's very good. It looks like it has a story."

Sarah looked at the chicken and then at Amber. "It does, but it's sort of tragic."

"I'd like to hear it sometime, if you ever want to share it."

Sarah thought about it for a moment. "Some time, but not right now, okay?"

"That's fine. How about we show you the rest of the apartment?"

She nodded and followed Amber and Maria through the tour.

"This is like a whole house in here," Sarah marveled.

"Yes. That's what apartments are. They're like a whole house with other houses glued to them," Maria explained as she led the way through the living room.

"Have you ever been in an apartment before?" asked Amber while flipping on the light switch in the bathroom.

"I don't think so."

She saw Amber and Maria's bedroom and asked, "How come you have to share a bed?"

"Because we want to; we like to sleep in the same bed."

Sarah nodded, not really understanding but not wanting to be rude.

Maria said, "How about lunch?"

They went into the kitchen and made lunch together, showing Sarah were everything was and how to use the appliances. "Am I allowed to use the stove?"

"Do you know how to use the stove?"

"No. In the hospital the stove was turned off by a switch that was locked. And in my little house I just had a butane burner." Maria looked at Amber, who said, "How about we teach you how to use the stove before you use it on your own? And for now at least, you don't use the stove without asking and one of us being home."

"Okay. What are we going to do this afternoon?"

"Well we were thinking…how about shopping? It doesn't look like you've had new clothes in a while and you're going to need clothes for school and a couple pairs of shorts for now. We have your school clothes requirements from Rabbi Cohen."

Maria picked up the itinerary. "Then we can come home, get something to eat and go to services. We've never been to Jewish services, so we're going to need some help."

"I can help you. How come you haven't been to services?"

"We aren't Jewish. Maria is Catholic and I'm Lutheran. We don't go to church much."

"I can show you services. Do you know Hebrew?"

"No," they chorused.

"Well, some of it is in English and some of it might not make sense but everyone is nice. Where are we going shopping?"

"Sarah, do you have a favorite place to buy clothes?"

"I bought my underwear at Jack's and the rest of my clothes at The Second Hand store."

"The one with the funny clock that only has a second hand?" Sarah nodded.

"I like that store. But do you shop there because you want to or have to?"

"Well, I didn't have very much money."

"How about we splurge today? Let's go to Macy's."

"Macy's is huge."

"So you've been there?"

"Of course; I like the perfume counter. And the clothes are really pretty."

"Then let's put these dishes in the dishwasher and go."

"We need to get you a Metro card."

"I have one. It's in my backpack. It was with my money when Joe brought it to the hospital."

"Great. Let's go to Macy's." They were able to pick up several pairs of shorts and short sleeve shirts on clearance. Then they bought a few outfits for school. Sarah tried on all her clothes and was happy with how they looked on her. "I haven't had brand new clothes since…." She stopped and looked down, not wanting to finish the sentence or think about the pretty dresses she used to have or what she did when wearing them.

Maria closed her thoughts by saying, "Then it's time you did. And you need some new shoes and sneakers."

"Both?" Sarah was wide-eyed at the extravagance.

Amber explained, "You need shoes for school and sneakers for gym class and play. Let's see what they have here and if we don't like these, we can go to Sketchers."

"I've never bought so much stuff in my life."

Amber was amused by her solemnity. "Do you think we got enough for today?"

She nodded.

"Then let's get all this home and get you cleaned up before services. You can wear your new dress if you like. Rabbi Cohen will be surprised when you show up in a new dress."

"Maria, can, um…"

"What is it?"

"Can you cut my hair?"

"How short do you want it?"

"Can I have it this long?" She held her hand a few inches below her shoulder.

"Sure you can. Actually I know a place on the way home that will donate the part that is cut off to Locks of Love."

"What's that?"

"They make wigs for kids who have lost their hair. People who are getting their long hair cut donate it."

"So, some kid could have a wig made out of my hair?"

"Yeah. Cool, isn't it?"

"Is it a Mitzvah?"

"It sure is a good deed."

"Rabbi Cohen will be proud of you," added Amber.

So they stopped at the salon and Sarah's hair, which was beyond her waist, was cut to just above her shoulder blades.

Shaking her head, she smiled and said, "It feels so different."

"Lighter?"

"Lots lighter. It was too long."

"How come you left it so long?"

"Taina used to trim it for me at each season but she just trimmed the ends because she thought that I had parents and she didn't want to offend them. And we didn't have scissors in the hospital. So it just grew."

Maria stopped and appraised Sarah. "You know what you need?"

"What?"

"You need a hair band." They went into a hair accessory store and purchased several barrettes and hair bands. Coming out of the store, Maria said, "I haven't had this much fun shopping in a long time, have you Amber?"

"Well, it was fun, but next time I think I will let you to tackle it without me."

Maria said, "Have you ever had a mani-pedi?"

"Taina cut my nails for me. But she said I couldn't wear polish so my parents wouldn't get mad."

"Tomorrow, let's you and I sneak out and get mani-pedis."

"How do we sneak out? You're a grown up."

"We leave Amber at home. She hates mani-pedis."

"And go to a nail salon?"

"Yeah, I'm due and you are definitely due so let's do it."

"You're funny." Sarah was relaxed and happy but also curious. "Maria, are you rich?"

"Nope, not even close."

"Then how come you could buy me all this stuff today?"

"Well, you actually come with some money attached. Today, we used your clothing allowance. It won't buy you everything you need, but it will get us started. And Amber and I both have good jobs. So, you won't be getting a fancy car but we can buy you what you need."

They had arrived home and entered the apartment. "Now, why don't you put these clothes away, take a shower and get dressed for services. You want to wear the blue shorts under your dress." Sarah stopped and looked at Maria. Seeing a dumbfounded look on Sarah's face she asked, "What did I say?"

"I never even wore underwear when I used to get dressed up in pretty dresses."

"It's a new world, Sarah. We are here to keep you safe."

August 10th   6:30 pm

Sarah felt like a new kid in her new clothes and new haircut. She led the way into temple and showed Maria and Amber into the chapel. Rabbi Cohen came over to introduce himself. "You look wonderful, Sarah, and I see you brought Amber and Maria. What a wonderful family you make."

Maria replied, "We're kind of new at it. But we had fun today."

"Maria, Amber, we are having a naming ceremony for Sarah tonight to welcome her back and celebrate her new beginning. We would like you to come up with her so that we can introduce you to everyone and bless your family. Are you okay with that?"

Maria and Amber looked at each other. They were both taken aback. Rabbi Cohen explained, "For various reasons, caregivers sometimes are left to raise children in the Jewish faith although they are not Jewish themselves. We feel that it is important to support these parents and caregivers who are willing to make the extra effort to raise a child in the Jewish faith. Sarah has been a part of this congregation for a long time. Having her back is cause for celebration." To Sarah he said, "You may see more people here tonight than is usual."

Amber spoke first, "I am a little anxious about this."

"Of course you are. You've never been to a service, have you?"

"No, neither of us has."

"And you are a little worried that people will not accept your lifestyle?"

"Uh, yeah."

"Let me assure you we are very friendly and accepting. Any family that will allow Sarah to be ours again is going to be not only accepted but celebrated. She looks wonderful and I don't just mean well dressed." He paused to allow them a moment to absorb what he had said. "You will allow the blessing?"

The looked at each other again and nodded in unison. Maria said, "We can be blessed."

Families came into the chapel used for smaller services. Some just went to their pews, but others came over and welcomed Sarah back and introduced themselves to Maria and Amber. By the time services started, Sarah was ready for a break.

Her work with Rabbi Cohen had paid off and she was able to sing, chant or say all of the prayers with the congregation. For the people who had known her as a furtive silent child, watching this confident speaking child was like watching a butterfly unfurling her new wings. Sarah did not flit about. She was no social butterfly yet, but she was able to look at people and speak to them.

After the Torah was read, Sarah, Maria and Amber were asked to come up to the front. Sarah had her naming ceremony in which everyone was told that her name was now Sarah Elizabeth Miller. She was blessed as a child and then all three were given a blessing as a family.

The congregation was tear-filled when Rabbi Cohen talked about the importance of children and of her coming from the wilderness to their doorstep.

After the service there was a party. There was always food after the service, but this time there was a Welcome Home Sarah sign and a Welcome Home cake. Sarah was asked to address everyone. She went up to the cake and, looking around and thinking for a moment, she spoke clearly. "I want to thank everyone who let me be here when I couldn't speak. Thank you for feeding me after services when I was too scared to get my own food. Thank you for leaving me be so that I could stay. Thank you for letting me go to Hebrew school even though I wouldn't participate. But most of all, thank you for letting me come back now that I can talk."

Everyone clapped and then the cake was cut. Rachel and Micah, who would be in Sarah's class, came up to her. Rachel said, "My mom says that you're going to go to school here."

"I am."

"How come you can talk now?"

"Because I went to the hospital and they made it so I could talk."

"Did you really live all by yourself?"

"Yeah, but now I'm going to live with Amber and Maria, and it's going to be better." Then, deftly changing the subject, she asked Rachel, "Did you get your school clothes yet?"

"I got some slacks and blouses. I don't have shoes yet. How about you?"

"These are my new shoes and I got sneakers and I got 2 outfits. I need a couple more."

Micah asked, "Do you have your laptop?"

"No, I didn't know we need a laptop."

Micah was now on proper footing. "Yeah, we have to do our homework on the computer and e-mail it in."

"I'll talk to Maria about it. Rabbi Cohen didn't tell me I needed one."

"Do you talk Rabbi Cohen a lot?" Rachel asked.

"He talks to me every week. We've been doing my Hebrew class and I'm getting ready for my bat mitzvah. Do you meet with him?"

"I'm starting in September. My birthday isn't until October. When's yours?"

"May."

"Do you know what your reading will be?"

"Not yet. It should be like Leviticus or Numbers because it's in May. But I don't know which chapters yet. Yours is going to be Genesis. Micah, when are you?"

"July, but not for a whole other year."

Rachel's mother called, "Rachel."

"I got to go. Sarah, I'll see you in school. Bye, Micah."

"I gotta go too. See you later, Sarah."

Sarah went over to Amber and Maria, who were talking to other parents. Amber put her hand on Sarah's shoulder. "Are you okay?"

Sarah looked tired but nodded. "I need to talk to rabbi."

"Okay, I'll be right here."

Sarah went over to rabbi. "Thank you for the party."

"You're welcome." Then, looking at her he asked, "What's wrong?"

"Micah said we need a laptop for school."

"Yes, you do."

"I don't have one. And Maria and Amber already spent a lot of money on me today."

"And you look very pretty." Sarah looked down at her new dress and new shoes.

"Sarah, you have a full scholarship for day school here. That includes your computer. Your teacher, Mrs. Rifkin, finished loading the software on it today. Would you like to take it home with you tonight?" She nodded and smiled.

They went together into his office and he handed her a box with a small laptop computer inside. "Do you think Maria or Amber can teach me how to use one of these?"

"You don't know how?"

"I've never touched one before. I think I'm probably the only kid in America that hasn't used a computer."

"You'll do okay with it. Bring it with you on Thursday."

"Thank you."

Sarah went over to Maria, who was talking to a congregant. "Hi, Sarah. What do you have?"

Beaming, Sarah said, "It's my computer for school. Can you teach me how to use it?"

"Sure, we can do that. Are you getting tired?"

"Yeah." She sighed and yawned.

"Are you ready to go home?"

"Yeah, it's been a big day."

"Okay, let's get us extricated."

"Amber, our little flower is wilting." Amber looked at Sarah and nodded. They quickly started to help with the clean-up but were stopped and told that tonight they were guests. They excused themselves to take Sarah home.

Sarah was half asleep by the time they had walked the six blocks. Maria took the computer. Amber took Sarah into her room and helped her get ready for bed. She slept soundly.

Amber and Maria sat in the kitchen after Sarah went bed. "We've never had one like this one," Amber spoke quietly.

Maria shook her head in disbelief, "I've never felt so supported. We usually have to fight for the kids to get them what they need. She is having everything given to her. I feel like we're in a new world."

"She really seemed comfortable there. She never stopped talking. She was just a kid."

"We should cherish this day."

"What are you doing tomorrow?"

Maria laid out her plans. "I am going to take her to the nail salon and then to the library. Then we need to start teaching her how to use the computer."

"We should have a quiet day tomorrow." Amber murmured.

"We need to get her a cell phone before she starts school."

"Next week."

"Sunday, let's go to Coney Island."

"Sounds like fun, as long as I don't have to get my nails done."

August 13th   8:30 am

The weekend was a fun one for Sarah. On Monday, the three walked to Dr. Feingold's office. He met with Sarah alone first.

"How was your weekend?"

"You were right. I like it a lot better than the hospital. We went to Coney Island yesterday. And we went to the aquarium. I never went there before. We saw a little white whale."

"The beluga?"

"Yeah, that's what it's called! And we saw the penguins. I've seen penguins before at Central Park but I never saw a whale." She continued happily. "Friday night we had a party at services and Rabbi Cohen gave me a laptop. I need it for school. Amber showed me how to use it on Saturday afternoon. And we went to the library. The librarians were very surprised to see me; they almost fell over when I asked for a library card."

Dr. Feingold appraised her. "And you got your hair and nails done. Whose idea was that?"

"The hair was my idea. I gave it to Locks of Love so kids that don't have hair can have wigs. The nails were Maria's idea."

"They look very pretty. Are you sleeping okay?"

"Yeah, I have my own bedroom. They have to share a bedroom but they said that it's okay because they like to sleep together."

"You seem pretty happy. Are you having any problems talking?"

"No, I haven't had a problem all weekend. I like Maria and Amber. Last night they let me help cook dinner."

She stopped and then asked, "Can I really do this?"

"Do what?"

"Live with Amber and Maria and go to school and talk to friends. I talked to Rachel and Micah Friday night."

"Who are Rachel and Micah?"

"They are in my class. I never talked to them before."

"How did it go?"

"It went well. I'm going to do my bat mitzvah before either of them." Sarah stopped again, looked around the office and bit her lip. "They spent a lot of money on me on Friday. I'm expensive."

"Are you worried about that?"

"Yeah. How am I going to pay it off?"

"By working hard here and in school, and being respectful to them. And most of all, you will repay them by becoming yourself."

"That's all?"

"Sarah, we are asking quite a bit of you. Would you mind if I spend some time with them?"

"No, I brought a book."

Amber and Maria came in. "How is it going?"

Amber stated, "Honeymoon period."

Maria expanded on the thought. "She is polite and respectful, helpful and curious. She also knows her way around. We have never had a kid who had a community surrounding her before. The temple is wonderful and the librarians were shocked to see her but very supportive."

Amber said, "We need to get her some more clothes but she seems overwhelmed by all the new stuff. We are going to have to get her a cell phone too."

Dr. Feingold confirmed, "She's a little worried about how much she is costing. Take it a little slow. If she just gets one outfit at a time she might do better." Then, "She said she didn't have any problems talking this weekend."

"She hasn't. You would never know she was mute. The only time she showed any baggage this weekend was when I told her to wear her new shorts under her dress."

"What did she do?"

"She said that she didn't even wear underpants under her pretty dresses before." Amber observed, "I think she is surprised by how much she has changed. She is walking around like she knows where she is but she isn't the same person."

"She isn't. She is very different than when they brought her in to the hospital. Have you had any word from Joe? She didn't mention him."

"We're all going out for Chinese tomorrow night. How much supervision do we need to provide? Can we let him take her places?"

"Play it by ear. I trust Joe. He wants the best for her. It's Sarah I am concerned about. She is the one who is going to get confused and test boundaries. He is going to need support maintaining them. So can you trust him with her? Absolutely. Can you trust her with him? For the time being, yes."

"Anything else?"

"No, we're good."

"Okay, why don't we bring Sarah back in here?"

Sarah came back in. "It sounds like you are all doing well. Sarah, can you come back here on Wednesday morning and on Friday morning?"

"I can do it."

"Okay, I will see you Wednesday."

They walked toward home, window shopping along the way. At Union Square they got a drink and sat down to watch the squirrels. "I never shot any squirrels in this park."

"You shot squirrels?"

"Yeah, I've shot squirrels and pigeons."

Amber asked with some concern, "Did you have a gun?"

"No, you can't have a gun in New York City. I had a slingshot."

"What did you do with the pigeons and squirrels?"

"I ate them. Joe said that all my stuff is packed up and stored for me. Am I allowed to have it at your house?"

"Your stuff or your slingshot?"

"Both."

"Why don't we talk to Joe about where your stuff is? You are not going to be running around the city with a slingshot. Your hunting days are over. But we can go through your stuff and figure out what you still want or need."

"What if I don't want it anymore?"

"Then we will get rid of it." Maria explained, "Your needs are different now than they were. As we change, we get rid of what we don't need so that we have room for what we do need. Otherwise, we'll just be too cluttered."

"Can we go by where I used to live? I know it isn't there anymore, but I want to go there anyway."

"Sure we can. Where did you live?"

"On 9th."

"We can go by there on the way home." They walked south to 9th and Sarah stopped when they got to a vacant lot.

"Was this it?"

Sarah nodded. She had tears in her eyes. Maria put her hand on Sarah's shoulder. "It's different to know something and to see it. Seeing something makes it more real." Sarah looked up at Maria and nodded.

After a few minutes of looking at the empty lot, Sarah asked, "I lived there for a long time. What are they going to do with it now?"

"I don't know. We can find out."

"What do you want them to do with it?"

"What if they built new apartments and I lived there? But not in the basement again; I like living in an apartment better than a basement."

"Do you like your room?"

"Yes. I like it even better than the hospital. Even if it doesn't have a ceiling I can climb in."

"What?"

"I used to climb in the ceiling at the hospital. It was against the rules but I didn't get in trouble. Some kids had time outs all the time at the hospital. I never had a time out. I had to do talking time instead of quiet time. Am I going to have time outs at your house?"

"If you need them you will have them. It sounds like you aren't a kid who needs to get attention by breaking the rules."

"Is that because I always had my own rules?"

"Maybe. What kind of rules did you have for yourself?"

"Well, don't talk to anyone was the biggest rule. I didn't break that rule until I was at the hospital and Dr. Feingold told me that I couldn't escape and they knew that I could talk. Don't get noticed. I broke that rule a few times. Like at the library and temple and the laundromat. But usually, I didn't break it. So, I didn't shoot squirrels in Union Square. People are always there and they would have seen me. I always put my food away because I hate rats. And I hate cockroaches."

"You had important rules." Maria spoke as they walked home. "I think that we have important rules too. I hope you are going to think they're important also."

"Like what?"

"You don't leave the house without saying where you are going and when you are coming back."

"Why?"

"We will worry about you if we don't know where you are."

Sarah stopped walking. She looked at both women quizzically. "You will? Why?"

Amber said, "Because we care about you and we would not want something to happen to you. Letting people know where you're going is part of being a family. You've seen us tell each other where we're going when we leave. That's a part of being connected."

"And you will tell me where you're going and when you're coming home?"

"We will. It's an everyone rule."

"What else?"

"You need to call if you are going to be late."

"Um, um," Sarah looked worried.

"What is it, Sarah?"

Sarah barely whispered, "I've never used a phone."

Amber started them walking again. "Then I think now is a good time to get you one. There's a phone store right up here. Getting you a phone was already on the agenda, so how about now and we'll teach you how to use it this afternoon."

"Okay." Sarah was amazed by all the phones. They chose a phone with a text keyboard and added it to their plan.

"Now you can even send us a message if you have something happen and you're having trouble finding your words."

Sarah smiled. "How did you know I was worried about that?"

"Intuition."

They spent the afternoon working on the new computer and charging the cell phone. Once it was charged, Amber showed Sarah how to program numbers into it. They programmed Amber and Maria's work and cell numbers, Joe's, Dr. Feingold's, and Rabbi Cohen's. By the end, she was programming them on her own. Then she learned how to make a call and how to text.

"Now that you know how to do this, you need to call Amber every day when you get home from school."

"So she can let me in?"

"What? Oh, no. We haven't given you a key yet, have we?"

"I got a key made for you yesterday. We need a nice key ring for you, but I'm sure we'll find one along the way. For now you have this lovely pink fob."

"You know what else you need? A backpack for your computer. If we find the right one it will have a place for your cell phone and your keys."

"I need a lot of stuff. I didn't need this much stuff when I was living on my own."

"True. But you have to admit, now is more fun."

"Yeah, it's more fun."

Amber said, "I need to go out to the market. Do you want to come?"

"Okay."

"Let me grab the grocery cart from the closet. We need to get some heavy stuff."

Sarah had been to the market. It was the same one that she had shopped in. But it had never occurred to her to actually buy most of the food. Maria, aware that Sarah was becoming overwhelmed, kept the buying to a minimum. Nonetheless, there were fruit, cookies, and a few days' worth of meats and vegetables.

"We need to think about what to make you for lunches. You need to take your lunch to school every day and the rule is no meat or shellfish. So this week, I want you to think about that... We can experiment this week and next."

"Can I have sandwiches?"

"Sure, sandwiches are a fine lunch; we just need to find stuff to put in them."

"I never had sandwiches when I was alone. A loaf of bread was too big. And I was afraid the rats would get it."

"I'm sure we can protect your bread from the rats. Why don't you pick out a loaf?" Sarah chose a loaf of bread and asked if they had peanut butter. "We have smooth. If you want crunchy, we will need to get some."

"Crunchy peanut butter?"

"You have never had it?"

"I never heard of it."

"Well, you will need to try it."

Sarah gasped at the total at the register. After they left, Sarah whispered, "That's a lot of money."

"Well, there are more people than you we're buying for. But Sarah, we need to talk about money and how much we are spending on you. You seem pretty concerned about it."

"I'm not used to it and there is so much."

"If you had lived with us all along, you would have gotten this stuff slowly over time. But you came here without anything except some clothes and Cody. You will notice that we are not getting you a new Cody. We aren't buying you stuff to buy you stuff. However, you need to be prepared for your new way of life and we need to get you ready in just a few weeks. Once we have you set up, you won't be getting new stuff every day."

"Where does all the money come from?"

"The state pays for you to live with us because you don't have parents. So some of what we spend on you comes from that. The temple has given you a scholarship to pay for your schooling. It pays your tuition—that is the cost of you going there, and for your books and computer. And both Maria and I work, so we get paid for working."

She continued as they walked. "When we put it all together, we can handle taking care of you properly. And we think that it's important that you be taken care of properly. How do feel about people thinking that taking care of you is important?"

"I don't feel like I'm as special as people are treating me."

"You are the only Sarah Elizabeth Miller in our lives and just you being you makes you special. All you need to be is you. We are all here to give you the tools to grow up well. That's all we ask for in return." They were almost home. "And Sarah, most kids in this city have always had all this stuff. What is different for you is that you never have. Now, what do you say we bake chicken for dinner? Have you ever baked chicken?"

"No, I didn't have an oven."

"It's time you learn how to bake chicken." They took the groceries into the kitchen and put them away. Then Maria said, "Grab an egg. I'll get the breadcrumbs and spices." They proceeded to dip the chicken parts in flour, then the beaten eggs, and then the breadcrumbs and spices to put together a nice dinner. Having a way to contribute helped to settle Sarah.

"What are we doing tomorrow?"

"You have an eye doctor appointment. But we can do whatever we want after that and then we're going out to dinner with Joe at 6:00. What do want to do?"

"You're on vacation, right?"

"Yeah, we are."

"What do you want to do? It's your vacation so you should get to do something fun." Amber looked at Maria and said, "She's right, you know. I mean mani-pedis, Coney Island, and shopping trips are not fun at all. We should do something fun."

Playing along, Maria nodded, "Good idea. You know what we haven't done this summer?"

"I'm open."

"We haven't ridden on the Staten Island Ferry. It's not officially summer without a ride on the Staten Island Ferry. Let's pack our lunch and ride the ferry."

Sarah lit up. "I love riding the ferry. I haven't ridden it since last summer either. We bought bread today so we can have a lunch experiment."

August 14th 9:00 am

Sarah had her first eye exam and it was determined that her eyes were fine.

When they arrived at the ferry terminal Sarah suggested that she pay for the ferry ride for everyone. Since riding the Staten Island Ferry is free, they saw for the first time that Sarah had a sense of humor.

"Thanks, kid." Amber chuckled as they made their way through the stations and security. They stood at the front railing as the boat started across New York Harbor.

"How did you know to ride the ferry, Sarah?"

"I don't know. Sometimes, there were other kids my size doing stuff and I would just join them. I wasn't really scared when there were a lot of kids my size so I would go places. It was like in the "_Mixed-Up Files_" book."

"So, you were a stowaway."

"Can you be a stowaway if you are on the deck and the ride is free?"

"You have a point," Amber conceded.

"I love this view. This is perfect day to be out here on the water." Maria was smiling with her face to the sun.

"I don't think I will ever get tired of seeing the Statue of Liberty," Amber agreed.

Maria pointed to the ferry just north of them. "Look at all those people on the Liberty Island Ferry. They have to pay and we get the better view."

"Yeah, but they actually get to go there," Sarah noted.

"There is that."

"I've never been there. It cost too much and the security always scared me."

"We will have to go sometime, but not in August," Amber interjected.

They sat down and ate their lunch. As the ferry approached Staten Island, the passengers disembarked and new travelers boarded.

As they were returning to Manhattan Amber commented, "The Freedom Tower is just not the same as the Twin Towers."

"I never saw the Twin Towers."

Maria and Amber both looked at Sarah. Then recognizing her age Amber said to Maria, "There is nothing like kids to mark the passage of time."

"Do you know what the Twin Towers were?"

"Yeah, I saw them in pictures and statues in tourist stores, but I never saw them for real."

"Do you remember the Freedom Tower not being there?"

"I remember it being built and getting taller but I don't remember it not being there at all."

"Wow, there is a half a generation that doesn't remember an event that was so defining for us."

"That's something to think about." Amber and Maria embraced in the thought and Maria reached out and placed her arm on Sarah's shoulder.

September 2nd 12:30 pm

The next few weeks were a whirlwind of activity. Sarah succeeded in going to her first dental visit without incident or cavity; she completed her school shopping and mastered operating her computer and cell phone. The visit with Theresa Meyers went well and Sarah seemed very happy. Amber and Maria began allowing her to stay home alone for short periods of time to get used to it. They even went for walks around the block together just to create the opportunity for Sarah to experience being alone.

She was responsible and followed the rules. They would leave her reading on her bed and come back as much as an hour later to find her still reading. Sarah was becoming comfortable with getting snacks and with having food around. She was the perfect child. Unfortunately, perfect children don't really exist. Amber and Maria were beginning to wonder what was really going on and what they were in for.

They found out on Labor Day Sunday. They were scheduled to go with friends and Joe to a picnic in Central Park. Sarah was dressed in shorts and sneakers and was wearing the NYPD hat that Joe had given her. She looked like any other small but healthy 12 year old. But as she stepped out of the building, she looked up and froze. She stepped back into the building and began quaking. Suddenly, she was unable to speak again and unable to move.

Sarah had her first full-blown panic attack. For several minutes Sarah was unable to respond. Maria talked to her quietly, letting her know that she was safe. Slowly, Sarah began to re-orient and calm herself. She wasn't speaking, but she could nod. Maria asked if she wanted to go back to the apartment but she shook her head no. She wanted to go on the picnic. She was quiet on the train. Amber and Maria exchanged anxious glances as they glimpsed the depth of Sarah's difficulties.

Sarah was quiet through the day. She played Frisbee and toss with the other party goers, but she seldom spoke. After lunch she walked off to the brambles, a wooded area, by herself. Joe saw her walk away and followed her. He found her sitting on a bench alone near one of the favorite bird watching areas. He sat down near her and let her be. She watched the birds for a while; the Nuthatches and Chickadees flitted about from tree to tree. The Downey Woodpecker hopped up and down the trunk. When a Northern Flicker came into the grove, he asked, "What's that one called? That's a pretty one."

She looked at him. "It's a Northern Flicker."

"Do you know what all of them are?"

"No, most."

"I haven't seen you this quiet in a long time. Is there something going on?"

She nodded.

"I know I am not Doc, but can I help?"

"No."

"Do you want me to stay here with you or leave you alone?"

She tapped the bench, indicating that she wanted him to stay.

"Did you watch the birds a lot when you were alone?"

She nodded.

"Show me how to watch them. I've never sat and watched the birds."

She moved over and he put an arm around her shoulder. She drew one leg up onto the bench and pointed to the birds she was focusing on. After a while Sarah turned to Joe and sighed.

"What do you want to do, kiddo?"

Sarah sighed again and said, quietly, "Practice."

"You are feeling pretty upset, aren't you?"

Sarah nodded.

"Did anything happen that brought this on?"

Sarah shook her head.

"Do you like living with Maria and Amber?"

She nodded.

"You've had a busy couple of weeks. I bet you've done more in the past two weeks than you've done in a year."

Sarah nodded.

"Has it just caught up to you, or is there something else?"

"Just."

"Are you going to tell Doc that you wanted to practice with me?"

Sarah nodded.

"You ready to head back?"

She nodded and stood up. As Joe stood, she touched his injured arm and looked at him as if to say, "Does it still hurt?"

"It hurts a little but it's getting better. I am going back to work next week."

Sarah looked scared.

"Just desk duty; I won't be going back on the streets for a while."

Sarah nodded.

They went home from the party shortly before dusk. Sarah was still very quiet. Amber asked, "Did you have fun?"

Sarah nodded.

"Tired?"

She nodded again.

"Sarah, I'm not sure what you need right now."

Sarah shrugged. "Does that mean you don't know what you need either?"

Sarah nodded.

Maria said, "I know what you need."

Sarah looked at her. "You need to go home, take a shower and climb into bed with Cody. We've done too much in the past two weeks and pushed you too hard. Now you need a night off to just be quiet and be with something familiar. Does Cody time sound like what you need?"

Sarah nodded and started crying. "Sarah, there is a word for what you are right now."

Sarah looked at her imploringly. "Sarah, you are homesick. You miss the hospital, don't you? And you miss all the nurses and the staff and you miss the routine." Sarah nodded.
"I have good news for you."

Sarah cocked her head.

"After you spend an evening with Cody and have a good night's sleep, you will feel better. And if there is something we need to change, we'll adjust it. But you don't need to be going all the time. If you need quiet alone time, that's okay."

September 3rd   10:00 am

Sarah spent the night with Cody. She slept late and found that Amber and Maria had already eaten breakfast when she came into the kitchen.

Maria came in and asked if she wanted eggs. She looked at the eggs and burst into tears. "Sarah, what's wrong?"

"My chicken...."

She fled the room and threw herself on her bed and held Cody, sobbing as if her heart were broken. Maria called to Amber and they both came in to see what was wrong.

Sarah pointed to her sculpture. Amber handed her the little chicken and said, "It's story time, isn't it?"

Sarah nodded and told them she had killed a chicken at the hospital. Amber was in disbelief. "You really killed a chicken, not pretend killed or you killed a pretend chicken."

"Real killed, real chick. Yellow fluffy chicken."

Maria asked, "Why did you cry now?"

"My chicken will never get to lay eggs."

"That never occurred to you before, did it?"

She shook her head. "Always a little chick, but if I didn't kill it, it would be laying eggs now."

"And you feel bad that it will never get to grow up?"

"I killed it."

"Do you feel differently now than you did when you made a statue of him?"

She nodded. "Then I wanted to honor him for what he did for me. Now, I feel bad for what I did to him."

"Sarah, you can't unkill him. So, what do you think we should do?" Sarah tapped Cody's head. "You want some time with Cody to work it out for yourself?" She nodded.

"Okay."

They left her alone in her room but looked in on her every 15 minutes. Sarah lay quietly on her bed for the morning. Amber and Maria spoke in the living room.

"Should we call the doctor?" Amber asked as she reached for Maria's hand.

"No, she's going to be okay. She just needs a day off to be quiet. She'll have a quiet day today and then she sees him tomorrow. She's got to be worried about starting school Wednesday. She's never been to school. She has got to be anxious about it. I bet that's part of what she's feeling; it's just coming out as freaking out about a chicken."

"She really killed a chicken, didn't she? Why didn't they tell us that she was dangerous?"

"They told us that she killed her father."

"Yeah, but look what he *did* to her. But a chicken? A fluffy yellow chick?"

"I don't think the doctor is too concerned about it. We weren't planning on getting a pet, were we?"

"No. I'm sorry. I'm just worried that we're not going to be enough for her. What will happen to her if we can't meet her needs?"

"You always worry that we aren't going to be enough for the kids."

"And you always know we will be. That's part of why I love you."

They were embracing and kissing when Sarah came into the room. She looked at them quizzically. Maria saw her first. "Hey, Sarah." She slowly released Amber. "We were just talking about you."

Sarah shook her head.

"Well, before we were kissing we were talking about you. We were talking about making sure you are going to be okay here. We're going to work very hard to meet your needs, okay?" Sarah nodded confidently.

Amber looked at her, "You're not just saying this because you think it's what we want to hear?"

Sarah shook her head and smiled.

"Well, at least the neighbors won't be complaining about you being too loud."

"Lunch anyone?" asked Maria. Sarah nodded. "What do you want to eat?"

Sarah got out the carton of eggs and the loaf of bread.

"Egg salad sandwiches it is," smiled Amber.

Sarah seemed to have found her center again. She was quieter but more comfortable. In the evening they all went out for ice cream cones, a happy new family.

September 4th   8:30 am

Tuesday was a chance for her to talk to Dr. Feingold about the past weekend, the panic attack, and feeling unsettled. They talked about feeling overwhelmed and how to handle it. And they talked about the upcoming first day of school. They reviewed all that she had learned over the past two weeks: how to use the phone, the computer, how to cook, how to handle the tough moments.

"I miss being in the hospital."

"You learned to feel safe there."

"Yeah, and I knew everyone and I knew what was going to happen."

"There are a lot more people in the big world."

"Yeah, there are more people every day. Amber and Maria know a bazillion people. I am never going to learn that many people."

"Actually, you will. But you need to take it slow. They've had more time to meet them. You're just starting out. For now you have your classmates to know, and your teacher."

"I know my teacher. Mrs. Rifkin is nice. She worked with me on Thursday when I met with Rabbi Cohen. We worked on how to use my computer and we talked about what to do if I can't talk in class."

"Really? What are you going to do?"

"The whole class is going to learn sign language this year. But if I can't talk I just have to put my finger to my lips like to tell people to be quiet and that means I can't talk right now. But I have to sign or use my computer to write the answer or I have to nod."

"And after it happens and I am okay again, we have to talk after class about what happened so she can help reduce the times that I am having trouble. She said she is in charge of her classroom and she wants to make sure all of her students are comfy in it. She said I have caught up with everyone else. She says I am ready for sixth grade."

"Do you feel ready?"

"I'm scared."

"Are you scared of anything in particular?"

"No, I just never went to a regular school before."

"You have 'anticipatory anxiety.' Good news Sarah—that is a very normal experience. Most people are scared before they do something they have never done before. But let's look at the parts and see if you know how to do them. Do you know your teacher and like her?"

"Yeah."

"Is she going to do everything she can to help you be successful?"

"Yeah."

"Do you know how to use your computer?"

"Yeah."

"Do you know how to eat lunch?"

"Yeah."

"Do you know how to listen and pay attention?"

"Yeah."

"Do you know your classmates?"

"Some of them."

"Do you know how to be friendly?"

"Yeah."

"So you have all the parts. You have never put it all together before but if you remember that you know how to do each part when it happens, I think you will be okay." He leaned back in his chair. "Just remember to breathe. Anytime you start getting anxious, take a deep breath and remember that you can do this. And after school you are coming here so you can tell me how it went. Sarah, I'm proud of you. You're doing very well."

"Even with getting scared and crying? People who are doing well don't cry."

"We are going to spend some time talking about that, but for now, just know that even people who are doing well cry."

"Are Amber and Maria here?"

"Maria is. Amber went back to work today."

"Why don't I touch base with Maria?"

"Okay."

Maria went into the office and closed the door. "Doc, I'm sorry. She was doing so well and we pushed her too far. She told you she had a panic attack on Sunday?"

"Please sit down. Yes, she told me that she panicked. She also told me that you stood with her and talked her down and let her choose what she wanted to do next."

"She said she wanted to still go on the picnic and we went but I think she did it for us rather than because she wanted to go."

"That may be part of it. But she went and she participated in a somewhat limited way but with a good attitude, correct?"

"Oh, yeah. She wasn't sulky; she was just quiet and reserved."

"So, she was able to move beyond a panic attack and have some fun?"

"Yeah."

"That's important."

"But she hasn't been right since."

"Not right how?"

"She cried about her chicken not growing up and she just laid on her bed yesterday morning."

"We talked about that too. Maria, she was always quiet and reserved in the hospital. She is not an extrovert. Introverts need quiet time and alone time. She spent the past two weeks in a high energy mode. That level of involvement and activity is always going to be taxing for her. The important part here is that she didn't run away from you. She let you comfort her and she was comforted. Those are big steps. Once she gets into the routine of school, she is probably going to do better. She likes routine. Even when she lived on her own, she created a daily routine. Rituals have meaning for her. She isn't rigid in them but she needs them."

"She's coming here after school tomorrow. And I will meet her here and we will walk home together."

"Okay. I'll see you tomorrow."

September 4th   5:30 pm

They spent a fun day together. They played at the park and had lunch at a diner. Maria said she needed a manicure before she could go back to work so they had their nails done. Maria approved of Sarah's choice of a natural pink. Then it was home to make dinner and hear about Amber's first day back at work.

Sarah was setting the table when Amber arrived home. She put her bag down in the hall and came into the kitchen and gave Maria and a hug and kiss in greeting. Sarah watched them curiously. "Hi, kid. Did you two have a good day?"

Sarah nodded. "We got our nails done and we went to the park. We fed the pigeons. We're getting them fattened up for when we have them for dinner."

Amber rolled her eyes. "What is it with you and killing birds? Were you a cat in your former life?"

"No, cats kill song birds. I just get hungry."

"Fair enough."

"What are we having?"

"Spaghetti and meatballs"

"Who made the meatballs?"

"We both did."

"Did you remember to wash your hands?"

"Of course; I may be weird but I'm not stupid."

The mood had gone from playful to angry and Maria turned around to find angry tears in Sarah's eyes. Amber followed Maria's gazed and said, "Hey, kid, I'm sorry. I was just playing with you. You are the first kid we have ever had that we didn't have to tell how to take care of herself."

Sarah sat down and tears started rolling down her cheeks. "It was hard."

"What was hard?"

Sarah crumpled to the floor. "Taking care of myself. I was hungry all the time. And I was always scared that someone would find me and kill me. I didn't want to die." Sarah's breathing was ragged as she continued. "And I hate the rats. I always had to kill the rats. One night one climbed in my sleeping bag and bit my toes. It woke me up and he was in my sleeping bag and I had to dump him out and I grabbed him by the tail and I slammed him against the wall until I killed him then I had to throw him in the alley so he wouldn't get fleas on me. You can't have dead rats around or the fleas will get on you and kill you."

She took a few breaths and continued. "I had to keep everything in metal containers or else the rats would eat it. I used to steal rat traps and put them outside my house so they wouldn't come in." The tears flowed freely and Sarah's shoulders heaved with the sobs.

"I was always alone. I would see kids with their parents and getting carried and held and fed and I was alone. Sometimes it hurt to see other kids and to think about it and I wanted to cry so badly." Sarah's tears streamed down her cheeks but she worked to calm herself. She had given them a glimpse of her life and was working on putting it back in its box.

Amber wanted to wrap Sarah in her arms and erase her horrible memories, but instead she handed her a glass of water. Sarah calmed herself and took a drink of water. Maria handed her the Kleenex box and she wiped her face and blew her nose.

"Sarah, I am sorry I kidded you about washing your hands. And I am sorry that life was so hard for you before."

"It's okay. I know you were just kidding. But what I don't understand is why I keep crying. I never cried."

Maria asked, "How come?"

"When I was with Zeke he would hurt me if I cried. And when I was alone, I was afraid someone would find me and kill me if I cried. I cried a couple of times in the hospital, but now I keep crying."

"Sarah, you didn't cry because it wasn't safe to cry before. Do you feel like you are safe here?"

She nodded. "You're nice and you don't want to do wrong things to me."

"Maybe that is why you are crying."

"Because you're nice to me?"

"No, silly, because here it's safe to cry, so you can."

Sarah looked puzzled.

Maria explained. "You have a lot of built-up tears and they are going to have to come out sometime. Here is a good place for that to happen. We can handle tears. So, it's okay to cry and it's okay to have feelings here."

"So crying is okay?" She wasn't crying anymore and she worked on regaining her composure.

"Crying is okay."

"And is it okay if I feel hungry?"

"No," replied Maria. "We need to make you full."

Amber said, "So let's eat."

They sat down together and began eating their dinner. "Amber? I was going to ask you how your first day back at work went."

"It was hell, kid. Don't ever grow up and get a job. Just stay a kid forever."

"I don't think that's a choice."

"No, I suppose not. So, just try not to have total air heads in your department who have no idea what's important. I had a pile of work on my desk that was all time sensitive for last week. I spent the morning putting out fires and getting stuff out the door, then this afternoon I was handed a big project that The Dork was supposed to do but didn't."

"You have a dork at work?"

"Everyone has a dork at work."

Maria interjected, "I think that it's a requirement."

Amber smiled at Maria and continued. "But overall it was a typical first day back from a vacation. I swear half the time I feel like a fireman."

"What are you really?"

"I am a systems analyst."

"What's a systems analyst?"

"I look at how things are working and find ways to make them work better or cheaper or make people happier about their jobs."

"Are we a system?"

"Sort of; we are a family system."

"Do you analyze us?"

"Um, sort of. I look at what we are doing and the effect it has on everyone. Then I look at how we need to change."

"Did I mess up the system?"

"Mess up, no. You changed the system. There is the Maria and Amber system and it works one way. So, when we don't have a kid our life is different. But each kid changes the system in a different way. So, our system has to change accordingly. How we are with you is different than we are with any other kid because you are different than any other kid."

"Is that because I'm weird?"

"No, you're different because your experiences and personality are different from anyone else in the world."

Sarah was listening closely and trying to understand.

"Look, I am the only me in the world. Maria is the only her. And you are the only you. So since each of us is unique, the system is unique."

"I'm not weird?"

"What's with this weird?"

Maria had an idea. "Are you worried about fitting in at school tomorrow?"

She nodded.

Amber explained, "Sarah, you are not the typical kid. You've had life experiences that no one should ever have and fortunately very few people do have. But you're just like other kids in many more ways than how you're different. We have set you up to fit in. You look just like your classmates. You have the same clothes and books and computer and cell phone. You're academically on the same level. You're going to a school where you're wanted. And let's face it: Rachel didn't act like you're weird, did she?"

"No."

"Yes, you've been through a lot. And I'm not going to minimize that. But you can do this school thing. We'll get through this. We have a system."

Sarah nodded and said, "I'm full."

"Good, then you should get a shower and get in your PJ's."

Maria asked, "Do you have clothes picked out for tomorrow?"

"Not yet. I've thought about it but haven't decided."

Together they chose an outfit and packed her backpack. She plugged her cell phone into the charger and made sure that she had her keys in the bag. Then they laid out her lunch for the next day.

The plan was for Amber to walk her to school and for Maria to pick her up at Dr. Feingold's after school.

Sarah went to bed early, anxious but organized.

September 5th   8:15 am

The planning paid off. She was ready to leave the house on time and in a good mood. Amber and Sarah talked about Amber's work on the way to the school and the rabbi was in place to greet her.

"Shalom Sarah, I am so glad to see you this morning."

"Shalom. This is a lot later in the morning than when I used to come here. Are morning prayers all done?"

"They are finishing up. I wanted to see my Sarah on her first day of school."

Looking up to meet Amber's eyes, he said, "Good Morning, Amber. Thank you for bringing her today. Will we see you every morning?"

"I think she can handle it from now on, but if she wants me to walk her, I will. I like walking kids to school the first day. It's nice to know they got there at least once."

Sarah smiled and told her, "Thanks; it made it easier."

Rabbi Cohen walked her into the school down the hallway to her classroom. Mrs. Rifkin standing was outside the door. "Good Morning Mrs. Rifkin." The rabbi modeled the typical morning greeting.

"Good morning, Rabbi Cohen. Good Morning, Sarah."

"Good Morning, Mrs. Rifkin," said Sarah gamely, trying to hold her anxiety in check. Before she went into the room, Rabbi Cohen said, "Rabbi Hug" and Sarah gratefully accepted a hug from him.

He whispered, "Have a good day" in her ear and directed her into the classroom. Sarah already knew where her desk was; in the second row, the 3rd seat down. She went to it and filled her desk with her new school supplies and then placed her computer on her desk top. The other kids were filing in and doing the same. She put her back pack and lunch in her locker in the back of the room.

When Mrs. Rifkin called the class to order, there were 15 students sitting at their desks, ready to learn.

The day started with the pledge of allegiance, which Sarah had never heard before. She was starting to feel anxious when they sang the Hatikvah, the Israeli national anthem. The singing of the familiar song settled her down again and she was able to focus. The rest of the day went smoothly. Sarah was able to participate in class and in the small groups that were set up to work together.

During lunch she sat with Rachel, Micah and Tara, the class chatterbox. They traded cookies and talked about their vacations. Sarah hadn't left the city like some of the kids, but she had had enough adventures and was able to make them sound fun enough that no one noticed. At the end of the day Rabbi Cohen came in to talk to the girls about preparing for their bat mitzvah. Half the girls were already seeing the rabbi and the rest were about to begin. He set up a schedule with them for meetings during the school day. He reminded the class that the boys would begin in the spring as they were one year behind the girls in Bar Mitzvah training.

After school, a happy and confident Sarah walked alone to Dr. Feingold's office. He ushered her in, trying to gauge how it went by her body language.

"So..."

A very happy Sarah said, "It was just like being in the hospital. I can do school."

"Relieved?"

She nodded and took a deep breath and relaxed. "We said the pledge of 'legence but I didn't know it and I was starting to get worried. But then we sang the Hatikvah and it all got better from there."

Sarah settled into her chair and continued. "Small groups are just like therapies and desk work is just like when I had my tutor. And lunch is like any meal at the hospital, except home food is better than hospital food." She leaned forward and said, "Some of school is in Hebrew and some of it is in English. I am ahead in Hebrew and I have my own reading book that is different from everyone else. Mrs. Rifkin said that I am way ahead in reading in English. We all have the same math book and I looked at it. Some of the stuff I did during the summer but I don't know how to do a lot of it."

"You will learn. That is what school is for. Do you have homework?"

"Yeah, but I can do it." Then she shifted in her seat and said, "I have to ask you about something."

"Okay."

"Remember you told me that grown up men and grown up women have intercourse?"

"Yeah."

"Well, is that like having a boyfriend or a girlfriend?"

"Yes…"

"Do people who hug and kiss have intercourse?"

"Sometimes. People may hug or kiss lots of people, but they usually only have intercourse with one special person. What are you wondering, Sarah?"

"Maria and Amber? But they are both women? But they act like married people do."

"Do you remember that I said usually a man and a woman?"

"Yeah, so they are the unusually?"

"That is one way of putting it."

"So, when I used to see guys walking down the street together and kissing—same thing?"

"Same thing."

"How come?"

"How come what?"

"How come it's different for different people?"

"Because people are different." Sarah's eyes demanded further explanation. "I know that is a non-answer, but without going into a lot of biology and psychosocial theory, it is actually a good answer. Each person is a unique individual so each person needs to find out what is right for them. For Maria and Amber, being together and getting married was the right thing."

"What about me?"

"Your story isn't written yet."

"What if I like boys?"

"Then you will want to be with boys."

"What if I like girls?"

"Then you will want to be with girls."

"If I live with Amber and Maria, are they going to want me to like girls, too?"

"What do you think?"

"I think they are not going to care."

"I think you are right. Do you have feelings about Amanda and Maria being married?"

"I was just curious, but I didn't want to ask them because it might be rude." Sarah thought for minute and then said, "So, they don't just sleep together in the same bed do they?"

"Probably not."

"What if I went in there and they weren't *sleeping*?"

"How about if you knock before you enter, then they can make sure that you're not walking into something that isn't for you?"

"Is that the same rule as for everyone?"

"It is."

"What if they hug me? Will they want to do girl intercourse?"

"No more than when Joe hugs you or Rabbi Cohen hugs you."

"Rabbi Cohen can't hug me after I have my bat mitzvah."

"Do you know why?"

"Because I won't be a little girl anymore and the rules for little girls and for women are different."

"How do you feel about that?"

"Sad. I like Rabbi Cohen hugs. They feel good. He hugged me this morning before school started. It got me started right. I am going to miss them."

"I think everyone misses some parts of being a child."

"Do they always miss it?"

"Sometimes, and sometimes they have other ways to have their needs met, or their needs change."

"What will happen to me?"

"We will have to wait and see. And now shall we see if Maria is here?"

Maria looked up as the door opened. Sarah and Dr. Feingold came out and greeted her with smiles.

"It looks like you had a good day."

"I did. I can do school."

Maria looked pleasantly surprised by Sarah's happy confidence. As Sarah led the way outside she said, "And you were worried." Maria could only shake her head and chuckle.

October 10   12:30 pm

School proved easy for Sarah, a willing student who applied herself. She was challenged by the many new concepts she was being taught, but she was learning quickly and usually wanted more. The work she had done in the hospital had prepared her well. She was liked by her classmates, who saw her as unique and somewhat exotic. It was just after the Sukkot break when she was sitting at lunch with Rachel and Tara. Tara started talking about the latest teen heart throb, a boy band singer whom Sarah had heard of from the girls at the hospital. Tara talked about wanting to meet him and what if he kissed her. In Tara's mind, being kissed was the penultimate sexual experience. As Tara was talking Sarah's face went blank. Tara looked at her and said, "Come on Sarah, wouldn't you just die if he kissed you?"

Sarah went silent as a perplexed, fearful expression crossed her face. Slowly she stood up, threw out her trash, and walked out of the cafeteria.

Tara was confused. "What did I say, Rachel? Is Sarah mad at me?"

Rachel, whose parents had explained that some things were going to be hard for Sarah because some bad things had happened to her, said, "I don't think she's mad at you. I think she just has something wrong."

"Should we do something?"

Rachel shrugged, "I don't know. Maybe we should send her a note when we get back to class. Sometimes Sarah just has her own thoughts."

When class resumed, Mrs. Rifkin asked where Sarah was. Tara and Rachel were scared but they spoke up. Rachel said, "We were having lunch together but then Sarah got up and walked out of the cafeteria. We thought she went to the bathroom or back here to the classroom."

Mrs. Rifkin checked the girls' room. Sarah was not there. She called Rabbi Cohen, who told her to continue teaching, that he would take care of finding Sarah. He checked the chapel and the temple then called Maria. Maria activated her GPS monitoring program for Sarah's cell phone and was able to let Rabbi Cohen know her location. "She's on the playground in Union Square. What do you want to do?"

The rabbi assured her that he would go get her. "After all, she's supposed to be at my school. Does she know that you can monitor her location?"

"I don't believe the topic ever came up. Some things are parents' to know and kids' to find out much later."

"I will call you when I find her or if I get there and she has moved."

Five minutes later he spotted her on the swings. He called and informed Maria that Sarah was found safe.

He walked into the swing area and watched her for a few moments before calling to her. She was in her own thoughts, swinging joylessly. He called her name but she was turned inward and didn't notice him. Looking closely, he saw that her face was tear-stained and that she appeared to be in a trance. He called her name again, but again she didn't respond. She was swinging at an even momentum, using the motion as a hypnotist uses a pendulum.

The rabbi knew he was out of his element and called Dr. Feingold, who suggested that he let her be, but monitor her. He would meet them in the park and either talk to her if she had stopped swinging by then or try to bring her back if she was still swinging. The rabbi sat and watched, and, as rabbis do, prayed.

Sarah was still swinging when Dr. Feingold arrived 15 minutes later. "How long has she been swinging?"

"About 30 minutes."

Doc watched her and agreed that she was in a trance-like state. "Do we know what precipitated this?"

"She was eating lunch then got up and left the room. No one knew she had left the school until the class went back from lunch."

"Has there been any change in her pattern?"

"No, she has kept the same rhythm."

"Okay, let me see if I can reach her."

He walked up to the swings and stood next to Sarah's swing. She was not aware of his presence. He started talking to her quietly. He let her know that he was there and that they could talk about what was happening. It took some time, but slowly her swinging slowed.

When she stopped, she sat still and limp in the swing. Dr. Feingold moved into her field of vision to get her attention. She was still in a trance induced by the swinging, but she was able to look at him. He spoke quietly, helping her refocus on the playground and orient herself to the world around her. She looked around as if she didn't know where she was or how she got there. He encouraged her to get off the swing and sit with him on the bench. She complied. She sat with Rabbi Cohen on one side and Dr. Feingold on the other, barely aware of them. She was very much in her mind. Then, rather than becoming more oriented, she started rocking again. Dr. Feingold tried to catch her attention to no avail.

"We need to take her to the hospital. I don't think we can take her in a taxi." He called for an ambulance and Rabbi Cohen called Maria. When the paramedics arrived, Dr. Feingold explained the situation and one of them simply picked Sarah up and laid her on the gurney. She lay still, except for one hand that she was moving rhythmically. Dr. Feingold rode in the ambulance to the hospital with Sarah. Rabbi Cohen went back to the school to see if he could find out what had happened to cause this reaction.

October 10th   2:00 pm

Neither the bumping of the ride nor being lowered from the ambulance into the hospital impacted Sarah.   Sarah was taken directly up to the pediatric psych unit, where she and Doc were met at the door by Mike and Nancy.

"What happened?"

"We don't know." Dr. Feingold related what they did know as Mike lifted Sarah off the gurney and placed her on a bed. He took off her shoes then rolled her on her side facing the door. She curled up and began rolling her head from side to side.

"Let's give her a moment." They stepped outside and watched her from the observation window. Sarah continued as she was.

Mike asked how she had been doing. "She was doing very well. She has been happy and adjusting well. We just don't know what set this off or where she is right now."

"Do we leave her alone or try to reach her?"

Mike said, "Let me try to reach her." He stood next to Sarah and brushed the hair away from her face. "You've been crying. Let me get a washcloth and wash your face." He returned with a warm washcloth and proceeded to wash Sarah's face and hands. He spent time on her hands, focusing on each finger as he worked. But Sarah remained unresponsive. Then Mike held her head still in his hands. Within moments her hand began to move rhythmically. He left her and went back into the hallway. "She doesn't want to come back."

"Let's get a vest for her and get her admitted."

She still had not moved when Maria arrived two hours later. "I'm sorry I couldn't get out sooner. How is she?"

"She's catatonic. She hasn't moved since she came in."

"Do we know what happened?"

"The girls were talking about some boy band heartthrob and Tara said she wanted him to kiss her."

"That is it?"

"That's it."

"What are we going to do?"

"We are going to support her and wait. We have done enough work for me to know that she does what she needs to do. We just need to support her and let her get back to a point where we can help her."

"Can I see her?"

"Of course." He led her to Sarah's room. "Sarah, Maria's here."

Sarah didn't respond. Maria went to her and brushed her face. She held her hand on her cheek for a few moments, feeling Sarah's head rolling under her hand. Then she said, "Let me try something." She untied the restraints and lifted Sarah out of bed. With Sarah on her lap, Maria began rocking and singing. After half an hour with still no change in Sarah, Maria thought her legs and back were going to fall off. The evening nurse tried having Sarah stand so she could be led to the bathroom, but she was beyond that too. Sarah was placed back on the bed and Maria helped change her into pajamas and tucked her in. She kissed her goodnight on the forehead.

The kiss was like a switch. Instantly Sarah began shaking and flailing, sitting up in bed with her feet under her and screaming. Dr. Feingold ran into the room to find Sarah fighting the nurse who was trying to hold her wrists. Playing a hunch, Dr. Feingold said "Marcia, stop it."

Sarah's transformation was instant. She stopped fighting and was once again still. She tried to get out of bed but, meeting the resistance of the vest, lay back down. "Sarah, you need to tell us what is going on. What are you feeling?"

She looked disoriented. "You are at the hospital, Sarah. Can you tell me what happened today?" Dr. Feingold was unwilling to lose her again. "Sarah, look at me." She met his eyes, before her gaze drifted away. He tried to refocus her, "Sarah, stay with me."

She looked at him again. "I want you to stay here now, Sarah." Sarah's eyes danced around as if she were watching scenes that no one could see.

"Stay with me. You're safe here, Sarah. Maria is here. You need to come back to here now." Sarah started shaking her head.

He held her head still and told her again she was safe. "You're going to stay here tonight, Sarah, and we will see how you feel in the morning. We're going to let you get some sleep now." They left her then, except for her one on one staff person, Molly, and she went to sleep.

Maria went into the therapy room with Dr. Feingold. "What's going on with her?"

"I think that she is experiencing flashbacks and to combat them, she is dissociating. She is separating herself from what she is experiencing."

"Does this mean she is getting better or worse?"

"Well, as bad as it looks, she is getting better. We'll let her be overnight and hope she works it out in her mind. I will work with her in the morning."

"Should I bring her clothes or Cody?"

"If you or Amber could bring her Cody and a couple of sets of clothes and in the morning, that would be great."

"I'll call Amber now. I know she's going to want to see her tonight."

"Okay. Make sure she knows not to wake her. At this point I think we have pushed her as far as she can go for one day."

Sarah slept fitfully through the night. Mike woke her in the morning with her breakfast tray. Although awake and oriented, Sarah was once again not speaking. Mike undid her restraint and helped her as she moved hesitantly and unsteadily to the bathroom. Nancy was in the room when she returned. She was wearing her pajamas— tops and bottoms—and Nancy and Mike exchanged a grateful look. Sarah climbed back into bed, curled up and went back to sleep.

October 11th   2:00 pm

Sarah was still sleeping when Dr. Feingold checked on her two hours later. He worked with his other patients, but checked on her throughout the day. Finally, he had Mike wake her and bring her into the therapy room.

She sat on the floor in a little ball. When she started rocking he said, "No. Look at me. We can get through this but you have to help me understand what is happening."

She looked at him and seemed to actually see him for a moment. "That was good, Sarah. Now I want you to find one word. Give me one word."

Sarah turned her head to the side and with a great effort she whispered hoarsely, "Rooster."

"Is this about Zeke?"

Sarah nodded then shook her head. "Roosters."

"Is it about all the people who did wrong things to you?"

She nodded.

"I want you to try to explain what you were feeling yesterday."

With difficulty she croaked out, "Touching me. Lots of hands touching me. Kissing me."

"Did you feel people touching you?"

She nodded. "See, feel, smell. Alive again all around me. Made it stop. Made empty all white."

"You made the images stop?"

She nodded. "Then all back again, the rooster people, then too tired so the rooster people touched me."

"Then they came back and you were too tired to go blank again."

She nodded.

"Sarah, are you here with me now?"

"Here, there."

"Can you see people from then, now?"

She nodded. "I see through them."

"Can you see through me?"

"Solid."

"I want to you to pay attention to the solid things. Look at the solid things in the room." Sarah patted the floor and then a few of the toys. She moved towards Dr. Feingold as she touched the solid things in the room. Regaining her focus, she was now sitting on the floor next to him. She reached out and patted his leg in the same way she had patted the other objects. She was clearly more tuned in to the here and now. Then she started to stroke his leg. Dr. Feingold took her hand in his and held it, using the contact to help her focus. "You are here with me now. Zeke is dead and the other men are gone. Look around; they aren't here anymore." She looked around, surprised to find that he was right. The transparent people were gone. It was just the two of them and he was holding her hands gently in front of his knees.

"Where did they go?"

"They weren't ever really here."

"I saw them. I felt them; they smell."

"They seemed very real, didn't they?"

Sarah nodded. "Where'd they come from?"

"Sarah, you were having a flashback."

"What is?"

"What's a flashback?"

She nodded.

"It's when your mind thinks that things that happened a long time ago are happening now."

"Crazy?"

"No, you're not crazy. You're safe now and your mind is trying to process what you went through when you weren't safe."

"Tired."

"Okay, let's get Mike to help you go back to bed. You can take a nap, then have some dinner. Maria and Amber will be here tonight to visit."

"Stay here?"

"You are going to stay here for a few days. Okay?"

She nodded.

Mike came in and took her hands from Dr. Feingold. Then he gently helped her stand, walk into her room and climb into bed.

October 11th   8:00 am

Sarah slept better that night and woke up quietly. She was up and dressed when the morning shift came onto the unit. She greeted Mike at the door with a hug. "Hey, you must be feeling better."

She nodded, "I missed you."

"I missed you too. I need to go into the staff meeting, but I want to talk to you after breakfast. I want to hear all about how things are for you now."

She nodded and went back into her room with her one on one staff person.

"You aren't going to be my person again tonight, are you?"

"I don't know."

"I know. You won't because I won't need one. I am going to sleep alone tonight."

"That's fine with me. Do you want to rest before breakfast?"

"Can I have my back pack? I want to read my social studies." She was working on her homework when Dr. Feingold came for her.

"How are you feeling?"

"Better, but confused."

"Well, I am glad you're feeling better. Come on into the therapy room.

Sarah climbed off her bed and followed him into the therapy room where she sat on the floor as before.
"Shall we talk about the confused part?"

"Yes. What happened to me?"

"What do you remember?"

"I was eating lunch and Tara was talking about that guy she likes in a band. She said that she wants to go to his concert and get invited back stage. Then she wants him to kiss her."

Sarah's eyes started to lose focus.

"Sarah, look at me. I want you to stay right here with me. Are you back?" She took a deep breath and nodded. Then she moved and sat in front of him on the floor and gave him her hands.

"Hold me here."

"You want me to hold your hands so you stay here with me?"

She nodded. "I don't want to float away again."

"Is that what happened?"

She nodded. "I felt, I saw, I heard, I smelled people I could see through. They were kissing me like when I worked but all at once and I needed to make it stop. I got up from the table and I got my backpack from the classroom. Everything was foggy but the hands were everywhere. People were talking to me and they smelled all different ways. Lots of different people smells. I went outside to try to make it stop but it didn't stop. I tried to go to your office but I saw the swings and I just wanted to swing. When I was swinging I could make them go away but I made myself go away too and everything was white and quiet and I didn't want the white quiet to stop. The white quiet was better than the touching."

"Okay, let's go back to Tara. Tell me what you pictured in your head while Tara was talking. Did you know who she was talking about?"

"Yeah, she talks about him all the time. He's all she thinks about."

"Tell me what you were seeing in your head when she talked about going back stage."

"I was thinking about him and there being a lot of people and everybody shoving around."

"Were you still okay?" She nodded. "How did it change when she talked about him kissing her?"

"First it was him coming towards her to kiss her and then it changed to him coming towards me to kiss me, but then he changed and all the people around him changed and they were are all trying to kiss me and touch me."

Sarah became jumpy and Dr. Feingold squeezed her hands, bringing her back to now. "Okay. Are you here with me?"

Sarah nodded. "It was so real."

"Flashbacks can feel very real."

"But it wasn't real?"

"It wasn't real now. Your mind moved the past to the present and hit play."

"I think it played a lot of the past all at once. I never had that many people at once. There were like 50 people trying to get near me and touch me. But in real I don't think there were ever more than five at one time. That was when I was little and they passed me around. When I was older there was only one at a time, or sometimes two. But it was never 50."

"Were there always 50 people?"

"No. At first it was but then it got less. When I was walking down the street a lot of the people were gone, but I didn't have pants on and I had my pretty blue dress on and I kept walking so they couldn't stay inside of me. But they kept moving in front of me and reaching out to touch me."

He squeezed her hands again to bring her back. "Are you back here with me?"

Again she took a breath and refocused herself. Then she let go of his hands and sat at the table across from him. "What are we going to do about flashbacks? I can't go to school if all those people are going to show up. What will the other kids say if they see all those people trying to touch me?"

"Sarah, you're the only one who can see the people."

"Am I crazy?"

"No. You are not crazy. You're processing."

"Well, can I just process when I'm not in school? I don't like see-through people coming to my school."

"We'll work on it. How do you feel now?"

"Worn out, but okay."

"Why don't we stop now and begin tomorrow on controlling the flashbacks? Then if you are ready, you can go home tomorrow."

"When can I go back to school?"

"Tomorrow is Friday. So take the weekend off and if you do well this weekend, you can go back on Monday."

"Can I e-mail my teacher and tell her that I am okay and ask for my assignments?"

"Sure. I will write an order to let you have your computer. You need to turn it in to the nurse's station to charge though. We can't have cords on the unit right now."

"Can I go to services?"

"I think I want you to have a quiet weekend without a lot of people. So no services, no coffee houses, no busy restaurants."

"You're going to be the bane of Amber's existence."

"I've been worse."

October 11th   2:00 pm

Sarah took a short nap before lunch. Mike supervised the lunchroom so Sarah was able to fill him in on her life. She talked about her classmates, her teacher, the places she had been with Amber and Maria, the fun she had with Joe and her worries about him returning to the street in a few weeks.

At two o'clock sharp Rabbi Cohen showed up just as he had before. Sarah greeted him with a tentative "Shalom?"

"Shalom, Sarah."

"Really?"

"Really."

"Am I in trouble for leaving school?"

"Leaving school without telling someone is not something we encourage. But I am not sure that you were thinking much about rules when you left."

"I just wanted all the people to go away."

"Yes, we need a plan in case the people ever try to come back."

"You have a plan?"

"It is my school and therefore I say who can be in it. If the people try to come back in the school, the plan is for you to come to me."

"What if you're busy?"

"For this, I am never busy. You may always knock on my door if there are intruders in the school. Can you do that?"

She nodded. "But what if I can't talk again?"

"We need a sign. This is the sign for 'people.'" He showed her the sign with his first finger in the air and moving his hand toward himself in a reverse pedaling motion, and she repeated it.

"Now if you knock on my door you can either tell me with your words or you can tell me with a sign. And I will help you."

"Okay. I would rather that they didn't try to come back."

"I understand that. I feel the same way. But we pray and we plan."

"Is Tara mad at me?"

"Why would Tara be mad at you?"

"Because I walked out on her?"

"No; they're very worried that they did something wrong that hurt your feelings."

"Will you tell her that she didn't do anything wrong and my feelings aren't hurt?"

"I will tell her. I'm glad that you have friends who care about you so much."

"I like Tara and Rachel. If Dr. Feingold and Maria and Amber say it's okay, do you think they will want to come over on Saturday? I have to take a quiet weekend without a lot of people but they are only two people. Maybe they can come over and play Sorry."

"I think that would be fun for all of you."

"I'll e-mail them after I ask. I could text them but I can't have my phone here."

"You sound like your old self again."

"I feel better having a plan."

October 13th   1:00 pm

After a meeting of the adults, it was decided that a "Sorry" party on Saturday was a very good idea. Sarah e-mailed her friends and they both accepted. Amber and Maria prepared to host the party. They baked cookies and prepared a veggie and dip platter.

Rachel was the first to arrive. She gave Sarah a hug, which surprised Sarah. Then she gave Sarah a card. Sarah opened the get well card and thanked her friend. "I never got a card before. Thank you."

Rachel asked, "Are you okay now?"

Sarah nodded.

Rachel was about to say something else when Tara knocked on the door. They opened the door and greeted Tara with smiles. "Hi Tara, come on in. Rachel just got here too. Come on into the living room. Tara, Rachel, you know Amber and Maria." Everyone said "Hi." Sarah played hostess. "Do want something to drink? We have water or we have cherry soda today."

Tara and Rachel's eyes lit up. "Cherry soda!"

"I'll get it," said Maria. "You kids just settle in."

Rachel said, "My mom said that you had to go the hospital."

"Yeah, just for a couple of days. I kind of got weirded out. But I'm okay. My doctor said I need to have a quiet weekend but he said I could have you guys over."

Tara, who had been unusually quiet for Tara, said, "But we are the ones that made you sick."

"No, you didn't. It just happened. It wasn't your fault. Besides, we have a plan now so if it ever starts to happen again, I know what to do. It's okay if you have a plan." She sat down in front of the coffee table. "I thought we should play Sorry, because Rabbi Cohen said you guys were sorry that you did something to upset me and I was sorry that I walked out on you. But he said that none of us has anything to be sorry for. So I thought it would be funny to play Sorry.

Tara laughed, "You are *so* funny." The ice was broken and the friendship resumed.

They played freely for a while, sending each other back to the start with a flourish of "Sorrys" and giggles. Tara relaxed and got caught up in the game. Then she forgot herself and started talking about her heartthrob. Rachel and Sarah laughed at her desire to go to a diner and find him there. She talked of sharing French fries. Suddenly realizing what she was saying, she looked stricken as she turned to Sarah. Sarah and Rachel looked at her and said together, "What's wrong?" Tara stammered how sorry she was and asked if Sarah was okay.

Sarah said, "Tara, I'm fine. You can talk about him."

"But I made you go to the hospital."

"No, you didn't. It was going to happen. It just happened then. It wasn't your fault. Well it was, but not in the way you think."

"It *was* my fault!"

"Yeah, you and Rachel and everyone at school and Maria and Amber: it's your fault because I feel so safe and comfortable that I can start thinking about stuff that happened a long time ago that I couldn't think about before. So, in a way, it is your fault, but in a good way."

Tara looked relieved.

"My going to the hospital wasn't the best way for things to happen, but it could be a lot worse. And stuff is going to happen. I like it at the hospital so it isn't bad. I like it better here, but the hospital is okay."

"I've never been to a hospital. Isn't it scary?"

"When I first went it was, but now I know all the people and they're all nice to me."

Rachel asked, "What are they like?"

"My day time nurse is Nancy..." Sarah talked about the staff and the routine and what it was like to be in the hospital. Tara and Rachel thought it sounded like summer camp.

Tara asked, "Are you going to go back?"

Sarah shrugged. "If I need to, I will. I would rather be here and go to school, but if I need the hospital it's there for me. I can't have my cell phone in the hospital but this time I got to have my computer so I could do my homework."

"You have to do your homework when you're in the hospital?"

"When I can; I didn't do it for the first day but Thursday and Friday I got it all done so I can be all ready to go to school on Monday."

"You have your homework done?"

"Yeah."

"You did your math?"

"Yeah."

"How did you do it? I don't get it at all."

And they were off again.

October 13th   5:00 pm

Tara and Rachel left at 5:00 and Sarah sat on the couch, surveying the mess they made. They had put the game away, but Sarah's laptop and the dishes were strewn about the coffee table.

She was about to get up and carry the dishes to the kitchen when her cell phone rang. It was Joe.

He wanted to know if she wanted him to come over after his day shift the tomorrow and bring Chinese. Sarah asked Amber, who said that sounded good. "What are we doing tonight?"

"Movie night!" Exclaimed Amber.

"What are we doing tomorrow?"

"Laundry and house cleaning and then I don't know. What do you want to do?"

"I want to go to the museum or the zoo but I'm not allowed. Can't we just go to the little zoo?"

"How do you propose we get there?"

"Oh yeah. Can we just go for a walk? Can we go now?"

"How about movie night tonight and we can go for a walk in the morning?"

"Okay. Amber, will you walk me to school on Monday?"

"You're feeling a little anxious about going back?"

"Yeah."

"I'll walk you to school. I know Maria is better at the talking stuff, but I am always here for you, kid. How about we load the dishwasher? Maria should be back with food soon."

"What are we having?"

"Pizza."

"How come she went to get it?"

"She had some other stuff she needed to do and said she would bring it home with her." They had a pleasant evening. The movie was a fun family movie and Sarah enjoyed lying on the floor while Amber and Maria curled up on the couch.

October 14th   6:00 pm

Sunday was another pleasant day. Amber and Sarah went for a walk in the morning on the quiet streets. They picked up bagels and brought them home for breakfast. The house was cleaned and everything was made ready for the upcoming week. Joe brought the take out after work and they all sat together eating.

Sarah brought up Joe's arm, which he was now using freely. "Is your arm all better?"

"Not yet, but almost. I went to the doctor on Friday and he said the bone is almost healed; a couple more weeks."

"If you touch it, does it still hurt?"

"A little bit."

Sarah was quiet. Maria picked up on it first and looked up to see Sarah starting to drift in her focus. "Sarah!" She spoke sharply, but Sarah wasn't hearing. Instead, she had gotten out of her chair and was holding her arm and wincing.

Maria stood in front of her and held her hands. Squeezing her hands and talking to Sarah worked and before long Sarah was able to focus on Maria. "Stay here Sarah. We're having dinner and you are here with us. Focus on the solid people."

Sarah nodded, shuttered, and started to shake. She was protecting her arm. "Are you with us?" She nodded.

"Can you eat some more?"

She nodded again.

Joe, who hadn't heard about the recent hospitalization, was dumbfounded. "What's going on?"

"Sarah, do you want to tell Joe what just happened?"

Sarah signed "people." Joe watched, confused.

"Sarah has started having flashbacks," Amber explained. "When she starts to fade out like that, she is starting to have a flashback. Squeezing her hands helps her focus on the solid people and re-orients her."

"Sarah, do you just see solid people now?"

She looked around and shook her head.

"Do you know where you are?"

She nodded and touched the table.

"Good, have some more dumplings. Dumplings will help."

Sarah gave Amber a look of incredulity.

"Really, the see-through people never get to eat dumplings." Sarah looked around and found that indeed, the see-through people were not eating dumplings.

Like a many a child raised in Manhattan, Sarah deftly picked up her chopsticks and took a bite. They finished dinner cautiously.

Sarah was holding her own. Amber took Sarah into the living room.

Joe stayed in the kitchen and helped Maria clean up. "What's going on?"

"She has PTSD and she's having flashbacks."

"Why did she have one then?"

"You know that she had her arm broken, don't you?"

"Yeah, I guess I knew that. They found it when she was first brought in."

"Well, she is very sensitive right now to anything that brings up back then. She had a flashback last week and spent a few days in the hospital. The Doc says we may be in for a tough time until she gets through this stage. We're not going to be able to stop them but we're trying to keep her from getting stuck in them. Sarah is having trouble separating her past experiences from her current life. It's as if the past is overlaid on the present and she can't tell which one is real."

"Is she in school?"

"She's supposed to go back tomorrow. She was fine yesterday and today up until now. We'll have to see if she is ready in the morning."

"Can I do anything to help?"

"You are doing it. Just keep her focused on the here and now. You want coffee?"

"Yeah, that would be great."

"Amber, do you want coffee?"

"Yeah, thanks."

"Sarah, do you want some juice?"

Sarah nodded and Amber relayed, "That was yes in case you didn't hear her head rattling."

Sarah was sitting on the couch when Maria came in with drinks and a plate of Oreos.

Joe sat down next to Sarah and tucked her under his arm as he did when they were watching ball games in the hospital. "I'm sorry you're having a tough time." Sarah patted Joe on the chest. Joe gave her a cookie. She ate the cookie and then had some juice and settled back into his arm.

"Sarah, you look so far away. What are you thinking?" Sarah put her hand on Joe's belt and then let her hand move further down. Joe set down his coffee cup and took her hand. "No, Sarah!" He was surprised and it came out more harshly than he had intended. "Sarah, look at me. I don't do that with you. I have never done that and I am never going to." Sarah started rocking.

Maria said, "Joe, I don't think Sarah is up for company right now. Why don't I walk you out?"

When they were in the foyer Joe asked, "What was she doing?"

"She is going back in time to when she was abused. She never did that to you before?"

"She said she wanted to practice once, but no, she never tried to touch me."

"Well, she's trying to go back to what's familiar. She is trying to find her center. Servicing guys was something familiar to her."

Joe was visibly shaken. "Look, she needs you and I need to try to wrap my head around this. I just never thought about what she used to do. She was a spunky little kid that I watched ball games with. I think I need to go."

"Goodnight Joe."

Amber was holding the rocking Sarah, trying to focus her when Maria returned.

"Do we try to keep her here or take her back to the hospital?"

"Has she refocused at all?"

"No, she's further away."

"Let me call the doctor."

After a quick consult, Maria called an ambulance and Sarah returned to the hospital. She was admitted directly to the pediatric psych unit and tucked into bed with a restraint vest.

Molly stayed with her for the rest of her shift. Sarah was holding her arm and moaning, then rocking off and on. Just to confirm that she did not have an actual injury, a portable x ray was taken. Although her pain was consistent with a freshly broken arm, her arm was fully healed.

Sarah slept poorly. She was restless throughout the evening and had had several bouts of nightmares.

October 15th   3:30 am

Mark walked by Sarah's room and saw Barry, a night attendant staff, standing next to Sarah's bed. He walked in to see if he needed help with Sarah and found that he was holding her head and guiding her movements. Barry was so involved in the moment that he had not heard Mark's approach.

He climaxed as Mark said, "What the hell are you doing?" He grabbed Barry by the arm to turn him around and, seeing his penis come out of Sarah mouth, drew back and punched Barry in the face. Barry dropped to the floor.

"Kendra!" Mark called for the night nurse.

Hearing his tone of alarm, Kendra was instantly at Sarah's door. Seeing Barry on the floor, his genitals exposed, and Sarah shaking her head as she lay on her bed, she understood immediately that she had a mess on her hands.

She called for another staff person to come and sit with Sarah, giving the clear instructions that Sarah was not to get out of bed or have anything to eat or drink. Then she called the nursing supervisor, who in turn called the police and Dr. Feingold.

A nurse brought a rape kit and swabbed Sarah's mouth. While there was no question about what happened, they worked by the book to collect the evidence.

When Barry was able to pull himself off the floor, Mark frog-marched him to the treatment room and held him until the police arrived. The police took statements from Mark and Kendra. Then they talked to Barry.

He was read his rights and cuffed without incident.

"So, you were caught with your dick in a kid's mouth."

"I want my union rep."

"We're not from the hospital; we're cops."

"Look, she wanted it. Ask anyone. She's always trying to give head. She likes it. Her old man trained her right. I just let her do what she wanted."

They just looked at him.

"Come on, I didn't hurt the kid. It's not like she's some innocent. She's a whore who wants to practice her trade. She's always trying to 'practice,' she calls it. I just let her. There's no harm."

"She's 12 years old and is in the psych unit and you don't see the harm?"

Barry was taken into custody and transported to the precinct house for processing. Once Barry was removed, the police asked to see Sarah. Kendra led the way, explaining that Sarah had come in the night before with flashbacks, having had a very difficult night before this incident. She also explained that Sarah may not be able to talk to them, as she is frequently mute.

They entered her room and Kendra nodded to the staff that they could leave. Then she went to Sarah and gently woke her. "Sarah, the police are here."

Sarah was suddenly awake and panicked. She sprang up in her bed and was on her knees with the vest restraint holding her back from launching herself off the bed. The detectives were startled by her reaction.

"Sarah, calm down. Lay back down." Sarah was shaking her head and flailing her arms. Kendra caught her arms firmly but gently and guided Sarah to lie back down in the bed. "Sarah, look at me. Breathe. Come on Sarah." Sarah met Kendra's eyes and began to focus. As she calmed, Kendra released her arms and asked, "Would you like me to raise your bed up so you can be sitting?"

Sarah nodded.

Kendra raised the head of her bed. "Now, the police are here to ask you some questions about what happened tonight. I'm going to stay here with you in case you need anything."

Detective Muller said, "We need to talk to her alone if you don't mind."

"She is my patient, she is under aged, and she is restrained. She needs to have a staff person with her."

Dr. Feingold entered the room at that moment. "Thanks Kendra, I'll stay with her."

Kendra left the room. Dr. Feingold introduced himself.

"I'm Detective Muller and this is Detective Laramie."

"Let me help you with the interview."

"Doc, no disrespect but we've been talking to victims for a long time; I think we can handle it."

Dr. Feingold smiled and stepped aside. Detective Muller approached Sarah. She was lying back against her pillow. She was shaking her head and squeezing her eyes shut as if she was trying to clear her head. "Sarah, I'm Detective Muller." Sarah looked at him and then at Dr. Feingold and then Detective Laramie. "That's my partner Detective Laramie."

Sarah looked at Detective Muller again. "Sarah, do you know why we are here?" She nodded and then held out her hands to be cuffed.

"No, Sarah, we aren't here to arrest you."

He turned around and asked, "Doc, does she speak?"

"When she can, she does." Then he addressed Sarah. "Sarah, are there people here that shouldn't be?"

Sarah looked around carefully, then at him and shook her head no.

"Are you with us?" She nodded then touched her arm.

"Your arm still hurts?" She nodded and rubbed the arm.

"Sarah, these detectives and I need to know what happened tonight. Can you find one word that will help us understand what happened?"

In a hoarse whisper she uttered, "Fallatio."

That was not the word that the detectives were expecting and they exchanged surprised looks.

Dr. Feingold continued. "You performed fallatio?"

She nodded.

"Who did you perform fallatio on?"

"Barry."

"Why?"

Slowly and with difficulty she replied, "He woke me up and said if I practice I will feel better. He said you wrote an order for him to let me practice so I would feel better."

"Barry told you to perform fallatio so you would feel better?"
She nodded.

"He woke you up to tell you this?"
She nodded.

"Did he ever do this before tonight?"

She nodded.

"When?"

"Last summer."

"How many times?"

Sarah shrugged.

"Was it more or less than 5 times?"

"More."

"What about 10 times, more or less?"

"Less, I think. Less."

"Sarah, did you and Barry do anything other than fallatio?"

"One time."

"What did you do?"

"Intercourse."

"When?"

"After my medicine time. He said you wanted to make sure I could still do rhythms after I took the medicine."

"Was this after you were seen by the gynecologist?"

Sarah nodded. "He said that after people take that medicine they have to be sure they can still do rhythms so he did it with me."

"Sarah, has anyone else done any practice with you?"

She shook her head no, then became upset. "What is it, Sarah?"

"I wanted to practice with Joe last night and I touched him and he got mad at me and he left. I don't think Joe is going to be my friend anymore."

"Sarah, we are going to spend some time together today and we will talk about that then, okay?"

She nodded.

Detective Muller asked, "Sarah, are you always restrained when you go to sleep?"

"No, just when I am not doing well."

"Why are you restrained?"

"So I don't go into the ceiling?"

He looked puzzled. Dr. Feingold helped her out. "Sarah has a propensity for getting into the ceiling. We don't have any rooms with solid ceilings and we would rather keep her on the unit."

"Have you gotten into the ceiling a lot?"

"When Joe got shot I almost escaped from the building."

Dr. Feingold explained what Sarah had done.

She sighed, "Almost got out."

"Sarah, when did you come to the hospital?"

"Last night."

Dr. Feingold explained her timeline of hospitalizations.

"So you were released on Friday and returned on Sunday night?"

She nodded. "But Saturday was a good day. My homework is all done for school." Then she lay back, yawned and rubbed her arm.

Dr. Feingold asked, "Sarah, does your arm still hurt?"

She nodded.

"What's wrong with your arm?"

"Broken."

"Sarah is having flashbacks of when her arm was broken," Dr. Feingold interjected.

"Can you give her something for the pain?"

Sarah responded, "Now medicine doesn't work on then hurts."

"Very good. Why don't you rest? I am going to have a staff person come in with you. The morning shift is here."

"Mike here?"

"I'll check. Do you want Mike?"

Detective Muller asked, "Sarah, does Mike ever do fallatio or intercourse with you?"

Sarah shook her head and said somewhat wistfully, "Mike doesn't practice with little girls."

"You sound like you have talked about it."

"I wanted him to let me practice. He won't."

"Okay. Have you wanted to practice with anyone else?"

"Dr. Feingold. He doesn't let me practice either. He holds my hands and talks to me instead."

"Thank you for talking to us, Sarah."

"Get some rest. We'll talk later." Dr. Feingold left the room with the detectives and directed a Kendra to sit with Sarah.

Once they were out of the room, Detective Muller said, "What's going on with her?"

"Come in the therapy room," Dr. Feingold directed. He laid out Sarah's history and the level of abuse she had suffered.

"So what Barry said about her being trained was right?"

"Unfortunately, she is extremely vulnerable to abuse right now. We're taking special precautions to try to prevent her further abuse but clearly we missed a bad egg with Barry. She will need another gynecological exam later on today. Do you need anything else for this?"

"No, I think we're good."

They looked in on Sarah as they were leaving. She was asleep but was restless. As they left, Detective Muller turned to Detective Laramie and said, "Let's go book this bastard."

A child being sexually assaulted by their attendant while restrained in a psychiatric unit is not a situation that anyone could take lightly. The day was just beginning for the hospital staff and the people who were supposed to be taking care of Sarah. While she tossed and turned asleep in a ball, the hospital administration began an investigation to determine if other kids had also been accosted by Barry. The legal department dealt with the ramifications of a sexual predator being in contact with children. HR dealt with his termination. Theresa was notified and came to conduct her own investigation. Maria and Amber were also notified. Amber was at the hospital in ten minutes. She demanded that she be allowed to see Sarah. Dr. Feingold let her onto the unit and showed her Sarah, who was sleeping, albeit fitfully. She was invited into the therapy room.

"What the hell happened?"

Dr. Feingold explained the situation.

"We brought her here so that she would be watched over and safe and you let her be sodomized. What the hell kind of place are you running? We don't leave her alone with anyone and you're letting some staff person stick his dick in her mouth?"

Amber was pacing while chewing out the doctor. She was careful not to yell to avoid upsetting the patients, but her anger could not be missed.

"Amber, I hear you and I share your anger. He has been arrested and you can be assured that he will be prosecuted fully. There are already at least three investigations underway that I know of. We are cooperating fully with all of them. And you may take some solace in knowing that Mark, the staff person that walked in on Barry, knocked him to the ground."

"I would have killed the bastard if had caught him."

"I know how you feel."

After she was assured that Sarah was in good hands and that her going home or to school was not an option, she left a note for Sarah that she would be back after work.

October 15th 10:00 am

Sarah was allowed to sleep until 10:00 am. Then Nancy woke her gently and led her to the bathroom to shower and dress. She was fed and taken in to see Dr. Feingold. His session with her was taped for the hospital administration.

She sat in a ball in the corner of the room. Dr. Feingold sat in the chair he had been using since they first started meeting.

"Sarah, how are you feeling?" She rubbed her arm. "Your arm still hurts?"

She nodded and signed people. "You are seeing people who don't belong here?" She held up her hands. "You want me to help you focus on here?"

She nodded.

"Come on over. I can't reach from there."

Sarah crawled across the floor and sat in front of Dr. Feingold and gave him her hands. He held them in front of his knees. She was in a ball with her head down but with her hands relaxed in his.

"Sarah, I am right here. I am here with you. I want you to focus on the solid things. Look at something solid." She looked at the bookcase lined with toys. "Good. Now I want you to look at one of the transparent people."

Sarah quaked at the request.

"It's okay, I'm here with you." She looked at the person who was standing closest to the door. She could hear him talking. Dr. Feingold squeezed her hand and said, "Now look at something solid."

She looked back at the bookcase and then at the transparent person.

"Are you okay?" She nodded and took a breath. "Now, tell me what he's doing?"

"He's standing."

"Is he doing anything else?"

"Talking."

"Can you tell me what he said?"

"Now, isn't she a sweet young thing?" She mocked the lascivious tone of her past.

"Are you okay to look at him again?" She looked in his direction and startled to find him closer. "What are you seeing, Sarah?"

Sarah looked up at the semitransparent man towering over her. "Sarah, I want you to tell him, 'NO!'"

She looked up and whispered plaintively, "No." Sarah looked down and winced.

"What is he doing?"

"Laughing and he hit me."

She heard him say, "*I paid good money for you. You wouldn't want me to tell Zeke you said no, would you?*" Sarah shook her head and tried to stand up to go with her flashback.

Dr. Feingold held her hands and called her back to him. Sarah shook her head as if trying to clear it.

"You're here, Sarah. You're with me and you're safe. Let's stay here for a few minutes. You are right here." Sarah looked up at the angry man looming over her and then ducked her head; bracing for the pummeling she was sure was to follow.

"Sarah, look at me."

She stayed in little ball for several minutes and then looked around in surprise when she hadn't been hit. The tall man was gone. Only Dr. Feingold was with her. She looked all around the room and then at him with pleasant surprise.

"Gone?" he asked.

She nodded, "How?"

"They can't actually touch you, Sarah. When you stand up to them, they have to back away. Now is different than before. You had to do anything anyone wanted before, didn't you?" She nodded in agreement. "Now you have a very powerful word. You can say 'No.' Let me hear you say 'No!'"

She quietly said, "No."

"Say it like you mean it."

"But I'm supposed to do what I am told."

"Not always."

"When?"

"When doing something is the right thing to do, you should do what you are told. When you are told to do something that is wrong, you shouldn't do it."

"How do I know?"

"We are going to work on that one together. Some things you need to do when you are told to do them. Eat your dinner, go to school, do your homework, brush your teeth go to bed. Those are all things you should do because they are all good for you. But no matter who tells you or asks you to do fallatio, or sodomy, or intercourse, the answer should always be no."

"What about Barry?"

"What Barry did was wrong and he will not be back here. Sarah, did you ever ask Barry to practice with you?"

"No. I didn't know Barry until he started testing me."

"How did he start testing you?"

"He put his finger in me like that first person did. I woke up and he told me that you wanted him to test me. Then he told me to tighten down." She took a breath and continued. "He said I was very well trained and we would do more tests on other nights. He said that I shouldn't tell other staff people that he was testing me because it would hurt their feelings that you chose him and not them."

"Sarah, I did not order Barry to do tests on you. And I will never write an order for you to perform fallatio, or for anyone to have intercourse or perform sodomy on you; no rhythms, no practice. I will also never have you do something that is a secret. Everything we do is out in the open and you are allowed to talk about if you choose to. Do you understand?"

"No. Why did he tell me that you said to do it?"

"Barry lied to you because Barry wanted to do things to you that he shouldn't be doing."

"You aren't supposed to lie to people."

"No, you aren't."

"I'm supposed to do what staff tells me to do."

"Except if it involves keeping secrets or practicing in some way."

"Grownups aren't supposed to practice with kids?"

"You're correct."

"What about if there are medical tests?"

"If there is a medical test to be done on you, you will have the nurse with you in addition to the person running the test. You should never be alone with a person who is running a test on you. Do you remember when you went to see the gynecologist?"

"Yeah."

"Do you remember that Nancy was with you?"

"Yeah, she was there and another nurse was there too."

"Good. That is how medical tests are done. They are never done during the night in a dark room with just an attendant."

"You're mad at me."

"Sarah, I am very angry and very frustrated but it is not at you. I'm angry at Barry and frustrated that with all the rules we've set up to keep you safe, you were transgressed here under my watch and weren't able to tell me that it was happening."

"I'm sorry."

"You don't have anything to be sorry about. I'm the one who should be saying that I'm sorry to you."

"You didn't write the order."

"So, maybe we should both put the blame on Barry where it belongs."

"Barry was bad."

"Barry was bad." Dr. Feingold repeated.

"Zeke was bad."

"Yes, Zeke was bad."

"Mike was good?"

"Mike was good."

"Joe was good. He didn't let me practice. He said he will never let me practice. If I promise not to try, do you think that he will still be my friend?"

"How about if I talk to Joe?" She nodded. "How about if you go get some lunch?"

"Okay." She left the treatment room and Dr. Feingold shut off the recording equipment, closed the door, and wept in frustration and anger.

He had composed himself when Nancy knocked on the door a half hour later. "Come in."

"Doc, I just wanted to let you know that Sarah is scheduled for another internal exam at 2:00 pm."

"Okay. Make sure you go with her. She knows now that if she is to have any type of testing or medical procedures that she is to have a nurse with her in addition to another person."

"Are you as angry as I am?"

"I…yeah, dammit. We're supposed to provide a safe place for her. That kid took care of herself and kept herself safe for four fucking years on her own. We have her here in our damn hospital and she was raped and sodomized Lord knows how many times because we told her that we were the good guys and she could trust us. What the hell are we doing? How did we miss this? How did we not see what was happening in this unit? If he did it to her, who else did he do it to? How many kids were brought in here and told that this was a safe place only to be exploited and abused? The death penalty is not good enough for this sorry excuse for a human being. He should be drawn and quartered. Slowly. With no anesthesia."

"Yeah, you're as angry as I am. I was thinking that he should be hung by the very parts of his body he likes to put where they don't belong. But drawn and quartered works for me. How is Sarah?"

"She is so damaged that she is just rolling with it like it is nothing. It's times like this that I realize just how little self she has. Even a two year old is able to say 'No, I don't want to.' She has no idea that she has that right. With her age and the work we are doing, she is going to hit the terrible twos and adolescence at the same time."

Nancy sighed and said, "I think that this is going to be her home or her second home for years."

Dr. Feingold looked at Nancy and smiled. "We've had worse. At least Sarah is a trooper. Have you ever seen another kid try harder?"

They were both smiling now as Nancy said, "Or climb in the ceiling?"

They looked at each other with caring respect and camaraderie. Nancy said, "Thanks Doc. I'll get things ready for her to go for that exam."

"Thanks, Nancy."

The gynecological exam showed that Sarah had a new STD. A warrant was issued for Barry to be tested for STDs. He was found to have the same strain of bacteria as Sarah and the charges against him were increased as Sarah's story was corroborated.

October 17th   1:00 pm

Over the next week, Sarah worked on facing her flashbacks and managing them. She was questioned by Theresa from child services and the Assistant DA. As the investigation moved forward, Sarah was struggling. The work on flashbacks was exhausting for her and the questions in the investigations were confusing. She could speak clearly and competently about what transpired. However, she did not understand the context of the investigations and began to worry, as children do, that she was to blame for all the investigations. When she spoke to Theresa, she asked if she could still live with Amber and Maria.

"Do you want to live with them?"

"Yes. Do they still want me?"

"Yes, why wouldn't they?"

"Because I'm so much work and now I'm more work and I'm not going to school. And because I'm stupid and bad."

"Why do you say you're stupid and bad?"

"Because I wasn't smart enough to know that Dr. Feingold didn't order tests and I let Barry do wrong things."

"Sarah, you aren't stupid and you aren't bad. Barry was manipulative and he gave you what sounded like a reasonable excuse for what he was doing. Barry is the one who was bad, not you."

"So, Maria and Amber still want me?"

"They do."

"Does my school still want me?"

"As far as I know, you still have a place at your school. Have you been able to do any school work?"

"Some, but not much; I have to try to do an hour every afternoon. But it's hard to concentrate."

"I'll let you rest, Sarah. You can call me if you need me for anything."

"No I can't. I can't have my phone when I'm here."

It was the first surly comment Sarah made. It would be far from the last.

October 18th   2:00 pm

Rabbi Cohen arrived. He brought cards from her classmates. Sarah looked at them, burst into tears, and swiped them all off the table. Mike was immediately in the doorway to assist if needed, but Rabbi Cohen said quietly, "You're angry today."

"I want to be at school and I can't go. I have to stay in this stupid place."

"Things are hard for you right now."

"I hate it here. I want to go home."

"Are you ready to go home?"

"No, I'm never going to be ready. The stupid people keep coming here like they came to school."

"You're having flashbacks."

"Yeah and I hate them." Sarah stood up and literally stomped her feet as she yelled. "I hate it all. I hate everyone." Then she crumbled into the corner and hid her face and cried.

Mike backed out and got Dr. Feingold. He came to the door and watched as Sarah wiped her face and yelled. "And don't tell me about Job. I don't give a shit about Job. Job can go fuck himself."

"You are having a very difficult day. Hearing that others had it bad just doesn't help, does it?"

"No. And if praying is helping I would hate to see what it would be like if I wasn't praying."

He asked, "You're praying?"

"Yes. But it's stupid. I keep saying the Sh'ema and the Kaddish and the Hashkiveinu but it doesn't help. What good are all the Baruch Ata's? The people keep coming here and I keep telling them to go away and they keep coming back. And the stupid suit people keep coming and talking to me and asking me questions. I already know that I am stupid to have listened to stupid Barry. I already know it's all my fault. I wish that first stupid suit guy that came here had killed me." And then she spoke the words they had all been dreading. "I wish I was dead. Why can't I just die?" Sarah sat in the corner with her knees drawn up to her chest and cried. Dr. Feingold went to the nurse's station and put Sarah on suicide watch.

Mike stayed in the doorway and watched Sarah. Rabbi Cohen began to pray quietly and slowly, asking for God to help Sarah. He spoke in Hebrew but used words he knew she would understand. She quieted. When she looked up, he was watching her. "Can you sit here at the table with me?"

She got up and sat at the table. She was shaking. "Sarah, there are many people who truly love you. We want to see you grow into a happy adult and are willing to help you do just that. But it is your choice. You can work hard and move beyond this very difficult time or you can stay in this hell. I don't think that you want to stay in this place that you are in." He paused and placed his hand over hers. "I don't want you to die. Working is not easy. But I think you will find the rewards are worth it. Will you think about it?"

"If I work hard can I come back to school?"

"You are welcome to return to school whenever you are ready."

"Will you tell everyone 'thank you' for the cards?"

"I will."

"Are you going to tell them that I want to die?"

"Do you want me to tell them that?"

She shook her head "no."

"How about if I ask that they keep you in their prayers for healing?"

"Okay."

Mike intervened, "Sarah, why don't you come with me now?"

"No."

Rabbi Cohen stood up and said "Rabbi-hug?"

Sarah fell into his arms and began crying again. He held her then blessed her and handed her to Mike, who led her to her room. At the doorway Sarah became defiant. "No, I don't want to wear the vest."

She challenged Mike, ready for a fight. "That's for the Doc and Nancy to decide."

"It's for me to decide and I say 'No.'"

Both Nancy and the Doc came to the hallway. "And I am not staying here anymore. I want my backpack."

Dr. Feingold said quietly, "Why don't we discuss this in here?" He gestured to the therapy room.

"Why don't you just let me have my stuff and go home?"

"That isn't going to happen, Sarah. But we can talk about how you are feeling."

"What if I don't want to talk to you? What if I hate you?"

"Then you can go sit on your bed."

"I don't want to sit on my bed. I want to go home."

"That isn't an option right now. You can come in and talk to me or you can sit on your bed."

"I hate you."

She stepped toward Dr. Feingold and inches from his face yelled, "I hate you. I hate you, I hate you." She had tears in her eyes when she started throwing punches. Mike caught her from behind before she landed her first punch. She struggled against him, but she was less than one third his weight and he had little trouble controlling her fury.

Dr. Feingold motioned to the therapy room and Mike duck-walked a protesting Sarah there. Dr. Feingold began, "Sarah, you are allowed to have your feelings but you are not allowed to hurt yourself or other people."

She pulled away from Mike and he let her go. She glowered at him and sat in the corner. Doc nodded to dismiss Mike.

"So, you are having a tough day."

"Are you going to let me go home?"

"No, I am not going to let you go home. I'm going to listen to you tell me what you're feeling."

"I don't know what I'm feeling."

"Let's figure it out together."

In a sarcastic tone that would make any teen proud, she mimicked, "Let's figure it out together." Then she crossed her arms and scowled.

"You're pretty angry."

"You're pretty angry." She mimicked back.

"Who are you angry with?"

"Why should you care?"

"I care because I care about you."

"No, you don't. You don't care about me. You don't care about me!" She was becoming more agitated with each repetition. "You can't care about me."

Calmly and quietly he asked, "Why can't I care about you, Sarah?"

"Because I'm too stupid."

"Why do you feel stupid?"

"Because I listened to everyone. I listened to Zeke and I listened to the men and I listened to you, and I listened to Barry. And now I'm in a lot of trouble and I don't know how to get out of it. It was better before I came here. I shouldn't have ever talked to you."

"You feel like people violated your trust."

"What is that supposed to mean?"

"You trusted people to take care of you and they didn't."

"I trusted Zeke and he did bad things to me and he let other people do bad things and I was too stupid to know that they were bad."

"Sarah, you were too young to know they were bad."

"I wasn't too young on Monday. I trusted you. If I didn't trust you, then Barry wouldn't have told me to do bad things. It's your fault that I did that stuff. It's your fault that I'm bad."

"You think that you are bad for people doing things to you?"

"People didn't do stuff to me. I did it to them. So now I am going to have to go to jail and I won't get to go home with Amber and Maria and I won't get to go to school and I won't get to make my bat mitzvah."

"Sarah, who told you that you're going to jail?"

"That's why I had to talk to the District Attorney and Theresa. So they can put me in jail. That's why you have to keep me tied up now."

"Sarah, you are not going to jail."

"I don't trust you."

"I can understand why you don't trust me but you're still not going to jail."

"Then I can go home?"

"Not yet."

"I hate you."

"You can hate me. But you're not ready to go home and I think you know that."

"Because I'll have the flashbacks again?"

"That's part of it."

"Because I hate you?"

"That's part of it."

"Because I hate me?"

"That's part of it too. Should we talk about why you hate yourself?"

"Because I'm stupid. I'm the stupidest person in the world."

"Sarah, you're not stupid."

"Then why did I try to touch Joe and make him not like me anymore?"

"You're pretty angry with yourself, aren't you?"

"I wish I was dead. How come you didn't let that guy kill me when they came the first time? It would have been easier and Barry wouldn't have lost his job and Joe wouldn't know that I am a little whore."

"Who told you that you're a whore?"

"Nobody had to; I figured it out for myself. I got paid to have intercourse and to do fallatios. That makes me a whore. Now I even know how they have to kill me."

"How do you know that?"

"It's in the Torah. Don't you even read the Torah?"

"Yes, but I wasn't aware that you had gotten to that part yet."

"I've read the whole thing. I mean, I read it in English, but it says the same thing in English as in Hebrew, right?"

"Pretty close."

"So when am I going to get stoned for being a whore?"

"You haven't made your bat mitzvah yet."

Sarah sat down. She understood exactly what he was saying. Quietly she said, "I haven't made my bat mitzvah. I'm not responsible yet. So, I can't get stoned and I can't go to jail."

"You are correct."

"But I was still pretty stupid."

"Stupid isn't the right word."

"What would you call it?"

"Innocent: you trusted people you should have been able to trust. They violated that trust. They are the ones who should be in jail."

"So, why did the DA lady come here and why did Theresa, the social worker, come here?"

"The DA lady, as you put it, came here to understand what happened so that she can prosecute Barry and put him in jail. Then Theresa came here to make sure that this is the best place for you to be right now."

"Is it?"

"Yes. I think so. I think that we've done a lot of work together and you've developed good relationships here. You work well with Nancy and Mike and Molly and Julia, correct?"

"Yeah."

"You're in your own neighborhood so Amber and Maria can come here easily and Rabbi Cohen can come visit every week."

"Yeah."

"Well, if we moved you to another hospital, you would need to get to know a whole new group of people and a whole new routine. And they would need to get to know you before you could get to work. All of that would take time. I would rather use that time to help you through this and get you back to school."

"I want to go back to school."

"So, you will stay here and work with us to get through this mess?"

"Yeah, I guess I don't hate you too badly."

"But you're still angry?"

"Yeah."

"You should be angry."

"What?"

"Being angry when someone takes advantage of you is natural. Barry violated your trust and he took advantage of my relationship with you. I am very angry with Barry too."

"You are?"

"Yes, we're all very angry with Barry. That's why you have seen so many suit people around here this week. We're on the same team. We are all on Team Sarah."

She cocked her head and smiled. "I have a team?"

"You have a team. And we're all working very hard to help you win."

"What happens if we win?"

"You grow up to be a happy, responsible adult."

"What happens if we lose?"

"Then either you don't grow up, you aren't happy, or you aren't a responsible adult."

"You want all three?"

"We want all three and we're in it for the long haul. How about you? Are you willing to be on the team?"

"I don't know. I'm not any of those things right now and I don't even know if I want to be any of them."

"You still feel like you want to die."

Quietly she said, "Yeah, mostly."

"Do you know how you would make that happen?"

She nodded. "And so do you. We've both known it for a long time."

"So you have had the thoughts before now?"

She nodded. "Since the first DA suit guy came and told me that he wasn't going to kill me. I just figured I would have to do it myself." She crossed her arms and continued. "Sometimes when I went into the ceiling at night it was to think about what it would be like to be dead and to try to do it. But I just couldn't step off."

"What do you mean you couldn't step off?"

"After I made a noose and put my head in it, I couldn't step off the wall."

"Is the noose still there?" Sarah looked down and bit her lower lip. "Sarah?"

She nodded and cringed, expecting to be hit.

October 18th   4:00 pm

Dr. Feingold sat still for a moment, trying to contain his feelings. Then he called Mike in to sit with Sarah. He went to the nurse's station and told Nancy to call maintenance to bring a ladder. They arrived and he asked them to go into the ceiling and see if there was a noose up there. There was and they untied it from the rafters and dropped it down.

"Is there anything else up there that can be used to make another?"

"Doc, no offense, but if you wanted to kill yourself and you was up here, you have your choice of ways."

"Okay."

He went back into the nurse's station and put the noose on the counter top. "It has been up in the ceiling since last summer. She has had this around her neck and just couldn't step off the ledge. All those times I had her restrained and we wondered if we were overreacting she had a fucking noose in the ceiling above her bed. We didn't have her restrained enough. She is never to be left alone in that room. She's on suicide watch until further notice."

"Doc, she's got a long road to go, but we can only take one step at a time. She told you she had the noose. That's progress."

"I need to go back in there. I'm so angry right now. Damn it!! I don't want to lose her."

Sarah was sitting at the table with her head on her arms when he returned. Mike started to leave and Doc said, "No, Mike, you need to know this. Sarah had a noose tied up in the rafters."

Mike dropped his arms to his sides and stood up straighter, pulling back from the news. Then he looked at Sarah. She sat up and looked at both of them. "Are you going to throw me out?"

"No, we're going to do everything we can to keep you safe. We are part of team Sarah. We are going to keep you safe until you are ready to handle that responsibility."

"Are you mad at me?"

"Do you want me to be mad at you?"

She shrugged. "I'm mad at you."

"I guess you wanted to show me how angry you are."

"Are you going to come back tomorrow?"

"Yes. I'll be back tomorrow."

"Are you going to talk to me?"

"Yes. I'm going to talk to you. What are you thinking?"

"Are you my team captain?"

"Do you want me to be your team captain?" She nodded tentatively as tears filled her eyes. "Will you stay on the team?" he pushed a little further.

"I can't promise that."

"That's fair enough. For now the job of Team Sarah is to keep Sarah alive."

"I'd rather you called a different play."

"Yeah, but I'm the captain and I'm calling the plays."

Sarah rested her head on her arms in resignation. Mike gave her a moment then asked her to come into the day room with him. He pulled out a puzzle and sat her at the table. Together, they started working the puzzle.

"Are you sure you want to be on Team Sarah?"

"It seems like a good team to be on. Sarah, I know that you feel pretty awful right now and this is going to seem like a platitude, but it is going to get better. You're a hard worker. If you weren't, I wouldn't bother being on Team Sarah. But you're the hardest working kid who has ever come through here. I want to see you succeed and I'll make sure that you stay safe long enough that you can work this through."

"Okay, but I really do feel crappy."

They worked the puzzle together in silence until Molly came to join them. "Hi, Sarah. I understand you are having a horrible day." She nodded. "Well, I'm hoping that you can have a better evening. I was also asked to tell you that I'm on Team Sarah. The Captain said that I'm to guard you from yourself tonight."

"It seems like a popular assignment."

Mike got up to leave. "I'll see you in the morning, Sarah."

"If I have to be here, at least you'll be here too."

Amber and Maria visited Sarah after dinner. She wasn't much for company but Amber went with her get her ready for bed. Sarah walked into her room. "I can get dressed by myself."

"Not for now, you can't."

She grumbled as she got into her pajamas. Molly started to put the vest on her but she drew away. "No, I'm not wearing the vest."

"Sarah, you can put this on cooperatively or we will put it on you, but you are wearing the vest."

"No I'm not and you can't make me."

Amber looked at Sarah and said, "You don't actually believe that statement, do you?"

"I'm sick of the stupid vest. He already knows about the noose."

"You need the vest because none of us is naive enough to think that you don't have a backup plan. Or to think that about now, you might test it out. You're not the first suicidal kid we've had. We know the score."

"Then why do you want to be on Team Sarah?"

"Because we want to see you beat all those bastards that hurt you."

Amber went to Sarah and embraced her. Sarah cried softly, "I just want to die."

"I know. Right now is pretty bad." While she held Sarah, she helped Molly secure her in the vest. "Try to get some sleep. Maria and I will be back tomorrow night."

October 21st   4:15 pm

After Dr. Feingold finished with Sarah's session he took the noose and went to the hospital administrator, who had been dealing with the Barry investigation. He dropped the noose on his desk demanding, "I want a solid ceiling installed in Sarah's room."

"Where did you get this?"

"She tied it in the rafters last summer."

The administrator blanched, inhaled and said, "Let me see what I can do."

The next morning Sarah was moved to another room while a solid ceiling was installed in her room.

Dr. Feingold showed her the room when it was finished. "Team Sarah 1, Sarah 0," she muttered.

"Now you don't need the vest."

"You're pretty serious about this Team Sarah thing, aren't you?" she said flatly.

"Yeah, you could say that. Are you ready to join the team yet?"

"How about if I just go to team practices?"

"That's a start."

"Um," Sarah froze, realizing what she had said. Dr. Feingold realized it too.

"Not *that* kind of practice," he stated emphatically with a smile.

November 8th   12:40 am

They worked hard during their sessions. Sarah was processing the memories with her new-found realization that she had been betrayed and violated. It was difficult and exhausting work which left Sarah with little energy for anything else. Eight years of constant abuse cannot be resolved in a few weeks, but Sarah was gaining enough ground that she could begin to function again. By the third week she was able to resume some of the therapies on the unit. She was able to concentrate on her schoolwork for an hour a day. She was taking several naps daily but could be left on 15 minute checks most days.

But Sarah was different now. There was a gravity about her that had not existed before. She no longer asked the staff for hugs and did not want to hug Rabbi Cohen when he visited.

Sarah was no longer the innocent child she had been. She was no longer mute, but she was very much alone. She had built a wall around herself.

Mike commented about it to Dr. Feingold. "Doc, I feel like we're losing her. She is more closed off now than when they first brought her in."

"I know it seems that way. She needs to sort this out inside herself. All you can do is be there for her so when she breaks through this wall she has built she isn't left standing alone. And Mike, don't trust that she is okay. She'll kill herself if she gets the chance. She can't see a future."

Sarah's life on the unit was again becoming routine. She now put herself to bed without Molly or Julia tucking her in. She was sometimes surly and often grumpy. Sarah had mastered the eye roll, the shoulder shrug and the slouch of total indifference. But she did what she was expected to do without actual complaint. She was up and dressed every morning for breakfast and attended the groups she was assigned to and did her school work. And she was the only kid on the unit that didn't have to be told to brush teeth and go to bed.

About a month after the incident with Barry, Mark looked in on Sarah during the night and found her pajamas lying on the floor.

"Kendra," he whispered. She came at his call and together they entered her room. Sarah had taken off her pajamas and was sweating profusely. "She's burning up" Kendra said, feeling her forehead. "Let me get the thermometer. Get some towels. We need to get this temperature down."

"104.6. Stay with her and put wet towels on her. I need to call the doctor." She had Jesse go in to help Mark. The on-call doctor was on the unit in minutes. Sarah was still sleeping. The doctor performed a short exam and a strep culture. "We had a boy admitted last week who turned out to have strep. We'll know if she has it in a few minutes. In the meantime, let's see if we can get that fever down before her brain cooks." The test confirmed strep and Kendra started an IV. They continued working to reduce the temperature until the morning shift came in and took over.

November 9th   9:15 am

Sarah's fever diminished and she went from sweating profusely to shivering uncontrollably. Mary dressed her in clean pajama pants and a hospital gown to accommodate the IV. Mike was holding Sarah, who woke up while they changed her bed. "I'm freezing."

"I know, sweetie. We are changing your bed and then we will get you tucked back in."

"I don't feel good."

"I know. You have strep throat."

"I...", and she threw up all over herself and Mike.

"Nancy!" Nancy came in to find Sarah horrified and shocked; Sarah wasn't mute —she was speechless.

"Help."

Grabbing a towel, Nancy cleaned Sarah quickly. Within moments they had her dressed and back into a clean, dry bed.

Mike excused himself and changed into a clean set of scrubs. When he returned, Sarah was asleep again, shivering profusely and moaning in her sleep. She slept throughout the day and Mike reflected on the last time she was sick. She wasn't the same little girl anymore. He noticed when she was being changed that she wasn't going to be a girl much longer. Her time as a pedophile's object of desire was coming to end. Now, she would be facing another class of perverts. He wondered what Zeke had planned to do to her when she was no longer wanted by his clientele. Would he have sold her, killed her, pimped her out to different group? What was going to happen to this little girl as she became a woman?

He brushed the hair from her face and felt her forehead. The fever was coming down. It was just a normal childhood illness in a child's life that was anything but normal. He tucked her blankets around her and let her sleep.

Within a few days, Sarah bounced back from the strep and gained a new equilibrium. She was more settled and more able to concentrate. She was less grumpy and surly. She was still a hard worker but she was playful in a way that staff had not seen in a month. She spent Thanksgiving in the hospital. It was her first Thanksgiving with a turkey and she enjoyed making paper decorations with the younger patients on the unit. When she was still on an even keel after a week, Doctor Feingold decided that she was ready to go home and return to school. She was caught up on her school work and had been e-mailing her friends and reconnecting. At first it was difficult because she and her friends had been apart for so long, but they focused on the school work and were able to bridge the gaps.

November 28th   4:30 pm

Amber and Maria picked her up and took her home. Sarah was glad to be back. "It feels like I haven't been here in forever."

"It's been a long time."

"I hope I stay here from now on."

Amber hugged her and said, "I hope so too. But the hospital is part of the system and if you need it, you shouldn't be afraid to utilize it."

"You don't think that I am done there, do you?"

"I'm a realist. I know how much work you're going to need to do and I would not be surprised if sometimes the best place for that to happen would be in the hospital. But for now, let's enjoy your being here. How about pizza for dinner? If there's one thing the hospital cannot get right, it's pizza."

"Here or there?"

"Let's have it delivered. We can get your clothes put away while we're waiting." Amber ordered the pizza, then together they unpacked Sarah's belongings and chose an outfit for the morning.

"Amber, will you walk me to school tomorrow?"

"Sure, kid."

"Amber, what will happen if I sort of want to die again? Will I have to go back to the hospital?"

"Everyone wants to die at some time. If you feel that way, we can talk about it and decide if we are able to help you stay safe or if you need the hospital. You know that Maria and I are signed on to Team Sarah. If you need us, we are here in whatever way you need us to be here." Amber turned to Sarah, "Now, all that being said, do you feel like you want to die?"

"The thought is there but it's like over in the corner. It's always sitting over in the corner now, so it's the same as usual."

"Will you promise to tell someone on Team Sarah if it starts moving?"

"That's a big promise."

"And?"

"I promise to try to tell someone. Is my teacher on Team Sarah?"

"Yes, and so is Rabbi Cohen."

"Are we having sausage on the pizza?"

"Yeah, cheese, pepperoni, and sausage, just like you like it."

"This is so totally not kosher."

"Do you feel like a rebel?"

"Yeah, and it's kind of fun."

They had a nice night and Sarah was ready for school in the morning. She was, of course, anxious, but she was ready and steadfast.

November 29th   8:15 am

As they approached the building, Rabbi Cohen came out. As he did on the first day of school, he greeted Sarah and walked her to her classroom. This time he did not hug her before she entered the room. He just wished her a good day and let her know that he would be in his office all day if she needed him.

Mrs. Rifkin greeted Sarah warmly. "The kids all know that you are coming back today and we are very glad that you're ready to return."

"It's been a long time."

"Yes, it has."

"Do they know why I wasn't here?"

"They know some of it. They know that you were in the hospital and that you have been working on some very difficult feelings. Sarah, these kids have known you for a long time. They know now that the whole time that they knew you, you were living alone without anyone to take care of you. They are in awe of what you have done."

"They don't know the bad stuff, do they?"

"They don't know your whole story, no. Everyone who needs to know does, and we're here to help you. But we have no intention of making your private life public. What we want to focus on is now and making sure you get the best education you can."

"Well, I did all my homework and read all my assignments."

"I'm proud of you. I have graded all your homework. You have a few tests to take, but we will work them in over the next week."

Sarah was putting her things in her desk when the other students started coming into the classroom.

Sarah found returning to school easier than she had thought it would be. Rachel was once again her best friend and Sarah found Tara's curiosity about the hospital amusing. She could give Tara bits of information and Tara would weave amazing fantasies about life in the hospital that did not resemble reality in the least. But Sarah enjoyed listening to Tara talk.

December 11th   4:30 pm

She explained to Dr. Feingold one afternoon, "Listening to Tara's Tales is like eating cotton candy: it's sweet but there's nothing really there. But she's so much fun to listen to. Rachel and I call her stories Tara's Tales. We said that at her house and her mom heard us and started laughing. They've been calling them Tara's Tales for years. I think Tara should be a writer. She has a huge imagination."

"How about you? What do you imagine?"

"I don't imagine. I mean, I can see Tara's imagines when she talks about them but I don't make imagines like she does."

"What do you think about?"

"I think about school, the work I have to do, and I think about where I need to be and what I need to have with me or done to be ready for it. I have a lot of planning thoughts. And I have a lot of how thoughts."

"How thoughts?"

"I have thoughts about how to do something, or how to solve a problem or how to make something work better." She changed her position on the floor before continuing. "And I have a lot of remembering."

"You have had a lot happen that would be difficult to understand. Are there memories that you want to talk about now?"

"Remember last summer when Joe used to come and watch baseball with me?"

"Um, what about it?"

"That was fun. Nobody ever did that with me before."

"Did what?"

"Watched a game and treated me like a person. I felt like I was just another person. Joe didn't want me to do anything. I could just be. Doing and being are very different."

"Try to explain it."

"Before, when I was doing stuff to the men, it wasn't about me. It wasn't about who I am as a person. I was just—I don't know how to explain it. I wasn't a person."

"You were seen as an object?"

Sarah thought for a few moments then nodded. "Yeah, I was an object. I wasn't me. Well, I was me but they didn't care who I was, they cared about what I could do."

"You were objectified by them and you didn't really like it."

"I liked the attention and I liked being told I was good at something. But Joe…it was different with Joe. He didn't tell me I was good at something and I didn't do anything for him except learn how to watch baseball games but I felt…." Sarah paused and looked around for the right word. "I felt like it was about me and not what I could do." She looked down. "I can't explain it very well."

"I think you have done a very good job of explaining objectification. The men before treated you like an object. Joe treated you like a subject. He saw you as person instead of a tool. Does that fit?"

"Yeah. Do you think he will ever see me as just a person again?"

"Does Joe spend time with you?"

"I see him sometimes when he is walking his beat. But it isn't like before. I know that it's my fault because I touched him. But I don't know how to make it better. Now, when I see him it's weird and he doesn't look at me like he used to. But you're not different and Mike is not different, so why is Joe different?"

"First of all, Mike and I have much more experience with girls who have been objects. You are the first person Joe met who has your experiences. When you met Joe, he saw you as little person who was in trouble and then a child whom people had done things to."

"Okay."

"But even though he knew in his mind what happened to you, he never really thought about you—the child— he knew actually performing fallatio and engaging in intercourse."

"But that's what I had to do."

"Yes it was, but until that night when you touched him, he was able to see you as a child and separate you from what you did."

"I pulled him out of Eden, didn't I?"

"You did."

"You can't go back to Eden once you leave."

"No you can't."

"Can I tell you something?"

"Sure."

"It's is sort of like Tara's Tale."

"Okay."

"Sometimes I get mad when I see Joe and I want to push him down and do all the stuff I used do. I want to do it to him."

"What do you think that's about?"

"I don't know. It's kind of all mixed up. I want him to feel bad and I want him to feel dirty because that's how I feel now when he looks at me. He makes me feel like I'm dirty. It's like he thinks that all I really am is a little whore. A tiny whore in nice clothes that acts like a little girl until you get her alone and then she attacks you and you see what a real harlot she is."

"That must not feel very good."

"It doesn't. I don't like feeling that way. So, I don't really like seeing Joe very much anymore."

"You see a part of yourself that you don't like."

"I don't want to be that anymore."

"And you have made some very clear choices in your life that show that."

"And I have made some really stupid choices that contradict that."

"Sarah, when you touched Joe, did you really want to perform fallatio or have intercourse with him, or did you just want to find something stable and familiar to hold onto?"

"I wanted the flashbacks to stop."

"So you weren't trying to be a whore. Your method may have been a bit off, but your motive was pure." He sat forward on his chair. "You are not a little whore. If you walked out of here right now and some man walked up to you and offered you $50.00 to perform fallatio, would you do it?"

Sarah sat back in disgust. "No."

"I rest my case. You are a not a whore. You are a girl who is becoming a young woman who was required to engage in behaviors that are not OK for any child. But given a choice, it is not what you would do for pleasure or money."

He continued, "Joe's problem with you is Joe's problem. He needs to reconcile what you did and who you are. Sometimes seeing a person for who they are instead of the fantasy of who they are is very difficult."

"Joe saw me like a Tara Tale."

"That is a good way of putting it. Shall we see if Maria is here for you?"

December 13ᵗʰ   4:30 pm

Sarah's after–school routine was to walk to Dr. Feingold's office for their sessions. While their work continued steadily, the pace was slower since Sarah lacked the supports at the hospital. Properly pacing the work was crucial to avoid overwhelming Sarah.

Most sessions started with an assessment of Sarah's suicidal thoughts. Her typical response was "they are sitting in the corner." But one afternoon she was surprised to find "They've left the room. Where did they go?" She was literally turning around and looking for them in his office.

"I don't know. Where do you think they went?"

The jovial Sarah replied, "I don't know, maybe they went out to buy Chanukah presents."

"Is that likely?"

"No, it's not their style."

"What do you think is going on that they were able to leave?"

"Has anyone talked to you about gift horses?"

He chuckled, "Sarah, I do enjoy your sense of humor but this is therapy time and you know me; always the questions."

"Okay, since you must ask about the stupid feelings, I think it's because I," she wiggled around on the floor, "I don't know, I just feel good right now. I like school and I got an A on my math test and even better I really knew I was going to get an A. I'm going to a party at Tara's on Saturday night and she's fun and her mom is going to let us bake brownies and make brownie sundaes and watch movies all night. I haven't been awake late at night in a long time." She moved around more on the floor. "Remember when I used to be up during the night?"

"I remember the reports. But why were you up during the night?"

"So I could go hunting. That was when I went dumpster diving. I found great stuff during the night and restaurants would put food out and if you were there, you got to have it. I have eaten behind some of the best restaurants in the Village."

She sat up and leaned over the ottoman. "You know what's funny? Amber and Maria will talk about a restaurant and I'll start talking about their food. They have the funniest look on their faces when I talk about having eaten the food."

"Do they know that you ate behind the restaurants?"

She rocked excitedly, "They do now. At first they didn't and Amber was like, 'No way have you had spaghetti at the Trattoria. They let you in?' So I told her that they didn't let me in, but they did feed me. Sometimes the restaurants would even make a 'to go' bag for me. And once in a while they, the pizza people especially, would call me in and sit me down and feed me. I've gone back to some of them and told them thank you. One guy, Luigi, he gave me a hug and told me I could always have pizza for free. But now I pay for it when I go in and I smile at him. He pinches my cheeks and tells me I'm beautiful. 'Not so skinny now,' he always says to his wife. And she says. 'Luigi, you no tell a girl she no skinny. She think she is fat.' But he's right. I'm not skinny anymore. I'm not fat, but I'm not skinny like I was."

Then she stopped and looked around, "Wow, that was a tangent."

"Are you still happy?"

"Yeah, now is a lot better than then. But you know who I miss and I am never awake to see her?"

"Who?"

"Taina."

"Who is Taina? I don't remember us talking about her."

"I don't think we ever did; we never did. Remember when I wasn't talking yet but I was writing?"

"Yes."

"Well I wrote about her but then we had a lot of other stuff to talk about and we never did talk about her and then I got busy with everything and I'm always asleep at night so I never went back to tell her that I'm okay. She called the police about me when I didn't show up. Joe talked to her and he told me that he let her know that I am safe. But I never got to talk to her again."

"How did this come up now?"

"At Tara's we are all going to stay up all night and I used to see Taina in the middle of the night. She works at the laundromat and she helped me do my laundry and she washed my hair for me every week and she used to trim my hair and nails for me. I used to take a bath in the laundry sink in the laundromat. Can you imagine me taking a bath in a laundry sink now?"

"No, I think you have outgrown laundry sinks. But it sounds like you would like to see Taina again?"

"I would like to say thank you to her. I knew her for longer than I knew Rabbi Cohen. She is why Rabbi Cohen thought I lived somewhere. She kept me clean and she kept my clothes clean. People thought I lived somewhere because I didn't look like a ragamuffin."

"Did she buy your clothes for you?"

"No, I bought my clothes. But she told me to buy all dark colors so they wouldn't go all grey. And she taught me Puerto Rican. It's useful sometimes to understand Puerto Rican."

"Sarah, you seem very happy today."

"I *am* happy. Does that mean the bad thoughts are sneaking outside the room and are going to come rampaging in and attack me?"

"Not necessarily. But I think Team Sarah should be on the lookout for rampaging feelings, just in case that's what they're doing."

"Okay, but they better not mess up Saturday night because I want to eat brownie sundaes."

"So long as you have your priorities straight. Shall we see if Maria is here?"

"You're notifying Team Sarah, aren't you?"

"I am just putting the team on standby."

"Am I too happy?"

"I'm not sure. But we have come this far and I don't want to have those feelings blindside you. I would rather that we be cautious."

"Why don't we just close the door so they can't get back in?"

"If only it worked that way. Shall we tell Maria together?"

"Okay."

December 18th   7:30 am

Team Sarah was activated and Sarah was assessed four times a day: before school, at lunch, during therapy and before bed. She attended the sleep over at Tara's and had a good time. Her mood remained very high for several days before it waned. It was Tuesday when Sarah woke up agitated.

Amber picked up that Sarah wasn't quite right at breakfast. "Hey, kid. What's going on?"

"I've just been having bad dreams. When I close my eyes I keep seeing them. How come the dreams aren't going away when I wake up?"

"Do you want to talk about the dreams?"

"Yeah, but I need to put them away until I get to Dr. Feingold. I need to talk to him about them and if I start to tell you about them, I'm not going to be able to go to school."

"Are you safe to go to school?"

"I don't want to die. I want to go to school but it's just hard to keep this contained. I wish I had a morning appointment but I think I can hold on until this afternoon."

Sarah was distracted at school. During art class the rest of the class was drawing portraits. Sarah put her pencil down and sat on her hands.

"Sarah, why aren't you drawing today?"

"I don't think it would be a very good idea right now. May I please read a book instead?"

With one look at Sarah's face, Mrs. Rifkin understood this was not an act of defiance or disinterest. "Would you prefer to be here or with Rabbi Cohen?"

"I can stay here. I just need to hold on for a few hours more and reading will help distract me."

"Let me know if that changes."

At lunch Rabbi Cohen checked in with Sarah.

"I'm okay but I don't want to walk alone to Dr. Feingold's. I know you have meeting with kids but do you think Rachel's mom is busy? Is it okay if I ask Rachel to call her mom and ask if they can walk me over there?"

"Let me talk to her. Then if it's okay, I will let Rachel call and ask." Rachel's mom was more than happy to help out. She even played along when Rachel called and asked if she and Rachel could walk Sarah to her doctor's after school. Rachel, bright and alert, had noticed Sarah struggling all day and felt very happy to have a way to help her friend. She was proud the she and her mom were able to share in a mitzvah.

December 18th   4:30 pm

Finally, Sarah was at Dr. Feingold's office. She said good bye to Rachel and her mom and thanked them at the door. "Sarah, I'm not sure what is going on but I want you to know that if you ever need an escort again, Rachel and I will be happy to take the walk with you."

Sarah walked into the office and sat down on the floor near Dr. Feingold.

"What's up? This isn't your usual spot."

"I might need you to hold me here like when I was having flashbacks."

"Are you having flashbacks?"

"No. These are different."

"Okay, tell me what's going on."

"I'm having bad dreams about when I killed Zeke."

"When did you start having them?"

"It started the night I was at Tara's."

"Okay."

"We stayed up really, really late and then Tara and Rachel fell asleep. I was lying in my sleeping bag on Tara's floor and everything was really quiet and really still. And when I fell asleep I dreamed about when I killed Zeke. The first dream wasn't too bad, but I keep having the dreams every night and now every time I close my eyes I see it again. It makes blinking very disruptive. I didn't draw in art today because I was afraid of what I would draw."

"How did your art teacher handle that?"

"She let me read a book."

"Why don't you tell me about what you see when you close your eyes?"

"I see Zeke's face when he opened his eyes after I stabbed him. His eyes were closed but he opened them and they got really wide and really surprised. It was like he was going to say something but then he couldn't. And then his face went blank and his eyes closed again. But then he did that shuddery thing and his eyes were open again and they were looking at me. They were scary. And now I keep seeing his face. I have to go back then, don't I?"

"I think we do need to visit back then. Are you ready to do this?"

"Yeah."

"You said that the nightmares started when you were at Tara's. Why did they start then?"

"It was really late at night at Tara's and quiet and even though we were in her bedroom the dark and quiet made me think about being outside in the summer with Zeke. You know that very dark and quiet time when almost all the animals are asleep. The bugs are all sleeping and nothing is flying around and all the frogs are asleep. There was a ton of stars but almost no moon that night. So we could see each other but not very much else."

"So being up late at night reminded you of the last night with Zeke and you have dreaming about then?

"Yeah"

"How are you feeling now?"

"I'm all shivery."

"Sarah, did anything happen in the dream that you haven't told me about yet?"

"No, it's all about killing him."

"Then what I would like you to do is to talk to me about what you were feeling during the dream."

"I see Zeke standing on the sleeping bag. He is telling me to kneel in front of him and get him ready for practice. She turned away slightly before continuing. "I was sore from all the work that night and it hurt when it touched me. Then he got mad at me and kind of snarled, "God, kid do I have to do everything around here?"

"What did you feel when he said that?"

"I'm angry. I do everything now. I'm the one earning all the money. He's giving it to other people and he isn't even getting food for us or a place to live. We're sleeping outdoors in the woods because of him."

Dr. Feingold noted the change of tense, but continued, "You're angry that you're not being taken care of."

"And frustrated"

"What did you do?"

"He started getting soft inside me. He said it was my fault that I'm becoming a lousy fuck. It really hurt my feelings and he didn't put stuff on it so it hurt going in my butt."

"So this was very painful for you."

"Yeah, Zeke didn't used to let me get hurt. He used to put stuff in me so that I would slide around him. But I was already sore from all the work and he wasn't using anything for me to slide. It hurt more than ever before." Sarah was near tears and her voice was almost whiny.

"But you did it."

"I had to. It was my job. But I wasn't liking it and I wanted to just be finished and go to sleep. I was wishing that he could stick his thing up his own butt."

"You wanted him to do that to himself."

"Yeah."

"Do you want to continue?"

Sarah nodded. "It didn't work anyway and he turned me back around and put it in my front and he exploded. He was sweating and he was panting and I was mad and I hurt everywhere and I was really tired and when he closed his eyes and had the last little explosion, I picked the knife up off the sleeping bag and I just lifted it up over my head and brought it down as hard as I could."

He squeezed her hands, "Okay, come back here for now."

Sarah opened her eyes and looked around.

"Are you okay?"

"Yeah." Sarah shivered and shuddered.

"Are you with me?"

Sarah took a few deep breaths, centering herself in the now. "I'm okay."

"What were you thinking when you picked up the knife?"

"Stop! I want to stop!"

"Was that what you were thinking then or is that what you want to do now?"

"That is what I was thinking. I was tired and sore and it just seemed futile and it was getting so much worse and I wanted it to stop."

"Had you thought about killing Zeke before?"

"No. The thought hadn't occurred to me before that night. It was when he picked the knife up and moved it that I thought about wishing I could stab him with it. I saw it in a picture in my head and then when he exploded I just did it." She took a shuddering breath. "I'm not really sure which of us was more surprised. The knife just went right into him all the way to the hilt. It didn't bleed at first but then I moved a little and there was this geyser that went up a couple of feet and I had blood on my face and in my hair and all over my clothes and Zeke's face. The geyser didn't last very long." She paused, and then continued matter-of-factly, "You know what I thought about?"

"What?"

"A whale spouting; it was like a whale spouting. And Zeke opened his eyes and he was going to say something and he moved his hand towards me like he was going to pick me up but then they just fell down and his eyes looked far away and then closed and I just sat there because I couldn't do anything. Then he did the shuddery thing and peed everywhere. And I closed my eyes and I was totally grossed out." She shuddered again. "He didn't move anymore. I just sat there for a little bit. I was blank. But then my stomach started hurting really bad and I had to get up and I pooped all over him and the sleeping bag. I felt sick all over. I used the clean part of the sleeping bag to try to wipe myself off but then I pooped again and I got it all over my legs. It smelled so bad that I threw up. I went to Zeke's bag and I got one of his shirts and I wiped myself off and I moved away from the mess."

She looked up and then continued. "I sat on a rock a little way away and I tried to calm down and decide what to do. My body was all out of control. And now my life was really out of control because I was pretty sure that Zeke was really dead. I was sort of expecting him to wake up but I knew he wasn't going to but I expected him to and if he did he was going to be very mad at me. Then I was just thinking that he would kill me if he found me. And anybody who found out about what I did would kill me. So I got my money from Zeke's pants and I got my back pack and I just walked away."

"What a very difficult night for you." Sarah nodded. "How are you feeling now?"

"Really tired."

"I am not surprised. You worked very hard today. You have talked about very difficult memories today. I am wondering how you feel inside having talked about them."

"Quiet and sort of empty; before I came here I felt like I was going to erupt. But I don't anymore. Now, I just want to eat some soup and go to sleep."

"Are you going to be okay at home tonight?"

"I think so. I'm a little worried about the dreams but I don't want to die now. Is it okay if I don't want to go to the hospital?"

"It's okay if you are safe at home."

"I don't want to do my homework tonight. Can I be excused from homework?"

"You are excused from homework. I want you to go home and have a nice bowl of soup and then take a nice bath or shower, get into clean PJ's and curl up with Cody."

"That sounds like a great plan."

"Let's share it with Maria."

December 19th   4:30 pm

Sarah was able to stay at home and despite the continued nightmares she was able to attend school the next day. She was less distracted but still not able to fully participate. She was anxious to get to Dr. Feingold's office that afternoon.

"How did you sleep last night?"

"Better, but I still had nightmares."

"Do you want to talk about the dreams?"

"They weren't picture dreams this time. They were scared confused trapped feeling dreams. They were just lots of scary feelings and everything was very dark."

"That was a very dark night in more ways than one. You talked about sitting on the rock after you killed Zeke. Can we talk about when you were sitting on the rock?"

"Okay."

"Tell me about the rock."

"The rock was about 2 feet tall and it's a table rock but just a bit slanted. It was about 3 feet square sort of. And…what do you call those flat stones that are sharp at the edge not round like granite?"

Dr. Feingold remained silent.

"That's what it was. And it was still warm from the day. This was nice because I was getting cold. Everything hurt on me. And I was shaking all over."

"What were you seeing?"

"Not very much; it was getting real dark and, I don't know, I was…I can't explain it."

"What were you seeing?"

"That's the weird thing. I couldn't see right. I could only see in front of me and even that was sort of cobwebby. So I just closed my eyes and I sat on the rock until I wasn't shaking so much anymore. But with my eyes closed I started getting scared. This is really stupid."

"What's stupid?"

"I was scared that when Zeke woke up he was going to be really mad at me for killing him and for messing up the sleeping bag and especially for messing up my dress and my sneakers. But I knew that dead is dead and you can't wake up from dead, but I still expected him to. I kept trying to see him to see if he was alive again yet. After a little while I stopped shaking and I was really tired. I wondered if I was going to just die too. But then I started thinking that if I fell asleep and Zeke woke up, he would kill me for sure. That was when I went back over and took his wallet and I checked his pants pockets and I took all the money and then I just started walking. Once I started walking I wasn't tired anymore. I wasn't anything anymore. I fell down a few times when I tripped but it didn't hurt and nothing hurt. And my thoughts just stopped. I just walked."

She stopped speaking for a moment before continuing. "Weird, isn't it? Remember when I had flashbacks and I swung on the swing?"

"Yes."

"Walking was like that. I wasn't attached to me. Except that when I was swinging I left my body and when I was walking I was just sort of dead."

"When did you start feeling again?"

"When I got into the river. The water was cold and I felt it and then I felt everything again and I could see clearly again like over to the sides. And the sun was up and the sky was a pretty blue. I washed everything off that I could and then I fell asleep on a rock in the sun. When I woke up my skin felt all stiff and I was sore again and I had a headache. And there were flies buzzing around me."

"So I went into the water again and washed more and then I waited until the water was clear again and I took a drink and then I started walking again. When I was walking I stopped feeling again. It was like I was in a numb bubble. Do you know where I was?"

"No, do you?"

"No. I'm not really sure how many days I walked for, either. I ate berries and leaves and I drank water in the streams but I don't remember how many days it was. Is talking about this going to make my dreams go away?"

"It should help. If you look at what happened when you are awake, your mind won't need to try to deal with it when you are asleep."

"I don't like thinking about it. It was scary and confusing. I didn't like being in the woods by myself. I was afraid that a bear would kill me. And then the bear would change into Zeke."

"Did you see a bear?"

"No, no bears. Lots of deer and raccoons and an opossum with baby opossums and I saw an owl. He scared me because he hooted from right behind me. Then another owl flew right by my head and I saw it catch a mouse and eat it like 20 feet away from me. That was kind of cool but gross. And a porcupine wandered across the path. I heard it making noise in the underbrush and I stopped and he just wandered across. He was almost as big as me. I thought porcupines were little. They are huge. Did you ever see a wild porcupine?"

"No, I've only seen them in the zoos."

"Trust me; you don't really want to meet one in the woods."

"I'll trust you on that. How are you feeling now?"

"Kind of excited; I liked seeing the animals. That part was fun. I would hear a noise and I would crouch down and stay really still and just wait until the animal came out. It was always a relief when it was an animal because it wasn't Zeke and it wasn't a bear. I did see a fox one time. It saw me and we looked at each other for a few minutes and then it just left."

"How did do find your way out?"

"I heard a train whistle and when I came to a clearing on the side of a hill I could see the train tracks. So I went towards them and I walked in the woods by the tracks until I came to a station."

"Why did you come to New York City?"

"It's where the train went."

"So, you didn't have a plan?"

"Plan? Are you kidding? I wasn't even thinking very much."

"When did you stop talking?"

"I didn't know that I had until the ticket taker man talked to me. He asked me where I was going and I couldn't answer him. I mean, I didn't know where I was going so I handed him a twenty dollar bill and he said Grand Central? And I just nodded because I couldn't say yes. He said that I was pretty young to be riding alone so I pointed to a lady that was a few seats behind me. He gave me a ticket and money and just went on."

"That's when I knew I couldn't talk. You know what's weird?"

"What?"

"It didn't matter that I couldn't talk. I wasn't worried about it. I just accepted it as the way it was. You'd think that I would be freaked out but I wasn't. I guess because I was in my numb bubble."

"Do you know why you couldn't talk?"

"I just figured that if I talked I would die. But it still happens that when I get really upset I can't talk. But now I can text. At least I can find words in my head now. Before, I didn't have words in my head. Just pictures. I could understand words so I knew what people we saying to me but I couldn't answer them in words. I just had pictures in my head."

"When did you start getting words?"

"When I was at the temple; when I was learning the prayers, they were in Hebrew so I didn't have pictures to go with them so I kept the sounds in my head and then they turned into words and I learned what they meant and as I learned the Hebrew words, the English words came back." She paused, "Rabbi Cohen made your job a lot easier, didn't he?"

"He sure did."

"What if I still didn't have any words in my head when I went to the hospital the first time? What would you do?"

"We would have started with finding your words. When did you know that you could talk again?"

"When you told me I could. That security guard that caught me told me that I couldn't get away and then you told me that I could talk. So I figured that it must be time for me to die and I decided to be brave and face my death."

"It didn't turn out that way, did it?"

"Nope. You were right. Talking is better than not talking."

"How come I didn't have bad dreams when I lived alone and now I have them?"

"Because now you're ready to look at what happened. Your dreams are your mind sending messages that you are ready to deal with it now."

"Are they going to stop now that I told you what happened?"

"They will stop when you are finished dealing with what happened. Sarah, I think that it's only fair for me to tell you that from time to time in your life, the dreams may come back. If or when they do, it means that you need to take another look at what happened because your mind is ready for you to understand it differently."

"But if we talk about it now, how come it will come back?"

"You may have them again because you are growing and as you grow, you will understand things differently. They may be uncomfortable and disruptive but I want you to think of them as a sign that you are growing in a new way."

"Does this growing have anything to do with the growing I am doing now?"

"What do you mean?"

"Well, I went to the doctor's last week and I gained five pounds and we had to get me new clothes and they aren't from the kids department anymore."

"How do you feel about that?"

"Okay, I guess. Is it okay to talk about this with you?"

"Yes, you can talk to me about anything you want and if something is concerning you, it is important that you talk about it."

"Even if you're a man doctor?"

"Would you prefer that you have a female doctor?"

"Sometimes, I wish you were a female doctor but I don't want a different doctor. I want you to be my doctor. But I wasn't sure if it's okay."

"It is okay. I can handle whatever you want to talk about."

"I have a question."

"Okay."

"Well, I'm kind of, well,"

"Is this embarrassing for you to talk about?"

"Yeah, sort of. Alright, I'm just going to say it. I'm getting boobs, sort of."

"And?"

"Well, Zeke and all those people that I did stuff with, they liked me because I looked like a little girl didn't they?"

"Yes, they were attracted to a little girl body."

"So, Zeke wouldn't like me anymore, would he?"

"No, pedophiles will no longer be attracted to you."

"So, I don't have to worry anymore, right? Getting boobs is good because now I'm free."

"Sarah, I wish I could tell you that all the bad that could possibly happen is done and you don't have to worry ever again about someone hurting you."

"It's not over, is it?"

"There are many different people in the world. The group of people that was attracted to your little girl body aren't going to want your early pubescent body, but there is a group of people that would find it very attractive, and as you get older and more developed, well then, there is another group that finds that attractive."

"I can't win for losing."

"Yes, you can. You now know that there are such people and we're going to work to keep you safe from them."

"So nothing bad will happen to me?"

"No one can guarantee that for anyone. But Team Sarah is going to do everything possible to reduce the likelihood of anything happening and we are going to give you tools to help you recognize danger, avoid it when you can, and fight it if you have to."

"What would Zeke do with me if I was still with Zeke?"

"I don't know. What do you think that he would do with you?"

"I think he would have me do fallatio on him and then instead of doing intercourse he would stick a knife in my vagina and cut me all up inside and then leave me to die."

"That is a pretty specific thought."

"Yeah, but it fits him. If I wasn't worth anything to him anymore, he would make me hurt. He was nice to me when I was really little because I was more valuable if I wasn't torn. He used to talk about how important it was that no one tears me inside. But those last nights, I was bleeding from both holes and Zeke didn't care. I think he would have enjoyed making me hurt inside."

"How are you feeling right now?"

"I'm kind of sad because that really is what he would do and kind of glad he isn't here to do it. Can I ask another question about me growing up?"

"Okay."

"Remember when you said that you won't do practice stuff with me because I was a little girl?"

"Yes."

"Well?"

"Sarah, I will not have sex with you now or ever. I do not have sex with my patients. I don't do it when they are children or when they are adolescents or even when they are all grown up and not my patients anymore."

"What if you love them?"

"Never do I have sex of any sort with a patient. I don't have sex if I love them or if I dislike them. I don't even have sex with them if they want me to. I don't have sex with a patient."

"Did you take lessons from Dr. Seuss? You sound like Sam I am."

"I guess I did, didn't I?"

"Yeah, but I get it, sort of."

"But not really?"

"Remember I told you that I knew Zeke was dead but I kept watching for him to get up and be alive again?"

"Yeah,"

"Same thing."

"You believe it in your head but not in your heart?"

"No, I know it in my brain and in my heart, but my body doesn't get it. It keeps expecting it to happen. It always expects it with everyone. Is that ever going to change?"

"Has it changed since we started working together?"

"It isn't as much now. So, yeah, it's a little better. I still think about doing it."

"With all guys or just some guys?"

"Just the ones I know. It was weird when I started thinking about doing it with Rachel's dad."

"Did Rachel's dad do anything to indicate that he wanted to do it with you?"

"No. He's really nice and we were playing in the living room when he came home from work and he came over and ruffled Rachel's hair and kissed the top of her forehead when she looked up and I just had this thought that he wouldn't be bad to have sex with."

"Do you want to have sex with him?"

"No, but it wouldn't be bad."

"Why not?"

"Because he's clean and gentle. I don't think that if he had sex with me that he would hurt me."

"Do you think that he would have sex with you?"

"I don't know; I didn't ask him."

"Sarah, I am going to make a rule as Team Sarah Captain. You are not allowed to have sex with anyone until you are at least 16. And I reserve the right to change that to higher when you turn 16."

"What if they want me to?"

"Then you can tell them that you aren't allowed to and you are to tell me about it."

"So, no sex with Rachel's dad if he wants to?"

"How long have you been having thoughts about having sex with men that you know?"

"When I was in the hospital it started. When I lived on my own I didn't think about it but now I do all the time. Tara talking about kissing guys doesn't really help because she thinks about kissing them but then I start getting pictures about what it would be like to do fallatio on them and what it would be like to have intercourse with them."

"Sarah, are you thinking about the mechanics of it or do you get pleasure from the thoughts?"

"What do you mean do I get pleasure from them? They're just pictures in my head. They're just there."

"So when you think about having intercourse with someone, does it make your vagina feel different?"

"No, is it supposed to?"

"At some point it may. I just want you to know that if it happens it is normal and you still are not allowed to have sex with the person."

"Okay. Do you want to explain that?"

"Let's just say that if or when it happens, you'll know it."

"Are you saying that someday, I might actually want to have sex with someone instead of just thinking about what it would be like if I had to?"

"Yes, and for now, even if you want to, don't do it."

December 20th

Amber had prepared spaghetti and meatballs and was finishing setting the table when Maria and Sarah arrived home. "Hi, great timing. Dinner is just about ready."

"It smells great!" Maria and Amber embraced as Sarah put her backpack in her room.

"Hey kid, how was school today?"

"Micah got in trouble in math."

"You sound happy about that."

"Well, it was really funny."

"Micah getting in trouble is funny?"

"Not him getting in trouble, how he got in trouble. Do we have parmesan cheese?

"In the fridge."

"I think there's a story here: let's hear it."

"Okay, in math we are doing algebra and have to solve for x but sometimes we've been saying that we have to find x. Well, today we had a whole bunch of find x problems and Micah, he's been kind of grumbly lately, said, 'If x would just freaking stay next to w we wouldn't have to keep finding it.'"

Maria and Amber burst out laughing.

"Yeah, that's what Rachel and I did. And Mrs. Rifkin heard him, too. She didn't laugh. Micah had to stay after school.

"What do you think is going to happen to him?"

"Knowing Mrs. Rifkin, he will have to talk about what's wrong. Micah is usually really quiet and respectful. It isn't like him to mouth off but it was really funny when he said that."

"Do you know what's wrong with Micah?"

"Yeah, his grandpa is sick and he's worried about him. His mom has been crying when she thinks he isn't around and he thinks his grandpa is going to die. He said he is going to miss him because he liked playing games and doing stuff with him."

"That's sad."

"Yeah, except I don't know what it is like to have a grandpa. I'm not going to have grandparents am I?"

Maria looked at Amber and asked, "Well, since you brought that up, how would you feel about going to my parents' house for Christmas?"

"Okay, I guess. What do I have to do?"

"Just be your delightful self. I've already bought presents for everyone and we will give them from you too. It just seemed wrong to have you buy presents for people you've never met."

"Okay. When do we go?"

"Christmas morning we'll take the Path Train over and my dad will pick us up at the station."

"Is it okay to celebrate Christmas if I'm Jewish?"

"Celebrating and being with people is always okay. Besides, Christmas is the celebration of the birth of Jesus and he was a Jewish kid."

"He was?"

"He was."

December 26th   4:30 pm

"We have to talk about something that happened on Christmas."

"Okay."

"We went to Maria's parent's house for Christmas day. They live in New Jersey so we took the PATH Train over and her dad picked us up at the station. Did you know they had to get permission to take me with them?"

"Because it's out of state?"

"Yeah. We could drive 8 hours to Buffalo and it would be fine but they needed permission to go 30 minutes away."

"Is this what we need to talk about?"

"No, I'm procrastinating. Okay, so we got to her parents' house and her sister and brother were there along with their families. It was a lot of people. If someone is Maria's nephew, are they my cousin?"

"Technically, they would be your foster cousins."

"Well, my foster cousin Brian is eight and I don't like him very much."

"Why not?"

"He is really greedy. He just wanted to know what we brought him and when we gave him his present he wasn't very happy about it."

"What did you get him?"

"Well, Maria said that his parents were getting him a Wii and a TV for his room so we got him Wii baseball. He wanted to know why he only got one game and said this was the worst Christmas ever because he only got a 42" TV and not a 50" and he only got four games for his Wii. And he said he got stupid clothes."

"How did this make you feel?"

"Angry."

"Can you explain why you felt angry?"

"I was thinking that he is eight and if I'm twelve, then I was his age when I killed Zeke. He's complaining that he only got a 42 inch TV. I was worried about finding food and a place to stay dry. He yelled at his dad that he hates him and he is the worst dad in the world. I don't think he's even in the running for the worst dad award."

"What did you do?"

"I wanted to really yell at him. I wanted to tell him how totally clueless he was. But that would have really wrecked Christmas for everyone and he still would have been clueless."

"So what did you do?"

"I asked to be excused and I went outside. Amber suggested that we take a walk around the block and she helped me cool off. But I cried."

"You look like you are going to cry now."

"It's not fair. How come everything was so bad when I was eight? I shouldn't've had to kill Zeke. I shouldn't've had to have intercourse all the time. I was just a little kid. Zeke should have been buying me Wii baseball, not pretty work dresses. It's not fair. He thinks chores are hard because he has to put his clothes in the hamper. He doesn't have to find and cook all his own food or worry about getting caught in the fountains picking up the change. He didn't have to learn the city all by himself. He is a lazy, selfish, greedy jerk."

"And you really envy his life, don't you?"

"Yeah, how come he has it so easy and I had it so hard? Am I really a bad person and do I need to be punished?"

"Do you think you're a bad person who needs to be punished?"

"I don't think I'm Christian enough to believe that."

"What?" Dr. Feingold sat up, startled by her anti-Christian sentiment. "Where did that come from?"

"The people on street— you know the people who want to know if you've been saved?"

"I know the ones you are talking about."

"They always talk about how you are going to be punished and that bad things happen because you were sinful. Well, I wasn't sinful. I was a little kid. And that kind of takes us to the other thing I really have to talk to you about."

"Oh."

"Maria has a niece named Gretchen. Gretchen is two and a half and she's still wearing diapers and she wet her diaper and Maria offered to change her. I went with her and watched.

When Maria took Gretchen's diaper off and wiped her with the baby wipes, I remembered Zeke putting his finger inside of me. I wanted to try it."

"You wanted to put your finger in Gretchen?"

Sarah nodded.

"What happened?"

"Maria looked up from Gretchen and she looked at me and asked me what I was thinking about. I could hardly talk and I pointed to Gretchen and Maria got the idea I think because she said that having thoughts about doing to others what I had been through was very common. But that I was not allowed to act on those thoughts and that she and Amber would help me to not do something that I would feel very bad about. And she put a clean diaper on Gretchen and sent her back to the living room."

"Then she just held me and I cried again. Amber came and checked on us and they asked if I needed to go home. I told them that I could hold it together. But it was just seeing kids that were those ages that really made me have a lot of feelings."

"We made it through dinner and then escaped. I think Maria told her mom that I was having a tough time because they were very nice but sort of too nice. Like we pity you but we don't really know you," she sighed at the memory of the excursion.

"It was a tough day."

"I really wanted to touch Gretchen. I keep thinking about it. I keep thinking about what it would feel like to put my finger in her. Would I feel like Zeke felt? Does it feel good to put things inside little children? You know what Maria didn't do?"

"What?"

"She didn't stretch Gretchen's legs."

"What do you mean?"

"There was a baby that came over sometimes and when Zeke changed her diaper he would take her feet and push them apart as far as they would go and then he would bend her knees and bring her feet together and her knees to the bed. He called them stretches. Stretches were fun and he tickled her and he laughed a lot. He played a game with his finger. His finger would move around hide and she had to find it and he would put it inside her and she had to point to his hand

and it would come back out again. It was almost like peek-a-boo. I forgot all about that until I saw Gretchen.

"How do you feel now about touching a little child?"

"I really want to do it. Remember how the sad feelings used to be sitting over in the corner?"

"Yeah."

"Well, these are bad feelings and they keep jumping up in front of my face."

"So you are telling me that you are not safe to be with small children."

"I wouldn't trust me. Maria said that I will not be accepting any babysitting jobs and that she is going to let Rabbi Cohen know that I am not to ever be alone with the little kids at school. I can still go to Rachel and Tara's because they don't have little kids there. Maria says that I am not a bad person. So how come I am having really bad thoughts?"

"Why do think you are having really bad thoughts?"

"I think it's your fault."

"Why?"

"It's your fault because when I come here I have to think about stuff and talk about stuff and if I think about it, and talk about it, then it's more real and then I have more feelings and more thoughts. So, I wouldn't have these thoughts if I wasn't coming here. I wouldn't even have very many words if I wasn't coming here and I would be all frozen inside and I wouldn't have feelings. So it's all your fault."

"You don't want to own these feelings?"

"No; they are horrible feelings. Only a mean horrible person would want to do that to a little tiny kid. I don't want to be a horrible person."

"You are not a horrible person. You are trying to understand why Zeke did what he did. It is important that you remember that thoughts and actions are very different. You can have any thoughts or feelings that you have. Have you acted on those thoughts?"

"No. I haven't had a chance to. Maria and Amber kept Gretchen away from me and I don't have any other kids around."

"Would you act on these thoughts if you could?"

"I don't think I could stop myself if I had the opportunity. Am I a pedophile?"

"No. You are working out the abuse you went through. It sounds like Amber and Maria are working to keep other kids safe while you and I work this through."

"Are we going to get through this and the feelings will go away?"

"Sarah, we will get through this, too. We need to talk about when you want to do things to other kids and what you want to do. But with enough work, we will get through this."

"I don't think I made a great impression on Maria's family. They probably think that I am a real nut job."

"I think that they will get over it. Remember, Amber and Maria had you alone when you cried. Maria's family didn't see it."

"Yeah, they didn't see the worst of it. But I have to admit, I wasn't my chipper self of late."

"You can't always be your chipper self. Why don't I touch base with Maria tonight before you leave?"

"Do you want me to stay or to wait in the waiting room?"

"How about if you wait in the waiting room?"

"I'll do my homework."

Maria was invited into the doctor's office.

"Sarah says you had an interesting Christmas."

"She told you about wanting to touch my niece?"

"She did and she told me that you redirected her and ensured your niece's safety and are setting up rules to ensure she does not have access to children."

"Am I over-reacting?"

"Do you think you're over-reacting?"

"Part of me says no, and part of me does not want to think that Sarah could actually hurt another child."

"Trust your gut. Given the opportunity, right now, Sarah would violate a child. She knows she would and she hates that she would but nonetheless, she would do it if she had the opportunity. You're right to ensure that she doesn't. She would feel awful if she hurt another child and we don't need another abused child in the world."

He continued, "I have reinforced the difference between thoughts and actions. So long as we are able to contain her actions, we're okay and so is she. Are there any other concerns that you have?"

"No. I almost wish we hadn't gone out to my parents. I didn't expect her to have so much trouble with meeting my niece and nephew."

"You can't protect her from everything that is going to trigger memories, nor should you. If she's going to recover, she has to remember and deal with those memories. All things considered, she did very well. She had memories but not flashbacks. She was able to contain her feelings and express them verbally and appropriately and she was able to remain safe and not abuse anyone else. I would say she had a great day. You and Amber have created a wonderful support system for her. You should be very proud of yourselves and her."

"Thanks, Doc. I needed the pep talk."

December 27th   4:30 pm

Sarah had a second bag with her. "Cody's mad at me and he wanted to come here to talk to you."

"Hello, Cody. I haven't seen you for a long time."

"He doesn't want to live with me anymore."

"Did something happen last night?"

"I couldn't help it."

"Can you tell me what you did?"

Sarah dropped her voice to a whisper, "I put my finger inside Cody."

"How did you feel?"

"Sort of weird. Sort of excited and I wanted to keep putting it in him but I wanted to put my finger in me too. But then Cody started to cry and I felt bad and I stopped. He said that he wanted to come here today and talk to you about it."

"So, let me get this straight. Cody did not like you putting your finger inside of him, but if I'm guessing right, you still want to do just that."

"Yeah, but he doesn't want me to and I don't want to hurt him."

"You're in a tough place. You want to gratify your own desires without hurting anyone else."

"Yeah. Will you tell Cody that it's his job to let me touch him?"

"Like it was your job for you to let Zeke touch you?"

"I'll be nicer than Zeke."

"Do you think that being nice is a factor?"

"No, but I wish it was."

"You need to explore what it would feel like to penetrate a child just like Zeke penetrated you."

"But I can't even go near a child and even Cody won't let me."

"Did you ask Cody why he doesn't want you to penetrate him?"

"He said he's not that kind of bear. He likes to be held and he likes to sleep with me but he doesn't like to have things inside him. You know what the problem is?"

"What?"

"I didn't start putting things inside Cody until now. He knows the difference."

"What difference?"

"The difference between how Rachel's dad touches Rachel and how Zeke touched me. Rachel's dad hugs her all the time and he kisses her and he picks her up. But he doesn't have her sit on his lap and put his finger inside of her like Zeke did. Well, if I trained Cody like Zeke trained me, then he would think that my doing it was just normal and he would be okay with it. But I treated him like Rachel's dad treats Rachel. I think Rachel would freak out if her dad ever put his finger inside of her."

"So you think that you didn't train Cody properly?"

"He isn't properly trained to let me do that to him."

"So what do you think we should do about you and Cody?"

"Will you tell him that it's part of his job?"

"No. I think he is expressing how you feel about actually engaging in penetration."

"What do you mean?"

"Sarah, Cody is your bear and you are the one who gives him his feelings, so if Cody tells you that he doesn't want to be penetrated, perhaps that is a way of saying that you see what you want to do as wrong."

"I don't know what to do. I don't want to hurt Cody but I want to see what it feels like."

"I may have a solution."

"What?"

"How about if we used a therapy doll? They are designed to let you work out feelings like this without hurting Cody or any children."

"So, it's okay to try it on the therapy doll?"

"That's what she is here for. Shall I get her for you?"

Sarah nodded and Dr. Feingold opened a cabinet and brought out an anatomically correct doll in a blue dress. He laid it on the ottoman in front of Sarah. Sarah just looked at the doll without touching it.

"What are you feeling?"

"Scared."

"Can you talk to me about the scared feelings?"

"I think she must feel scared. Did you tell her what I'm going to do to her?"

"No, I thought I would let you talk to her about it."

Sarah stared at the doll. She started to tear up and asked, "Can I have Cody?"

He handed Cody to her and she held him tight and began crying in earnest. "I'm sorry. I wanted to know. I don't want you to hate me. I want you to still be my bear. Please still be my bear."

"You feel pretty bad about hurting Cody."

Sarah nodded though her tears.

"It sounds like you really don't want to hurt someone. You would feel very badly if you touched a child, wouldn't you?"

Sarah nodded. "I think it would be even worse than Cody."

"I think you're right." Sarah's tears were spent. She wiped her eyes on her sleeve, then wiped the tears off of Cody. "Cody got a little wet."

"I imagine he has gotten wet before."

"Yeah, he doesn't usually mind. Do you think that he'll come home with me?"

"You'll have to ask him."

"Will you come back and still be my bear?" She held Cody on the edge of the ottoman facing her. He sat quietly, as bears do. He was waiting.

"If I promise not to do that again will you be my bear again?" Cody continued to sit quietly on the ottoman.

"And get you honey graham crackers for dinner tonight?" Cody nodded and Sarah breathed a big sigh of relief and hugged the bear that had been her companion for years.

"You look very relieved."

"I am. I was afraid he was going to move out on me."

"I think we've done enough work for today. But I'm going to leave the therapy doll out when you are here so if you want to work with her, you can."

"Okay. Maybe we can do it when Cody isn't here. I think it might upset him."

"You need to take good care of your bear."

"What is her name?"

"What do want her name to be?"

"She doesn't already have one?"

"If she is doing therapy with you, you get to name her if you wish. She is all about your therapy." Sarah looked at the doll for a few minutes and then she started to look sleepy. As much as Dr. Feingold wanted to explore where she was headed, there wasn't enough time and she had already done enough therapy for one session.

"Why don't I put her over here in this bed and let her sleep until tomorrow afternoon?"

"Okay. Is it time for Maria?"

"Just about."

"Are you going to tell her that Cody was mad at me?"

"I was thinking that I would let you tell her about it if you choose. How are you feeling now?"

"Tired. I want to just go to bed after dinner."

They went to the waiting room and met Maria as she was coming in the door. She looked at Sarah and then Dr. Feingold. "Is she okay?"

"Just tired. She has requested dinner and bed."

Sarah looked at Maria and asked, "Can we take a taxi home?"

"Tough day, huh?"

"Yeah, you could say that. I just want pizza and to go to sleep."

"Let me call Amber and see what we can do about that."

December 28th   4:30 pm

Sarah arrived for her next session without Cody.

"How was last night?"

"Cody was exhausted too. We went to bed at 7:00 and slept all night. Cody wanted to stay home today. He said that if I was going to violate that doll, he wasn't going to watch."

"He has some strong feelings about this."

"Yeah, he doesn't want me to do it even if it is a therapy doll."

"Did he say why?"

"He said that if I do it to the doll, then where will I draw the line? Will I go to FAO Schwartz and molest all the stuffed animals there? What about live animals? And if I do it to a doll that looks like a child, will I do it to a real child?"

"You are very scared of these feelings, aren't you?"

Sarah nodded.

"You don't want to become like Zeke."

She shook her head.

"And you are afraid that if we explore these feelings, we will not be able to control them?"

She nodded.

"They must be very big feelings."

Sarah nodded again.

"This wasn't the first time you've had these feelings, is it?"

She shook her head.

"When did you feel them before?"

"When I used to play at the playground I would watch the little kids in the sandbox and think about putting things inside of them. And when I saw kids eating popsicles I thought about them sucking on my penis. But it always confused me because I don't have one so I didn't understand what I was thinking."

"You were relating your experience to them and you were seeing yourself as Zeke."

"Am I really weird?"

"No, you are really normal. We have a term for what you are going through. Would you like to know what it is?"

Sarah nodded.

"You are identifying with your abuser. You are trying to sort out why Zeke did what he did."

"So having these feelings is a good thing?"

"Feelings just are; they aren't good or bad. What you do with a feeling is what is good or bad. If you touch a child to explore these feelings, that would be very bad. However, if you work in this office to explore these feelings, that is good. It is important that you understand the feelings and deal with them so that they don't get explored in an inappropriate way."

"So touching the doll is really okay?"

"It is really okay if you want to touch the doll. It is a tool for you to use if you chose to."

"It's still scary."

"These are scary feelings to have. Do you want to hold the doll?"

She nodded and he placed the doll in her arms. She sat with her back against the couch and the doll on her lap facing her. She looked at a loss as to what to do.

"Did you ever have a doll when you were little?"

"I don't remember one. What do regular kids do with dolls?"

"They pretend that they are babies and they take care of them. They dress them and change their diapers and feed them and hold them and put them to sleep and play games with them."

"Why?"

"Because it is how they learn how to take care of people and how to get practice with daily life skills. Sarah, you look very sleepy. What are you feeling?"

"I'm really tired."

"Sarah, are you still scared?"

"Yeah."

"Tell me about the scared."

"Even if doesn't make sense?"

"Yes, even if it doesn't make sense."

"What if I was the doll and I lived here; if I went to sleep would you put your finger in me?"

"You're worried that this might not be a safe place for you if I will let you penetrate the doll."

Sarah nodded.

"Sarah, you aren't the doll and I will not let someone penetrate you."

"But you would let me hurt the doll."

"You don't see a difference, do you?"

Sarah shook her head.

"For you, dolls and bears all have thoughts and feelings, don't they?"

Sarah nodded.

"So, this must have been very confusing that I would let you hurt a doll with feelings."

Sarah nodded.

"Sarah, I am very proud of you."

"Why?"

"Because even though you wanted to touch inside something and even though I said you could touch the doll inside, you still listened to your own sense of what is right and didn't do it."

"It's okay."

"Yes Sarah, it is okay. How does the doll feel about it?"

"She is a little mad at you and she is a little mad at me."

"Why is she mad at me?"

"Because you would have let me touch her."

"Why is she a little mad at you?"

"Because she is a therapy doll and I'm supposed to touch her so I work it out and I won't do it."

"So she is mad at me for letting you touch her and mad at you for not doing it?"

Sarah nodded. "You just can't please some dolls. Sometimes it is better to put them in the corner and not even try."

"Sarah, you do know that we will be revisiting this at some point, when you are ready."

"Yeah, I kind of figured. But I don't think I'm ready yet."

December 29th   5:00 pm

Sarah was at Rachel's house on Saturday afternoon. She and Rachel were helping to make dinner.

"How come your kitchen isn't kosher?"

Rachel's mother explained, "Keeping kosher is not a part of Judaism that holds meaning for me or Rachel's father. So, we don't keep kosher."

"So, I'm not the only one at school who doesn't live in a kosher home?"

"No, Sarah, you're not the only one. Very few Reform Jews actually keep kosher."

"Then how come the Temple is kosher?"

"It is kosher so that it is ready for anyone who does keep kosher. We don't want to exclude anyone, so everyone respects the kosher rules in the Temple."

"That makes sense. Thanks for explaining it. You know what the best part of not being kosher is?"

"What?"

"Bacon. I think I could do everything else okay, but I would really miss eating bacon. Rachel, what is the most non-kosher thing you can think of?"

"BLT with mayo."

"Shrimp and lobster bisque."

"Cheeseburgers with mayo."

"Hey, you know how you can have kosher pigs?"

Rachel's mom interjected, "Girls, pigs are never kosher."

"But if you made pigs in a blanket with Hebrew Nationals, they would be kosher pigs." Rachel and Sarah were rolling on the floor laughing when Rachel's father came home.

"What's so funny?"

"We figured out how to make kosher pigs!"

He looked at his wife and the two girls on the floor and asked, "Do I want to know this?"

Rachel stood up to give him a hug and said, "You wrap Hebrew Nationals in crescent rolls and make kosher pigs in a blanket." He just shook his head and walked out of the room.

Sarah's evening at Rachel's was a joyful respite from the work she had been doing with Dr. Feingold. During her time with Rachel and her family, she was just a normal giggly twelve year old.

January 10th   2:00 pm

Sarah was meeting with Rabbi Cohen for her bat mitzvah preparation. "Rabbi Cohen, I looked up what my reading is supposed to be for my bat mitzvah."

"Yes, what did you find?"

"I am supposed to read Leviticus 16 through 20."

"Are you worried that it is too much to read?"

"No, it's a lot but that isn't it." She looked up at him, "You know what it is. You're going to make me say it, aren't you?"

"Yes, you are going to be an adult soon and that means that you need to stand up for yourself and speak for yourself."

"Part of it is going to be weird to read out loud."

"So, you have read your portion."

"Yeah, I've read it. How long have you known that this would be my portion?"

"Since you chose your birthday."

"How come you didn't tell me?"

"Because no one else can choose their birthday and I did not want you to change yours because you were worried about something you might have to do."

"You think I would have wimped out if I had the choice?"

"I think that last summer you were not ready to face this."

"What about now?"

"You read the portion and you are here talking about it. I would say you have grown since last summer."

"You know what we learned about in English?"

"What?"

"Irony. I think that me reading this portion is very ironic."

"You know what I think?"

"What?"

"I think that it is poignant."

"What does poignant mean?"

"Sarah, the reason that you were able to be hurt by people was because you were a child and did not know the proper rules. Who better to read this portion as they become an adult than a child who was so affected by the violation of these rules as a child?"

"You make a good point. I hadn't thought about it that way."

"How had you thought about it?"

"I thought about standing up in front of everyone and talking about sex."

"God is very clear about who a person should and should not be with in that way. He made those rules because he wants individuals and the community to be happy and healthy."

"All the rules are for men."

"That is because the Bible was written for a male audience."

"Do the same rules apply to women?"

"Yes."

"What about Maria and Amber?"

"We now recognize what people a long time ago did not. Sometimes, two people love each other and share their lives together like Maria and Amber. If God made them that way, who are we to say that it's wrong? But if a person is made to be with the opposite gender and sleeps with his own, that is not acceptable."

"Do people do that?"

"Unfortunately yes, and you can imagine how disruptive it is to all the people involved. That creates turmoil and the purpose of the rules is to avoid turmoil."

"I get it. So, the rules are there to make life easier in the long run."

"Exactly. And the Torah talks about rules governing all parts of life. From how we get up and when and what we eat to how we grow and prepare our food and how we keep our bodies clean and healthy."

"Why is it we don't follow all the rules anymore?"

"You need to look at what makes sense for you. Some people do not eat pork and some people do now. The Torah says that we don't eat pork because although pigs have a fully cloven foot they don't chew their cud. When the Torah was written, eating pork was not a very safe thing to do. The pigs ate from the garbage pits and carried disease. There is very little health risk from eating pork in the United States now, so some people say the rule is outdated. Other people say that not eating pork is part of what makes us Jewish; it is our tradition. You need to decide what makes sense to you."

He paused until Sarah looked up at him. "I want to get back to your reading. No one reads five chapters during their bat mitzvah. You only need to read one. You may read any one of the five that you choose. "

"I don't have to read 18?"

"No, you don't need to read 18."

"I like 19 a lot better."

"Would you like to read 19 for your reading?"

"Yes, I want to read 19. It talks about what Zeke did but it isn't all about sex."

"Sarah, I am very proud of you."

"Why?"

"Because you recognized how something would make you feel and you made a decision that you would feel comfortable with. You did what was right for you, not what you thought was expected. That is what being an adult is about."

Sarah sat quietly, absorbing his words. "Now shall we go over the text in Hebrew and make sure you know all the words?"

They were in the final preparation mode. Sarah and Rabbi Cohen began holding their sessions completely in Hebrew to help Sarah to read and speak more fluently.

January 19th   4:30 pm

School was going well in January. Her work with Dr. Feingold was proceeding and Sarah was finding herself in a new way. She was mastering the changes in her body and dealing well with her past.

"I had to go get more vaccines this morning."

"How is your arm?"

"Sore. I wish Zeke had me vaccinated when I was little but the doctor said that some of my vaccines are for kids my age. Maria and the doctor had to talk to me about one of the vaccines."

"Which one?"

"Gardasil."

"What did you talk about?"

"I've already been exposed to HPV. They found it last summer when the doctor tested inside me. But my doctor said that they are going to give me Gardasil anyway because there are more kinds of HPV and I may not have been exposed to some of them that it protects for. Did you know that I might get cervical cancer?"

"Yes, I knew that you were exposed to HPV and that is one of the causes of cervical cancer."

"How come you didn't tell me?"

"We've had a few more pressing issues. Did the doctor tell you what you need to do?"

"Yeah, I am getting the Gardasil and I need to have a pap smear every year to make sure that I am okay."

"She said that they are going to start my pap smears now because I may have been exposed the first time I had intercourse and that was a long time ago. She didn't have to do it this time because they did it last summer. Maria talked to Theresa and I'm going to have a gynecologist and a pediatrician. Maria said that is an unusual combination. Can I have a lady gynecologist like last summer? That lady was nice."

"I'll talk to Maria."

"If I have the Gardasil, do I still have to have the no sex until I am 16 rule?"

"Gardasil does not give you permission to have sex, nor does it make you ready to have sex. It protects your life so that when you are ready, you can do it with one less worry."

"Humph."

"Humph what?"

"That's what Maria said too."

Sarah laughed as a small pillow gently grazed her head. It was rare, playful moment.

February 19th   1:20 pm

It was February vacation and Sarah was spending the day at Tara's. They had been to the library in the morning but were now playing a game in the living room with the TV on Nick. Sarah was half paying attention to the TV and watching in between chess moves. Sarah was a strategic player and Tara an impulsive player, so the game required Sarah to have numerous contingency plans, but she was none the less aware of the show with lots of kids on the TV. She started paying attention when she heard one of the girls being called Marcia. When Jan exclaimed with famous exasperation, "Marcia, Marcia, Marcia," Sarah stared and began to shut down. Tara noticed when Sarah did not respond to her move. "Hey, it's your turn."

"Sarah? Sarah? Mom there's something wrong with Sarah!" Tara's mom knew that tone that every mother knows and fears, the one that says *this isn't right.* She was in the living room instantly. Tara pointed to Sarah. "Sarah isn't okay."

"Sarah, what's wrong?"

Sarah pointed to the TV.

"What's wrong with the TV? Sarah, can you talk?"

Sarah looked around and signed phone. Tara was learning sign along with Sarah in school. "You want your phone?"

Sarah nodded vaguely.

Tara pulled Sarah's phone from her back pack and Sarah opened it and called up Maria's number. She showed the name to Tara's mom and handed her the phone.

"You want me to call Maria?"

Sarah nodded.

She placed the call and told Maria that Sarah was not talking and was upset by something on TV.

"What were they watching?"

"The Brady Bunch."

"The episode with Jan freaking out about Marcia?"

"Yes, how did you know?"

"Can you ask Sarah if she is safe?"

"Sarah, Maria wants to know if you are feeling safe?"

She nodded.

Then she signed "I go home. I want Cody."

Tara translated and her mother relayed the message.

"That is fine. Can she walk to Dr. Feingold's or does she need to go to the hospital?"

Sarah signed "We walk?"

Tara translated and her mother said yes, they could walk her home and then to the doctor's. Maria said she would call the doctor and then meet them there. Tara and her Mom helped Sarah get into her coat and back pack.

Tara held Sarah's hand as they walked. Tara's mom asked if there was anything they could do.

Sarah signed "Talk."

"You want us to talk?"

Sarah nodded.

"I don't know what to talk about."

Sarah was having trouble focusing on the world around her. Even keeping her eyes open was very difficult. Tara's mom understood the need for Sarah to have something to try to hold her focus and prompted her daughter. "Why don't you tell Sarah about the trip we took over the New Year's Break?"

"We went to Vermont and went skiing at Stowe. You should have seen the mountains and all the snow and there was this really cute…." Tara prattled on and Sarah found it impossible to follow but comforting to hear. They made it to Sarah's apartment and Sarah picked Cody up off the bed and held him.

Tara's mom saw the relief in her face and decided that Sarah might not know it, but she wasn't coming home from the doctor's. She quickly packed a set of pajamas and a change of clothes and directed the girls out as they continued to the doctor's office. Dr. Feingold was walking down the sidewalk from one direction as they approached from the other. They met at the front door of the building. He greeted Sarah, who was no longer able to keep her eyes open and focus on the world. He introduced himself to Tara and her mother.

"I packed a set of clothes and pajamas for her." She handed him the bag. "She was playing chess with Tara when she saw the Brady Bunch and just stopped talking. It was the one with Jan freaking out. I didn't know she shouldn't see the Brady Bunch."

"It's okay. She needed to see it at some point. Now is as good a time as any. Thank you for bringing her." He dismissed them and turned to Sarah.

"Sarah, should we go inside?"

Sarah nodded and reached out for him. "Let's get you up to the office."

"Can you open your eyes?"

She nodded and complied but then signed "Small."

"Are you having trouble seeing?"

She nodded. He guided her to the elevator and then to the office.

He unlocked the office, turned on the lights, and started to take off his coat. Sarah turned the light back off. He turned around and looked at her. She dropped her coat on the floor and then walked to him and hugged him.

Gently extricating himself from her embrace, he looked at her face. "Sarah, why did you turn the light off?"

She touched her eye with the hand that was not holding Cody. Then she signed "pain."

"The light is hurting your eyes?"

She nodded.

"Okay, we'll leave the lights off. Can you sit down over here so I can understand what's going on?"

Sarah curled up in a ball on the couch. She was facing him, but her eyes were closed.

"Sarah, can you look at me?"

She extended her head and opened her eyes but they were unfocused.

"Sarah, I want you to sit up."

Sarah again opened her eyes and tried to focus, but was less successful.

"Sarah, do you need to be in the hospital?"

Sarah made no response.

He sat on the ottoman and held her hands as they held Cody. "Sarah, can you come back here? I want you to come back here Sarah. Squeeze my hands." But her hands were still.

He stood up and covered Sarah with a throw, called Maria to give her an update, then called for an ambulance to take Sarah to the hospital. He called the unit to arrange for the child in Sarah's room to be moved and began the intake so she would be taken directly to the unit.

When the EMTs arrived they decided to carry her to the lobby. A gurney wouldn't fit in the elevator and she was small enough to be carried easily. She didn't respond when she was lifted.

February 19th   3:15 pm

At the hospital it was Mark who lifted her into her bed. Julia was taking her shoes off when the Doc remembered that Tara's mom had packed clothes.

"I think there are pajamas in here for her. I will let you get her changed. I need to write some notes. I'll be back in a few minutes."

Julia took the bag and found a pair of green pajamas with yellow ducks. She talked to Sarah as she undressed her and put her in pajamas. It was only when she took Cody out of her hand to take her shirt off that Sarah reacted at all and that was to blindly reach for Cody. Julia quickly finished changing her and then handed Cody back. "Cody is right here, Sarah. He's right here." Sarah relaxed her breathing and curled up on her side in a little ball holding Cody. Julia tucked her in and then sat down to keep watch.

Maria arrived a few minutes later. "How is she?"

"She's completely catatonic." Dr. Feingold apprised Maria of Sarah's condition.

"What are you going to do for her?"

"We have her in bed. Tara's mother had the foresight to bring pajamas and clothes for her. Julia changed her into pajamas and tucked her in. Now we wait until she works out enough in her head that she can come back and lets us help her."

"Can I see her?"

"She's in her room."

"The same room?"

"It's the only one with a ceiling and since it was built for her, it seemed appropriate to put her in it. It will be less disorienting for her to be in the room she knows."

Maria went in and Julia smiled in greeting. "I will let you visit with her. I'll be out here if you need me."

"Thanks. It's Julia, isn't it?"

"Yes. I'll be right outside."

Maria sat down at the edge of Sarah's bed and touched her face. Sarah lay passively holding Cody. "Oh, Sarah. I'm sorry sweetie. I am here with you and Cody is right there with you. We're going to take good care of you so you can come back when you are ready. We are going to let you take a nap and then when you wake up, it will be time for dinner. How about a nice bowl of chicken bouillon?"

Maria rubbed her back for a few minutes then re-tucked her and kissed her forehead. If Sarah was aware of her presence, she made no indication.

February 20th   9:00 am

Sarah did not move for the next six hours. At 9:00 pm the nurse called the unit pediatrician who wrote orders for catheterization and IV. Sarah did not resist when she was laid on her back and the tube inserted but she rolled back into a ball when they had finished. She didn't flinch when the IV was inserted.

In the morning Sarah was still catatonic when the doctor arrived.

"Sarah, it's time to wake up. Come on sleepyhead, we have some work to do. Sarah, open your eyes. Cody is getting hungry; he wants some breakfast." Sarah tapped her fingers on Cody. "Yes, Cody is with you but he missed dinner last night and he wants some breakfast."

She tapped Cody again and continued to tap for a few minutes before she faded away again.

He left her to sleep and saw other patients on the unit. After each patient he looked in on her, but each time he found her unchanged.

At lunch he again tried to reach her, "Sarah, it's time for lunch. Cody is going to take a little break so he can get some honey." He gently took Cody from her. She didn't resist him leaving but moved her hands in a feeble grasping movement. He gave her his hand and she held it. "I'm here Sarah. I'm right here. Now I want you to start coming back here. It is time to come back now. Just follow my voice and hold my hand and come on back. You can do it. Come on back here." Sarah's breathing changed. She began breathing more erratically and there were hitches in her breath. "You're doing great. It's just a little bit further Sarah. You can come back here. I want you to sign your name."

Sarah was holding his hand with her left hand. With her right she made the letter S.

"Good job, Sarah. You look like you need to take a little rest. I want you to look around where you are. Is there a nice chair that you can sit in and relax?"

Sarah signed "Yes."

"Okay, are you feeling safe where you are right now?"

Sarah again signed "Yes."

"If I have Cody come sit with you, will you stay right there and take a nap?"

Again she signed "Yes."

"I need you to stay right there so I can find you again later. I am going to talk to some other kids while you take a nap. Then I will come back and help you come home. Here is Cody. He's going to help you stay right where you are until I get back."

She held Cody and, based on the evenness of her breathing, was asleep.

The doctor had lunch and worked with another of his young patients before returning to Sarah.

"Sarah, it's time to wake up. Did you have a nice nap? Cody, you've done a great job watching over Sarah while she slept. You are a very good watch bear. Do you need to take a little break while Sarah and I get ready to walk back home?"

He took Cody away from Sarah. "Yes Cody, you can run ahead if you want, but don't go out of sight. We need you to stay close by."

He handed Cody to Mike, who was sitting in the room with Sarah. "Okay Sarah, take my hand and we will walk home together." He gave Sarah his hand and she held it. "Good. Now I want to you to tell me what you see up ahead?"

She signed "C."

"You see Cody?" She nodded.

"Can you wave to Cody?"

She waved her loose hand. "That's good. Can you feel the sunshine? Feel the sun warm on your face. Turn you face to the sun." Sarah extended her head and moved under the covers. She extended her legs so although she was still lying on her side, she was no longer in a ball. "You're doing great, Sarah. If you open your eyes, you will see Cody is here waiting for you."

She signed "Want."

"I know you want Cody. You need to come back here to join him. He is already back here. Open your eyes."

Sarah blinked and grimaced against the brightness. Nancy entered the room and upon seeing her face asked, "Lights off?"

The doc nodded.

"The sun has gone behind a cloud now; it's okay to try opening your eyes. Look who is here." Sarah opened her eyes again and saw Cody in Mike's lap.

She shuddered as she came back to herself. She lay very still, looking around. "I'm glad you're back. We missed you. Sarah, what are you thinking?"

She signed "Want Cody."

Mike stood up and handed Cody to her. "He's right here." Sarah finally recognized Mike and signed M. There was a hint of a smile on her face.

"You're going to be okay, Sarah; we'll get through this. Can you stay here now?" Dr. Feingold asked quietly.

She nodded "Yes."

"Good. Cody, I want you to stay with Sarah and don't let her wander away. Can you do that?" Sarah tapped Cody's head.

"He's a good bear. I'll let you visit with Mike and Nancy. I'll be back before I leave."

He called Maria and suggested that she and Amber come together and bring a pizza.

"Is she back?"

"Not all the way, not yet, but she is responding and signing. I think seeing you two and eating pizza will help. I'll be staying late, so I will be here when you arrive. I want to do another session with her when you get here. I would like her more grounded before we leave her for the night."

Sarah held Cody and watched Mike and Nancy. Nancy checked her IV and emptied her catheter bag. She was aware of what Nancy was doing but not able to show any interest. She did focus on Mike but didn't know what to say. He started to engage her when Nancy had finished. "Hi Sarah."

She raised her fingers in greeting.

"Did you learn to sign in school?"

She signed "Yes."

"Did your whole class learn or just you?"

"Whole."

"Wow. That must be fun to all be able to talk to each other using sign language."

"Yes."

"Have you needed it before now?"

"No. When?"

"When did you get here?"

"Yes."

"Yesterday. It was after I went home so I wasn't here when you came in."

"Time now?"

"2:30."

"You work tomorrow?"

"Yeah, I'll be here tomorrow."

"Me?"

"You will be here tomorrow too. We've hardly had a chance to catch up."

"No, you me."

"Oh, will I have you tomorrow?"

"Yes."

"I'll talk to Nancy about it. Do you want me to be assigned to you?"

"Yes." Sarah yawned.

"Are you getting tired?"

"Yes."

"Okay, you've worked hard, why don't you take a nap? But remember, no running away inside again."

She nodded and closed her eyes for a nap.

February 20th   6:00 pm

Maria and Amber arrived together with pizza. Julia was with Sarah when they came in. Dr. Feingold also came into the room. "Is she sleeping?"

Julia nodded.

"Let's go in the other room for a minute. Why don't you leave the pizza here? The smell might wake her up." They closed her door as they moved to the therapy room to discuss Sarah's current state.

"She's coming back. This afternoon she was able to open her eyes and sign the answer to a few questions. I don't how long this is going to take or where she went," They spoke about expectations and treatment for a few minutes before Dr. Feingold asked, "Shall we see if she is awake yet?"

The smell of pizza was indeed rousing Sarah. She was sniffing when they went in. Maria went to her and touched her face. "Hi Sarah, can you wake up? We brought you some pizza. With Sausage and pepperoni and extra cheese."

Sarah stretched and with her eyes still closed she signed "No K."

"Very not kosher, just the way you like it. Let's put your bed up so you can sit up and eat dinner in bed. Our girl of luxury." Sarah opened her eyes and then covered them. "Too bright?"

She nodded. The doctor turned off the room light, turned on the bathroom light, and opened the blinds to the hallway some to create a low light condition. "Try now." Sarah opened her eyes again and was able to look around.

She nodded. But she was moving her head from side to side to take in everyone. "Sarah, can you see okay?" She shook her head no. "Let's try something." He tested her peripheral vision and found that she was still experiencing tunnel vision. "Okay, when you look at me, am I clear?" She shook her head no. "Can you explain what's wrong?"

She signed spider.

"Everything looks cobwebby?"

She nodded.

"Okay, we're going to see how it is in the morning. For now I think you need some pizza."

Amber served the pizza. Sarah took a few bites and then leaned back on her pillow. She reached for Cody and started tapping on him.

"Sarah, are you feeling okay?"

She shook her head no.

"Is your tummy okay?"

She nodded.

"Sarah, do want to go back to where you were?"

She nodded.

"You need to stay here with us Sarah. We want to help you, but we can't if you run away. You are the bravest kid I know. Together we can face whatever it is and beat it. Can you find one word that will help us understand where you are?"

In Hebrew Sarah said "Real."

Everyone looked at Sarah and then to Dr. Feingold. He shook his head. "Sarah can you sign it?"

She shook her head.

"Can you find the English?"

She shook her head again then signed "cell phone."

She signed "Rabbi Cohen."

Amber smacked her forehead, "Duh, he would know." Sarah lay back while her phone was retrieved and Rabbi Cohen was called. Then Sarah was asked to tell him the word.

He translated.

"Real? Are you trying to sort out what is real?"

She signed "sort of."

"Okay. I think that was enough for tonight. I can see you are getting pretty tired. You did a great job coming back here today. I know it wasn't easy. I'm going to let you spend a little more time with Maria and Amber and then I want you to get a good night's sleep so we can do some work tomorrow."

"Sarah, what language are you thinking in?"

"ASL and Hebrew."

"What about English?"

She shook her head.

"Okay. Rest."

With encouragement Sarah ate another few bites of pizza and had a drink of orange soda.

Maria followed the doctor out of the room while Amber stayed with Sarah.

"What's going on?"

"Her brain is trying to process information and it's not working properly. Hearing her old name on TV has really shaken her and we are going to need to explore exactly why it has shaken her so badly, but I think she will be better organized tomorrow. She has several languages to work with and that is a plus."

"Why can she find words in Hebrew and Sign but not English?"

"They are stored in different areas of her brain and they have different associations for her so she is able to access them differently. We'll work this out. Once she sorts this out in her mind, she will come back and be stronger than before."

February 21st   8:30 am

Sarah slept very soundly and during the night she started to unfold from her little ball.

When she awoke in the morning, Mike was again watching over her. "Good morning, sweetie."

She signed "Morning" as she stretched and rolled over in her bed. She wanted to go back to sleep.

"Orders are to have you up and dressed when the Doc shows up."

She signed "No, Sleep."

"Come on Lazy Bones, Nancy will be in here in a minute to remove the catheter." Sarah reached under her covers and felt the tube then looked puzzled.

"You didn't know it was there?"

She shook her head no, then curled up again and fell back to sleep.

Nancy came in a half hour later and tried waking her again. She was barely able to keep her eyes open and Nancy decided to leave the tube in for the time being. Sarah was not ready to respond to her body.

Dr. Feingold visited with her but she still not ready to work. At lunch, Mike sat her up to encourage her to eat but after a few bites she returned to sleep. She slept heavily until dinner when Molly woke her and encouraged her to take some food. Then she slept soundly until morning.

February 22nd 8:30 am

Sarah woke in the morning alert and ready to get up. Nancy removed the catheter then untethered her and helped her stand. She was able to shower and dress before breakfast arrived.

When Dr. Feingold arrived she was sitting on her bed, finishing her breakfast and talking with Mike using Sign.

"Hey, I see you decided to join us again. Are you ready to talk about where you have been?"

She pointed to her breakfast.

"Okay. You finish your breakfast and I'll get settled in for the day. Then we can go into the therapy room. I have something to show you."

She cocked her head in question.

"In the therapy room in five minutes."

She nodded and worked on finishing her breakfast.

Dr. Feingold had his laptop set up on the table when she came in with Cody.

"We will get to this. But first, we need to find your words again and we need to understand what happened."

They were sitting on opposite sides of the table in the center of the room.

Sarah started to sign but he stopped her. "We need to find your English words. How can we do this?"

Sarah looked anxious and thought for a moment then signed. "I sign, you say, I say."

"Okay let's try it."

She signed "I was at Tara's house."

"I was at Tara's house," he translated slowly.

She tried several times, opening her mouth, but she could not speak. She looked disappointed and frustrated.

"It's okay. Let's take a break."

She pointed to the computer and he said, "No, that's for later. I see Cody came to join us. Maybe we should see if he has anything to say." She sat Cody on the table. "Cody, I've been watching you the past few days; you have been working very hard. Have you been getting enough to eat?"

Sarah helped Cody nod "Yes."

"That is great. I wasn't sure that we had bear food on the unit."

He nodded again.

"And have you been able to sleep at all?"

He shook his head.

"No sleep? You must be tired."

Cody looked at Sarah.

"I see. Taking care of Sarah is a very important job and you have been doing it very well. Do you know how to seek and find?"

Cody cocked his head to the side. "Some bears can find things that their people lose and hold them until the people are ready to have them back. I was wondering if perhaps you were one of the bears and if perhaps you found Sarah's words."

Cody looked around him then shook his head.

"You really aren't ready, are you?"

She shook her head sadly and signed "You mad?"

"No, Sarah, I am not mad at you. I know that you are very brave and if you say you aren't ready to face something and deal with it, that you really aren't ready. I am wondering what we need to do to get you ready. How can I help you?"

Sarah looked around but then shrugged.

"Sarah, how do you feel now?"

She signed "Alone."

"Alone. Do you feel disconnected from everyone?"

She nodded. She signed "I went away. You stayed here. You didn't hold me here; I went away. Bad place. Now you want me tell you. I don't want to go back."

"Are you mad at me?"

She nodded and her tears started.

"I failed you because I couldn't hold you enough to keep you here with us."

She nodded again.

"When you came to my office, you held me so you wouldn't be swept away in the storm and I didn't hold you, I set you on the couch."

"I wanted to stay." She gestured.

"But you needed to go. You needed to go to the bad place and you needed to see what you saw and now you need to report back and talk about what was in the bad place."

She shook her head. "I talk, I go back."

"Well, in a way you are right. If you talk you will go back, but you won't be alone. If you talk, I can go with you. We can go together if you talk me there. But I can't go to the place back in time without you taking me."

"Cody?"

"Cody went because you took him. He can't go by himself."

"You walked me home." She motioned.

"Because you and Cody were looking for the path and I was able to lead you with my voice, I talked you home. But if I am going to the bad place, you need to talk me there." He paused and looked at her, "You're getting tired, aren't you?"

She nodded.

"It's time for you to take a nap. I want you to stay here. Don't go back to the bad place without me. And don't worry, Sarah. When you're ready, we'll go together."

She was fading fast and he walked her back to her room and covered her with a blanket when she lay down. "Cody, keep her here."

She was asleep.

February 22nd   11:30 am

A child services worker arrived to see Sarah. The unit social worker greeted her and asked why Theresa, Sarah's assigned worker, was not with her.

"Her worker is on vacation. I'm covering her cases. I just received word that Sarah was brought in 3 days ago. We're supposed to see a child within 24 hours of arrival at the hospital. So, I need to see Sarah."

"She's sleeping right now. But you seem upset; perhaps we should discuss your concerns first."

"I was looking through her file and this is her fourth hospitalization in a year. I am very concerned about her treatment and I am questioning her placement."

"I see."

"According to her file, she is not on any medications. Why is she not on any medications if she's being hospitalized?"

"So you think that she should be placed on medication rather than working through her issues in a safe environment?"

"Nearly every child in foster care is on medication. And they're not being hospitalized. With the budget constraints, I can't help but wonder if it would be less expensive to put her on medication and not have her spending taxpayer's money in the hospital."

"That's an interesting point. Have you read Sarah's history?"

"Well, she was abused by her caretaker, but most kids in foster care have suffered some abuse."

"Perhaps her file is not explicit; Sarah has suffered more abuse than any other child we have ever seen. Sarah has post-traumatic stress disorder. There is no medication for PTSD. The best we can do is to use medication to reduce the discomfort of the symptoms. Sarah is receiving cognitive behavioral therapy. So far, she has not needed long-term medication for her symptoms. The benefits of the medications are no greater than their risks to Sarah."

"I also have some concerns about her placement. The file says that she is living with married women."

"You're concerned about Maria and Amber?"

"They are lesbians. I can't help but question Sarah's safety."

"You are more concerned about her safety with two women than with her living with a female and male caregiver?"

"I am concerned about her growing up normally, aren't you? How is she going to understand how to behave in a marriage if she doesn't experience one while she's growing up?"

"She is experiencing a healthy family but you think that she should be in a traditional family rather than with a family of an alternate orientation?"

"Of course.

"Children learn what they witness."

"Exactly, I see you understand."

"Yes, I do understand. You said your name is what again?"

"Virginia Mathews."

"Virginia, how long have you been with children's services?"

"Well, just six months but let me tell you, I can see why they are in such a mess. Placing kids with anyone, letting kids get away with anything. They just say they don't want to stay at one home and we have to take them out and move them somewhere else. If they don't want to go to school, they say they want to hurt themselves and they know we have to take them to the hospital."

"Well, Virginia, I'm going to make your life easy for you today. Sarah is going to stay with us until she is ready to go back to her foster home with Maria and Amber. She will continue to attend her private school where she is doing very well despite having missed several months early in the school year. Sarah is on vacation now and she's not here because she wants to get out of anything. She is one of the hardest working patients this unit has ever seen and we will do everything we can to ensure that she grows up to have a normal adulthood. You are required to see a child and as I walk you out you can look in on her. But Sarah is currently not able to speak and you will not talk to her. Do you have any questions?"

"If she can't speak, how do you know that her foster parents didn't do something to her?"

"Sarah was at a friend's house and watching the Brady Bunch and playing chess when she lost her speech. We know why she lost speech and it was to her foster parent that she reached out for help."

"You want me to believe that she can't talk because she watched the Brady Bunch? That's a kid's show. That can't make someone unable to speak."

"What can I say? Sarah has some issues to work out that we are not going to discuss. But I can assure you that she is not being abused in her foster home; she is actually doing very well in school and with the exception of moments like this one, she is typically a happy, bright, cooperative child. Now can I show you out?"

They looked in on Sarah as the children's services worker was escorted off the unit. A phone call to children's services revealed that reports were piling up on this worker and that no one should worry about Sarah's placement. Sarah's life was secure; the child services worker's job was not. The social worker wrote up the incident and e-mailed the report to the supervisor.

Sarah was awakened for lunch, never knowing that everything she had grown to depend on had been threatened and then reinforced while she slept.

February 22nd   12:30 pm

"Mac and cheese, Sarah."

She touched Cody. "He had some honey grahams while you were sleeping." She looked at him and smiled at Mike.

Mike sat with her while she ate her lunch.

"Doc says you two are going to go back at it after lunch."

Sarah signed "Work, work, work."

"He's a slave driver."

She was signing, "I want to get out of Egypt" as he came in the door.

"What was that?"

She repeated the sign then said it in Hebrew.

"I'm the right person for you. My whole job is helping people out of 'de-Nile.'"

Sarah lay back on her bed and covered her face, shaking her head at the really bad joke.

"Come on kid, give me a break, have I not been like Moses leading you through this wilderness?"

"We go another walk?" she gestured.

"I'm afraid so. There are lots of journeys and I think we need to go on another one, what do you think?"

In Hebrew she said, "Can't we just kill a calf or a goat and call it a deal?"

"Or a chicken?"

Sarah lay back, thinking about that. She shook her head and then nodded.

"This isn't like the work we have done before, is it?"

"No." It came out small and weak and much like a question but it was audible English.

"You said that it was about reality. Are you wondering about what in your life is real?"

She looked at him imploringly and then said, "Hold here."

"You want me to hold you so you will stay here while we talk?"

He grabbed a chair and sat next to the bed facing her and held her left hand, leaving the right for her to sign with if she needed.

"Okay?"

She tucked Cody in under her head as a pillow.

"How do we get there?" Sarah asked.

"How about if we start at Tara's house? What were you doing at Tara's?"

Sarah began speaking. "Playing chess." Then she smiled, "Tara is a crappy player. She doesn't think ahead. It makes it harder. I have to think about every possible move, not just the good ones. The TV was on and a show about a lot of kids, then 'Marcia, Marcia, Marcia'. I turned and looked at it but then everything started to go black at the edges. I started getting sucked up by the black. It was like 'The Nothing'. It was all black. I tried to hold on. I got Cody. Tara talked so I could hold on then I held you but you let go and I got sucked away. I couldn't stop." Sarah's voice was getting stronger as she continued.

"Let's talk about where you went."

"I went to my house when I was little. 'Marcia, Marcia, Marcia.' It kept calling me to Zeke. It was weird."

"How was it weird?"

"I was watching him do stuff to me when I was little but it wasn't me anymore. I'm Sarah and I'm bigger. He didn't see me. I watched him with me when I was little. I was very little. I watched him change me and touch me. I watched how he looked at me. I listened to how he talked to me." She turned and faced Doc. "He hated me. He liked to hurt me. He always talked about how important it was to not hurt me but there was a tone in his voice that I never understood before. He didn't hurt me because it would decrease my value in the long run. He would have loved to torture me if he could have. At the end when he was letting people do whatever and he was making me do stuff to him so much, that's what he always wanted to do." Sarah rested for a few moments, then asked, "Was he my father?"

"I don't know and unless you learned something during your trip, we may never know. Did he say anything about where you came from?"

She quoted Zeke, "You look just like that fucking skank we got you from. I hope you turn out to be a better fuck than she was. We get you trained up and you should be worth a pretty penny. You hear that? You're going to be worth a pretty penny."

She shook her head as if to clear it and continued. "I don't think I was really his daughter. I think I was just a... a... I don't know what to call me."

"A way to earn money? You weren't a person, were you?"

"No. Everything he did was to make money off me. The playground was to build stomach muscles and he liked to touch me and he liked to make me hurt a little. He found me contemptible."

She paused before asking, "I'm not the only kid this is happening to, am I?"

"You tell me."

"I saw another kid. A boy. He was mostly grown but he wasn't a man yet. He didn't have any clothes on and Zeke did fallatio on him and then they told him to lie down on the floor. Zeke told me to 'kiss his little mansicle' so I did and everyone laughed. Then Zeke told me that we were going to do something really fun. He was going to be my split stand. One of the other guys held the boy's penis to guide it in me and Zeke lowered me all the way onto him. It hurt and I wanted to get up, but Zeke would lift me an inch and then put me back down. Then the other guy put the kids' hands on my hips and showed him how to do rhythms with me. Then he touched the boy's balls and the boy started to move on his own. The boy exploded and the guys started laughing and said they were sure he was a man in there somewhere. They were mean laughs. After Zeke lifted me up one of the guys held me and put his finger in me while another person had the boy perform fallatio on him and then sodomized him. He said that pretty soon I would be just as good as that boy. 'You see how he does that. You can do that too pretty soon.' They made it sound like an achievement. Zeke made everything sound like an achievement."

"It wasn't long after that that Zeke started having intercourse with me. I watched the first time. He brushed my hair and then he unzipped his pants and told me that it was time to practice. So I started to do fallatio and then he stopped me and said that he wanted me to do a split onto him like I did to that kid. He held my body instead of my hands and when I touched him it was hard and it hurt and then he was inside and it really hurt and I couldn't get away and he held me and said just relax. But I could see his face now and he really liked that I was in pain. It made it more exciting for him. He didn't do rhythms but he wanted to. I could see it. He just held me until I relaxed. Then he told me that I was the best kid in the whole world."

"I think it was the next day that he used a bunch of lubricant and did it again and this time he exploded. Then he checked me and I was bleeding. His 'Marcia, Marcia, Marcia' wasn't very nice. He looked like he wanted to throw me against the wall. I watched him kick me and lock me the closet and put me in the shower with just cold water. I watched his face. I don't know how I lived through it. When it was happening, I thought that what he did was right because he was all I knew. I didn't know what that tone meant until I saw it on TV. He hated me. The only thing he liked about me was the practice sessions and sometimes he didn't even like me then. He called me a robot a lot. And he would say that I was a trained monkey. Those aren't very nice and I know why he said them now."

"Why?"

"Because I wasn't like that boy."

"What do you mean?"

"That boy did his own rhythms and he exploded. I don't know if this is possible, but can girls explode?"

"Yes, we call it having an orgasm."

"Do you think that Zeke got mad at me because I never learned to have an orgasm?"

"I don't know. Did you ever feel excited by the intercourse and want to do rhythms of your own?"

"No, I just did what I was supposed to do. Am I defective?"

"No, you are not defective, you were a young child and young children are not able to have orgasms."

"How did you feel watching this happen?"

"Very sad and disillusioned and I felt kind of broken hearted. Part of me still believed that he loved me. But even my name was a mockery. I just kept seeing our life until you came and got me. I couldn't look away and I couldn't walk away. I think Cody kept me from being seen. If Zeke saw me, I don't think I could have come back here."

"What do you think would have happened?"

"I think he would have tied me down and raped me a lot of times. I'm glad he didn't see me and I'm glad you came and got me."

"Sarah, you know that Zeke is dead and he can't hurt you anymore."

"Part of me does but part of me doesn't. He was very alive when I was there and that was just a few days ago."

"But you were seeing things that happened years ago."

"I didn't have Cody years ago and he was with me."

"Okay. What's real and what's a memory is pretty confusing right now. We will talk about that another time. You are looking pretty tired now. Is there anything you want to tell me about your trip now?"

"I'm glad I'm home here."

"I'm glad your home here, too."

She took Cody from behind her head and held him as she curled up and went to sleep.

February 22nd   4:30 pm

Dr. Feingold called Maria to let her know that Sarah was talking again. After dinner Sarah asked for her computer and e-mailed Tara.

> *Hi,*
>
> *I just wanted to let you know that I am okay. I'm sorry I freaked out at your house. Please tell your mom thank you for walking me to the doctors and for packing clothes for me. I don't think I will be back at school on Monday but at least I'm back from the freak out trip and I can talk again.*
>
> *I can e-mail but not IM and no cell phone. Bummer. Maria and Amber will be here soon.*
>
> *Later,*
> *Sarah*

Then she sent an e-mail to her teacher:

> *Hi,*
>
> *I am at the hospital again. I have my books here and would like my assignments for this week coming up. I won't be gone for a long time, this time; at least I don't think I will. Thank you for teaching us sign. I freaked out at Tara's house and she was able to translate for me when I could sign but not speak. It made life easier at the hospital too.*
>
> *Please give Tara a Mitzvah star on the board, she deserves it and it would mean a lot to her to be given it publicly. She doesn't get to shine very often. She translated for me and then she told Tara tales while we walked to the doctor's. I don't think I would have made it to the doctor's office if she wasn't telling Tara tales. She doesn't know that part and I wasn't planning on telling her. I think if she knew how bad off I was during the walk it would scare her.*

Thank you,
Sarah

Maria and Amber found a smiling Sarah waiting for them. She hugged them both and told them that she missed them. "We were here last night." Amber looked at her quizzically.

"Yeah, but I wasn't. I feel like I haven't been here for a long time I'm glad I'm back here. I'm not going home for a while, am I?"

"Do you think you're ready to go home?"

"No. I think I have to do more work about the trip before I'm ready to come home and go to school. Remember last time I came home we talked about me coming back here?"

"About this being a tool that we use when appropriate?"

"Yeah. I'm glad here is here. I thought I would feel like a failure if I had to come back. But I'm not a failure. I didn't do something wrong, did I?"

"No, you didn't. We've wondered if we did something wrong by not showing you that TV show and talking to you about it."

"You knew about it? How did you know?"

"Because we all watched the Brady Bunch when we were growing up and in fact most Americans have seen the Brady Bunch. It was on for years and then it was in reruns and it's been on Nick forever. That episode is very famous and it's actually amazing that you had never seen it before now."

"When would I see it? Zeke didn't have television. I lived in a hole in the ground without electricity for four years and then I was here where we hardly see television and you guys have TV but we hardly watch it. The only person I know that has the TV on all the time is Tara. Maybe that's why she is so good at Tara Tales. I sent an e-mail to Mrs. Rifkin and asked her to give Tara a Mitzvah star for helping me when I freaked out. I love her Tara tales".

Amber groaned, "Oh, God, not Tara Tales."

"They're funny."

"I really enjoy Tara but they are stupid stories."

"Yeah, but they're funny because they're so stupid."

Maria looked at the two of them and said, "You know, Sarah may be onto something. She could be a sitcom writer some day and do very well for herself."

They all burst out laughing.

Then Sarah sobered up and asked, "How come you didn't tell me?"

Amber took her hands. "Honey, you've had so much on your plate. We've been focusing on dealing with whatever was in the forefront and when you haven't had something pressing, you need to have a break, not have something else piled on top."

"Maybe we should have brought it up and watched the episode with you, but I'm not sure that it would have stopped you from going on this journey or made it any easier for you. We may have thought that Zeke was a bastard, but it really wasn't right for us to rub your nose in it and that's what it feels like we would have been doing. We're here to support you. We can't remove all of the speed bumps. But we're here to make sure you're wearing your helmet and to clean the skinned knees."

"That makes sense. We did have a system that worked for getting me help quickly. I'm not going back to school on Monday, am I?"

"What do you think?"

"I think I am going to be here for a little while sorting this out. Can I tell you something?"

"Of course."

"I need to be here."

"What are you saying, Sarah?"

"I haven't told Dr. Feingold yet, but I don't feel very safe with myself. Remember before when I wanted to die?"

"Yeah,"

"This is different but the same."

"Can you explain that a little?"

"Before, I hurt really badly and the pain was very overwhelmingly big. This time it's a small sad pain that is deep inside and it feels like I have something dead in my middle. I want to cut myself open and take it out. Last summer there was this girl Kim that was here. She used to cut her arms and legs. She said that when she cut herself all the pain went away. It didn't make sense then but I understand it now."

"Have you cut yourself?"

"No, it's in Leviticus 19. I can't cut myself; it's in my Torah portion. But I'm not sure that if I was at home that I could resist the urge. So, are you okay with me staying here for now?"

"Of course we are. We are part of Team Sarah. Our first goal is to keep you safe and we are proud of you."

"For what? I want to hurt myself; how can you be proud of me?"

"We're proud of you for recognizing what you're feeling and for asking for help with it. You're getting more grown up all the time."

"You're not disappointed in me?"

"Not at all; we're both very proud."

"What are you going to do if I am not at home?"

"Um, I don't know, stay up all night, have wild parties; we'll probably trash the place."

Sarah smiled. "You can have the weekend off without a kid."

"Woo hoo! Really, Sarah, we would rather have you at home, but you need to stay here until you're ready. You look exhausted. How about if you get in your PJ's and we tuck you in like you were at home?"

"That would be good. Are you going to tell the staff about what I said?"

"Would it be easier for you to tell them or for us to?"

"You tell them."

Maria went to the nurse while Amber helped Sarah get ready for bed. Then they both tucked her and Cody in and kissed her goodnight before Molly arrived to sit with her through the night.

February 23rd 7:30 am

Sarah was up and dressed before the morning shift arrived. She tried reading but was restless and irritable. When Mike arrived she met him at the door and hugged him. "Hey, good morning. You're up early."

"I couldn't sleep anymore."

"You don't look very happy."

"Did you ever want to just kick everything and throw everything?"

"Is that how you feel?"

"I want to punch somebody."

"Can you hold that feeling while I get my coat off and get report?"

"Then can I kick you?"

"No, but I'll kick your butt at chess."

"You can't kick my butt at chess."

"Go set up the board; I'll show you how to play chess."

Sarah started for the therapy room when Marge, her night staff, told her she wasn't allowed in there. Giving Marge a withering look, she got the chess set and went back to her own room to set it up.

"You aren't supposed to go in the therapy room except for during your therapy time."

"Trust me. Dr. Feingold would approve of me borrowing the chess set. It isn't like I'm stealing it and if it keeps me from breaking something or hurting myself, then it is therapy."

"Do you want to hurt yourself?"

"Do chickens hatch from eggs? Why do you think you have to be with me? I'm on suicide watch, duh?" Sarah continued to rant at Marge. "How many kids in here have someone with them all the time? Hardly anyone in case you didn't notice. But they're all on drugs and I don't take drugs. It would be better if I whooped Mike's ass at chess then if I whooped Mike's ass for real."

Mike walked in at that moment. "As if. You are going to learn how to play chess this morning."

He nodded to Marge in dismissal, "Unless you want to see how we take down the patients with chess men."

"I'll leave you to it."

Sarah held out the men for choosing. Mike chose white. Within just a few moves Sarah knew she wasn't playing with Tara. Mike knew how to play. The intensity of the game helped to hold her anxiety and frustration in check until she saw her loss four moves out. She saw it before Mike. She stopped, looked at the board and then at him. She saw it in his eyes when he saw it. Then she reached over, and laid down her king quietly and reverently. She looked in his eyes again and the frustration and rage she was bottling up burst forth. The chess board and pieces flew across the room as she lunged for Mike. Expecting it, Mike caught her fists and was in the process of restraining her when most of the staff converged on the room, drawn by the noise.

Sarah was kneeling on her bed with Mike holding her wrists and her head hitting his chest gently when Nancy came in. "Sarah, do you need some medication?"

"I don't want any." She screamed.

"I asked if you need it, not if you want it." Nancy replied calmly.

"Maybe, but I want to try to wait until after I work with Dr. Feingold." Sarah's voice trembled in her response.

"Okay, we can try, but you need to stop beating up the staff. You don't want to bruise Mike; you know how delicate he is."

The humor helped and she was able to relax a bit more and stop hitting her head. She let him hold her and rub her back. "Feel better?"

She nodded. "I have to pick up the chess men. Dr. Feingold is going to flip out if he sees this mess."

Dr. Feingold walked in the door. Sarah looked up at Mike, "Uh, oh. I think my ass is grass. Am I in a lot of trouble?"

"I think you have some 'splaining to do."

"Therapy room?"

"Therapy room."

"Now?"

"Can you think of a better time?"

"Ten minutes ago would have been good." Disengaging from Mike, she said, "Maybe we should have a rematch later. You just got lucky."

"We'll see what kind of shape you're in when the doc finishes with you."

She went into the therapy room and sat on the floor.

"Have a seat." Sarah sat down, expecting to be reprimanded. But Dr. Feingold instead said, "We're going to watch this together."

"What is it?"

"The Brady Bunch."

"The episode that freaked me out?"

"The very one. Are you ready?"

"Um, I guess so. What if I freak out again?"

"Then we will deal with you freaking out. But if we deal with this now, you won't be blindsided by it out in the world."

"I'm scared."

"What are you scared of?"

"I don't want to go back to the bad place."

"Do you think that you will go back?"

"I don't know."

"Well, when you are ready to watch this, start the video."

Sarah took a deep breath and clicked on the screen. She watched the episode in its entirety.

February 23rd   11:30 am

"What do you think?"

"I think that Jan was jealous and sick of living in Marcia's shadow. I don't think she hated Marcia, I think she was just frustrated. I think the only way Zeke was like Jan is that he used the same name for me as Jan used when she was really frustrated, except Zeke used it all the time. I'm not going to freak out from the Brady Bunch."

"That's good. You have one less thing to worry about in the world. Now, how do you feel?"

"About this or in general?"

"About this."

"Relieved. I don't have to worry about freaking out and that's nice."

"In general."

"Frustrated and hurt."

"Talk to me about it. And I want to know what happened this morning."

"Mike was helping me hold on until you got here. He knew when he came in today that I was on edge and trying to contain myself until you got here. He suggested a game of chess and I was doing okay until I lost. Then I just couldn't contain it anymore and I sort of had a temper tantrum."

"Did you throw the chess board because you lost?"

"Not really. It didn't matter who won really. It was about the distraction but then I lost and some of it was about not being good enough and some of it was because I was frustrated inside and what if I'm not good enough to stop myself? I needed to know that Mike would stop me. This all sounds lame when I say it."

"So, you tried to punch Mike so that he would stop you from punching him?"

Sarah nodded. "I know it sounds stupid. But I had to know."

"You needed to know that if you couldn't keep yourself safe, that he could protect you."

Sarah looked at Dr. Feingold. "Yeah. That's exactly it. Am I stupid?"

"No. You were testing your resources. And I'm sure that you intend to clean up the chess pieces and put them back away."

"Is it okay if we play some more first? Mike is a good chess player. But don't tell him I said that. Chess keeps my head busy."

"Why don't we talk about why you need to be distracted?"

Sarah's agitation was growing palpable. "Where did I come from?"

"Where do you think you came from?"

"A junkie skank is a heroin addict right?"

"I am almost afraid to ask how you know that."

"I Googled it last night."

"Okay, what are you thinking?"

"If Zeke wasn't just using junkie skank in the pejorative, then they bought me from my mother who was a heroin addict and would rather have a hit than me. So, what do you think they paid her for me: just a hit or a day's worth?"

"How you feel if it's true?"

"Mad at her. What kind of person would sell her kid for drugs?"

"A sick person. A very sick person."

"I don't want her excused."

"You want to be angry with her."

"Do you think she is dead?"

"I don't know, Sarah; I know that she is probably either dead or she got into a rehab program."

"Do you think she ever thinks about me?"

"If she is alive and went to rehab, she probably wonders what happened to the little girl she gave up for drugs and is guilt ridden."

"I want to kick her."

"What else do you want to do to her?"

"I want to yell at her."

"What would you say to her?"

"How could you do that? How could you choose drugs over me? Why couldn't you just take me someplace safe and drop me off if you couldn't take care of me? Why did you have to sell me? Didn't you think about why they wanted me? Was I that bad of a baby?"

"You have a lot of questions for her."

"Am I going to be a heroin addict?"

"No."

"How do you know?"

"You are able to face yourself even when it's scary. To take drugs you need to be afraid to face yourself or unwilling to feel your feelings. You can face yourself and your feelings, so you will never need to take drugs. And if you never take drugs, you will never get addicted."

"I hope you're right. Do you think I might be right about my mother?"

"You could be. If you were kidnapped, you would be in the missing child database."

"I'm not, am I?"

"You aren't in any database anywhere in the world."

"They checked all around the world?"

"Last spring when you were found the police looked in every database and checked every missing persons report going back 14 years to find someone matching your description. You aren't in there."

"So either Zeke was my father or he took me from someone who didn't report me missing."

"Or both."

"I don't know if I would feel worse if Zeke was my father or if he wasn't my father."

"His behavior was pretty horrible either way, wasn't it?"

"Yeah, if he hated me so much, how come he didn't just get rid of me?"

"Sarah, do you really see him dropping you off at a firehouse?"

"No, he would have taken me out in the back woods and shot me, or dumped me in an incinerator."

"How do you know what an incinerator is?"

"It's a 55 gallon drum and you put trash in it and burn it. It's out in Zeke's way back yard."

"Can you picture yourself standing near the incinerator?"

"Yeah."

"Turn around and describe the house."

"It's white and it's a double wide trailer. And there are fields around the house and only the yard around the house is mowed."

"Are there other houses around?"

"No, just alfalfa fields. At night there are lightning bugs and I can catch them and put them in a jar."

"Did Zeke burn anything in the incinerator that wasn't trash?"

Sarah stopped and looked worried. Very quietly she whispered, "Before we left the trailer he burned everything of mine that we weren't taking with us." I cried when he burned my books and he said, 'Cut it out or I'll burn you with them.' He burned all my clothes except what we were taking in the back pack. He was already being mean by then and I stopped crying.
He was being paranoid, wasn't he?"

"Sounds like it."

"I think he was taking drugs. Are there drugs that line up on the table and you take with a straw?"

"Is that what he did?"

"I did too but mine were colored and I sucked mine up with my mouth. His were white and he used a razor blade to line it up and then he put the straw in his nose."

"Were yours called pixie sticks?"

"Yeah, that's what they were. They tasted good and when this guy came over to do stuff with Zeke he would bring me pixie sticks."

"What was his name?"

"John. How do I know that? How come I can remember so much now?"

"Because you're ready to remember."

"Zeke was on drugs, wasn't he?"

"It sounds like it."

"What was he taking?"

"From your description, he was snorting cocaine."

"Is it expensive?"

"Yes."

"Is that why Zeke sold everything and then we left?"

"That would fit."

"John wanted Zeke to sell me to him. Zeke didn't do it. Maybe part of Zeke did care about me."

"Or maybe he was being selfish."

"Can we be done for today?"

"After you tell me how you feel."

"I want to hurt myself. If I had a razor blade, I would scourge myself. You know those religious people who whip themselves bloody?"

"Flagellants?"

"Yeah that's it. I kind of feel like being one of them."

"You sound like you're angry with yourself."

"I want of get rid of the bad feelings inside of me."

"Hurting yourself may seem appealing, but I know a better way."

"What?"

"Doing just what we're doing, talking it out."

"But I still want to hit something and I still want to hurt myself."

"It doesn't go away overnight. But we will get through this."

"Promise?"

"If you won't give up, I won't give up. Now, go pick up those chess pieces."

February 23rd   2:00 pm

She did as she was told and then lay down on her bed. She didn't want to play chess again. And she couldn't concentrate on a book. By the time lunch arrived, she was short tempered and very irritable. Nancy informed her that she was to stay on her bed.

She tried playing with a fantasy of being marooned on an island in the middle of the ocean, but she couldn't hold onto it. At 2:00 she started crying. "I give up. I want medicine."

"Okay, I think Doc just finished with another session." Mike went to the door and called Doc into the room.

"What's going on?"

"I want medicine. I feel like I want to unzip myself and climb out. I can't take it anymore. I'm going to hurt myself."

"You want something to take the edge off?"

Sarah stood up on her bed and started jumping. "I can't take it anymore!"

"Sarah, *stop*! Get down, *now*!" She jumped forward off the bed and hit the wall before anyone could catch her. She crumpled into a pile. She was stunned by hitting the wall and shocked by her own actions. Nancy heard the noise and was in the room instantly. Sarah was awake but not responding. She looked terrified by what she had done.

"Get a vest. Let's give her a shot of Lorazepam."

As Mike put the vest on Sarah, she looked at him but didn't reach out for comfort. Once the vest was secure, he told her to stand up and she complied.

"You're going to lie back down on your bed."

Sarah shook her head. "Yes, Sarah." Sarah closed her eyes and shook her head again. Mike saw the melt down coming and grabbed Sarah from behind to restrain her. Dr. Feingold went to the door and called for staff.

Very quickly, Sarah was on the bed and strapped down. She was tossing and turning and kicking wildly when Nancy returned with the shot. The staff held Sarah still as the shot was given, then released her. The medication took effect quickly and Sarah calmed markedly.

The last thing she noticed before falling asleep was Mike holding her hand and telling her that she was okay.

Once asleep, Sarah resumed thrashing. Fury and fear ran across her face as she fought demons invisible to those around her. Mike covered the bed rails with blankets to prevent injury while the team debated four point restraints.

Dr. Feingold explained, "Further restraining a child who has been abused like she has may cause her more damage. If we can keep her safe without restraining her more, I would rather do that. She isn't fighting us and she isn't trying to hurt herself. Let's let her work this out."

"Is this what she was holding back? My God, I knew she was trying to contain herself this morning but I had no idea it was this bad. Do you know why now?"

"She is seeing her life through a new perspective. She is remembering a lot more of it and she is able to apply five years of knowledge to what she experienced in order to understand it. This trip may make the last one look like Disney World."

Sarah cried "No!" in her sleep.

Dr. Feingold woke her up and asked her what she was dreaming. She was barely awake and dazed from the medication. "He's burning my clothes. That's my pretty green velvet dress. And he has a box of my toys. Not Bop-bop. He's burning Bop-bop."

"Who was Bop-bop?"

"He is my bunny. I sleep with Bop-bop and I get to hold Bop-bop if I am good. He's burning Bop-bop." She was fighting to get to the incinerator and suddenly she went limp.

"What happened?"

Sarah shared Zekes's words. "Shut your fuckin' mouth or I'll put you in the damn incinerator too. And turn off them infernal tears or I'll give you something to cry about. Now get inside and bring out another box of your shit. We can't leave no trace. You don't leave footprints. You don't leave a trail. No evidence, you hear me? No fuckin' evidence. Now get goin'."

Sarah took a few deep breaths and then drifted back to sleep.

Mike stepped out of the room with the doctor. "I want to cry. That bastard burned her bunny right in front of her and her life was so bad that she was willing to climb into the incinerator to be with it. No wonder she's having a tough time. Sometime it amazes me that these kids that show up here are still alive."

"Let's hope we can keep her that way when her walls come down."

They woke Sarah every few hours to walk her to the bathroom and to have her eat and drink. The medication made her very unsteady on her feet and very groggy. Before he left, Dr. Feingold stopped in to check on her.

"How do you feel?"

"Like a World War One battlefield after the cavalry came through."

"Do you think you need more medication?"

"Do you want me dead?"

"No, I definitely do not want you dead."

"No more medicine, please."

"Do you still want to hurt yourself?"

"Is my punishment more medicine if I do?"

"No, medicine isn't a punishment but I do need to know if you still want to hurt yourself."

"I do. But I don't really have enough energy to try right now. I really feel like just going to sleep and not waking up." Sarah started to drool and her eyes closed.

"Okay, lay down before you fall down. You're going to feel better in the morning."

"I wish Dennis was here."

"Who was Dennis?"

"He used to like me to sleep on him."

"Can you tell me about Dennis?"

"One time I had a bad dream and I went to Zeke in the living room and I tried to practice like I did to you and Mike, but Zeke let me. I got him hard and then I got on him to do intercourse. Everyone thought it was funny. Zeke said 'You have to service the wenches sometimes.' But after Zeke exploded and said he had to put me back to bed, Dennis said he would do it. He picked me up and took me in my room and he took off his shoes and his pants and he lay down in my bed next to me. Then he took my pajamas off of me and he held me until I was quiet then he took my hand and he showed me how to touch him softly and quietly. And he rubbed my back and talked quietly to me. He called me his sleeping beauty. He touched my chest and it felt funny. Good, but funny. And then he asked if I wanted to sleep with him inside so I was safe all night. He put stuff in me and I got on top of him and he didn't want to do rhythms right away. He wanted me to relax and go to sleep. When I was asleep then he would do the rhythms and I would wake up a little and he would tell me to go back to sleep so I would pretend I was asleep and he would explode. But then I really would go back to sleep and he would fall asleep too. The first time he only did it once and then he went back in the other room. But after that he would come and sleep with me a couple of times a week. Sometimes when Dennis was holding me and touching me, I wanted to do rhythms. He would let me do it for a couple of minutes and then he would tell me to relax. He said I was still too little for that. I was his sleeping beauty."

"You wish Dennis was here now?"

Sarah nodded. "I liked sleeping with Dennis. It was warm and close and quiet."

"You felt protected and cared about."

Sarah nodded. "He was as bad as the rest of them, wasn't he?"

"What do you think?"

"He didn't feel as bad. He sort of acted like he cared. Or maybe he was just quieter. I liked how I felt when I was with Dennis."

"You would like to feel quiet inside now."

She nodded and drifted off to sleep. She slept quietly for a few hours before the violent dreams started again.

February 24th   12:15 am

She woke at midnight, startled to find herself in a bed and dry. She was still gasping for breath.

"Talk it out. What happened? Come on, talk it through." Mark started the recorder the doctor had ordered them to use if Sarah woke during the night.

"Zeke took me to Bill's house. He has a hot tub. Bill said I could play in the hot tub. I had to take off all my clothes and Bill took off his clothes and he got in first and he lifted me in. It was hot. When I stood up in the middle I could just keep my head out of the water but if I sat on the benches I was under water. I could kneel on the bench and I could swim in the water. I got used to it and I swam to Bill and I swam to Zeke. It was fun. Then they showed me how to hold my breath. I could do it and I was proud of myself and I was happy and I was swimming. Then Bill stood up and told me to lick him. I made him get hard and he wanted me to take him all in and I did but then he was holding my head and he went under the water and he exploded but I couldn't breathe. He didn't let go of me and I couldn't get away and then everything went white. And then I think Zeke hit me and I was coughing and I was in a snow bank and I threw up. And Zeke wiped my face off with snow and he gave me a drink and then he handed me back to Bill and said 'Guess she does better if we keep her above water.'"

"What did Bill do?"

"He washed the snow off of me. I was shivering and he said that there is no sense in wasting that little motor I got going. So he held my head above water and Zeke had intercourse with me. Then Bill said he was ready for more and he sat on one of the steps and sat me on his lap and he went in the back. I was mostly under water so I was warmer but I was shaking all over. He said it was better with me shaking. He was in my butt and he had his fingers in my front and he held me tight to him and he started doing rhythms really slowly and the water was making splashing sounds against the side of the pool. Then the waves got bigger and he held me tighter and then he pushed me under the water when he exploded. I held my breath and he pulled me back out and against him as he finished."

"He told Zeke I was worth every penny. He said I was the best trained little bitch he ever had."

"I played in the hot tub a couple of times. Then Zeke said I wasn't going back there anymore because Bill liked to almost kill me before he had sex with me and Zeke said that one day he was going to go too far."

"Zeke didn't just get excited when I did stuff to him. He like to watch me do stuff to other people. He would get hard watching me do stuff. After we went to visit people or they came to our house to play with me, Zeke would do a session with me. He always said that it was to make sure I was in good shape. It wasn't about me. He just wanted to explode. It didn't take him very long to explode if he watched me work. He would say that he needed to do a quick check up."

"Sometimes when Dennis slept with me, he would pick me up out of bed and make me do stuff with him then he would put me back."

Then she lay down and went back to sleep.

February 25th   11:00 am

Sarah slept fitfully for the rest of the night and throughout the next day. As the medication wore off, she was more awake but very subdued. When Dr. Feingold saw her on Monday she was wrung out.

"I don't ever want to go through that again. I'm exhausted and I have so many pictures in my head. I'm just not right."

"It's going to take another day for the medication to finish getting out of your system."

"Is that what it was supposed to do?"

"Not quite. Most people sleep and calm down with that medication and it usually makes thinking a little clearer."

"It gave me dreams and I couldn't stop moving. I don't want that medicine again. If I need medicine again, can I have a different one?"

"If you need medicine again, you will have a different one. Do you need medicine?"

"Not right now."

"You'll tell the staff if you need medicine?"

"You promise it won't be that stuff again?"

"I promise."

"Then so do I. But I would rather not need to take medicine."

"I would rather that too. I want you to have today off. Just relax and sleep and settle. Can you do that?"

"I can try. We have a lot of to work to. Am I ever going to go home?"

"Probably sooner than you think. Do you think you will be able to get some school work done today?"

"You're kidding, right? I can't read."

"What do you mean you can't read?"

"Everything is all blurry. I can't read anything. I can't watch television and I can't play games because I can't hold thoughts in my head. I hate this and my mouth feels really bad. I keep brushing my teeth but it doesn't help. And I'm grumpy."

"It sounds like you feel all out of sorts."

"Do you want me to punch you?"

"No. Why do you want to punch me?"

"You always say what I say. It's annoying!"

"You find me annoying."

"Now you are doing it on purpose. You're being mean."

"You haven't punched me. Do you know what that tells me?"

"What?"

"That you have a frustration tolerance."

"What?"

"You can handle getting annoyed without being inappropriate."

"You were testing me?"

"I was."

"And I passed?"

"You did."

"Am I done for today?"

"You are."

"What day is today?

"Monday."

"What happened to Thursday at two o'clock, sharp?"

"You weren't up for the visit so I called Rabbi Cohen. He will be here this week if you are up for it."

"Will I be out of here in time for my bat mitzvah?"

"That isn't for ten more weeks. You'll be out of here in plenty of time. Now how come you aren't leaving the therapy room?"

"That would require standing up."

"And?"

"Standing up is hard."

"Out."

"Okay, I'm going."

February 26th   6:00 pm

Sarah spent the day waiting for the medication to clear her system. The staff encouraged her to drink plenty of water and they decided that if she would stay on her bed and calm she could be untethered.

Amber and Maria arrived together after work with Chinese take-out. "We thought you could use some real food."

"You were right."

"Are you feeling any better?"

"I can see better and my head's clearer. But I still need to be here." They started eating dinner. "I love egg rolls. Dr. Feingold said I don't have to take that medicine again. If I need medicine, they'll give me a different one."

"You didn't like that one?"

"Well, no. I think I would feel better if I was a blade of grass on the Serengeti during a stampede of wildebeests."

"That bad?"

"I hurt everywhere. I had so many dreams about having sex that I hurt inside."

Amber and Maria both started to laugh. "We're sorry, honey, but dreams can't make you hurt like that. Your muscles are all sore because you didn't stop moving for a couple of days. You were in motion the whole time you were asleep."

"So how come I hurt in here?" She touched her zipper.

Amber and Maria stopped smiling and looked concerned. "When did it start hurting?"

"A couple hours ago and it's getting worse."

"And you've been awake all day?"

She nodded.

"And no one has had sex with you?"

She shook her head, no.

They both relaxed and looked at each other. "I don't think it's from the medicine, honey. Why don't we finish dinner?"

They talked about their days and plans then Sarah excused herself to visit the bathroom "for the 6,000th time."

She came back white faced, "I have a problem."

Amber and Maria looked at each other and then Sarah. "What's wrong?"

"I'm bleeding."

Amber was the first to reach Sarah. She hugged her and asked, "Is it your period?"

Sarah pulled away and thought for a moment, trying to organize in her mind.

Then she nodded, "That makes sense. I thought I was hurt or something. Yeah, but I don't have anything here."

Amber pulled a pad out from her back pocket.

"You have one in your pocket?"

"Sure, you never know when your kid will need one. Remember the long part goes in front. Do you need fresh underwear?"

"No, I'm okay. I'll be right back." Sarah came back and sat on her bed. "Am I stupid?"

"No, just drug addled. You probably can't add three numbers together right now. How would you put this together when you hadn't experienced it before?"

"I wish this happened at home."

"You would rather be in the comforts of home for this?" Maria asked.

"I would rather everyone not have to know about it. Everyone knows everything here. They're all going to look at me funny tomorrow. I wish it could be private."

"I'd hate everyone knowing too. There's nothing worse than having everyone know something intimate and personal."

Amber nodded and smiled, "I know this is a very big deal for you. It's your first period and that is a big deal. But to grownups, periods are part of the routine and we just take them in stride. I think you'll find that if the staff mentions it all, it will be to ensure you have what you need. Everyone here really cares about you. I've never seen a kid treated like you are treated. They really care about you here."

"I've spent a lot of time here. Is it weird that this feels like my other home?"

Maria spoke quietly. "It's sort of sad that you need another home, but you certainly found yourself a good one."

"Can I still come here now that I had my period?"

"Of course, just because you've had your period doesn't mean you have to move off the peds unit. You will probably no longer need the hospital long before you outgrow this unit."

"Really?" Sarah sat up and looked surprised.

"If you keep working with Dr. Feingold, you won't need to be here many more times. Look how much you've grown in the past year. You went from living on your own and terrified that everyone was going to kill you to being the top of your class in a private school and talking about subjects that would put most adults to shame. The only reason you need to come here is to deal with things that most adults couldn't handle and you are doing it very well. You're going to get through it and once you do, you won't need to come here because you will know how to handle bad things when they happen."

"I'm really not going to have to keep coming back here all of my life?"

"You're going to outgrow it, just like you outgrew the clothes we bought you last summer."

Sarah sat quietly.

"What are you thinking?"

"I'm trying to wrap my drug addled brain around the concept of not coming here. It will be sort of weird."

"This is home for you. But someday, you will even leave our house."

"I will?"

"You are going to college, aren't you?"

"Yeah, but I guess I never thought about where I would live."

"Well, since that isn't for another seven years, I don't think we need to dwell on it now."

"How is your stomach? Do want some ibuprofen?"

"No, I'm okay. I have to tell the nurse, don't I?"

"Someone does. It's your call as to who that is."

"I'll tell her. I'll be right back." Sarah went to the nurse's station. She whispered to Marge, the evening nurse, "I got my period."

Marge whispered back, "Do you have supplies?"

"Amber gave me a pad."

"Do you need ibuprofen?"

"No, I'm okay."

"Okay, let me know if you need anything."

"Do you have to tell everyone?"

"I have to put it in your chart, but I also understand that you would like your privacy. I'll put it in your chart for people to respect your privacy, okay?"

"Okay." Sarah came back to the room looking pleased. "She's going to put in the chart that I want my privacy."

"That's great." Maria smiled and hugged Sarah.

"Hey, we need to take off."

They each hugged her and Amber said, "Welcome to womanhood, kid. We'll see you tomorrow. Keep drinking the water. I think it's helping."

February 27th   8:00 am

Sarah woke early and found a brightly colored gift bag in the bathroom. Inside was a package of pads and a card from Amber and Maria that read:

"You are growing up in many wonderful ways. We are very happy that you have allowed us to be a part of your life.

Love, Amber and Maria"

She was showered and dressed when the first shift arrived.

"Hey, you look bright eyed." Mike spoke as he came in the door.

"I think I got the drugs out of me. I need my cell phone for a minute. I need to text Maria and Amber."

"Is everything okay?"

"Yeah, I just have to tell them something and it really shouldn't wait until tonight."

"Show me the text before you hit send."

"Nosy!" She texted "thanks" and showed Mike.

"That's it?"

"That's it. They will know exactly what it means and be happy." She hit send and gave the phone back. "Can I have my laptop? I want to get some work done before breakfast."

No one objected and Sarah spent a few hours on school work.

February 27th   11:00 am

"Hey, you ready?"

Sarah followed Dr. Feingold into the therapy room. "I understand you've been feeling pretty good this morning?" He closed the door and moved to sit down.

"The medication is out of my system. So I can think clearly again and I got up early because I wanted my privacy."

"You didn't want to discuss what happened last night?"

"I didn't, so I figured I would get up and dressed before anyone started talking about it."

"Did it work?"

"Yup. I guess we probably have to talk about it, don't we?"

"At some point we will probably talk about it. But we can talk about it when you're ready. I don't want to violate your sense of privacy."

"For now can we just say that we are okay with it?"

"Are you okay with it?"

"Yeah, I am. I kind of feel like it's a shield; or a wall maybe between my old world and my new world. It's just one more way that now is different than then."

"I can see that. And how is your head today?"

"It's clearer. That medicine really messed me up."

"It opened you up to a lot of memories."

"Yeah, but they weren't good memories."

"No, they weren't, but the more memories we look at together and get out into the open, the better you're going to feel. How are you doing with wanting to hurt yourself?"

"This is going to sound really weird."

"Say it anyway."

"I'm bleeding so I don't feel like I need to make myself bleed. So, the thought of cutting myself is still there but it isn't as much of an urge as it was. You know when I started jumping on the bed?"

"Yes it would be hard to forget."

"I wanted to jump out of myself. I felt so creepy. It was like I had bugs crawling under my skin and I wanted to get them out of me. Were the bugs the dreams that I had?"

"I think so."

"They are only a little bit now. There is more stuff in me that I have to remember, isn't there?"

"There probably is. Did you just remember the stuff that you dreamed about this past week?"

"I hadn't thought about any of it. It's like when I came back here last time and I walked in the kitchen therapy room, I was surprised that it was yellow. Then I remembered that it was yellow last summer. I thought about my chick being so much brighter than the walls. But if you had asked me before I came back what color the walls were, I couldn't have told you. It was like that with the dreams and the pictures in my head. I forgot all about Bop-bop. Now I'm sad about him."

"What was Bop-bop like?"

"He was a fluffy stuffed rabbit with really long soft ears. He was light brown and he had big brown eyes and a little fluffy bunny tail."

"Where did you get him?"

"Remember the man that told Zeke how to train me?"

"Yes."

"I'm not sure, but I think he gave him to me. It's kind of fuzzy in my head but I think that he gave me the bunny for being good. I guess that probably means that he did something wrong to me, but I don't remember what it was. I do know that Zeke would take Bop-bop away from me when I had to work and tell me that I would get him back if I did a good job."

"How did he get the name Bop-bop?"

"Well, I think it was supposed to be Hop-hop but I didn't say it right and Zeke called it Bop-bop and it stuck. How come Zeke stopped me from getting in the incinerator?"

"Why do you think he stopped you?"

"Do you think he cared about me sort of?"

"That is possible. He stopped taking you to Bill's house."

"Yeah, Bill was pretty weird. Is there a word for people who want to almost kill you before they have sex with you?"

"Yes, we call them weird. But let's get back to Zeke. He did a lot of things that harmed you, didn't he?"

"You mean you're not supposed to rent your kid out? And you aren't supposed to have sex with them a couple times a day? And you aren't supposed to get jealous and excited if they do what you told them to do with someone else?"

"But he also cared for you."

"He fed me and clothed me and taught me to read. But then he burned everything I owned and blew up my house." Sarah sat back and sighed, "I just want to know one thing."

"What is that?"

"Is there any way to know if Zeke was my father?"

"I don't know. But I'll try to find out. What would it mean if he was your father?"

"It would mean that he did a very horrible thing. God talks about it in my Torah reading. It says that a father shouldn't prostitute his daughter. If Zeke made me and then defiled me, he defiled himself too. Why would someone do that to themselves?"

"I think Zeke was very disturbed."

"If I am his daughter, am I going to be a weirdo too?"

"Whether you are his daughter or not, you have free will. You can choose what you're going to do with your life. You can use your experiences for bettering the world or for destroying it, or you can step away from your experiences and go in a different direction all together. It is your decision."

"Okay. But will you try to find out for me? I don't know why it really matters, but it does."

"I will do my best."

"Now, I want you to start attending therapies again, okay?"

"Okay. Am I still on close watch?"

"Do you need to be?"

"15 minutes will be good. We can try 15 minute checks."

"Okay. Fifteen minute checks unless you need more."

Sarah began attending groups and continued working on her school work. She participated well for several days.

February 28th   2:00 pm

As Rabbi Cohen arrived, Sarah said gleefully, "Thursday, two o'clock, sharp."

"Have you been waiting?"

"I missed you last week. But since it was Saturday before I knew it wasn't Thursday, I guess it's okay."

"You were having a tough time."

"Yeah, things got a little squirrelly. Can we work on my Torah portion? I haven't practiced in like two weeks and I'm starting to get anxious about it. My bat mitzvah is only like ten weeks away."

"You are going to do fine. But let's start at the top." She began reading in Hebrew with Rabbi Cohen correcting her pronunciation and discussing the translations of the words. They worked for an hour before Rabbi Cohen called a halt. "You are doing very well, Sarah. I see you are gaining new understanding. It isn't enough to say the words; it is about understanding God in the meaning."

"Now, before I go, I have some things for you from your classmates." He brought out several cards and a letter from her teacher as well as three books. "And now, I must go."

"Tell everyone that I said 'Hi' and I will be back to school as soon as I can. I just have to work a few more things out before I come home."

"Home and school will wait. You are doing important work and it is always right to be in the right place for each job." He sang out "Rabbi-hug" and enfolded her in a hug before placing his hand on her forehead and blessing her.

Sarah sat at her table in the day room and was reading her cards when a boy and his mother came into the room. The boy rocked as he walked then began hitting his head with his hands. Julia quickly intervened and redirected the boy. Sarah watched with curiosity and then recognition. When the boy was calm and engaged with Julia, she walked over to the mother.

"Excuse me?" She looked up with very tired eyes. "You were here a year ago, weren't you?"

"Yes."

"I remember you and your son. I don't know if you remember me, or probably more accurately, I don't know if you recognize me. I had just come here then and I couldn't talk and a staff person wouldn't let me have dinner."

The woman's eyes shifted and she looked in wonder at Sarah. "You?" Sarah nodded and then smiled.

"You called the hospital administration and told them. Thank you."

"You were that little girl?"

"Yeah, I've grown a little this year. And I can talk now. And I just wanted to say thank you for seeing what was happening and caring enough to do something."

"I didn't want something like that to happen to my son. He can't speak for himself either."

"I can assure you that nothing like that will happen here now."

"Have you been here all this time?"

"No, I have a foster home and really nice foster moms. I'm just here to work a few things out and then I will go back home and back to school. I guess he needs to work a few things out too."

"He needs his medication adjusted. He is growing and we can't get the dosage right. He isn't sleeping and if he doesn't sleep, then I can't sleep."

"That sounds really hard. I hope you can get some sleep while he's here and get caught up. Julia and Molly are great at tucking people in. They were my tucker inners. We each have a team of bedtime people so we have the same routine every night. They will get him to sleep."

"You sound very confident."

"It's experience talking. If you'll excuse me, I have to go work on my homework, but I wanted to say thank you, now that I can."

"You're welcome. And thank you."

"For what?"

"Reassuring me that Timmy will be okay here."

"He'll be fine."

Sarah packed up her books and went into her room. She was lying on her bed reading when Julia came in. "Sarah that was a very nice thing you did."

"I just told her thank you."

"No, you let her know that her son would be safe. You let her know that she could trust us with her son."

"So, it was a Mitzvah?"

"It was. And I want to say thank you for the compliment and your trust."

"You're welcome. You earned it."

February 28th   6:00 pm

When Amber and Maria arrived, they found a happy, chipper Sarah awaiting them. "Wow, you look happy."

"I am."

"Any particular reason?"

"Well, I can think clearly and I feel in charge of myself. And I can see again. I got some homework done and I had a good session with Dr. Feingold and I saw Rabbi Cohen. It was a good day."

"How are you doing with your Torah portion?"

"I'm still stumbling over a few words but I'm getting there. I'm doing okay since I missed last week and I wasn't even saying my prayers for days. Rabbi Cohen speaks to me mostly in Hebrew now. You know what would be fun?"

"What?"

"To go someplace and just speak in Hebrew. Maybe Rachel and I can do it together."

"What about Tara?"

"Tara couldn't do it even if she wanted. She can barely read Hebrew and she can't translate. She just knows the sounds. But Rachel could do it."

"Do you want to go somewhere where they speak Hebrew or where they wouldn't understand you?"

"Someplace where they would understand. Like B&H. You know, the photography store with all the orthodox Jewish guys. Or someplace like that. Doing it where they wouldn't understand us would be mean. It's rude to talk in a language that people around you don't understand. That's why Rachel and I switch to English when you come in the room."

"You speak in Hebrew when you're alone?"

"Yeah, it's fun. But we only do it when we are alone or with her dad. Her mom can't do it and Tara can't do it. So we don't do it around them. And of course you guys can't do it.
What if I could go to Israel and talk to people there? Wouldn't it be cool?"

Amber nodded. "I went to France when I was in high school and spoke French while I was there. I understand what you mean. It was cool."

"I went to Italy in college. Yeah, it was hard with the dialect being so different but yeah, it was cool."

"Do you guys still speak French and Italian?"

"I can get by if I need to. But I don't use it enough to keep it all."

"So if I learned them would you talk to me in them?"

"We could try. You would probably out-strip either of us."

"You pick up language quickly," Maria observed.

Sarah started laughing.

"What's so funny?"

"Do you realize the irony of that statement?" Maria looked puzzled for a moment. Then the three of them burst out laughing.

When they had all recovered, Maria asked, "Sarah, have you thought about who you want to invite to your bat mitzvah?"

"I've thought about it, but I don't know who I can invite."

"Have you got a sheet of paper? We can start making a list." Sarah pulled out a spiral notebook from her backpack and handed it and a pen to Amber. "Okay kid, start listing people."

"You and Maria of course, and Rachel and Tara, and their parents and Rabbi Cohen of course." Sarah started to squirm.

"What is it, kid?"

"I want to invite some people but I don't know if it's allowed."

"Who do you want to invite?"

"I want to invite Mike and Nancy and Molly and Julia and I really want to invite Dr. Feingold. They are all like my family but only when I'm here."

"Have you talked to Dr. Feingold about this?"

"No, we have been a little busy with me having had sex with every third guy on the planet. And I'm afraid he'll say no."

Amber burst out laughing, "I'm sorry. I know that wasn't meant to be funny. It's just the way you said it. We need to come back to you having sex with every third guy on the planet. But let's talk about inviting Dr. F. You really want him to be there?"

Sarah nodded. "I wouldn't be doing it if it wasn't for him. We've worked hard for me to get to do my bat mitzvah. It just seems right for him to be there. He's part of my family too. You know what's weird?"

"What?"

"I'm not part of his family. Do know what I know about him outside of our work together?"

"What?"

"Almost nothing; I know that he belongs to my temple but he never goes."

"Is he married?" Sarah shrugged. "Does he have kids?" Sarah put her palms up. "How old is he?" She shrugged again. "Where is he from?"

"I don't know."

"What *do* you know about him?"

"I know that I can trust him and he won't hurt me or let me hurt myself. I know that he is really smart and that he uses the smartness to help people understand and not make them feel stupid. I know that he wants people to grow even if it means they don't go visit him anymore and he will miss them. And I know he loves me."

"Did he tell you that he loves you?"

"Of course not. Doctors can't tell patients that they love them."

"Then how do you know?"

"Because he always does what I really need instead of what I think I need or what I want. And he won't let me do things that will be bad for me even if I really want to do them."

"That sounds like love."

"Just don't tell him I said so; it might freak him out. He would probably have to go to therapy or something."

"We wouldn't want that."

"This is probably a novel concept, but why don't you ask him if the staff can go to your bat mitzvah and if he can go?"

"Should I give them invitations or just ask them?"

"Let's put them on the invitation list. If we're going to do this, we should do it properly. This is a big deal for you; let's send out formal invitations."

"Is there anyone you guys want to invite?

Maria said, "I think if it's okay with you, I would like to invite my parents. My mom was asking about it just this past week."

"Does she know I'm in the hospital again?"

"I told her. She said she is sending you her positive thoughts."

"Is she okay with going to a temple?"

"I think she's intrigued by the whole idea. She's never been in one and I think she sees it as an adventure."

"Okay."

"Anyone else?"

"I don't think so. Is there anyone you think I'm forgetting?"

"Do you want to invite Joe?"

"No. It would weird him out."

"Do you ever see Joe?"

"Sometimes we cross paths while he's on his beat. Pete is friendly with me but Joe just doesn't know what to say to me. Pete took me aside a while ago and told me that I shouldn't worry about his lame-brained partner. He said that he was really of proud of me and I should just keep working and growing and not try to drag Joe into the complex world of being a whole person. If Joe ever got there, he would find out just what a terrific kid I really was, warts and all. Now I just wave to them and say hi but Joe isn't my friend. He isn't my enemy or anything, but he couldn't handle who I am, so he's not my friend."

"You're okay with that, aren't you?"

"I was mad at him for a while but yeah, I'm okay with it. I guess I can let him have his warts."

"You've done a lot of growing. Are you too grown up to be tucked in?"

"Not quite yet. I'll get my PJs on."

March 1ˢᵗ   10:15 am

Sarah was walking from her room to the day room to work on her school work when the pet therapist arrived with a bunny and a cat. Sarah ignored her.

Nancy called to Sarah, "You're scheduled for pet therapy."

"No."

"What did you say?"

"No, thank you."

Sarah's bright disposition turned hard as she walked into the dayroom muttering, "I'm not going to fucking pet therapy." She sat down at her table and opened her book but kicked her feet angrily under the table.

Dr. Feingold had just finished with a patient and was standing at the door of the therapy room watching the exchange. Nancy looked at him. Their eyes met, went to Sarah, and returned to each other.

Dr. Feingold called for his next patient.

Sarah was still sitting at her table working on her schoolwork when he finished the session. Her agitation level was lower, but she was neither relaxed nor working happily.

He went over to her and asked if she was ready for her session. She nodded, signed off her laptop, and followed him into the therapy room.

"What's up?" She set down her books on the table and then sat in her little ball and shrugged. "What are you thinking?" She shrugged again.

"Are you remembering something?"

"No. I just hate her and her stupid animals."

"Tell me about why you hate her stupid animals."

"I don't know. I just do."

"Come over here and give me your hands."

"Are you going to make me remember something?"

"Is there something to remember?"

"Yeah, but I'm not sure what it is and I know I don't want to remember it."

"So, you know something bad happened to an animal or to you with an animal."

"I don't want to know."

"Knowing that something happened is scary, isn't it?"

"I don't want to know."

"When you closed your eyes just now, what did you see?"

"I don't want to know!" She curled into a smaller ball, faced the wall, and began rocking.

He started to speak and she covered her ears, "I don't want to know." He went over to her and sat on the floor next to her with his back against the wall.

"Sarah, I'm right here. When you are ready to tell me what you are seeing."

"I don't want to see it."

"I know you don't. But your mind knows that you are ready to know."

"Why do I have to know?"

"Because your mind thinks you're ready. Shall we start?"

"Do I have to?"

"You're going to see it, we both know that part. The question is whether you will see it now while you're awake or if you're going to have nightmares of it tonight. Who is in charge of this; you or your mind?"

"Okay. Let's do it the regular way. Your sitting on the floor is too weird."

"Okay, I'll get in my place." He sat back in his chair and Sarah sat at his knees and gave him her hands.

Quietly, Sarah asked, "I'm the only one you do this with, aren't I?"

"You're the only one."

"You won't let me go?"

"I won't let you go"

"Okay, I'm ready."

"Okay, close your eyes and take a deep breath and let it out slowly. Now take another deep breath. Good. Do you feel my hands? I'm right here. I'm going to keep you from getting lost. Now, I want to you to take another deep breath and let your mind go to where it needs to take you. Can you tell me where you are?"

"I'm at the picnic table in the backyard."

"What are you doing?"

"I'm eating cheese."

"Tell me what you see."

"I'm wearing my green dress and I'm not working because I am wearing underwear. And it's summer and the grass is green and the sun is bright and warm. And I'm eating my cheese and there is a black and white kitty in the yard. 'Here kitty, come here kitty.' I get off the picnic table and I'm walking toward the cat and it came up to me. I sit down in the grass and I pet the kitty and I gave it the rest of my cheese. 'Nice Kitty.' It has a long tail. The kitty is soft. It's meowing. It likes me. He is rubbing me with his head. I'm hugging the kitty and it's purring. Zeke came out the back door. 'I have a kitty. He wants to be my kitty.' Zeke came over and he picked up the kitty. 'You want this kitty?' 'I want him.' 'Let me show you what we do with kitties.' He pulled the knife out of his pocket and opened it and 'NO!!!!'"

Dr. Feingold held her hands. "What did Zeke do?"

"He cut the cat's head off." Sarah started choking, "There is blood all over me. The cat is trying to meow but nothing is coming out it's moving its eyes and it's on the ground and it's still alive but it's just the head."

"Zeke has the body in his arms and the blood is coming out of where the head was and I am underneath it and its bleeding all over me." Sarah pulled away from Dr. Feingold and curled into a ball face down on the floor at his feet. Her hands were balled into fists covering her eyes.

"Sarah, what is Zeke doing now?" Sarah rolled sideways and looked up. Then she covered her face again. "Tell me what happened, Sarah."

"He cut open the cat and all the guts are on me. Get them off of me. They're hot and slimy and they smell. No more. No More."

"Okay, Sarah. Is Zeke still there?"

"Yes."

"What is he doing?"

"I don't know. I don't know."

"Okay Sarah, can you come back here? I want you to take a deep breath and come back to the hospital."

Sarah took a breath and screamed.

"Sarah, what is it? Open your eyes. Sarah, open your eyes. You're in the hospital. You're safe." Sarah opened her eyes and looked dazed and horrified and disoriented.

"I hate you."

"You're okay, you're here and you're safe and you're okay. Take a deep breath."

"I hate you."

"Do you want Cody?"

"I don't want to get blood on him."

"Sarah, open your eyes. There is no blood on you. It was a memory. It happened a long time ago. You're here with me now and you are safe and you are clean and dry."

"What about the cat skin? Where's the cat skin?"

"What cat skin?"

"Zeke skinned the cat and he covered me with it. He put the slimy side against me and said that now I can be the cat. He said if he ever catches me touching another animal he would do that to me. Take the fur off of me."

"Okay, Sarah, I'm taking it off of you and I am going to get everything else off of you too. Sarah, I want you to hold my hands and we are going to come back to the therapy room. Hold tight. Take a deep breath and on three you are going to come back here. Ready? One, two, three, now open your eyes."

Sarah opened her eyes and found herself lying on the floor in the therapy room. She touched her arms and found that she was wearing a navy blue long sleeved shirt and denim jeans and a little vest. She was startled to find was that she was clean and dry.

"Just take a couple of breaths. Are you okay?"

"I hate you." She sat up and shuddered. "I really hate you."

"Hold my hands. I want you to stay here." She gave him her hands and looked around. "It's not here. It was a memory. It was just a really horrible memory."

"I'm still not going to pet therapy. I keep seeing it when I close my eyes."

"Just sit with me. Just let yourself be for a minute. Stay here."

They sat together just being while Sarah found her center again. Then she looked up at him. "Sometimes, I really hate you. I could have gone the whole rest of my life without remembering that. That was the grossest most horrible thing I have ever seen. Why did you make me remember that?"

He just held her hands together and sighed. "I'm sorry. It had to be done for you to heal. You're not all the way back here, are you?"

She shook her head. "I'm both places and I'm both people. I want to go back and get her."

"You want to rescue yourself."

Sarah nodded. "I was really little then. I want to go get me so more bad stuff doesn't happen to me."

"You need to stay here now. Sarah, you need to look at me." She complied. "You need to stay here."

"I want to get her and bring her here."

"Sarah, you are her and that was a memory. It isn't happening now."

"It feels like now."

"I know. But it was a long time ago and she isn't there anymore. She is you and you are already here." Sarah looked around the room and became more oriented to herself and the therapy room. She shook her head as if to reorient herself. Then she sat back.

"Are you okay?"

"Wow."

"Yeah, wow."

"Can we put a road closed sign on that memory lane? That was the worst memory ever."

"How do you feel now?"

"I don't feel right. I'm really tired. And I hate you."

"You've mentioned that."

"I think I need Cody."

"Do you need the vest?"

"I don't think that would be inappropriate."

"Do you need medication?"

"Not Lorazepam."

"But you need something?"

"I think so and I need the vest now. The jumpy feelings are coming."

"Okay, can you stand up?"

Sarah nodded and then walked to her room. They hailed Mike and Nancy on the way. Sarah kicked off her shoes and let Nancy remove her denim vest and put on the restraint vest. Then the shakes started.

"Sarah, what you are feeling right now is the adrenaline release. If you can hold together through this, I think you will be okay without medication."

"I'm freezing." They covered her with a blanket and Nancy sat on the bed with her and held her hands and rubbed them.

"Bill would love it if he was here now. This is how he liked me." She was shaking violently.

"Nobody is going to hurt you now. Just relax and let the shakes go through you and leave. You are going to be okay." In only a few minutes, the shaking stopped and Sarah yawned.

"Are you suddenly exhausted?" She nodded. "Okay, Cody, I want you to keep Sarah here. Can you do that?" Cody nodded. Dr. Feingold placed Cody in Sarah's arms. She rolled on her side and went into a deep sleep.

Mike stayed with Sarah as Dr. Feingold and Nancy stepped into the hallway. "We heard the scream. Is she okay?"

"I think she will be, but you should expect another round of nightmares. She befriended a cat and Zeke beheaded and gutted it over top of her then skinned it and covered her with the skin." Nancy shuddered. "Oh, the poor kid. God, does this ever end for this kid?"

"No wonder she doesn't go near the animals. Oh my God. It's a damn good thing that guy is dead. I would have to kill him myself if he was still alive."

"Yeah, I know the feeling."

"I am going to write an order for medication if she needs it."

March 1st   2:00 pm

Sarah slept for an hour before the nightmares started. She woke herself with her thrashing.

"Sarah, you're okay, honey. I'm right here with you. Wake up Sarah, you're in the hospital."

She awoke and looked around. "What time is it?"

"About 2:00. Do you want something to drink?"

"Yeah. I don't suppose I can have a vodka and tonic."

"No, but we can get you some water. Or, if you play your cards right, I might be able to arrange a ginger ale."

"Yeah, that will work."

"Will you be okay while I get it?"

"Yeah, I'll be okay."

Dr. Feingold stepped into the room as Mike stepped out.

"How do you feel?"

"I still hate you."

"I understand that."

"Am I ever going to be okay?"

"It doesn't feel like it right now, does it?"

"No. It feels like it just goes on and on. Will I ever run out of bad memories?"

"I hope so. And I hope that we're able to get you making good memories very soon."

"Are you going to be here this weekend?"

"I am going to check in with you."

"Okay. I'm going to have nightmares tonight, aren't I?"

"I wouldn't be surprised. But you have Cody and you will have staff with you. I've written an order for medication for you if you need it. I don't want them to just give it to you because I know that you don't like taking medication and want to tough it out. But it's there for you if you need it."

"Medicine won't make what happened not have happened."

"No, but sometimes it makes it easier to deal with the symptoms of the results. But for as long as you are safe, it's your decision. If you aren't safe, the staff will make that decision for you."

"I am in charge of me now?"

"To the degree in which you can be so safely, you are in charge of you. You have shown very good decision making and you have a done a good job of raising yourself. I don't want to take that away from you."

"I wasn't in control at all before, was I?"

"No."

"Zeke was a bastard. Did you find out?"

"Sarah, you are in no condition to talk about this right now. I want you to relax and regroup this weekend. I will have news for you next week, one way or the other."

"Okay."

"Looks like Mike has some lunch for you."

"That's good because I've missed a lot of meals here."

"We'll try to make it up to you. Are Amber and Maria coming in tonight?"

"Yeah, they're coming after work and then they are going out to dinner with some friends. They have another weekend without a kid."

"I need to see them when they come in. Do you want to be a part of the meeting?"

"Are you going to talk about cats?"

"We are."

"I'll pass. I don't really want to think about cats right now."

"Um, instead of medicine, could you write an order for me to play shots?"

"Have you ever played shots?"

"No, but I saw people play shots and there are times like now when getting really drunk seems appealing."

"You're really shaken up by this one, aren't you?"

"I keep seeing it every time I close my eyes. I remember that green dress. It was a pretty mint green and it had lace across the bodice."

"Do you have any idea how old you were?"

"Probably 3 or 4; I was pretty little. Sitting down petting the cat, my head was below Zeke's knees."

"Have some lunch and try to focus on something else for a while. We'll get back to the cat in due time."

"If we must; in the meantime, Mike and I should play shots."

"Yeah, we can play shots; let me get us set up."

"I have the best staff people."

Mike left the room again.

"What do you think he's up to?"

"I'm not sure, but I bet it'll be fun."

"You can fill me in later."

Sarah finished her sandwich and fell asleep again before Mike came back. She was still asleep when Maria and Amber arrived. They met with Dr. Feingold who filled them in on the events of the day.

"I want to put her on medication. I know she doesn't like the idea and I am not talking something long term. But I would like to put her on a very low dose of Risperdal. It is very fast acting and has a short half- life. I think it will help her sleep better with fewer violent nightmares and make her more able to process during the day."

Amber was immediately concerned, "Risperdal- that's like thorazine- the oldest drug out there. That's that drug for drooling and shuffling. I don't want Sarah to be a zombie."

"Those are higher dosages. I want to give Sarah a very small dose. It seems to be effective for this. Also, it doesn't need a couple weeks to take effect. She will feel herself relax in about 10 minutes. If it doesn't work for her, it will be out of her system in just a few days."

"Okay. Let's talk to her about it together."

March 1ˢᵗ   7:00 pm

They went to Sarah's room and found her in the throes of another violent nightmare.

"Sarah. Wake up, Sarah. You're in the hospital, you're okay."

Sarah woke frightened and disoriented.

"Hey kid. We're here and you're with us now. You're okay."

Sarah sat up. "I can't take it anymore."

"Dr. Feingold has a medication he wants you to take that he thinks will help."

"Do you think I should?"

"I think it's worth a try."

"Does it make me a wuss?"

"No, medication is a tool and the more tools you have in your tool bag, the better off you are. It's just like the hospital is a tool. You need to be brave enough to deal with what you can and know when to buy a new tool. I think it's time for medication."

"Do I have to take it forever?"

"No; just until you don't need it anymore. Let's worry about getting you through now."

"Okay."

"You're going to take it before you go bed and it will help you sleep without so many nightmares. Then the sleepy part will wear off for morning and you should be good for the day. It might take a couple of days to adjust but I think it's worth the try."

"Okay. I can't do this anymore. Living alone was a lot easier."

"Back when you didn't remember any of it?"

"Yeah, I sort of wish I was in my numb bubble again. Is it going to get better?"

"Yes, but we need to work our way through it. If we stop here, this is what you will be stuck dealing with. If we keep working, you will get beyond this and be in much better shape."

"I think I need new sneakers."

They all looked her.

"Don't I need Nikes so I can 'just do it'?"

Amber and Maria both rolled their eyes, "We're going to dinner."

"She's all yours."

March 2nd   1:30 pm

Sarah took the medication and although she still had a few nightmares, they weren't as vivid or as violent. She spent Saturday alternating between trying to do schoolwork and annoying the staff. She was irritable and frustrated. Dr. Feingold arrived in the early Saturday afternoon.

"How are you doing?"

"If this medication is helping, we should be very glad I took it."

"You're having a tough time."

"I don't know what to do with myself. I don't know what to do with the pictures in my head and they just don't stop."

"Why don't we talk about the pictures?"

"I don't want to go back there. I don't want the blood on me again."

"Okay, can we talk about it without you going back there?"

"We can try."

"Why don't you tell me what you are seeing?"

"It varies; it's flashes of that day. Sometimes I see the dress, sometimes I see the blood, or the cat's head rolling on the ground, or the cat's eyes blinking and its mouth opening and closing. Sometimes I feel it and I have to look to make sure I'm not covered in blood and guts. Cats have a lot of guts. A couple of times I felt the weight of the skin on my back. I don't think I'll ever wear a fur coat."

"How do you feel talking about this?"

"I don't know. It kind of makes my stomach hurt. Mostly, I feel really sad inside. It was my fault."

"How was it your fault?"

"I was my fault because I petted the cat. If I didn't call it over to me and pet it and feed it then Zeke wouldn't have killed it."

"So, if you pet a cat it will get killed?"

"That sounds stupid, doesn't it?"

"It sounds like it's what you've believed."

"I didn't even know I believed it. I guess I had a good reason for not doing pet therapy. That lady was lucky that I didn't go her stupid group. She would have been pretty upset if Zeke came to her house and killed her animals."

"Do you think he would do that?"

"Sort of; when I really think about it I know he's dead and dead people can't do that. But when I just think about it in the corner of my mind, sort of, he is alive and he wouldn't have any problem doing stuff. Is Zeke ever going to be dead and stay dead?"

"Zeke already is dead. He will stay dead in your mind when you're ready."

"Saying 'I'm Ready' isn't good enough is it?"

"No, I'm afraid not."

"Do other people have cloud thoughts?"

"What are cloud thoughts?"

"They're like Zeke being alive. When they are floating around they seem solid but then when you get in them they are like fog and you can't hold onto them and they aren't real."

"Do you have a lot of cloud thoughts?"

"Yeah, they get confusing."

"What kind of cloud thoughts do you have?"

"Well, a lot about Zeke being alive or coming back alive and I have thoughts about people having sex with me."

"Who do you think is going to have sex with you?"

"In cloud thoughts I think you will, but not in real. But I have the cloud thoughts all the time. Then when I catch the thought, it disappears. Am I weird?"

"No, you aren't weird. But we do need to talk more about the cloud thoughts."

"Now?"

"No, but over time. For now, how do you feel?"

"The medicine made the nightmares better but I feel sort of floaty today."

"Floaty?"

"I have a lot more cloud thoughts and it's like I'm floating around with them. That's the good part about having my vest; I don't have to worry about floating away with my thoughts."

"Are your thoughts floatier today than usual?"

"I'm floatier. I'm not sure about my thoughts. I'm tired. Can we be done?"

"We can be done. Are you going to be able to hold yourself together tonight?"

"I don't feel as itchy inside. Are you taking tomorrow off?"

"I am. I'll see you on Monday."

March 2nd   3:00 pm

Sarah spent Sunday reading and working on her school work. She was quiet and subdued and sedate. Amber and Maria stopped by to visit, but Sarah was not interested in visiting. She wasn't grumpy or rude, just detached.

"Are you feeling okay?"

"I don't know. I'm just not anywhere. Yesterday I felt all floaty but now I feel like there is a boulder holding me down and I'm not really having any thoughts. I'm not tired but it's hard to stay awake and I probably could think if I tried hard enough but it just seems like too much work."

"I was trying to read Anne Frank for school but I gave up. I'm reading Nancy Drew but I really don't care if she finds out what happened to the clock."

"Haven't you read Anne Frank before?"

"Yeah, a couple of times. But right now I don't care about her and boring Peter. I'm stuck inside all the time too and at least she has nice parents. I have you guys now but I'm not home. I'm not being very nice today and I don't know why."

"Hang in there. We all have an off day and I bet you're going to feel better in the morning."

"Am I ever going to come home?"

"As soon as it is the best place for you to be, you will be coming home."

"I miss home."

"Are you still having thoughts of hurting yourself?"

"Yeah, but I'm too tired right now to try."

March 4th   8:30 am

Monday brought a heavy snow storm. But on the unit, the routine continued. Sarah was up and dressed when the first shift arrived but was lying down reading when Mike came in to say good morning. She barely acknowledged him.

"Are you okay?"

"Someone made my head too heavy during the night."

"I'll let the Doc know. Are you ready for breakfast?"

"I guess so." Sarah got off her bed and stood up, then stopped and fell to the floor.

"Sarah! Nancy!"

Nancy was in her room in moments.

"She fainted when she got off her bed."

Sarah mumbled, "This floor is cold."

"Okay, just stay put for a minute. I want to take your blood pressure." She took Sarah's BP and assessed her for injuries. There were none. Then she had Mike hold her as she stood up and took her BP again.

She again passed out when she stood, but Mike had her and she did not hit the floor again. Once Nancy had taken her BP he placed her on her bed.

"What's wrong with me?"

"Were you dizzy when you got up this morning?"

"Yeah. Everything went black when I got out of bed but it got better while I was sitting on the toilet and then I sat on the floor to get dressed and I got back on my bed."

"You have postural hypotension."

"Is that bad?"

"You have earned breakfast in bed and an extra orange juice. For now, you need someone with you if you need to get up."

Mike got her breakfast and extra juice and Sarah seemed to be perking up. She was chatting with Mike when Dr. Feingold came in.

"Hey, how are you feeling?"

"Did Nancy tell you that I have developed an affinity for the floor?"

"She did mention that you had a syncope episode. How are you now?"

"Better. The juice is helping me feel better."

"Do you want to go into the therapy room or should we stay here?"

"I can try getting up."

"Let's go slowly." They got her up in stages and although she went dark, she didn't hit the floor.

"Is this from the medicine?"

"I think so. I think we need to reduce your dosage a little bit. Is it helping with the nightmares?"

"Yeah, I'm definitely sleeping easier. But it's too much."

"Okay, let's try dropping your dosage in half and see what happens." They had a light session because Sarah was not up to thinking very quickly. She spent the day quietly trying to read and do homework and drinking water to flush the medication. By dinner she was able to stand up without blacking out.

March 5th   11:00 am

On Tuesday she had slept well and was feeling clear headed and organized.

"How are you doing today?"

"Okay."

"Do we have the medication level about right?"

"Yeah. I have nightmares but they aren't as bad and I can stand up without falling down. So, did you find out?"

"I did find out."

"So, tell me."

"Are you sure?"

"I'm sure. I want to know. Was Zeke my father?"

"They took DNA samples when they found Zeke and they took your DNA when you were first found in order to run it through the data bases."

"And…"

"Zeke is not your biological father."

"So, I didn't commit patricide."

"You did not kill your biological father. "

"Was I kidnapped? Do they know who I am? Does anyone know where I came from?"

"No, Sarah. No one knows who your biological parents are. We do not know where you came from or how you came to be with Zeke. But we do know who you are now."

"He wasn't my father. Somehow that does make it better. I think one of the few ways that all of this could have been worse would be if he was my father. That would have been worse."

"How do you feel now that you know?"

"I want Cody. Well that's not really true. I don't want Cody. I want you to hold me. I want to belong to someone."

"You do belong. You belong to Maria and Amber and you belong to Rabbi Cohen and the temple."

"And I belong to you?"

"And you belong to me."

"You belong to me too. I like now people better than then people. You know what is different than cloud thoughts?"

"What?"

"Real thoughts. In cloud thoughts you are going to have sex with me. In real thoughts, you love me and would never do something that wasn't good for me. I like real thoughts better."

"Me too. You have some processing to do."

"I think I'm going to do some math homework while I'm processing. I'm way behind in school. Do Maria and Amber know about Zeke?"

"Not yet. Are you going to tell them tonight?"

"Yeah. Does the staff here know?"

"Not yet. I wanted you to be the first to know."

"This is bigger than multiplying fractions. I might just need some time with Cody today too."

"I think Cody time is a good idea. I'll check in with you before I leave."

"Okay."

March 28th   11:00 am

Sarah found a new emotional footing and with the information and medication, she quickly was able to find a solid foothold. She was discharged in a few days and was back at school on Friday. She was behind in school but was able to spend the weekend getting caught up.

The following week was Purim and she got dressed up in a costume for the Purim party at school and at temple. Amber and Maria experienced Hamantaschen, the prune filled tri- cornered cookies. They both decided that Purim was "way better than Halloween."

March went quickly with school, daily therapy, and bat mitzvah studies. The last week of March was vacation week for Passover. She attended services and worked with both the cantor and the rabbi to prepare for the bat mitzvah. Sarah spent part of some days with Rachel and Tara, but for the first time she was allowed to stay home alone. She was still seeing Dr. Feingold daily, but it was decided that she could be trusted to call for help if she needed it and was responsible to be where she was supposed to be and to do what she was supposed to do.

April 16th   4:00 pm

Sarah was walking from school to Dr. Feingold's when she noticed the headlines on the newspaper as she passed the newsstand. She stopped and reread the headlines, then purchased the paper and began reading as she walked. She quickly found that she could not read and walk at the same time without bumping into people so she folded the paper and ran to the doctor's office.

She burst into the office panting and trying to catch her breath. "What?"

Sarah opened the newspaper on the ottoman. "I haven't read it yet. I just saw it on the way here."

"What is it?"

"That is Dennis and that's Bill. That is the man that told Zeke how to train me."

'Child Sex Ring Shut Down' was the headline and there were pictures of 26 men. Sarah recognized all of them.

Together they read the article. The child sex ring had been discovered, infiltrated and all the adults involved had been arrested.

When they finished reading, Sarah was shaking.

"This was them?"

She nodded. "That's them. It's Westchester. How long do you think it's going to be before the DA comes to talk to me?"

"If anyone mentions Zeke, I don't think it will be very long."

"Or if they find pictures of me."

"Are there pictures of you?"

Sarah looked at the doctor. "You're kidding, right? How could there not be pictures of me? I had my picture taken. We did studio shots and I had to pose in different clothes and stuff. They even did movies."

"You never told me about that."

"It's not one of my prouder moments. But what if someone else had copies and they weren't all burned in the incinerator?"

"Sarah, you've been through all of this. You did what you did because you had to. But you have a choice now. What do you want to do?"

"Part of me wants to call the DA and tell him that they have the right people. And part of me is really dreading the knock at the door. I want to be in control of it. I don't think that I can give very good testimony against any of them. I can't tell them where things happened or exactly when they happened. I can say what happened. But I don't know if that's good enough. I don't want to be looked at by a lot of people for what happened to me. I don't want to be branded. I don't want to be famous for this. I don't want it public. I don't think that I can really help and I don't want to get hurt. Am I being selfish?"

"No, you are being self-preserving. L'chaim."

"He's going to call me, isn't he?"

"I can't imagine that he isn't."

"I need to give a deposition again, don't I?"

"You might need to."

"Maybe he won't call me."

"What was that river you were studying last summer?"

"I know, your name should be Moses because you won't let me live in Denial. Can't I just sit on the shores for a couple of minutes?"

"Okay, but watch out for alligators."

"Crocodiles, not alligators, live along the Nile. So I don't have to worry about alligators."

"You know a year ago, you didn't answer me back."

"A year ago I thought you were going to kill me. Aren't you just so glad that you disillusioned me?"

"You're really anxious, aren't you?"

"Does it show?"

"Just a little bit."

"Should I call him now or should I have Maria and Amber with me?"

"I think you need your lawyer."

"I think Amber would do a better job of preserving my rights and speaking for me, but okay. I will tell them what is going on and that I need my lawyer. They know how to get in touch with her. I kind of just want to call the DA myself but that might not be too smart, right?"

"You are learning about the adult world."

"If I have to see the DA again, what do you think he will say about me? Do you think he will be surprised at me?"

"What do you mean?"

"Well, I know it's been, what? Nine months since I saw him, right?"

"That's about right."

"Since last summer I have grown three inches taller and I am not the same shape and I'm pretty fluent in two languages and have a pretty good handle on a third. Do you think that I am articulate now?"

"One could say that."

"Do you think I was articulate last summer?"

"You made yourself understood."

"I can't believe I said 'mansicles' and splits to the DA. He must have thought I fell off the last turnip truck."

"Sarah, what would you have done if you saw this headline last summer?"

"I would have been hiding in the ceiling and you wouldn't have gotten me out. And I wouldn't have talked about it."

"You would have been a victim?"

"Yeah."

"How do you feel now?"

"I don't want to deal with this, but if I have to, I'll do it. And I'll do my best to preserve myself and my dignity. I'm glad JK Rowling wrote *Harry Potter.*"

"Why?"

"Because he shows how to handle the things that you have placed upon you even if you don't want them."

"It's how to be brave."

"Do you think that if I was a witch, I would be in Gryffindor?"

"I don't think the sorting hat would even have to think about it. But I think we need to share this with Maria. She should be here now; shall we check?"

April 17th   4:00 pm

"How did you do last night?"

"It was okay. This morning I stayed home and Amber talked to the DA. They already knew that I was involved and they are going to try to keep my testimony out of it if they can. I may need to give a deposition but the whole thing happened a little faster than they planned so they aren't sure yet. I won't know for a while but they will keep in touch."

Sarah paused, and then asked, "Do you think that the DA can ask them where I came from? They have to know where I came from. They were there."

"We can ask the DA."

"Okay. You know why I don't want to testify?"

"Why?"

"Those people all knew me when I was really little. I don't want them to know what I look like now."

"How are you feeling?"

"I don't need to be in the hospital. I can do this. I can tell my story if I have to and they can't shame me into silence, you know why?"

"Why?"

"Because I hadn't made my bat mitzvah yet; I was a little kid and I did what I was told to do. It wasn't mine to know right from wrong yet. And without knowledge, there is no shame. The people whom they arrested were the ones that were wrong. They were the adults and they were supposed to do the right things."

"You sound very confident."

"In two weeks I am going to make my bat mitzvah and I am going to be responsible for my decisions because I am able to reason. I can know right from wrong and I can think things through."

"Sarah, you have learned quite a bit in the past year and I am very proud of you. But I don't want you to get too far ahead of yourself. All that you have just said is true, but we still have work to do and you need to know that you will always have a way of looking at things and experiencing them that is not like other people."

"Am I ever going to be all okay?"

"I hope so and that is what we are working towards. But your life experience is part of who you are and it will always be there in some way."

"Will you be there with me, too?"

"I will be there and no matter what happens we will get through it together."

The End

ABOUT THE AUTHOR

Annie-Laurie Hunter is a home inspector by trade who likes to write, quilt, and rescue domestic rabbits in the Central New York area.